The Rainy Day Killer

Also by Michael J. McCann

THE DONAGHUE AND STAINER CRIME NOVEL SERIES

Blood Passage
Marcie's Murder
The Fregoli Delusion

SUPERNATURAL FICTION

The Ghost Man

The Rainy Day Killer

A Donaghue and Stainer Crime Novel

Michael J. McCann

The Plaid Raccoon Press
2013

The Rainy Day Killer is a work of fiction. Names, characters, institutions, places and events are either the product of the author's imagination or are used fictitiously. Any resemblance to actual persons, living or dead, events, or locales is entirely coincidental.

Front cover photograph: Yury Zap/iStockphoto
Back cover photograph: Jupiterimages/Thinkstock
Author photo: Tim D. McCann

www.theplaidraccoonpress.com
www.mjmccann.com

To Lynn, once again.

1

It was raining.

A warm, steady drizzle, it was carried ashore from Chesapeake Bay by gusting winds from the southeast, blurring the red tail lights of the cars ahead of them through the steady pulsing of the cruiser's windshield wipers. The roof lights were flashing, and the uniformed officer behind the wheel had blipped his siren once or twice, trying to push through the morning rush-hour traffic, but Homicide Lieutenant Hank Donaghue finally told him not to bother.

"She'll wait for us," he said, rubbing his temple to try to clear a nagging headache.

"Sorry, sir."

Hank closed his eyes. No one liked working outdoor crime scenes in bad weather. Responding officers hated standing around doing nothing for hours in bulky rain gear, crime scene technicians and medical examiners cursed as the rain washed away trace evidence before it could be collected, and detectives grew short-tempered as everyone else at the scene vented their bad mood and made the job that much more unpleasant.

Hank dreaded rainy day crime scenes because he disliked getting wet and because the rain often gave him a nagging headache, just like the one he was nursing this morning.

They passed the on-ramp for the Howard K. Chase Bridge and took the next right onto Levitt Street. Ahead, through the wipers and the rain, Hank could see the flashing lights of the emergency vehicles gathered on the pavement beneath the massive, arching span of the bridge. He released his seat belt and fastened the top button of his trench coat as they stopped at the wooden barricades marking the outer perimeter of the crime scene.

"Thanks for the lift," he told the officer, getting out.

"No problem, Lieutenant."

Ignoring the cameras and the shouting journalists, Hank held up the wallet containing his badge and identification to a uniformed officer who moved aside the barrier for him. Twenty feet ahead, barely within the shelter afforded by the bridge, Hank handed the wallet to another officer behind a line of yellow tape. The officer wrote down his name and badge number and gave the wallet back without comment.

Hank lifted the tape and moved forward, a little uncomfortable beneath the tons of concrete and steel above his head. He joined a circle of people watching other people work in the rain beyond the protection of the bridge, down near the water's edge.

"How are they coming?" he asked Detective Jim Horvath.

"Morning, Lieutenant." Horvath ran the sleeve of his police windbreaker over his damp forehead. "They got the body tent up but there isn't going to be much. Stains is getting the rundown from Chalmers, but the vic was dumped naked and has been out here all night. It doesn't look promising."

Tim Byrne, the crime scene unit team leader, handed Hank a tablet. Hank began to swipe through photos of the scene.

"She was found halfway in the water," Byrne said, watching as Hank studied a close-up showing the victim's submerged head. "Posed that way. Given the amount of time it's been out here, the body was probably dumped when the level was slightly lower, about three inches, so either it's coincidental that she was found this way—"

"Or he planned it, and this is how he wanted her to be found," Horvath finished.

Hank looked up from the tablet. "With the head completely underwater, and the rest of the body on shore?"

"How the hell would I know how he wanted her to be found?" Byrne snarled. "I'm not a fucking telepath."

Horvath raised an eyebrow at Hank. Thirty-three years old, he stood three inches shorter than Hank at an even six feet tall, and he was twenty-five pounds lighter at a slim one hundred and eighty. His short, black hair was neatly groomed and his green eyes, a gift from his Irish mother, normally danced with good humor. This morning, however, they looked tired and stressed.

Hank shrugged and went back to the photos. The body had been posed by the dumper in a provocative, obscene manner. The arms were extended and slightly bent at the elbows, palms up, as though inviting an embrace. The legs were splayed and bent at the knees, exposing the pubic area. The skin was pale and the long, straight blonde hair drifted on the surface of the water like fine angel's hair. He stopped at a photo taken after the body had been moved to the spot it now occupied on the pavement, about twelve feet from shore. The multiple ligature marks around the neck were clearly visible.

"Did you want to question the witness?" Horvath asked. "He says he's late for work and has to get going."

Hank gave the tablet back to Byrne and shook his head. "He called it in?"

"Yeah. He was the third who called but the only one who stopped. Name's Fred Adams, works as a pipe-fitter for a construction company. Says he was coming off the bridge and happened to look down. Saw the body and looped around down here from the off-ramp. That's his truck over there."

Hank looked at a black Dodge Ram with Maryland tags parked inside the crime scene tape. "Thought he could help?"

"We've all taken turns giving him shit for messing up the scene," Byrne said. "We've gone through his truck already. He swears he didn't touch the body. The footprints left by the dumper are a lot smaller than his boots, which fit his feet, so I'm fine with that."

"He says he came close enough to see that the eyes were open under the water," Horvath added. "That's when he called it in."

Hank looked at the young man sitting on the chipped cement footing of one of the bridge piers. He wore a plaid shirt, jeans, and scuffed work boots. He glanced up and nodded as a paramedic handed him a bottle of water, but he didn't smile. He looked very upset by what he'd seen.

"You're done with his truck?"

Byrne nodded. "He signed off on prints and a search, gave us a DNA sample, the works. We know where to find him if we want him. I've got no problem letting him go."

"Let him go," Hank told Horvath.

As the detective left in search of the sergeant in charge of the scene, Hank flipped up the collar of his coat and stepped out into the rain. After processing the body in situ, Dr. Sarah Chalmers, the assistant medical examiner, had moved it up onto the pavement where it was now hidden inside a blue eight-by-four body tent.

"Don't you just love this weather?" Detective Karen Stainer shoved her fists into the pockets of her tweed jacket. "She's gonna be as clean as a whistle and there's not a damned thing we can do about it."

Thirty-eight years old and a seventeen-year veteran of the Glendale Police Department, Karen was short, athletic, and about as intense as they come. Her shoulder-length blonde hair was plastered to her head, drops of rain clung to her slightly-pointed nose and chin, and her pale blue eyes smoldered in anger as she stared at Hank, her lips pressed tightly together.

Chalmers joined them. She wore a bright yellow rain jacket with OME emblazoned on the back. The hood was up, hiding her wavy red hair, and the drawstring was tied tightly beneath her chin. She looked like a freckle-faced schoolgirl.

"She's been here all night. We're about to transport. Do you want to see her?"

"I've seen the photos," Hank said, glancing down at the tent. "Walk me through it."

"She's in full rigor, so she's been here at least six to nine hours. She would've been positioned like that no more than two, possibly two-and-a-half hours post-mortem."

Hank nodded, understanding her point that positioning of the body must occur before rigor mortis sets in, which generally begins to appear two to three hours after death. It gave them a time frame in which the body would have been dumped, and a hint as to approximate time of death.

"Internal body temp also suggests a TOD of about ten to twelve hours ago," Chalmers went on, using the cuff of her jacket to dab at rain on her cheek, "although given the weather, I trust the rigor more. Once we've done the autopsy, I'll be able to give you a reliable time frame."

"So he kills her early last night at about seven thirty," Karen said, "brings her here when it's dark, wheels her body down to the water with some kind of hand truck or something—"

"Yeah, I saw the tracks," Hank interrupted.

"—then drops her there and poses her before rigor starts."

"You think he wanted her discovered with her head under water like that?" Chalmers asked.

Hank ran his hand through his frizzy brown hair. It came away wet. He shook off the drops. "It's possible. Low tide last night was at about eight o'clock, this morning it's at nine twenty, sunrise is about six thirty, he's got to figure the body will be seen by commuters as soon as it's daylight—"

"Probably counted on it." Karen took her fists out of her pockets and folded her arms.

"Maybe. Maybe he wanted the body found exactly the way it was found. So he checked the tide charts and did his calculations, brought it out and positioned it exactly where he wanted it after measuring it out." He looked at Chalmers, his thoughts shifting. "I saw the ligature marks on the neck."

"Yes. Overlapping. The most prominent being the final one."

"Sexual assault?"

"Oh, yes."

"Any mutilation other than the removal of the breasts?"

"Not that I could tell."

"They look like clean amputations."

"Yes, with a very sharp instrument and no hesitation."

Karen muttered something under her breath. Hank didn't ask her to repeat it.

Chalmers stoically stared back at him.

"Restraint marks on the wrists and ankles," he prompted.

"Multiple marks consistent with plastic locking straps."

"She was held for a while, maybe several days," Hank said. "Freed to use the washroom, then restrained again."

"Could be," Chalmers said.

Hank turned now to Karen. "Anything left behind?"

"No. Crime Scene found jack that hasn't been here less than a week, other than the wheel tracks and his footprints. They're still looking along the shore in case something blew over there." She pointed.

Hank stepped to his right and saw two yellow GPD FORENSICS rain coats about twelve feet apart, stooped over, creeping along the edge of the river where it met the vacant lot on this side of the bridge.

"He washed her," Chalmers put in.

Hank cocked his head. "Oh?"

"I could smell a faint odor of disinfectant, despite the rain. We'll be lucky to find anything at all, never mind DNA. I've bagged her hands and feet, but her nails looked like they've been trimmed and scrubbed."

"Anything he missed, the rain probably got," Karen groused.

"We'll see."

"All right. Thanks, Sarah," Hank said.

"You're welcome."

Hank turned away to stare out across the river.

"Man, I hate the rain," Karen said.

"Join the club." He went back under the bridge and spoke to the sergeant in charge of the scene, who pointed out the public information officer. Unlike some PIOs Hank had worked with, this one was sworn personnel who wore a patrol officer's uniform beneath her police rain jacket. Water dripped from the brim of her hat.

"Officer Eleanor Montgomery," she said, shaking his hand. "If you have a minute, I'd like to run over the statement with you."

"Sure." Hank watched her tap the screen of her tablet. She was short, slender, and pretty enough to be a model in a toothpaste commercial. Her makeup was subdued and natural-looking, in conformity with departmental policy for female officers, but done with an eye to enhancing her appearance before the cameras. Her long, blonde hair was pinned in a bun at the back of her neck, just below the brim of her hat. Her fingernails were carefully manicured to the permitted quarter-inch length and done with a light-colored polish. It was probable that her looks had been a contributing factor in her selection as a PIO.

"The victim is unidentified," she began, "white female in her early to middle twenties. She was sexually assaulted and strangled, then left unclothed on the river shore by the killer, who brought her body here from a location currently unknown. I'll polish up the wording. Detective Horvath suggested that I omit the mutilation, but said I should check with you first."

"Omit it for now," Hank said. "It's early."

Montgomery nodded. "We should include an appeal to the public for any information they may have about suspicious activity around the bridge last night, or any missing female matching the description, which I'll go over for them."

"Sounds fine."

"The eyewitness, Mr. Adams, got away without having to talk to them. They filmed him and took his picture, but there was no statement. They'll track him down, though."

"I would imagine. You'll schedule a press conference for later in the day?"

"I'm not sure," she said, "the D.C. may want to." She was referring to Deputy Chief Alonzo Philbin, who ran the administrative division in which she worked. "I'll repeat this statement at our regularly-scheduled briefing at ten—pending updates, of course—but we could do a three-o'clock conference if everyone thinks it's needed."

"Did they get any shots of her before they got the tent up?"

"I don't think so," Montgomery replied, "but traffic's slow at this time of morning coming off the bridge and someone may have gotten something on their cell phone from a vehicle up there before they moved her. We'll have to see what turns up. Will you make a statement at this time?"

Hank shook his head, causing droplets of rain to fall from his frizzy brown hair. They ran down his cheek. "It's all yours."

"All right, Lieutenant."

He watched her walk away, eyes on her tablet, index finger tap-tapping. He turned to see uniformed officers holding up a tarpaulin as Chalmers supervised the movement of the body from the tent to a body bag. The bag was then shifted onto a gurney for transportation to the morgue.

Behind Chalmers, Karen looked over at him.

The raindrops on her face could have been misinterpreted as tears, but the anger in her eyes was unmistakable.

2

Karen pulled into an empty spot in the parking lot of the Glendale Forensic Medical Center and killed the engine on the brand-new, unmarked Ford Taurus. One of the police interceptor models, it had just been assigned to her on Monday by the motor pool, replacing her beloved Crown Victoria. She hated it. It drove well enough, admittedly, but it wasn't a Crown Vic, so for that reason alone she hated it with a passion.

"You'll get used to it," the guy had told her as she'd signed the paperwork for it. "Couple of days, you'll think you should've been driving one all along."

"It looks like a fucking pace car at a harness race." She handed back the clipboard. "I'm lucky it doesn't have advertising on the doors for Pizza Hut or some fucking thing."

"You'll love it. Trust me."

Karen trusted no one, especially a weasel-necked goober in coveralls who parked cars for a living, but when she floored the accelerator on the expressway she found that it had a little zip to it after all. But it wasn't a Crown Vic. So it sucked.

Inside the smaller autopsy theater Karen found Harry Shaniwatru and Sarah Chalmers completing the external examination of the body from beneath the bridge. Chalmers was measuring the restraint marks on the right ankle while Harry wrote down the numbers as she recited them aloud.

Harry looked up and grinned weakly at Karen.

"Wow," she said before he could speak, "did you win or lose?"

Harry was sporting two black eyes and a butterfly bandage on the bridge of his nose, which had obviously been broken again. A small cut just above his right eyebrow held three stitches, and his lower lip was scabbed in the middle. His left hand, which gripped the pen he was using to write down the measurements being fed to him by Chalmers, was red and puffy.

"I won," he said quietly, "but it took some doing."

"Obviously." Karen shook her head. "You really should be worried about head injury, Harry. You don't need the money anymore, do you? You should be thinking about hanging them up."

"That's what I told him," Chalmers said without looking up from her work.

The son of Thai immigrants, Harry had started boxing as a student, first as an amateur and later, after failing to qualify for the Olympics, as a professional to help pay his way through college. His record as a pro stood at twenty-one wins—counting last night's bout—and twelve losses, which was good but not great. At five feet, four inches tall, he stood about an inch and a half shorter than the current champion in the flyweight class, but the fact that he was a southpaw sometimes compensated for his lack of height and reach, as did his complete fearlessness in the ring.

Harry had begun working for the Office of the Medical Examiner four years ago as a contract forensic investigator while completing his MD at State University. His objective was to become a pathologist, but last summer he'd put those career plans on hold when his father passed away and he was forced to move back home to look after his mother, who spoke no English and seldom went outdoors. Dr. Jim Easton, the medical examiner, considered Harry to be the best diener currently on contract and offered him a position that would allow him to move from the midnight shift to full-time days as a pathologist assistant. He was a favorite not only of Easton but also of Chalmers, who'd begun to nag him about giving up boxing while his brain was still intact.

"I'm thinking about it," he admitted to Karen. "But enough about me. Would you like to know who your victim is?"

Karen raised an eyebrow. "Hell, yeah. What've you got?"

"We got a hit on her fingerprints right away," Chalmers said, turning away from the dissecting table to pick up a tablet. "She was a school teacher, so her prints are in the system."

Karen took the tablet and looked it over. Theresa Olsen was born on March 12, 1989, which made her twenty-four years of age.

Born and raised in Glendale, her education degree was from State University. She'd taught Grade Two at Thomas Jefferson Elementary School in Springhill. Her home address was just around the corner from the school. The security check that had recorded her fingerprints was less than a year old, meaning that Theresa Olsen had not yet completed her first year as a teacher. The kids would be upset when they found out what had happened to Miss Olsen.

Karen made a face.

"I know," Chalmers said, as though reading her thoughts.

"What can you tell me?"

"First of all," Chalmers said, "I have to apologize, because we're not going to be able to do the internal until four this afternoon. I hate to make you come back, but the schedule's bad right now. Harry and I shoehorned in the external, though, because I said we'd have something this morning and we know you want to get moving on it."

"Don't sweat it," Karen said. "Horvath would love to come over this afternoon. He's that kind of guy."

"It's apparent she was held for several days," Chalmers continued, "judging by the number and aging of the contusions on her neck, ankles and wrists, plus indications of dehydration. I expect the stomach will be empty, or nearly so. The ligature looks to have been manila rope, three-eighths of an inch. Harry used adhesive tape in the hope that we might pick up any trace fibers the killer missed when he cleaned her."

Karen glanced at Harry, who was sitting at the computer at the far end of the room.

"His hands are as steady as a surgeon's," Chalmers said, following her eyes. "I don't know how he does it. I really wish he'd quit, though. He's going to seriously hurt himself."

"Yeah." Karen turned back to the body. "So you're sure it was strangulation and not drowning."

"I expect to find very little water in the lungs, if any. There's no doubt she was left on dry land, and that she was already deceased." Chalmers leaned forward and pointed at a mark on the left side of the neck. "I'd say this was from a stun gun, and this," she moved down and indicated a tiny puncture wound on the left thigh, "is an injection site. See the bruising around it? The syringe was applied with some force, several days ago. There are other injection sites over here," Chalmers edged past Karen and walked around the table to point at the right shoulder. "See? One, two, three, four, five. No bruising, though. We'll see what the toxicology report tells us, but I can guess."

"So can I." Karen went back around to the other side of the table and pointed at the mark on the neck. "Stuns her here and then pounds in a sedative right away, here," she motioned with her fist at the bruise on the left thigh, "then later on gives her injections in the right shoulder while she's tied up, to control her."

Chalmers nodded.

"Stunned and injected on the left side," Karen said, staring at the body. "Passenger seat of a car, maybe. He talks her into a car and then stuns and drugs her from the driver's seat."

Chalmers tucked an errant red curl back under her hair net.

Karen leaned closer. "What the hell did he cut off the breasts for? What'd he do with them?"

"I hate to think."

"Christ. Tell me about the sexual assaults."

"We've done the swabs," Chalmers said. "It appears as though the cleaning process included an enema and douching in an attempt to eliminate all traces of semen, but we've only just begun our work and we'll see what the internal yields." She looked at Karen. "I can assure you, Karen, the last word hasn't been spoken on this one. Not by a long shot."

Karen remained silent, looking at the body.

"There are the expected injuries to the vagina and the anus consistent with repeated rape," Chalmers said. "He shaved her as part of the cleaning process, nicking her once, obviously post-mortem. There wasn't a single loose hair to be found. Harry never misses them, and neither do I."

"Like he had all night," Karen said.

"He was very careful. Meticulous. But one thing to keep in mind is that he only had two to three hours after killing her to do all this, plus transport her to the river and position her, before rigor would begin to stiffen the limbs."

"You said before you thought time of death was about seven thirty last night. Anything change your mind on that?"

Chalmers shook her head. "Not so far. I'll be able to answer the question better once we've done the internal, but I think it's a fairly safe bet."

"All right. Thanks, Doc."

"Karen, do me a favor?" Chalmers asked, her voice rising.

Karen turned from the body, raising an eyebrow. "Sure, Doc. What?"

"Nail this son of a bitch's ass to the wall, will you? Please?"

Karen's pale blue eyes were steady.

"Count on it."

3

After picking up Horvath downtown, Karen drove across the river into Wilmingford to notify Theresa Olsen's parents of their daughter's death. At the curb outside the modest ranch-style house on Strathton Road, they waited for only five minutes before they were joined by the chaplain from Victim Services. By mutual agreement Karen took the lead, drawing on experience in giving bad news to parents that had been developed over several years as a detective working family-related crime. Horvath was more than happy to take a back seat on this one.

Tom Olsen was a longshoreman who worked at the marine port of entry in Wilmingford. It was his habit to have lunch with his wife Brenda every day, and so both parents were at home when Karen knocked on the front door. She sat them down in the living room to break the news, holding Brenda's hands as she cried her way through it and answering Tom's angry questions as delicately as possible, given the circumstances. It was necessary that they know at least as much as they might see on the six o'clock news, but it couldn't be piled on them all at once. She led them through it in small steps, using their questions as an opportunity to release a small detail, working through the emotional reaction to it, then finding a way to move on to the next thing they needed to know. It was time-consuming and stressful work that demanded sensitivity and patience, and the chaplain spelled her off occasionally, offering the well-intended, meaningless words that innocent, wounded people like the Olsens need so desperately to hear at such times.

Eventually they reached the point where it was time to stop giving out information and to start asking for it. Choosing a moment when Brenda's sobbing and Tom's cursing had subsided, Horvath leaned forward. "When was the last time either of you spoke to Theresa?"

"Last Friday," Brenda said, staring at a wad of tissue poking out of her right fist. "I called her after supper to see how she was doing."

"How did she seem?"

"Fine. She was fine. There wasn't nothing wrong, nothing at all."

"Did she say whether she had any plans for the weekend? Either that night or the next day, for example?"

"Nothing I know about."

"Did she have any close friends?" Karen asked. "Someone who might be able to help us figure out her whereabouts on Friday or Saturday?"

Tom shook his head. "She was a real quiet girl, didn't go out much. Kept to herself. There was Melanie, another girl from school she talked about sometimes."

"Cheryl Kasten," Brenda said. "From high school. But I don't think she went out with Cheryl since Valentine's Day. They went to a party together, but Theresa didn't stay very long. She went home by herself and then talked to me on the phone for an hour about it."

"Oh?"

"Cheryl picked up some guy and left Theresa by herself. Theresa didn't know no one else, so she called a taxi and went home."

"Did she have a boyfriend?"

Brenda shook her head. When Karen looked at Tom, he shook his head as well. "She was shy."

"What about neighbors?" Karen asked. "She ever mention any-one where she lives?"

Tom shook his head. "She didn't really know the other people, except the superintendent or whatever she calls herself, and that was just to give her the rent checks and one time to get her to fix the toi-let."

"When did she move there?"

"Last August, before the school year started."

"And before that?"

"Here. At home."

"While she was a student?"

"Not her first year," Tom said, "because they told her she had to live a year on campus. Residency requirements. After that she came home, because we couldn't afford it no more. We were barely able to make her tuition and expenses."

"So she'd lived away from home before, but this was her first place of her own?"

"Yes. She was real proud of it."

They asked a few more questions, building up a picture of a young, inexperienced, and lonely young woman tentatively starting out in life. When they reached the point where they'd gathered about as much information as they were liable to get, Karen and Horvath left the chaplain with the Olsens and went out to the car.

As he got into the passenger seat of the Taurus and buckled up, Horvath looked up through the windshield at the sky.

"Looks like it's starting to clear up."

Karen started the engine. "Let's go get something to eat. I'm supposed to meet Sandy at The Brass Pump for lunch. That okay? We can still talk. He won't care."

"Sure," Horvath said.

Karen eased away from the curb and accelerated slowly, in case one of the Olsens might be watching from the window. At the corner she stopped, signaled, looked both ways, turned left onto Hinson Road and then floored it, snapping Horvath's head back against the headrest.

Sandy had reserved a table at The Brass Pump but hadn't arrived yet, so Karen and Horvath ordered strong coffee and plates of nachos that they devoured while going over photos Horvath had brought along in the car with him.

Although he was five years younger and more comfortable with the technological devices that had been everywhere at the crime scene this morning, Horvath shared Karen's preference for eight-by-ten glossies from the big laser printer on the ninth floor. They were still pawing through them with salsa-sticky fingers when Sandy Alexander slid into the booth next to Karen and pecked her cheek. "Sorry I'm late. Meeting ran long."

Karen squeezed his thigh. "Don't sweat it. I'll punish you later."

"Ow." Short, slim, dark-haired and neatly groomed, Sandy

wore a tidy blue suit with a white shirt and a dark blue tie. He looked like a shoe salesman. He smiled at the server who immediately came over, ordered coffee, then gave his attention to the table for the first time. "What's this?"

"Rape and murder, early this morning."

A special agent with the local field office of the Federal Bureau of Investigation, Sandy's eyes roved across the photos spread out on the table, his professional curiosity immediately aroused. He reached out and picked up a close-up shot of an ankle, noticing the layered restraint marks. "Nasty."

Karen looked at Horvath. "We should put these away. Sandy wants me to talk about wedding stuff. He's got a whole checklist of crap I have to do, for cryin' out loud."

Horvath held up his hands. "Oh, hey. Don't mind me." He began to gather up the photographs. "We can do this later. I'll get some takeout."

"No," Sandy said. "Wait."

Karen and Horvath both looked at him.

His eyes were roving the table with sudden intensity. He put down the photograph of the ankle and suddenly snapped up a full-length shot of the body with the head still submerged in water. "Oh, shit." He picked up another photo showing the body from the waist down. "Oh, Christ."

Karen frowned at him. "What?"

"What is it?" Horvath asked.

Sandy picked up another photo, then another. "This was this morning? Here?"

"What do mean, here?" Karen asked.

"I mean here. Glendale. She was found here this morning?"

"Of course she was. Weren't you listening? What the hell, Sandy?"

He carefully put the prints down on the table, rubbing his upper lip with a knuckle. He glanced at Horvath and turned to Karen. "I've seen this before. Same dump MO, same basic positioning. Ligature strangulation, right? Multiple? Like he strangled her to the point of unconsciousness several times over the course of several days, before finishing her off?" He turned his attention back to the photographs on the table. "I didn't see all the pictures. Is there breast mutilation as well?"

"Oh, shit," Horvath said.

"Spill it, Sandy," Karen ordered. "What the hell have you got?"

"I've seen photos like this before," Sandy repeated. "I've seen this modus operandi before. I think your victim was done by a serial killer. He's been in Missouri, Indiana, Pennsylvania, and West Virginia that we know of. Now it looks like he's here."

Karen's shoulders slumped. "Christ."

Sandy nodded. "It looks like she was a victim of the Rainy Day Killer."

4

Although Hank Donaghue was responsible at the moment for all administrative and supervisory duties in the Homicide Unit, which currently carried four detectives, he did not occupy the vacant captain's office, which had remained without a tenant after Ann Martinez's promotion to commander of Detective Services. Instead, he continued to work out of his own office next to it, although it had a third less square footage and cheaper, less attractive furniture. The buzz was that Barkley, deputy chief of Investigations, was about to order Martinez to move someone into Major Crimes as acting captain until a competitive process could be held to fill the position. Barkley's choice was said to have narrowed down either to Lieutenant Bill Jarvis, currently heading up the chief's special Chinatown task force, or Lieutenant Helen Cassion, currently the supervisory lieutenant in Missing Persons. Hank was apparently not in the mix, and he figured it would be prudent to stay where he was to avoid the awkwardness of having to move back out on short notice.

Everyone was petrified that Barkley would insist on Jarvis, who was universally despised as an obnoxious, self-centered son of a bitch. Jarvis was perceived as a favorite of Chief Bennett, which was said to be helping him in his career advancement. The smart money, though, was on Cassion. Like Barkley and Bennett, she was ex-FBI.

Martinez had already explained to Hank that she'd had her say on the subject, that she'd insisted on Hank for the job, and that she'd been bluntly told to forget it. Her theory was that it had to do with Hank's perceived ties to the local Triad society, resulting from an earlier case in which he'd saved the life of Peter Mah, a well-connected Triad official. It was also a carry-over, she'd been told, of old internal political baggage that had effectively stalled his career at the rank of lieutenant for the past fourteen years. According to her, though, the upcoming staffing action was another matter. Everyone could see that Hank's star was once more on the rise thanks to the recent Jarrett case, which had garnered him positive press and the gratitude of influential people outside the department.

For his own part, Hank wasn't so sure about his future prospects. He was still debating whether or not to throw his hat into the ring when the captain's job was posted. On the one hand, he wasn't sure he wanted to move up to a level that was wholly managerial, giving up the participation in casework he currently enjoyed, and he also dreaded the loss of face that would come from having his ass handed to him by someone else if the game played out to the conclusion he thought it likely would. On the other hand, he believed in the axiom that you don't screen yourself out of an opportunity, you force *them* to screen you out. At any rate, he still had time to decide what to do.

He was sorting through the paperwork in his in-basket when Karen pounded on his doorframe and walked in, Horvath trailing behind her. She threw herself down in one of his visitor's chairs, draped her arm over the back, and motioned to Horvath to take the other chair. He did so with a self-conscious glance over his shoulder.

Ever polite, Sandy Alexander rapped a knuckle on the open door and smiled. "Hey, Hank. How's it going?"

Hank stood up and moved around his desk, holding out his hand. "Great, Sandy. Good to see you. Let me get another chair."

Sandy shook his hand. "No, it's okay. Please. I can stand."

"Feebs are used to having to stand up in other people's offices," Karen said.

"Ha, ha." Sandy leaned against a filing cabinet as Hank perched on the corner of his desk. "I saw the photos from your crime scene this morning. We need to talk."

Hank liked Sandy, and there were no qualifications about it. The FBI special agent was smart, personable, and very, very patient. At five feet, seven inches he was a small man, only four inches taller than Karen, but he shared her passion for physical fitness and moved with quiet confidence. He didn't bother to hide his affection for Karen and his tolerance of her fiery personality, which earned him top marks in Hank's book. Today, however, his usual good humor was missing.

"Talk about what?" Hank asked.

"I think the guy who killed Theresa Olsen this morning may be the same guy who's killed six or seven other women of similar appearance in other states, using the same or very similar MO. The press is calling him the Rainy Day Killer."

Hank sat back. It was not good news to be told that a serial killer had moved into his jurisdiction, and Hank took a moment to think about it. He vaguely remembered the nickname, but had read little, if anything, about the previous cases. "How sure are you?"

"I'm not an expert," Sandy said, "but I'm the NCAVC coordinator for our office, so I keep up on the files and talk to the Quantico analysts on a regular basis. I've seen pictures of his previous victims, and I'm afraid to say they look a lot like yours."

As a coordinator of the National Center for the Analysis of Violent Crime, Sandy processed all requests for assistance made by local and state law enforcement agencies to the FBI center's four units which included, of course, the famous Behavioral Analysis Unit responsible for crimes against adults, including serial, spree, and mass murders.

"Who's the analyst assigned to the case?" Hank asked.

"Ed Griffin."

Hank knew Griffin, having met him while on course at Quantico many years ago when he was a young detective and Griffin was an instructor at the academy. "Maybe we should talk to him. If he's available and we need him, we'd go through you?"

"Yeah." Sandy took out his phone. "I can give him a call right now to see if he'll take a quick look. He can tell us if you should put in a request for service."

Hank looked at Karen, who shrugged. He looked at Horvath.

"Sure, go for it," Horvath said.

Sandy looked up the number and called it. Griffin answered on the fourth ring, just before it went to voice mail. Sandy identified himself, explained the situation and who was in the room with him, and asked Griffin if he'd be available for a meeting.

"Unfortunately," Griffin said, "I'm in London, delivering a paper at a conference. London, as in England? In fact, I was still on stage answering questions when you called. It's early evening over here."

"Oh God, I'm very sorry."

"Relax," Griffin replied easily, "you had no way of knowing. I was glad to have an excuse to cut it short and let the next guy have the podium. These things drag on forever if you let them, and I'm getting hungry. You said Hank's there now?"

"Yes, do you want to talk to him?"

"It would be a pleasure."

Sandy handed the phone to Hank. "He's in the UK," he explained.

Hank put the phone to his ear but said nothing, as Griffin was talking to someone at the other end.

"No no, I'll send you a copy as soon as I get back. I'll even autograph it for you, how's that? Okay. Look, I've got to take this. It was nice meeting you. Yes, likewise, I'm sure. Hank, are you there?"

"Yes," Hank said. "Sounds like we caught you in the middle of something."

"No problem, my friend. It's been a while."

"Yes, it has. Should we call back another time?"

"No, just somebody sponging a copy of my first book. It's out of print and hard to find, except in my basement, of course, where I keep tripping over boxes full of the damned thing."

"Sandy thinks you might need to look at a homicide we caught this morning."

"Yeah. He thinks RDK may have moved into your fair town, does he?"

"RDK?"

"Give me a moment." Noises came over the line suggesting that Griffin was moving to a quieter spot to continue the conversation. "Look, Hank," he went on after a moment, "I refer to him as RDK in my notes and whatnot for the sake of convenience, but I apologize. I don't like to use the term in conversation because it's not only disrespectful to his victims, but those kinds of nicknames and acronyms turn these guys into celebrities and anti-heroes, and that's not what I want to do, by any stretch of the imagination."

"I understand, Ed. How long will you be out of the country? Do you think you'll be able to help us with this?"

"I'm flying back on Friday. Unfortunately, I'm not as young as

I used to be, so when I get home I'm going to have to crash for a while to deal with the jet lag. You're not far from Quantico, an hour and a half, I think it is, so I could drive over on Saturday. Will that be soon enough?"

"I'll take it," Hank said.

"Sandy can explain what you need to do in the meantime. Tell me something, have you had any contact yet with anyone claiming responsibility for your victim?"

Hank frowned. "Contact? No, not at all. Why?"

"Oh. Yeah. It just happened this morning, right? Sorry, I'm a little tired. I'm like a good French wine, Hank. I don't travel well. This guy tends to contact local law enforcement, but it's still too soon for that. I'm getting ahead of myself. Just continue your regular investigative process, work with Sandy on the service request, and I'll see you Saturday. Sound okay to you?"

"Sounds fine, Ed. Thanks."

"No problem. Hand me back to Sandy, and take care of yourself."

Hank returned the phone to Sandy, who listened and nodded as Griffin explained what he wanted in terms of first steps.

When Sandy ended the call, he exhaled loudly. "Okay, Hank. Let's get started."

5

Grateful that Hank was the one stuck with the paperwork and red tape, Karen and Horvath made good their escape and drove down to Thomas Jefferson Elementary School in Springhill. Karen drove the unmarked Taurus. Horvath, because he'd agreed to attend the autopsy of Theresa Olsen at four o'clock, followed in his personally-owned vehicle, a red 1974 Triumph Spitfire. School buses lined the curb in front, waiting to pick up their loads when the bell rang at three o'clock, so Karen took the narrow alley between the school and the rowhouse next door, parking in the lot at the back. Horvath pulled in next to her and got out. As they strolled toward the rear entrance, Horvath buttoned his suit jacket and self-consciously touched the knot of his tie.

"Got your invitation," he said. "Thanks."

Karen rolled her eyes. "You mean *Lane's* invitation. You'd think she was the one getting married."

"Hey, it's nice of them to pay for everything. You have to admit. My parents wouldn't do that."

"Whatever," Karen shrugged. Their buck, their wedding."

"I don't think I'm going to be able to make it."

She whacked him on the elbow. "No problem. They only invited a thousand frigging people."

He opened the back door for her with his other arm, flexing the one she'd hit. "Sorry to hear that. What a nightmare."

"I know. They must have me confused with Princess Kate." Karen stepped into the corridor and held up her badge to the middle-aged woman who was minding the door in anticipation of dismissal time. "Detectives Stainer and Horvath, GPD. Where's the principal's office?"

"I'm Assistant Principal Miller," the woman said, leaning forward to stare at the badge. "May I help you with something?"

Karen shook her head. "What's the principal's name?"

"Mrs. Audrey Humphries. She's likely busy right now."

"Where do I find her?"

Miller pointed. "Down the hallway and turn right, all the way to the end. The office is on the right."

They walked past a couple of closed classroom doors and turned right at the main hallway that ran the full length of the building.

"I hated school," Horvath said. "Grade school, anyway. Little kids can be really vicious."

"Yeah. Anyway, I thought you and Mandy would jump at the chance for a weekend getaway. It's only three or four hours from here."

"Mandy and I, we're not doing so hot right now." Horvath glanced at his reflection in a large glass display case.

"Sorry to hear that."

"I thought we had an understanding, but she started seeing some guy she works with. She was always bitching about my hours, that I cancel out on stuff, blah blah blah."

"So you dumped her."

"She dumped me. On Saturday."

Karen grinned up at him. "You're just too pretty for them, Horvath. They hate the competition."

"Hey!" Horvath looked hurt. "What a thing to say."

"Don't sweat it. They'll be kicking down your door, guaranteed, as soon as word spreads you're back in play. Right? Am I right?"

Horvath opened the office door and gestured her inside, his lips peeling back in a fake grin.

They signed the visitors' log on the counter and were shown into the inner office of Mrs. Audrey Humphries, a tall, slender African-American woman in her late thirties. They sat down in the chairs she offered and Karen once again took the lead, explaining the reason for their visit and their need to ask questions about Theresa Olsen. Her identity had not yet been made public, she explained, but it would be released to the media during a press conference at three o'clock this afternoon.

As she listened, Humphries slowly leaned forward, covering

her mouth with her right hand, elbow on her desk. Her eyes slowly closed. Tears began to run down her cheeks.

Karen gave her a few moments to recover.

Humphries leaned back, opened a drawer, and took out a box of tissues. She grabbed a handful and pressed them to her eyes.

"I'm sorry," Karen said. "I understand how upsetting it is, but we need to ask a few questions right now."

Humphries blew her nose and straightened abruptly. "Of course. Forgive me. It's the very last thing I expected you to come in and tell me. I heard the report on the news this morning, and Miss Olsen has been absent without an explanation since Monday, and we've been trying to reach her, but never in a million years would I have put the two things together. It's inconceivable. Completely horrible."

"How well did you know Theresa?"

"Not very well. She was young and inexperienced, but she was completely relaxed in the classroom. A natural. She was quiet, sweet, and had a very pleasant disposition. She was going to make an excellent teacher. The children loved her. They'll be devastated when the news comes out. We'll have to arrange for counseling right away." She picked up a pen and wrote it down on a lined pad next to her telephone.

Horvath turned a page in his notebook. "We understand she was friends with another teacher here. Melanie?"

"Melanie Peters teaches Grade Four, but I don't know if she was friends with Theresa. I don't know either of them that well."

"Is Peters here today? Could we talk to her?"

Humphries picked up the phone, the pen still jutting from between her fingers, and spoke to her secretary. As soon as she replaced the receiver, they heard the page go out over the public address system.

"Were there any reports of Theresa having problems with anyone?" Karen asked. "Male teachers here, or men coming onto school property to see her? Boyfriends, anything like that?"

Humphries shook her head. "Not at all."

"I saw cameras at the front and rear," Karen said. "I take it that you could supply us with video footage going back a week if we got a warrant for it."

"In response to a court order, yes, we could do that." She made another note on the pad, then shot a look at Karen. "Do I need to be worried? Is there a security problem I need to know about?"

"Not that we're aware of," Karen replied. "We're just trying to cover all the bases."

"Well, I need to cover the bases, too," Humphries shot back. "As you saw, we haven't yet converted to a buzz-in door system, which is currently only a priority in middle and high schools in this city, nor do we have an SRO assigned to us, for the same reason. We have a bit of money for the camera system and that's it. Until and unless our budgeting changes next year, elementary schools will continue to be regarded as lower risk comparable to the higher grades."

"You don't have access to a school resource officer?" Horvath asked, referring to the program in which uniformed police officers were present in some schools in the city, often once a week, to provide a variety of preventive and counseling services.

"No. As I said, the funding isn't there right now to include elementary schools in the program. The focus currently is on adolescent students and bullying, where retaliation has more potential to be violent, and while I agree with that policy, it leaves us out in the cold, trying to make do and praying that what happened in Connecticut won't happen here. I'll have to talk to the board security supervisor but the bottom line is, there's nothing currently in place." Her shoulders slumped. "We're probably going to be barraged by the media, on top of everything else. I need some help right away. My God."

Horvath glanced at Karen, who nodded. "We'll look into it from our end," he said. "We'll have them send a patrol car over in the morning before school starts."

"Thank you." Humphries looked up at a knock on her door. "Yes?"

The secretary opened the door. "Miss Peters is here."

"Ask her to wait in Mrs. Miller's office." Humphries stood up and looked at Karen. "Is there anything else? I need to make some phone calls."

"Not at the moment." Karen gave her a card. "Please let us know if you think of anything else that might be important."

Humphries was tough and very professional, but Karen saw the emotion coming to the surface as they shook hands.

"Damn it, Detective," Humphries said quietly, locking eyes with her, "this is epidemic. We can't escape it any more. No woman is completely, ever, 100 percent safe, no matter how careful we are. Does that bother you as much as it bothers me?"

"You have no idea," Karen replied.

According to Melanie Peters, she and Theresa Olsen occasionally ate lunch together and had met for coffee once or twice on weekends, but other than that were not especially friendly. She knew nothing about Theresa's other friends, didn't believe she had a boyfriend, knew of nothing out of the ordinary that had happened recently to her, and had had no contact with her after three o'clock last Friday afternoon when school was dismissed.

They let her go, burned another half hour questioning support and building staff still on the premises, and found themselves out in the parking lot with their hands in their pockets.

"That didn't get us much," Horvath said, leaning against his car.

"I know. She was like a damned ghost girl, here five days a week and nobody knows the first thing about her. We probably would've gotten more from her kids than from the adults."

"No thanks," Horvath said. "I'd rather interview bikers on death row than a bunch of little kids whose teacher just got raped and murdered by a psychopath."

"Yeah, well, pray it doesn't come to that." Karen slapped the palm of her hand down on the roof of the Taurus. "Rain's stopped, let's walk around the corner to her place."

"Fine by me." Horvath led the way across the parking lot. In the narrow laneway between the school building and the rowhouse, he glanced down at her.

"Mind if I ask you a question?"

"What kind of question?"

"Promise you won't hit me again?"

"Sure," Karen said easily. "Ask away."

"I notice your language has improved a little these days. Usually it's fuck this, fuck that, fuck the other thing. Is something wrong? Maybe, you know, I could help?"

Karen laughed. "Fuck off, Horvath. For your information, I'm trying to clean it up until I get this wedding over with. I seriously doubt the new in-laws would appreciate the rougher edges of my personality. But thank you for noticing."

Horvath turned right, onto the sidewalk. "You're welcome." He slowed, looking around the street. "So, every day after work she makes this walk home. Since the FBI analyst wants a full victimology report, this is a good idea. Walk a block in her shoes."

Karen glanced over her shoulder at the school. "The front camera only gets the entrance, and probably the sidewalk and the street right in front. We could see traffic passing, but not what's parked down here."

"Wonder if it's always jammed like this. There isn't an empty spot on the entire block."

"Usually you got parents camped out picking up their kids," Karen agreed, "but these cars look like they belong to people living here, or visiting. Nobody waiting behind the wheel."

"If he was surveilling her before he grabbed her, it'd be tough to do it on this block," Horvath said.

"Yep."

They reached the corner and turned right onto North Clanton Street. Theresa's address was four doors down, on this side. Traffic was more brisk here, and there were more empty parking spaces. Karen jumped over a puddle in the middle of the sidewalk. "It rained all weekend," she said. "Did it rain Friday night?"

"No," Horvath said, stepping over the puddle, "I don't think so." He led the way up the sidewalk to 1175 North Clanton Street, the second of four rowhouse units on the block. A police cruiser occupied the parking spot directly in front. Inside the front door was an enclosed entry with two inner doors, one leading to the upstairs unit and the other into the downstairs unit where they found two uniformed officers with a short, stubby woman in an ankle-length, flowery print dress and sandals.

"This is Mavis Williams," one of the officers told Karen. "She's the superintendent for all eight rowhouse units. The vic lived upstairs in this one. We cleared and sealed it. There's a fire escape exit off the little kitchenette that's locked."

Karen nodded. There was a noise at the front door. She turned around and saw crime scene technician June Allenson walk in, carrying her evidence collection kits. Allenson and Horvath went upstairs to process the victim's apartment while Karen remained downstairs to interview Mrs. Williams, who confirmed that Theresa was home Saturday morning. She heard Theresa walking around upstairs beginning around eight o'clock or so, she said. At about ten thirty, she heard Theresa's bell ring. Theresa walked downstairs and answered her door. Mrs. Williams heard her run back upstairs, as though to get her purse or a sweater or something, then run back downstairs and out the front door.

She never returned.

"You didn't see who rang her bell?" Karen asked.

"No."

"Did you hear a voice?"

"No, sorry."

"Did you see Miss Olsen leave in a car? See a suspicious vehicle of any kind on the street?"

"No. I didn't look out. I was doing my sewing, and didn't get up. Sorry."

Karen continued to dance in circles with her until it was obvious it wasn't going to produce any useful information. She went upstairs and found Horvath looking through Theresa Olsen's bookshelf.

"Nothing much here, Stains." He gestured around him. "Open-concept living room and dining room, tiny little bedroom back there, bathroom, kitchenette. That's it. Very little furniture, a few framed pictures on the walls, computer desk, TV and DVD player, these books. That's it. Butternut's in the bathroom pulling hairs from the shower drain." He glanced at his watch and began removing his latex gloves. "I better get a move on if I'm going to make it to the autopsy by four o'clock."

"Careful on the way out," Allenson called from the bathroom, "I haven't dusted for prints out there yet."

"Oh, sorry," Karen replied loudly, "I was just pawing through all the stuff on the desk. I hope that was okay."

"Smartass."

Outside, they stood on the sidewalk while Karen gave him a quick update on her uneventful interview with Mrs. Williams.

"So much for the stereotype of the nosy super," Horvath said.

"Speaking of which." She nodded in the direction of the next unit down, where she'd just seen a curtain move in the downstairs window.

Horvath turned. "Someone there?"

"Yeah. Go ahead. I'll check this out."

"Thanks, Stains."

As he hurried off, she walked up the steps of 1177 North Clanton Street and pressed the button labeled "A." Tapping the toe of her boot on the immaculate cement porch, she gave it a moment and pressed again, this time holding the button down for a full ten-count while pounding on the door with the heel of her fist. She heard the inner door open. She stopped pounding and the door opened, revealing a tiny, white-haired woman who looked like she was dressed for church in a black jacket and skirt combination with a white blouse and heavy black shoes.

Karen held up her badge. "Police, ma'am. I'd like to come in and ask you a few questions."

"I'm expecting a caller, Officer. Couldn't it wait until another time?"

"No, it can't. Please let me in. It'll only take a few minutes."

"Oh, all right. This way, please." The woman let her in, leading the way into the downstairs unit. It was laid out identically to Mrs. Williams's unit next door but was furnished much differently, with antique furniture, large oil paintings, and Tiffany lamps. "I've made some tea," she said over her shoulder. "Would you like a cup?"

Karen opened her mouth to decline, registered the hopefulness in the woman's tone, and shifted gears. "You know what, ma'am? I'd love tea."

"Sit here." The woman pointed to a large armchair with a green velvet throw draped on it. "I'll be right back."

As the woman disappeared into the kitchen, Karen mooched around, admiring the Art Deco statuettes, Toby jugs, and mantle clocks. In record time, the woman returned with a silver tea service and two cups with matching saucers. "Would you care for a biscuit? I have them already set out."

"No, thanks. This is fine." Karen accepted a cup of black tea and sat down in the armchair. "My name's Detective Karen Stainer, ma'am. May I ask your name?"

"Miss Esther Banks. You're not from around here, are you, Detective Stainer?"

"No, ma'am, I'm not. Texas born and bred."

"Northeast Texas, I'd say. Close to Dallas."

Karen's eyebrows went up. "Ponder, ma'am. Then Fort Worth. How'd you guess that?"

"From your accent, of course, just as you should be able to tell from mine that I'm a Maryland girl who's lived all her life within a stone's throw of the Chesapeake. How exactly may I help you?"

"We're looking into the disappearance of the young woman who lives upstairs next door. Do you know her at all?"

Banks sipped her tea. "You're referring to Miss Olsen?"

Karen recognized in the coyness of her tone that Banks had something to tell her, so she nodded as she raised the teacup to her lips and drank.

"I thought as much." Banks set down her cup and crossed her legs demurely at the ankles. "I heard on the news at noon the description of the woman they found at the bridge. It was her, wasn't it?"

"Yes," Karen admitted. "We believe she went missing on Saturday morning, and we're canvassing the neighborhood to see if anyone noticed anything out of the ordinary between ten o'clock and noon."

Banks leaned forward. "Do you mean to tell me, Detective Stainer, that he held her captive the entire weekend? Oh, my lord. They said she was sexually assaulted. Is it true?"

"Ma'am," Karen put her tea cup down, "I'm not at liberty to discuss any details of the case. I just want to know whether or not you saw or heard anything unusual Saturday morning."

"What a terrible thing to happen to that poor girl. I can't believe the world we live in today."

"Miss Banks? Did you see Theresa Olsen on Saturday morning or not?"

Banks raised an eyebrow. "Of course I did. I saw her on the sidewalk with that man carrying the umbrella. I saw her get into his car, and I saw them drive away."

6

The block between Clegg Street and Marson Avenue down at the river was part of what was known as Harborfront, a large redevelopment project begun in the 1980s when Maryland's economy as a whole was growing faster than the national rate. The abandoned warehouses and tenements in the neighborhood were torn down, and a sprawling, two-story complex was constructed with space for upscale restaurants, boutiques, and a small movie theater. Close to the waterfront, an outdoor seafood and produce market sprang up, and beyond that the developers included a bandstand and seating area. The wharves were rebuilt to accommodate boat traffic, and the entire complex was connected to the rest of the waterfront by the boardwalk that ran all the way along the river.

It was a three-block walk along the boardwalk from their high-rise building to Harborfront, and although they were normally very careful with their money, Karen and Sandy decided this evening to treat themselves to an expensive dinner at Nathaniel's. The oysters were fresh from Prince Edward Island, the crab cakes featured a mustard mayonnaise, and Sandy's seared red grouper came with jumbo lump crabmeat, capers, and lemon beurre blanc. Unsurprisingly, Karen chose a ten-ounce center-cut filet mignon, black and bleu, but condescended to have the sautéed crab meat enhancement to placate Sandy, who pretended to be upset that she was treating the best seafood restaurant in town like a mere steakhouse.

As they ate, she filled him in on the progress they'd made late in the day on the Olsen case. The eyewitness, Esther Banks, had agreed to sit with Butternut Allenson, who was trained in the use of the facial composite software used by the department, to produce a sketch of the man she'd seen getting into a car with Theresa on Saturday morning. Banks had begun with a very accurate description of the umbrella the man had carried. When pressed by Karen, she explained that the man had held it on an angle that prevented his face from being clearly seen.

Butternut found it amusing, but Karen did not. Doggedly, she continued to question Banks until, when Karen was at the point of strangling her, the woman finally acknowledged that the man had lowered and closed his umbrella before getting into the car. She then described a man in his early thirties, white, about five nine or five ten, slender build, with short dark hair and no prominent or unusual features. Butternut went to work and coaxed from her a few extra details: his nose was straight and a little pointed but not too pointed; his jaw was narrow but not too narrow; his lips were regular-looking; his eyes were slightly hooded; his eyebrows may have been thin and his eyes were a little small; his hairline was slightly high and a little rounded, with a part on the left side; and his ears seemed in normal proportion to the rest of his head.

Butternut worked diligently on her laptop and produced a sketch, after many adjustments back and forth, which Banks finally agreed bore a passing resemblance to the man she'd seen getting into the car with Theresa Olsen. Karen unfolded a copy from her jacket pocket and gave it to Sandy.

"The software makes everybody look the same," he said, studying it. "You should stick to the forensic artist, like we do."

"Not everybody has your massive budget, darlin'. I e-mailed you a copy, so you guys can do your thing with it. We're going to be releasing it to the press tomorrow morning. The powers that be have decided not to mention this Rainy Day Killer thing yet, so we need you guys to hold off on it at your end, too."

Sandy nodded, studying the sketch. "Ed Griffin can help make that call on Saturday."

"Does it look like any of the sketches you've seen from the other murders?"

Sandy shook his head. "It's the first one, as far as I know."

"You're shitting me."

Sandy put the composite aside and forked in a last bite of his grouper.

"We've never worked the same case before," Karen said. "It feels weird."

Sandy patted his mouth with his napkin and smiled. "It's your case, Karen. As I told Hank, Marie-Louise's instructions are that I should follow and not lead, provide on-site assistance as requested, and make our lab available on a priority basis. Ed Griffin's role is what it always is, to analyze the data you give him and provide a profile. He'll explain his part on Saturday. If you decide to hook up with the other cops who've worked the case in Pittsburgh and the rest, we can help set up the task force, but Hank will have the lead."

"You Feds are always so damned hard to deal with."

Sandy laughed. "We're supposed to be talking about the wedding, Karen, not work."

"I know, I know."

"Are you still okay with all this?"

She set down her fork and picked up her glass of wine. "Yes and no, same as before. I don't like weddings, and I still think we should get it done in the court house right here, but you promised your parents and I've got your six on it. I'll do my bit."

Sandy put the sketch in his jacket pocket and took out another piece of paper, which he unfolded and spread on the table next to his dinner plate. "She sent me this list, so we'd better go over it. Your brother's already begun the barn renovations, and they're going to build the gazebo and the barbecue pit in two weeks. I can't believe she agreed to a Texas ranch-style reception thing."

"You said it was her idea."

"It was, but I thought she'd change her mind after she talked to Bradley, that it'd be too—"

"Texan?"

He grinned. "Yeah. But she's all gung-ho about it, and she seems to have taken a liking to Bradley, so there you go."

"Brad's a charmer," Karen said, sipping wine.

"In fact," Sandy went on, "I don't think I mentioned that they liked his ideas so much they've decided to sink six figures into the project and turn the barn into an events venue. My father thinks he can draw a lot of tourists down from Bath County and recoup his money in three or four years. They've already installed a septic system for it, and

Brad's modified his design to include two washrooms with three stalls each."

"Good. There'll be modern facilities for me to go into and throw up."

Sandy smiled tolerantly.

Karen put down her glass. "Are you sure you're okay with me keeping my last name?"

"Of course. I already said I was."

"Your parents aren't going to be all up in arms?"

"My parents aren't marrying you."

She pushed her glass to one side. "What else you got there?"

"I talked to Meredith and she confirmed she can't make it, so Louise, the minister's daughter, has agreed to replace her. I take it Molly's still a go?"

Karen nodded. Molly Archer, a parole officer who was one of Karen's few friends in Glendale, had agreed to drive down to Virginia for the wedding and serve as a bridesmaid. Hank's friend, Meredith Collier, had also originally agreed to participate, but a situation had arisen in California that required her to fly back home that week. This Louise Tench person, instead, would be her other bridesmaid. Sandy's sister would be matron of honor. The whole thing made her feel very uncomfortable, but at least Molly would be there to lighten it up a bit, although Karen wasn't sure how the face piercings, tattoos, and spiked hair would go down in rural Virginia.

"Bolingbroke's confirmed as best man," Sandy went on, "and Hank and Delbert are in as ushers, so the wedding party's set. Mom's ordering the gifts for them, and she'll look after the gowns and tuxedos. She wants to know if you have any suggestions for gifts."

"Handguns. Body armor."

"Not funny. She contacted a florist here who'll show you the arrangements that she's considering. Pick what you like and she'll look after it."

"I'm not into flowers, Sandy."

"Just close your eyes and point. Nobody will care. Did you buy your shoes yet?"

"Yeah, garden boots."

Sandy looked up from the piece of paper. "Come on, dearest.

Help me out. Did you buy your shoes?"

"Yes, I bought the shoes."

"Thank you. The only other thing for now is the dress. You need to pick out what you want and book the fitting. Don't forget, okay?"

"I still don't see what's wrong with getting married in my Class As."

"I told you, save the uniform for the honeymoon. You know how much it turns me on. One other thing, I just need to ask you again about a bridal shower. She said to remind you she'd pick up the tab if you changed your mind and wanted to have one up here."

"No shower, Sandy. I don't do the girl thing. That's out."

"Okay." He folded up the paper and put it back in his pocket. "I'm done."

"Thank God."

"She sent out the invitations, and she's starting to get the RSVPs back. Marie-Louise's coming, but Will Martin can't make it."

"Too bad. I could've broken another one of his fingers for him."

Choosing not to react, Sandy went on, "There's still time if you want to invite anyone else from your side of the family, or any other friends."

"There's no one else. That's it."

He nodded, understanding the reason for the sharpness of her tone. "All right. That's fine. Tell you what, let's grab the check and get some air on the boardwalk. It's a nice night tonight, and the moon's up."

"No more wedding talk?"

"No more wedding talk. You could whisper dirty stuff in my ear, though."

"That's more like it, pal. Let's get out of here."

As they stepped out into the night, after Sandy had paid the check and left a tip, Karen slid her arm through his and pulled him close. "I'm glad we're doing it."

"We've been doing it for a couple of years. You're only glad now?"

She shook him playfully. "I'm glad we're getting *married*, you little prick."

42

"So am I." They stopped at the corner and waited for the light to change. Sandy took a deep breath. "We should talk."

The light changed and they crossed the intersection.

"I know," Karen said.

They reached the wooden stairs that led down to the boardwalk. Sandy stopped, slipped his arm out of hers, and took her hand. "We need to decide. Should we have a kid, or should we just let that part of it go and keep it the two of us? You need to tell me what you want to do."

Karen looked up at the sky and slowly let her eyes fall to the river below. The moon was hidden behind an office tower, but its reflection cut a diagonal path across the surface of the water. The tide would be rising again at this time of the evening. Theresa Olsen's bloated face flicked through her mind, and the face of Mrs. Olsen, red and tear-stained. The memories were immediately followed by the face of her mother, bruised and swollen, after an incident in a mental hospital in Arlington where she'd been briefly confined while Karen's father was still alive. "Gentle restraint" had been required to calm her down during one of her episodes, the nurse had explained defensively. It had taken a month to get her out of there into a better hospital in Dallas, where she remained to this day.

Mothers and daughters. In a violent, confused world. Karen grimaced. "I will, Sandy. I promise. Just not right now. I need to stay feeling happy, just for a little while."

He squeezed her hand. "Be happy, then."

7

The ninth floor was a busy place this morning. In the interview room at the end of the hall, Detective Frank Kaplan was interrogating a teenaged suspect from a downtown drive-by shooting while his partner, Detective Harold Belknap, questioned a witness at his desk in the Homicide bullpen, not far from Hank's office door. The witness, a friend of the victim, was upset and very loud. On top of that, Warren Seed, a cranky young detective from Robbery, had come all the way down from the other end of the floor to complain to Horvath at the top of his voice about his raids on their coffee.

As icing on the cake, building maintenance had chosen this morning to change all the ceiling fluorescent light tubes. A guy in coveralls with a visitor's badge pinned on his chest pocket walked through Hank's open door without a word, set up his aluminum step ladder, flicked off the light switch inside the door, and climbed up to remove a ceiling light panel. Dead insects pattered on the top of Hank's filing cabinet as he lowered the panel, propped it on its end against the filing cabinet, and proceeded to remove the light tubes which, as far as Hank could tell, were still working just fine.

Hank turned a set of photographs face down on his desk and switched on a reading lamp. He was going over the autopsy report on Theresa Olsen, sent to him this morning by Sarah Chalmers. Tipping up the folder to prevent its contents from being seen by the man on the ladder, he continued to skim through the report.

Chalmers had confirmed that time of death was between 7:30 P.M. and 9:30 P.M. on Tuesday, April 23. Cause of death was ligature strangulation as a result of pressure obstruction of the larynx, producing asphyxia. This finding was supported by significant multiple injuries to the larynx, a fractured hyoid bone, bruising and some slight rope abrasions around the neck, and conjunctival and facial petechiae. The ligature was judged by the pattern and size of the markings to have been natural-fiber, three-eighths-of-an-inch twisted manila rope.

Manner of death, Chalmers concluded, was homicide. Place of death was unknown. Regarding the latter point, lividity suggested that death occurred while the victim was lying on her back, and that she apparently remained in a supine position, legs and arms straight, for approximately an hour after death, during which time lividity began to fix. That the victim was moved after death was therefore obvious, because the lividity markings on the limbs did not match the position in which the body was discovered.

Examination of the gastro-intestinal tract revealed no signs of solid food consumption for at least fifty hours before death. There was evidence of mild but not severe dehydration, and tests suggested the victim may have consumed glucose-replacement liquids during that time period.

Penetrating genital injuries were discovered that were consistent with repeated sexual assault. Inspection of the mouth revealed no lacerations, hairs, or fibers. Chalmers had washed the mouth cavity, and the washing tested negative for spermatozoa, as did anal swabs and vaginal washing.

The entire body showed evidence of having been cleaned by the killer, and traces of a commercial detergent soap with bacterial disinfectant were recovered.

Abrasions and contusions on both wrists and ankles confirmed prolonged and repeated confinement with plastic locking straps.

Removal of both breasts was post-mortem and—

Hank became aware that someone was speaking his name. He looked up and saw Horvath in the doorway. The detective ducked aside as the worker returned with fresh fluorescent tubes and noisily climbed back up the ladder. Hank closed the file folder and set it aside.

"Sorry to bother you," Horvath said, glancing at the man on the ladder. "I've got our reports." He waved the folders in his hand.

"Just a minute." Hank stood up, gathered up the stuff on his desk, and headed for the door.

The worker came down off the ladder and nodded at him. "Won't be too much longer, Chief." He grabbed his ladder and scuffed it across the carpeted floor to Hank's desk, above which was another light panel.

Hank led the way out into the bullpen. Thankfully, Belknap had walked his witness down to the elevators, and the noise level had dropped significantly. Kaplan was still in the interview room. Karen was down at the lab. The other desks were vacant because currently there were no other detectives in Homicide to sit at them. He dropped the autopsy file on Karen's desk and sat down. Horvath perched on the corner and handed his file folders to Hank.

"We finished up the victimology report, since you wanted to send it to Quantico today. Along with that, there are reports from the responding officers," Horvath ticked it off on his fingers, "our notes and sketches from the dump site, witness statements from the school principal and a teacher who knew her slightly, a list of male school employees, a witness statement from the Banks woman, the comp sketch of the guy she saw, photos from the dump site, et cetera, et cetera. Stains is trying to shake loose some lab reports as we speak."

The worker strode out of Hank's office with the old fluorescent tubes from the light fixture above Hank's desk. He walked between the desks to a pushcart parked in front of the gun lockers on the far side of the room, removed fresh tubes from their cardboard sleeves, and strolled back into Hank's office.

"Bottom line?" Hank asked.

"A shy, quiet kid with no friends to speak of, no social life, no boyfriend. No indication of trouble with the parents or other relatives whatsoever. No problems reported in her past that we could find. Clean record. Driver's license, but no vehicle. Reasonably physically fit, rode the bus on a monthly pass to go shopping and stuff, had a bicycle that was kept locked at the back of the building and looked like it was being used. Ate sensibly and didn't consume alcohol or drugs. At least, we didn't find anything in her apartment at all. Not even beer. Aspirin in the medicine cabinet was as strong as it got."

Another worker wandered into the bullpen. This one wore a Department of Public Works identification card on a lanyard around his neck. He saw the pushcart in front of the gun lockers and looked around. Hank caught his eye and pointed at his office.

The man nodded and sauntered over, sticking his head in the

door. "Where's the other guy?"

"On the tenth," came the reply from above Hank's desk. "I've got this floor almost done."

"Need any more tubes?"

"Nope. Got enough."

"Sounds good." The man slapped the door frame, turned away, winked at Hank, and headed back down toward the elevators. On the way, he passed the mail clerk, who was heading toward the bullpen with his cart.

"Sometimes," Horvath said, "I think we might as well be working at the bus station. It'd be a hell of a lot quieter."

The man switched on the lights in Hank's office and came out carrying his ladder. "Thanks, Chief." He headed down the corridor leading to the interview and observation rooms.

Hank gathered up his stuff and went back into his office. He sat down at his desk, dropped the pile in front of him, and turned off the desk lamp.

Horvath leaned against the door frame. "I don't want this to be a self-fulfilling prophecy," he said, "but from what I've heard so far about this serial killer, I'm starting to think it may have been him. It looks absolutely, completely random. The father's no good for it, the men at her school are all coming up with alibis, and there are damned few other candidates. It doesn't feel like someone she knew. It doesn't feel personal, it feels completely impersonal."

"It's too early to tell," Hank said. He tapped the stack of files. "This is still preliminary."

Horvath held up a palm. "Understood. Absolutely. Like I say, I don't want to fall into some self-fulfilling prophecy where we decide it was some elusive serial killer nobody can catch and the case never gets closed. I don't—"

"Excuse me," said a voice.

Horvath turned around.

The mail clerk was standing behind him with a package in his hands. "This is for Lieutenant Donaghue."

"Oh. Thanks." Horvath took the package and put it down on the desk in front of Hank.

It was a manila cardboard carton, twenty-two inches by eighteen inches by ten inches. A shipping label with a bar code was stuck on top, generated from the website of the local courier company who had delivered it. The lid was sealed shut with clear packing tape. Oddly, the carton was also secured with manila rope, passed lengthwise and widthwise around the box and tied with a knot at the top.

Hank reached for the carton, puzzled. His attention suddenly gravitated to the manila rope, which looked as though it might be three-eighths of an inch. His hand hovered above the box as he stared at the rope, holding his breath. A faint humming came from the newly-replaced fluorescent lights above his head. Air gently buzzed through the vents. Horvath shifted his weight. A clock on the wall above his filing cabinet ticked.

Hank slowly withdrew his hand and picked up the phone. He punched a speed-dial number and stared at Horvath, who frowned, puzzled.

"Tim," Hank said when the call was answered, "can you send Butternut up to my office right away?"

He listened for a moment and compressed his lips. "No, I understand, but could you please ask her as soon as she's done the next one to put it on hold and come upstairs immediately?"

Eyes still locked on Horvath's, Hank nodded. "Yes, it is. I think you could definitely call it an urgent priority. I think the Olsen killer just sent us a package, and I think I know what's in it."

8

As he was getting out of the airport limousine with Meredith in front of the departures entrance of the Glendale International Airport, Hank's cell phone vibrated. He took it out, looked at the call display, and walked a few steps away as the driver began to remove Meredith's baggage from the trunk.

"Donaghue."

"The package connects to the victim, Theresa Olsen," Tim Byrne said without preamble. "Fingerprints on the driver's license and credit cards, hairs; the report will include everything. It's her stuff. Clothing, shoes, handbag. We'll wait on the test results, but the breasts are obviously hers, too. The son of a bitch."

"Thanks, Tim."

"Marcotte's processing the DVD, but I'm not hopeful. We're not getting anything connected to this bastard. No prints, no hairs, no fiber, no DNA traces, no nothing. Zip. Not on the clothes, the wallet, her keys, or the plastic container he put the breasts in."

"I understand, Tim."

"We viewed the DVD. Marcotte's pretty upset. This bastard's inhuman. He's talking directly to you, Hank. Where are you now?"

"At the airport. I'll be downtown later this morning."

"I'll see you when you get here," Byrne said. "I'm going to get some breakfast. Not that I've got any appetite left."

Hank put the phone away and told the limousine driver to wait. He walked Meredith as far as the security checkpoint in the departures area on the upper level before saying goodbye. They embraced and kissed. He watched her push aside a lock of hair and felt again a selfish sense of relief that there would be a continent between her and a serial killer who preyed on blonde women.

"I called Karen to tell her I wouldn't be back in time for her wedding," she said.

"Just as well. It might have given you ideas."

She touched his cheek. "I'll miss you. Stay out of trouble."

"No promises. Give my best to Patsy."

Patsy Wallace, Meredith's cousin, was the closest family member she had left. They stayed in touch, speaking every other week on the phone. On Monday, Meredith had received a call from her Uncle Donald, telling her that Patsy had been struck by a car in Sonoma, California, where she lived. She was in hospital, Donald said, with serious injuries. Seventy-four years old and living in a residence for seniors, Donald didn't know what was going to happen to Sherry, Patsy's twenty-two-year-old daughter. Sherry had Down's Syndrome and lived at home with Patsy, who had never married.

Meredith managed to speak to her cousin on Wednesday. She'd been moved out of intensive care into a room in the hospital, but was still in serious condition with a broken pelvis, broken leg, and a fractured skull. The conversation was brief. Patsy was groggy from the after-effects of a concussion and the pain medication she was receiving. Her attending physician happened to be in the room at the time, and she spoke to Meredith afterward. Patsy was stable and would recover. The doctor went on to explain that she'd made a few calls to ensure that things would be taken care of in the short term. A neighbor in Patsy's building was looking in on Sherry. The bookstore Patsy owned in Sonoma, her only source of income, would be kept open by her two employees. Her cousin would likely remain hospitalized for at least two weeks, however, if not longer. Things were still very much up in the air.

Meredith promised to fly out as soon as possible. She'd stay with Sherry until Patsy came home, and would remain after that for as long as she was needed. Sherry often spent time with Patsy in the bookstore during the day, so Meredith and she could do the same.

It was an early flight, departing at 6:50 A.M., and would be a long one. She had stops in Dallas and Los Angeles before she would transfer to an Alaska Airlines Dash-8 to complete the final leg to Santa Rosa, where she had a rental car waiting for her. She would drive down to Sonoma from there. She was an experienced traveler, but she knew she'd be tired by the end of the day.

"Will you visit the winery?" Hank asked.

"Probably."

Meredith was a native of Napa County and grew up on a winery in the Carneros region, east of Napa, owned and operated by her parents. Former beatniks from wealthy families in San Francisco, they'd used inherited money in the early sixties to buy an estate that had fallen onto hard times. Discovering an unsuspected talent for wine-making, they began to turn out superb lots in the varietals that made Carneros famous—pinot noir and chardonnay. Their only child, Meredith grew up in what was for her a veritable paradise. She had fond memories of the early-morning fog and the cool, persistent wind blowing off San Pablo Bay. In the afternoon, she could see as far south as San Francisco Bay from one side of the hill, and across the broad expanse of the valley from the other side.

Yes, she'd probably take Sherry for a little drive while she was there, and they'd probably take a run across the county line into Napa for a quick look at the Casa Carneros estate.

"I love you," Hank said. "Come back."

Meredith laughed, a little sadly. "Oh, I will. Don't worry about that, darling."

9

"I'd like to welcome everyone here this morning," said Deputy Chief Douglas Barkley, standing at the end of the long cherry wood table. "I'm very grateful to Supervisory Special Agent Ed Griffin for coming down from Quantico to help us with this very difficult and horrifying case." He nodded at Griffin. "I imagine this isn't quite what you expected to be confronted with, a board room filled with senior management giving speeches and all that, but I assure you as soon as we're done speaking, our intentions are to get the hell out of here so you folks can get the job done and nail this son of a bitch."

Barkley paused to allow the nervous chuckles and coughs to work themselves out. "I think it's a good idea that Commander Martinez has turned over her board room to the team for the duration of this investigation, and I've told her I'll authorize any expenditure within reason to make sure it meets your requirements while it serves as your war room. I've also told her that while you're occupying hers, she can have the use of mine on the second floor for her meetings. During off-hours, of course."

Another wave of polite laughter rippled around the room. "A special welcome not only to SSA Griffin but also to FBI Special Agent in Charge Marie-Louise Roubidoux and Special Agent John Alexander. On my left, going down the GPD side of the table, is Deputy Chief Alonzo Philbin, Officer Eleanor Montgomery, Commander Ann Martinez, Detectives Horvath and Stainer, and at the end of the table Lieutenant Donaghue, the lead investigator. To his left, on the FBI side of the table, Captain Michael Turcotte, who's in charge of our Criminalistics section. Mike, I hope you're not thinking of defecting because, believe me, after eighteen years with the Bureau I can tell you personally that the grass is definitely *not* greener on the other side of the table."

When the laughter had run its course, he said, "I'm about to sit down and shut my mouth, but before I do, I just wanted to thank you all for giving up such a beautiful Saturday morning to attend this meeting. For most of us, it'll be very brief, but I think you'll agree, very necessary. In a case like this, it's essential to straighten out the respective roles and responsibilities vis-à-vis local law enforcement and the Bureau, and I think it's very important to take a few minutes right up front to make sure we're all on the same page. With that in mind, I'll ask SAC Roubidoux to say a few words."

Barkley dropped his bulk into his chair and grabbed his cup of coffee as Roubidoux, a small, precise woman in her mid-forties, got to her feet and removed her reading glasses.

"Thanks, Deputy Chief. We're very glad you asked us over this morning. I'll let SSA Griffin speak for himself, of course, but as far as the Glendale city field office is concerned, we're more than happy to provide whatever advice and guidance we can to your investigative team. Special Agent Alexander will be your primary point of contact, but I'm also available at any time if Sandy can't be reached."

She touched the back of her carefully-styled dark hair. "Having said that, I can't spare Sandy or any other agent from their current workload for active participation in this investigation. There's a possibility you may want to set up a joint task force with police departments in other cities who have open cases on this UNSUB. If so, Sandy can help you and SSA Griffin set it up, but beyond that, he really won't be able to give you any assistance in terms of the investigation itself."

She put a hand on her hip and turned to Hank. "Lieutenant Donaghue, this is your case. We're here to help, but the burden of responsibility for calling the shots lies on your shoulders. I know that's what you want to hear, so I'm making it clear up front. Regardless of whether your UNSUB turns out to be the Rainy Day Killer or someone entirely different, it's up to you to investigate, identify, and arrest."

She shifted her eyes to Turcotte. "I'll say one more thing. Captain, our laboratory facilities are completely at your disposal during this investigation. I understand your difficulties in terms of backlogs and priorities. Sandy's empowered to facilitate the processing of any evidence on this case on a highest-priority basis. We can have one of our evidence response teams work with your people, if it'll help. You have our business cards: don't hesitate to call."

Turcotte nodded briefly. His expression was guarded, but his lack of trust was obvious to everyone in the room. It was his under-standing that when an FBI evidence response team went out to a crime scene, they generally secured the area with their own personnel and took over the evidence gathering and processing, shutting out other agencies. Although Roubidoux seemed to be making a genuine offer of cooperation, it was clear Turcotte didn't believe it would be that sim-ple.

"Thank you," Barkley said from the other end of the table. "We appreciate your generous offer, and we'll definitely take you up on it, if necessary."

"I hope so." Roubidoux smiled politely, sitting down. "That's all I want to say, other than thanks for the coffee and pastries, which I really shouldn't have touched, but they looked so good." She looked at Griffin. "If there's anything you'd like to say while we're all still here, please go ahead. Otherwise, I think we should probably clear out and let you get to work."

Griffin shrugged. He didn't stand up, just swiveled his chair back and forth, looking up and down the table. "What Marie-Louise said about jurisdiction is as plain as it gets. I'm here to discover what I can about the behavior of your offender, what made him select your victim as opposed to other potential victims, and tell you what I can about him. But don't expect me to be out there running around with my gun in the air helping you chase down suspects. It's been a long time since I worked in the field and, believe me, that's something that makes me very, very happy."

As everyone laughed, he swung around to look at Barkley. "Actually, there's something I was going to discuss later with Hank that I'll bring up right now, if you don't mind."

Barkley raised one of his football-sized hands and swallowed a mouthful of coffee. "Mmm. By all means."

Griffin looked at Montgomery. "You're the PIO on this case, right? I'm sorry, I don't remember your name."

"Officer First Class Eleanor Montgomery," she replied. She was the only person in the room wearing a uniform.

Griffin nodded. "Officer Montgomery. Right. I watched some of your tape. You're very good."

"Thank you, sir."

"Unfortunately," Griffin went on, "since your UNSUB's pretty obviously the Rainy Day Killer, one of my first recommendations to Hank is that he take over as the public information officer for this case."

As Philbin stirred in his chair, Griffin raised an eyebrow. "Don't you see it? A key part of this guy's post-murder behavior is to start a dialogue with the lead investigator. That's already happened with Hank through the package he got on Thursday with the video and the victim's amputated breasts. He'll establish telephone contact next, and he'll expect Hank to be the one who tells the world all about the horrible exploits of the killer who kidnaps women when it's raining outside. He's not going to be satisfied with some anonymous PIO reading prepared statements to the microphones—with all due respect, Officer Montgomery—because he's not interested in a relationship with you, he's interested in a relationship with the guy running the investigation. He wants Hank to feel the pressure, he wants to squeeze him, and he wants him to slip up on camera and reveal stuff that'll crank up the fear level in the community."

He tapped his hand on the table. "You *have* to have a single person making all the statements to the press. If you say one thing in the press room, Officer Montgomery, and then they catch Hank outside on the sidewalk and he says something different, the public gets confused and upset. Surprisingly, this guy also gets upset. He's been known to contact the media himself to correct erroneous statements or anything else he didn't like, and you definitely don't want that. You want full control of all information going out to the public, and you want to keep this guy focused on Hank and not on some loose-cannon reporter eager for attention. Understand what I'm getting at?"

"I don't agree," Philbin said. "Montgomery's an experienced, trained PIO who can deliver whatever message this department needs to have delivered. That's her job. I say, let her do it."

Griffin leaned forward suddenly onto the table. He clasped his hands together and pointed both index fingers at Philbin. "I *get* that. I get where you're coming from, I get that she's trained and experienced, but you gotta remember, this guy absolutely, every time, wants to play the game with the lead investigator. Only the lead investigator. Not some detective, not some spokesperson, and not you. *Him.*" He moved his hands and pointed at Hank, as though firing a gun. "This guy. You didn't see the video, did you? You didn't hear him speak directly to Hank like he already knew him from way back. Like they were such good pals."

When Philbin shook his head, Griffin nodded. "I don't recommend that you *do* watch it. Or you, Deputy Chief, or anyone else who's not boots on the ground on this case, because it's not something you want replaying in your head at three o'clock in the morning while you're lying next to your spouse trying to get back to sleep. The game's between Hank and the UNSUB. It has to stay that way."

No one spoke.

Griffin slumped back in his chair. "Look, you're all nice people, and I appreciate the welcome and the coffee and good humor and all, but the fact of the matter is, this is not a happy business that brings us together. We're here to hunt a cold, inhuman monster who does unspeakable things to young women whose lives end in horrible, terrible pain and fear. It's time you let us get to work."

10

"I've always been a pretty good meeting killer," Griffin said when the room had been cleared of senior personnel, "but it's been my experience that when they reach a certain level in the hierarchy, some of these people forget what it's like down in the trenches. They lose the stomach for it. Anyway, I suggest we get right at it. This is going to take a lot of time to go through, and we're going to be here for a while."

As Horvath rolled the television and DVD player out from the corner of the room, Sandy leaned forward. "Mind if I stay?"

Griffin shrugged. "Fine with me. Hank?"

"Glad to have you," Hank told Sandy.

"Thanks."

"Every time I turn around," Griffin said to Hank, "this guy's showing up at one of my courses. I can't get rid of him."

Karen snorted. "Christ, I know the feeling."

Sandy smiled but Griffin looked surprised, so Hank explained, "Karen and Sandy are engaged to be married. The wedding's in a month and a half."

"Six weeks from today," Sandy confirmed.

Griffin rolled his eyes. "My God, I had no idea. That's great. Congratulations." He leaned over to shake Sandy's hand. "But have you thought this through? Do you think it's wise to be marrying local law enforcement? Mightn't that lead to all kinds of complications?"

"It'll get real complicated if he *doesn't* marry me," Karen said.

Griffin nodded sagely. "Now I understand everything."

Hank held up the video received two days ago from Theresa Olsen's killer. "Do you want to run through this first?"

"No." Griffin bent down and picked up a battered leather case that had been leaning against the wall. "Let's go over your case work. I have a couple of questions."

Everyone's eyes settled on Griffin, who pulled files out of his bag and sorted them on the table in front of him. He was a small man, slender and clean-shaven. His wiry, dark hair was touched up to hide the gray, his eyebrows were thick and black, and his forehead was high. His hands were small and precise. Deep lines bracketed his mouth, and the crow's-feet at the corners of his eyes suggested a sense of humor which served as a modest defense, at best, against the constant weight of knowledge he carried around with him.

Originally from Las Vegas, Ed Griffin had spent six years in law enforcement with the LVPD before joining the FBI, working first in Albuquerque and then in Little Rock, where he had his first experience investigating a series of sexual homicides that turned out to be the work of a single serial killer. In 1989, shortly after he had successfully closed that case, his wife moved back to Las Vegas with their two young daughters. Griffin subsequently transferred to Memphis, where he worked for three years. During this time he began to publish articles in law enforcement journals and other periodicals. His work and his writing soon drew the attention of the chief of the national academy at Quantico, who recruited him as an instructor. It was there that Hank had first met Griffin, while on course as a young, up-and-coming homicide detective.

During the 1990s, Griffin earned a Master's degree in psychology. He wrote his thesis on sexual homicide and later published it as his first book. Two more books on the subject followed, and Griffin found himself a reluctant celebrity. After joining the National Center for Analysis of Violent Crime as an analyst, Griffin became more introverted, more focused on his work than ever before, until finally he'd slipped into a monastic lifestyle. He lived in a small house in town, he had very few personal possessions, his diet consisted of fish, chicken, rice, and vegetables, and he swore off all alcohol. Caffeine, along with blackjack three times a year in Atlantic City, were his only vices.

"What would you like to know?" Hank asked.

Griffin rubbed his face. "Did you do background on the witness, Esther Banks? How credible do you think she is?"

"She's credible," Karen said. "I interviewed her and vetted her written statement. It's okay. No history of dementia, although she's seventy-four. She's lonely, but still pretty sharp. I'm good with what she gave us."

"All right. So now we've got a composite likeness to work with. In terms of the victim, do you have anything to add to your report?"

Karen shook her head. "It's all there. Young, no regular friends, just starting out in life. No red flags in her past."

Griffin looked at Horvath.

"Stains is right," Horvath said. "We couldn't find anything that would've drawn this guy's attention to her. It seems completely random."

"Random." Griffin closed his eyes, rolling the word around in his mouth. "It's kind of a misleading word, random. It suggests she was grabbed out of thin air, that it could have been anyone, really, and just happened to be her. But we'll come back to that later."

He opened his eyes again and looked at Hank. "Are there any other lab reports you're waiting for, related to the crime scene or the autopsy? Or is this it?"

"This is it," Hank said. "For now. There was essentially nothing in terms of physical evidence, other than the footprints and wheel tracks from the hand truck he used to move the body from his vehicle to the river bank."

Griffin nodded. "Which brings us to his package."

"The breasts were hers," Hank said, "and so was the clothing. Jeans, underwear, top, bra. No shoes. The container he put the breasts in is a typical re-sealable plastic tub you can buy anywhere for leftovers. No fingerprints, trace evidence, hairs, fibers. Nothing. The DVD we sent you yesterday is a copy, of course. The lab processed the original, which again is common stock that could have been purchased anywhere. No prints."

Griffin nodded. "Let's watch it."

11

First there was darkness. Then a patch of faint light became evident in the top right portion of the frame, filtering through high, filthy industrial window panes, taking on an amber tint as it fell across the silhouette of a man sitting in a chair facing the camera.

The man stirred, as though to draw attention to himself.

"Hello, Lieutenant Hank Donaghue," he said. His voice was unremarkable, a mid-range tenor, neither forceful nor weak, with a slight Midwestern accent. "It's a pleasure for me to make your acquaintance, though I don't imagine the feeling's mutual yet."

The man's face could not be seen, of course, because of the shadows. He sat with his right leg crossed over his left knee. His hands were folded calmly in his lap.

"This is a little something I like to do in all the towns I visit," he said. "I feel like it's a good idea to connect with the man whose job it is to find me, to reach out and say 'hello, here I am.' Hello, Hank. Here I am. You seem to be the go-to guy in this town, from what I've seen, so I'm guessing you and I will be getting to know each other over the next while. By the time I'm done here, you'll feel like we're old friends."

He shifted slightly, moving his hands to cup his raised knee. "Of course, there's the little problem of what to call me. If you don't know already, the press in other towns called me the Rainy Day Killer. Actually, I suggested the name to a reporter myself quite a while ago, I forget where it was. Evansville? I'm not sure. Anyway, it's not important. Rainy Day Killer's kind of a mouthful, so why don't you just call me Bill? That's my name, after all."

He released his knee and put his hands to his cheeks in mock horror. "Oh no! Did I just give myself away? A vital clue! First name William! Last name—oh oh, we're not sure." He lowered his hands back to his lap. "It could drive you insane after a while. Sifting through all the tiny clues you think I'm stupidly giving you, trying to find two pieces of the puzzle to fit together. Well, good luck with that, Hank. Join the long list of cops who've been in the same seat you're in now, watching and listening to me as I take you to school on the hard realities of life in the cruel lane."

His hand moved slightly, and the camera began to pan left. When it stopped, the dark, indistinct shape on the left now filled the screen. There was an audible click, and a floodlight on a six-foot tripod suddenly illuminated the foreground.

Theresa Olsen's body lay on a low cot. She was naked, her legs straight and only slightly apart, arms at her sides. Her breasts were still intact.

"Speaking of school," he said, "isn't she lovely? Oh, don't worry. She's dead. I still have some work to do, of course, but this is the time when I like to take a little break, still feeling that post-coital warmth from our final lovemaking, and have this little one-way chat. It's kind of cool, actually. Like projecting myself forward into the future. The now-Bill speaking to the future-Hank while the future-Bill's already busy with his next hunt."

The camera zoomed in on the body. "Look at these breasts. Aren't they lovely? Not enormously large, but such a fine shape. Perfect, really. But of course you know that, don't you? You've already sent them to your lab, or whatever you do with that sort of thing, but trust me, they're hers. It's not so much a matter of identifying them as figuring out why on earth I would cut them off. Why would I do that, Hank? Why, oh why?"

The camera zoomed back to its previous setting and panned right until he was once more near the center of the frame. The spotlight went out. "If you haven't already done so, I suggest you contact Supervisory Special Agent Edward Griffin of the FBI. The famous Behavioral Analysis Unit has already been called in on my case, and Ed's the analyst who's been following me from town to town, picking up my bread crumbs and trying to put the loaf back together again. In fact, if I can project myself into the future once more, this may be the third or fourth time you've watched this, and Father Ed's probably right there in the room with you."

He leaned forward. "Are you there, Ed? How're you doing? Do you think this cop's going to have any more on the ball than the others? Have you made any improvements to the profile? I'm sorry if I keep feeding you misinformation through these hopeless saps, but it really is a lot of fun."

He leaned back again and folded his arms across his chest. "You see, Hank, I've read Ed's books. They're required reading, really, for anyone in my line of work. I've studied very carefully everything he's written about antecedent behavior and planning, characteristics of the crime, post-murder behavior. Fascinating stuff. Gave me a few ideas, I have to admit, but mostly they gave me openings to exploit. In some of my early experiments, I'm afraid I lied rather shamelessly to confuse things and mess with Ed's profile. Ed will explain; I don't have much more time right now. Anyway, your job is to figure out, with Father Ed's help, what part of this message is bullshit and what part's golden. Good luck."

He unfolded his arms and put his palms flat on his knees. "Here are the basics. My pretext, if I can use that word, was simple with this little beauty. I knocked on her door, told her I was a police detective, showed her this great-looking badge I have in my collection, and said her parents had been in an accident and we needed her to come to the hospital right away. Simple and straightforward. I prefer taking them out in the street, it's more of a challenge, but as Father Ed will explain, I've gone up on their doorsteps before, and I knew this would work like a charm. It did. I had her out onto the sidewalk and into my car before she knew what was happening. Wham, bam, and she was out for the ride.

"I know you'll watch this video many times, and I appreciate the attention, believe me, but if you're trying to figure out from the background behind me where I am right now, don't blow a gasket. I like to work in abandoned buildings. Ask Father Ed. I have to say, there's a real crisis in America right now. Did you know there are fifteen thousand fires a year in vacant buildings in the United States that cause a hundred and twenty million dollars' worth of damage? Do you realize in your own city that the cost of police and fire service for a city block goes up by fifteen hundred dollars for every vacant building on it? Did you know there are over one hundred violent crimes committed in abandoned buildings in this city every year?"

He waved a hand at the body on the cot. "Here's my contribution to your stats, Hank. By all means, step up the patrols of vacant buildings now, because you'll really want to find your primary crime scene, as they call it on TV. I may stay here, but then again, I may not. I scouted out a number of different spots, so I have some options. Something else for you to think about. And think about. And think about."

He folded his hands in his lap again. "I have to get moving, because there's still lots to do and she'll be stiffening up soon, but let me leave you with a couple of thoughts. First of all, she was great. She screamed and yelled and begged and moaned the whole weekend. I love it. That's why you won't find any signs of gagging, because I let them talk away." He waved a hand. "Who could hear, around this place? Second, we explored some things sexually I hadn't been able to try before, for one reason or another that I won't get into now, and she was wonderful. I came so hard I thought I'd see stars.

"The key word here, Hank, is lust. Ask Father Ed what it means in terms of my profile, will you? It'll be so helpful." His laugh was low, chilling. "He's such a great guy. Have you attended any of his courses or presentations before? I have. He's a great speaker. He explains things so simply. Lust murderers, organized and disorganized, nonsocial and social. All that bullshit. It just rolls off his tongue. He's so smooth. But honestly, Hank, these guys couldn't find their own ass in the dark with both hands. And neither can you, because I don't intend to leave you any physical evidence. Gasp! But anyway, don't mind me. I only work here."

He stood up and held out his hand, which gripped a wireless remote control device.

"Come and get me, you idiot."

The screen went blank.

12

"He's intelligent," Griffin said, leaning back in his chair, his knee propped up on the edge of the table. "Not as smart as he'd like you to believe, but smart enough. Studies have shown that 80 percent of serial murderers have an average or higher than average intelligence, and he certainly falls into that category."

"He said to ask you about lust and what it means in terms of his profile," Horvath said. "I don't know a whole lot about behavioral profiling. What are we supposed to understand, here?"

Griffin shrugged. "It's another game he likes to play. He's trying to use our own tools against us to confuse things and have a little fun. If you want, I can go over some of the basic stuff first, to get it out of the way."

"Feel free," Hank invited.

"Lust murder is a term that goes way back," Griffin said to Horvath. "Different analysts have different preferences when it comes to terminology, never mind the concepts themselves. Even the pioneers in the field like Hazelwood and Douglas have fundamental disagreements on a lot of this stuff. Here's my take."

He lowered his knee and folded his hands on the table in front of him. "I prefer to use the term sexual homicide when it comes to guys like this, because in its simplest terms it means we're dealing with a crime where the sexual element is the primary reason why it happens. It drives the whole thing, it determines the various acts committed during the period of captivity and rape, and it climaxes, pun intended, with the murder."

"So as we put together the sequence of events," Horvath said, "to figure out what he did, step by step, we need to ask ourselves why each thing was important to him in terms of sexual gratification?"

"You won't need to get quite that fancy," Griffin said. "You can just come right out and call a spade a spade. This is a sexual homicide. Let me explain." He gestured at the blank television screen. "He mentioned organized and disorganized, social and nonsocial. Suffice it to say, this guy is what's commonly called an organized offender. Despite all his playing around, there are definite characteristics that let us make this basic assumption." He held up a hand to tick off the points on his finger. "He's fairly smart, where disorganized offenders are usually less so. He's socially adept, because he can talk his victims into his trap, where a disorganized offender usually has to use a blitz attack to subdue them. He's sexually competent, whereas disorganized killers usually act out of sexual frustration or confusion. He has pretty good control over his emotions during the rape and murder, instead of being all over the map in his behavior. He follows himself in the media closely, where a disorganized offender either wouldn't bother or would be too upset."

He switched hands and continued to count off the points. "He plans ahead, controls the event, is comfortable hunting anywhere, targets strangers, uses restraints, and requires a submissive victim, where disorganized offenders usually grab a victim on impulse, improvise as they go along, may act against someone they already know within a geographical comfort zone, and blitz in a sudden attack that makes restraints an afterthought. Our UNSUB's not afraid of personalizing the victim, where a disorganized offender often depersonalizes or dehumanizes them."

"Where does the torture come in?" Karen asked, her voice flat.

"The asphyxiation routine is not uncommon with organized offenders," Griffin replied. "They use the ligature to strangle the victim to the point of unconsciousness for their own arousal. It's a control thing, and I expect the rapes occur at this point."

"Which fits with what you said about wanting passive victims," Horvath said.

"Yes. The mutilation, though, is something else. It doesn't quite fit with the rest of the picture." Griffin leaned back. "Let me explain by talking first about sexual substitution. Insertion of a foreign object is something you often see with a disorganized offender, a stick or screwdriver or some other phallic object that compensates for the offender's own inability to penetrate his victim. There's never been any indication of this with the Rainy Day Killer, as far back as we can go." Griffin waved at the television. "You could see the arrogance about his sexual prowess and, as far as I'm concerned, that rings true. So it doesn't surprise me there's no use of foreign objects because their absence is consistent with his type, if I can use a negative to prove a positive. See what I mean? There's a certain consistency.

"Mutilation, now, is often seen as a form of depersonalization. Either the offender wants to hide the identity of the victim, thinking maybe it'll hinder the investigation, or he wants to desexualize or dehumanize the body. There are different conclusions that might be drawn from this, including regret and a wish to deny that he's just killed a human being, misogyny and a feeling of contempt, resentment or hatred of the female body, and a desire to androgynize his victims and rob them of their sexuality. You could go on, but the point here is that you're much more likely to see this kind of behavior with a disorganized offender, which this guy clearly is not. So there's an inconsistency here."

"So why does he do it?" Horvath asked.

"Why, indeed." Griffin glanced at Hank. "This is the first time he's talked about it specifically in one of his videos. 'Why, oh why?' I'm thinking maybe he's getting a little bored with it. In the first case linked to this UNSUB, in St. Louis, there was mutilation of the breasts *and* the genitals, and they never turned up. In the second case, in Evansville, there was mutilation of the breasts only, and he sent them to the investigating officer, his pattern ever since. Looking back, I think he may have been experimenting in the first one. Maybe he wanted to try cannibalism because he'd read about it and thought it'd make him appear that much more horrible."

"And didn't like it," Horvath said.

"And didn't get the kick out of it he thought he would. But he'd already included it as part of what he was viewing as his signature, so the next time, he skipped the genitals, skipped whatever he did with the breasts the first time, and just sent them to the police instead."

"What the fuck's the point?" Karen demanded.

Griffin nodded. "That's the five-dollar question. As far as I'm concerned, there's no sexual component. They're removed post-mortem, and it's pretty evident he doesn't engage in sexual activity with his victims after they're dead. It's not depersonalization, because he wants their identity known and he likes to brag about how they performed sexually for him. I think it's strictly for shock effect. He lives for the fear factor. He wants to get inside the investigator's head and freak the hell out of him. Plus, it inevitably ends up in the news, and it upsets the public. That's the other thing that's so important to this guy. He wants the community to be afraid of him. It's part of his power-and-control thing."

"He's a fucking inhuman monster."

"Yes," Griffin said. "That's exactly what he wants everyone to think."

13

Hank ordered in lunch, after which they watched the other videos the Rainy Day Killer had sent to law enforcement in previous cities. Griffin had made copies of the case files, and he gave them a brief overview of each one before playing the corresponding video.

"The first one we know of occurred in St. Louis in October 2006," Griffin said. "The victim was Pearl Mortenson, a twenty-one-year-old prostitute and drug addict. She was the first in the basic victim profile—white, small, reasonably fit, blonde hair. She disappeared during a rainstorm in the middle of a Friday afternoon from a street corner on Jefferson Avenue in south St. Louis. He held her for four days, raped and tortured her multiple times using ligature strangulation, and left her along the river pretty much the same way he did here. This was his first video."

It was longer than the Olsen video, rambling and melodramatic, and shot with different equipment that obviously didn't include a remote device. He moved back and forth several times between his chair and the camera, at one point removing the camera from its stand and carrying it over to the body, all the while narrating as though he were filming a documentary. The movement gave them a look at his body, and it more or less matched the description given to them by Esther Banks of a slightly-built man who was not very tall. Griffin remarked that he likely wasn't a very strong individual, which would explain the use of the stun gun, drugs, physical restraints, and the hand truck when disposing of the body.

Karen asked if he thought the killer might have some kind of disability or condition that resulted in abnormal weakness. Griffin thought it was probably not the case; it was more likely he simply wasn't a very strong man, his sexual prowess notwithstanding. He likely spent most of his time in sedentary activities, such as sitting in front of a computer. If he worked, it was likely at a job that didn't involve manual labor.

In this first video, the Rainy Day Killer had already mutilated the body. He spent several minutes describing what he'd done, holding up a bloodstained KA-BAR combat knife with which he'd removed the breasts and genitalia. He went on to describe the erotic strangulation and compared himself to the Dating Game Killer, who had been active in California in the late 1970s, then invited the investigating officer, Detective Len Capers, to call him the Rainy Day Killer. He described where he'd leave the body now that he was finished with it, and explained he was bringing her to the river to let her soul cross the Styx to the afterworld.

"You could see he was in a warehouse," Griffin said, ejecting the DVD and loading the next one. "They were never able to find it. Capers suppressed a lot of information, including the Rainy Day Killer nickname and the mutilation. The case went cold. They were handling a rash of sexual homicides at that time and had their hands full. I've looked at some of them and I think our UNSUB was responsible for at least three, possibly five, between 2002 and 2006, in which he was experimenting with different victims and different MOs. Personally, I think he had a near-miss on one of the other ones and left the city before they got any closer to him."

The second video had been sent to Lieutenant Jim Feeley of the Evansville, Indiana police department. The victim was Jane Anne Meecher, twenty-four, a convenience store clerk who was abducted on a rainy Saturday afternoon in June 2007 after finishing her shift. Again, she was white, single, slightly over five feet tall, one hundred and nine pounds, and her medium-length hair was blonde. He held her for three days before she died on him, which he complained about bitterly in the video before removing her breasts with the KA-BAR while the camera recorded it.

He explained his intention to leave the body on the banks of the Ohio River as a human sacrifice to the spirits of the Angel Mound builders. Angel Mound, Griffin explained, was a Native American historical site eight miles from Evansville. Feeley spent a lot of time investigating this angle, and for some time worked on the theory that the killer was Native American.

"By the time he'd decided that the human sacrifice bit was bullshit," Griffin said, "the case had grown cold."

Because Capers had held back the nickname and the mutilation in the Mortenson homicide, Feeley didn't connect his case to St. Louis. Additionally, Feeley made the same decision, hoping that the suppression of this information would help weed out false confessions and dead-end tips. Unfortunately, he made no progress before the Rainy Day Killer struck again, walking onto the campus of the University of Evansville on a wet afternoon in April 2008, where he abducted nineteen-year-old Jackie Pilcher, a sophomore majoring in business administration.

The video he sent to Feeley this time was shorter and more to the point. He reminded Feeley that he wanted to be publicly known as the Rainy Day Killer, he pointed out the similarities between Pilcher and Meecher so that his modus operandi would be clearly understood, even by a moron like Feeley, and he explained he was dumping Pilcher on the riverbank close to the riverboat casino to apologize to the water spirits for the defamation caused by the presence of such a hollow temple of materialism and greed.

"This time," Griffin said as the video ended, "Lieutenant Feeley told the press he believed the two homicides had been committed by the same person, but again he didn't use the nickname. Like many of us, he didn't appreciate the way these individuals become popularized in the media. However, the UNSUB finally figured out it would be simpler just to go to the press himself, so he called a reporter with the local newspaper and gave him the works, including the fact that he was responsible for other rapes in the area but that the Meecher and Pilcher murders were what he liked to think of as his signature kills."

"He really wanted the publicity," Horvath said as Griffin changed DVDs again.

"It's the fear factor," Griffin agreed, sitting down and picking up the remote control. "Evansville's not that big a place, just over a hundred thousand people. The publicity forced the local authorities to step up their investigation, and once again it got a little hot for this guy and he left town. Just over a year later, another victim turned up in Louisville. This time, things were a little different."

The fourth video was addressed to Lieutenant Cindy Kowpacki, the lead investigator with the Louisville police department. The victim's name was Sarah Towson, and at age twenty eight she was the oldest so far. She was married, where the previous victims had been single, and she was a real estate lawyer, where the others had worked at lower-income jobs. Most noticeably, instead of approaching her on the street, he abducted her from the front porch of her ground-floor apartment in the trendy Belgravia district on a Sunday morning in June.

The quality of the video was higher than the other three and included the use of a remote control device for the first time. The UNSUB had upgraded his equipment upon arrival in Louisville. The routine was similar to what they'd seen in the Olsen video.

"This is the first time he explains his pretext on camera," Griffin said.

Hank watched as the man leaned forward in his chair and clasped his hands between his knees, his face still hidden in shadow.

"It was easy, Cindy. Can I call you Cindy? It gives me a bit of a tingle when I do. Anyway, it was very easy. I knew her husband played basketball every Sunday morning with a bunch of buddies downtown. I rang her doorbell and told her Frank had just been in a horrible car accident only a few blocks away. They were still trying to get him out, and he was calling for her. I told her I witnessed the accident and volunteered to come and get her. I was on my way to church, but this was much more important. She wasn't any brighter than the others, Cindy. She fell for it right away."

He leaned back. "Why am I telling you this? Maybe it's because I think females are stupid. They're dumb and trusting. Some guy they've never met before in their miserable little lives is completely believable because he's wearing a nice suit and carrying an umbrella to protect them from the rain in their moment of need. But what about you, my dear, sweet Cindy? Are you dumb too, like the rest of them? Or do you think you can catch me? Just the thought of it gives me such a rush. Being hunted by a woman. You have no idea how arousing that is."

Karen grunted something under her breath.

"I'm going to leave her on the riverbank, Cindy," the killer went on. "Another soul commended to the Ohio. Were you paying attention when I said I'd done this before? I'll give you a little tip, sweetheart.

There's no big spiritual meaning to it. It's not a signature thing. Do you know what that means? Look it up if you don't."

When the video was finished playing, Griffin ejected the DVD and put it back into the plastic case. "A victim like this is considered at low risk because she's married and her occupation and lifestyle don't expose her to targeting the same way as with someone working the streets, like Pearl Mortenson. The UNSUB was definitely taking a high risk to abduct her from her doorstep."

He picked up another DVD. "Victim number five, Patricia Skeldov, Pittsburgh." He put it down and picked up another. "Lise Larsen, Pittsburgh." He held up the final DVD. "Annabelle Witten, Harrisville, West Virginia." He wagged it back and forth. "This one was the most unusual. He was clearly in transit. He found her waiting on tables at a truck stop, heard her talking about her trucker husband who was on the road, followed her home to a ten-acre farm, and used the barn as his captivity site. He says he liked hitting a rural target for once, as opposed to hunting in a city. It's also the first time he mentions me by name. Kowpacki wanted to consult us in Louisville but her captain blocked it, so we didn't get involved until Pittsburgh, where, of course, the press made a big deal of it. You could see he was playing around the edges of the whole profiling business in the first four videos, but when you watch these last three you'll see him really getting serious about it. It raised the stakes for him and made the game that much more interesting."

"It's not a game," Karen objected. "He's raping and killing innocent women. Only a fucking sicko would think that's a game."

Griffin tossed the DVD on the table with the others. "You're right, it's not a game. I've devoted the past twenty-five years of my life to hunting guys like him and, believe me, I'm tired, depressed, and utterly devoid of religious faith or belief in a higher good.

"Do I think this is a game? Do I feel like I'm playing a game where we keep track of the points and decide who won and who lost at the end of the day? No. This is my work, my life's work, and it sure as hell isn't a game.

"But to him? Damn right it's a game to him. Look, everybody's got their own theories about what causes them to be the way they are. Some say it's genetic, others say it's a difference in brain structure or an unstable family background of violence or abuse, or a combination of things. Take your pick. Nobody knows for sure, although plenty of people *think* they know."

He pointed his finger at the TV. "This guy? I'm convinced he came from a relatively stable home and didn't experience any childhood abuse. In one of these videos he tries to claim he was abused by a baby sitter when he was a boy, but I'm convinced it's just more of his bullshit. I think he *doesn't know* why he is the way he is."

"I don't understand," Horvath said.

"Don't you see?" Griffin waved his hand. "He's sexually aroused in situations where he has complete power and control over females. He holds them for three or four days, as long as they can physically last, and he goes on a sexual binge, but for a reasonably intelligent guy he doesn't understand why he does it. His self-image is all over the map. He thinks maybe he's Hannibal the Cannibal, then he thinks he's the Dating Game Killer, then he thinks he's somebody else again. He likes the fact that an FBI analyst is on his case, so he keeps adding and subtracting stuff to yank on my chain and keep me interested, but at the end of the day he knows he's showing me enough to form a reasonably accurate profile, and he'd love to know what that profile is, because—"

"He wants *you* to tell him who he is," Horvath said.

Griffin nodded. "Exactly."

14

Every Sunday morning at seven o'clock, Chief Wilson Bennett arrived at the Silver Moon Grill on Clergy Street for breakfast. He sat in the same table near the back, ordered the same spread that included scrambled eggs, bacon, toast with orange marmalade, and a pot of coffee, and he read the Sunday morning newspapers while his driver drank coffee at the lunch counter and kept an eye on his boss in the big mirror on the wall. An hour and a half later, the chief stacked the papers on the table, walked to the cash register at the front, made a big show of paying his bill, and was driven two blocks to All Saints Episcopal Church at Clergy and Simpson, where he sat in his usual pew next to his ex-wife and their four children for the duration of the service. Afterward, he spent two hours with the kids—miniature golf was a favorite—and then took them to a restaurant for lunch. When their mid-day meal was finished, he dropped the children off at his ex-wife's house in Granger Park and had his driver take him to the country club, leaving behind his former family for another week.

This morning, however, his routine at the Silver Moon was interrupted to accommodate a meeting.

Hank arrived at ten minutes after eight o'clock to find Bennett and Ann Martinez waiting for him. After he accepted a cup of coffee, he watched the chief tap a folded-up section of newspaper with his index finger.

"According to this morning's Op-Ed, Lieutenant Donaghue, this department is ineffectual, quote unquote, when it comes to violence against women. Apparently Theresa Olsen's becoming the central focus of several lobby groups with longstanding grudges against us." He picked up a spoon and scooped sugar into his coffee. "Despite the fact that our violent crime statistics have been going down over the last eighteen months, this case is like an incendiary flare to these people. We need to show some sort of progress."

"I agree." Hank said. He saw Martinez tilt her head slightly to one side and took it as a cue to assume Bennett wanted a full accounting. "We prepared a statement that I'll release at this morning's regular briefing. It'll contain new information. There's—"

"What's your sense of the FBI's contribution so far?" Bennett interrupted, stirring his coffee.

"Good. Very helpful."

"How detailed is the profile?"

"It's good. What helps is that the description and composite sketch we got from the eyewitness on North Clanton Street seem to be a fit. For once we have a reasonably reliable eyewitness. In a nutshell, we're looking for a white male, mid-thirties, short, slight build, not all that physically fit or strong but with good coordination and hand and wrist strength, well-groomed dark hair, fairly intelligent, may be a college graduate, may work part-time in a white-collar position, probably drives a late-model van or SUV that's reasonably well kept. There's more."

"You're confident it's this Rainy Day Killer?"

"Reasonably confident," Hank said. "Everything's qualified, of course, until you have a suspect in custody with sufficient evidence to convict him, but it's clear this is the direction we need to take."

Bennett set down the spoon and sipped his coffee. "Okay. What about a task force with the other jurisdictions?"

"It's not in the cards." Hank had already spoken to Detective Capers in St. Louis, Lieutenant Feeley in Evansville, and Detective Hegman in Pittsburgh, none of whom had had the time for or interest in a meeting, let alone a joint investigation. Capers had been rude in his dismissal of any form of cooperation, Feeley had sounded distracted and overloaded, and Hegman had told him both cases were already flagged as "open-unsolved" and had been moved to the back burner. Lieutenant Cindy Kowpacki in Louisville had shown an interest in comparing notes, but her captain blocked a request to travel to Glendale. That left only Sheriff Tom Anglehart in Harrisville, West Virginia, who couldn't afford to make the trip but said he was available by telephone at any time.

"We have copies of their case files," Hank said, "or at least copies of what they gave the FBI, and that will have to do."

Bennett nodded. He began to doodle on the newspaper with a fountain pen.

"The plan is for me to appear at this morning's regular media session and deliver an impromptu statement," Hank said. "PIO Montgomery wrote it, and SSA Griffin and I vetted it. I'll announce that we have reason to believe the Olsen homicide is connected to a series of homicides in other states attributed to an individual known as the Rainy Day Killer. I'll mention that we received a communication from someone claiming to be this individual and taking credit for the Olsen homicide. For now we'll withhold the fact that it was in the form of a video. We'll also withhold what else was in the package. I'll state that the FBI has been consulted, and an analyst who's familiar with the Rainy Day Killer is providing assistance. I'll then state that I'll be the sole departmental spokesperson for this case, and that all other sources will have no comment. We'll give them a handout including the composite and a TIPS number the public can call with information, I'll repeat our request for assistance from the public, and then I'll walk out without taking any questions."

Bennett continued to doodle. "Sounds fine. Philbin's agreed to lend PIO Montgomery to Homicide. Ann tells me you've already decided how she'll spend her time."

Hank didn't look at Martinez, understanding now that she had briefed Bennett beforehand, but that the chief wanted to hear it from his lips. Was there a problem waiting to bite him on the ass?

"Montgomery will set up a series of meetings with Block Watch captains," he said, "to distribute the handout and encourage people to phone the TIPS line if they see or hear anything suspicious. She'll also work directly with TIPS to screen the calls and collate anything useful. She'll give me two reports a day. She'll also draft all my statements."

Bennett nodded again.

"Hank feels a proactive strategy is key at this stage," Martinez said.

"Explain," Bennett said to Hank.

"The use of a single spokesperson and the irregular timing of statements is one part of it," Hank said. "As Ed said yesterday, it takes control of the information flowing out to the public and gives us a chance to manage public perception of the threat. Going out to the Block Watch program is a logical next step, because then the neighborhoods can see us following up on what's said to the media. Also, the district commanders will step up patrols of areas with large-sized vacant buildings. We'd love to find the primary scene, or catch him moving to another site."

"Good," Bennett said.

"You're also covering the dump site," Martinez prompted.

"Yes." Hank glanced at her now, but she was staring at Bennett. "We're not sure if this guy's the type who returns to his disposal sites afterward to relive the crime, but we wanted to cover it. Midtown was sending a car under the bridge twice a day but it's not practical, so Tim Byrne set up a few motion-activated video cameras to give us twenty-four-hour coverage of the site. Midtown's extending their patrols along the river in any event, in case he's scouting for another dump site. We have to work on the assumption that he's planning his next kill."

"You know," Bennett said, putting down his pen, "you can call him an UNSUB if you like. If it's a good enough term for the FBI, it should be good enough for us."

"With all due respect, sir," Hank replied, "I think when it comes to catching offenders in our own jurisdiction, we need to be better than the FBI."

Bennett smiled. "What I want to hear." He turned to Martinez. "With one exception. I want their lab to handle all future physical evidence collection and analysis, if, God forbid, he does act again." He held up a hand as Martinez opened her mouth. "I know Turcotte will have a problem with it, but that's how I want it done. I want their evidence response team at the next crime scene. With our people maintaining functional authority, of course, but I want the FBI using their protocols and equipment to collect and analyze everything. Plus, I want everything we have so far on the Olsen case sent to their lab for a second look. Negotiate it with Roubidoux, and make sure it's given top priority, as she promised. I want rapid turnaround on everything from here on out so we can move quickly on whatever it tells us. We're going to show everyone how the GPD does it."

"Yes sir," Martinez replied, her tone neutral.

"Good." Bennett leaned back and picked up the coffee pot. "Get to it."

Martinez stood up, black portfolio in hand. Hank pushed out his chair and, as he was about to stand, Bennett put a hand on his arm. "A word, Lieutenant."

Her face blank, Martinez left the table.

Hank sat back down.

Bennett refreshed his coffee, then topped up Hank's cup as well. "Ann has what it takes to make the next step up."

"I couldn't agree more, sir."

Bennett looked at him. "We don't know each other very well. Socially, I mean. Professionally, I've made it my business to become thoroughly familiar with your jacket."

Hank said nothing.

"The Hero Cop," Bennett said. "Saved the young son of then-councilman Adolphus Post single-handedly as a twenty-three-year-old patrol officer. When Post was elected mayor, he appointed Gerald White as our first African-American chief of police, and White, word has it, became your rabbi. You made detective at twenty-five, sergeant at twenty-nine, and lieutenant at thirty-one. Lightning speed, and just in the nick of time before Mayor Post finished his second term and his Democratic replacement got shellacked at the polls by Darrien Watts. When Watts replaced White with Orvell Jenkins, your many sins as special assistant to the chief came back to haunt you."

Hank sipped his coffee, waiting.

"You stepped on a lot of toes during your time in the chief's office," Bennett said. "You developed a good rapport with the media, but you don't seem to have inherited your mother's sense of internal politics. I have no doubt you're aware that Myron Heidigger still wants your hide nailed to his door, years after the fact. When you make enemies, Lieutenant, you make good ones."

Hank nodded, knowing that Heidigger, who was now deputy chief of Internal Affairs Division, still deeply resented public statements Hank had made about ongoing investigations while Heidigger was captain of the Homicide unit. It had resulted in friction between Heidigger and Chief White that had interfered with Heidigger's career advancement at the time and caused the man to hold a grudge ever since.

"You've been the subject of three IAD investigations," Bennett went on. "One for selling information to the Triad, one for falsifying the performance reports of a subordinate while you were her supervisor during your first stint in Homicide, and one for improper use of force."

Hank kept his mouth firmly closed.

"In the use-of-force case you made an off-duty arrest of a biker who was engaging in a knife fight with two other men outside a bar. Internal Affairs contended you inflicted the knife wounds yourself, but the complaint went away when one of the other men insisted he get the credit for cutting the biker. Is that how it went down?"

"That's how it went down."

"Falsifying performance reports to hide the incompetence of a subordinate in exchange for sexual favors is an extremely serious charge," Bennett continued. "The fact that Ann Martinez's competence is and has always been beyond question, plus the fact that absolutely no evidence of sexual impropriety was uncovered, took the wind out of the sails of that one. Is there anything negative related to Ann's abilities that you saw at the time that I should be aware of?"

"No, sir."

"I didn't think so." Bennett shifted in his seat. "Your personal history with her is of absolutely no interest to me unless it interferes with her ability to do her job now. Will it interfere with her ability to do her job now, Lieutenant?"

"Of course not, sir."

"Wonderful." Bennett sipped his coffee. "The thing with the Triad. I saw the photo, with the money passing between your hand and someone else's hand at an outdoor stall in Chinatown. Cropped, of course. It took two requests, which is one too many, but I finally saw the original sequence of photos in which you were buying a carton of noodles from a vendor. I mention this investigation last because it relates to the wider question of your ongoing relationship with known Triad officials and associates. This thing with Mah, is it a problem I need to worry about?"

"There is no thing with Mah, sir."

A frown flitted across Bennett's face. "Try again."

Hank sighed. "I saved Peter Mah's life in an alley in South Shore East two years ago. He believes he owes me some kind of debt of honor. I've told him he doesn't. He insists. His family, particularly his father, are likewise deluded, despite my attempts to set them straight. Peter Mah's currently out of the country, but his associates occasionally contact me as confidential informants. They won't accept CI money; they believe it's part of the repayment of the debt. I've been rolling with it, because their information has been useful in several cases. A CI's a CI. I believe Peter Mah's committed more than one homicide during his rise through the Triad ranks, and I believe once he comes back, if he does come back, he'll pick up exactly where he left off, at which point I hope the next one lands on my desk because I'll bust his ass and go for the death penalty like a point guard driving to the hoop for an easy lay-up."

Bennett nipped at his coffee and set down the cup. He picked up his napkin, patted his lips, and nodded. "Heidigger's priorities have been re-evaluated," he said. "His people have too much work to do to waste time on personal vendettas."

Hank remained silent.

"That said, I have a favor to ask."

"I see," Hank said, his tone guarded.

"I've discussed the upcoming staffing action at the captain's level with Doug and Ann. They agree with me that Lieutenant Cassion needs the kind of seasoning an acting stint in your section would give her. Her field experience with the Bureau was somewhat limited, and since joining the department she's mostly worked on the administrative side. I'd appreciate it if you'd give her the benefit of your experience and support while she gets her legs under her."

Hank hid his disappointment. "Of course, sir."

"Fine. Good." Bennett looked at his watch. "I have to leave. I should add that the competitive process will be posted in a week or two. It won't be a lot of time for her, but it'll be something."

Hank nodded.

"I expect to see your name on the list of applicants."

Hank looked at him. "I wasn't planning to apply."

"Then change your plans, Lieutenant." Bennett stood up and pushed in his chair, looking for his driver. "Change your plans."

15

Karen took a last look over her shoulder and slipped through the door, her SIG Sauer P-226 at the ready position.

The abandoned factory was being cleared by an eight-member tactical entry team. The property was completely surrounded by a twelve-foot chain link fence topped with barbed wire. Strathton district had established a perimeter, sealing all entry points. Four members of the entry team breached a side door at the west end of the building, which led into the raw materials handling area, while the other four and Karen went in through the loading dock area at the east end.

Tactical had chosen not to breach the building through the main entrance at the front because surveillance had shown the big glass doors were solidly chained and locked. They probably hadn't been opened since management had snapped the padlock shut five years ago. More importantly, it was tactically preferable when entering a building at ground level to enter through the end of the structure rather than the middle, in order to minimize threats in front of the team.

Karen smelled dust, wet cardboard, oil, and an overlying odor she associated with rats and feces, but no seafood. The smell was one reason why she'd elected to come in through the loading dock area and not the other end of the abandoned cannery, where the raw seafood had been sorted and cleaned. The other reason was that she was betting whoever was using this place also found the stink repulsive enough to avoid that end of the dump, and she wanted to be in on the bust, not doing mop-up out in left field.

A drive-by patrol last evening had spotted suspicious activity, and the Strathton district commander had authorized Tactical to do their thing at sunrise. Because the exact location of the suspected individuals inside the building was unknown, a stealth entry had been ordered by the team commander. This approach relied on a quiet breaching of the building, brief and preferably silent communication among team members, and swift but systematic clearing of each successive area.

The team Karen was following got off to a good start, for although the roll-up door leading into the loading area was closed and locked, someone had conveniently left the steel security door next to it propped open with a chunk of two-by-four. The first man inside moved left and cleared from the center to the far left corner. The second man moved right and cleared from the center to the far right corner. The third and fourth, right behind them, entered and cleared the other two quadrants of the loading dock.

Inside, Karen peered through the gloom at stacks of old wooden pallets and shredded garbage bags. Refuse was scattered about the cement floor. The ceiling above her head was high, and the long-disused fluorescent light fixtures were filthy. The team's lights probed the shadows back and forth, up and down. She saw two shapes parked inside the big rolling door and, moving toward them, realized that they were two motorcycles. She used the light attached to her SIG to check them out. They were both Harleys, a few years old, and appeared to be in good working order. Tire tracks on the floor seemed fairly recent. She put the back of her hand against the muffler. Cold.

She looked at the team leader, who was watching her. She shrugged and shook her head.

On the left of the loading area was a security door, propped open like the door they'd just entered. It led into the main front corridor of the factory that ran the full length of the building, east to west. Two team members slipped through this door as Karen watched. Their job was to sweep the main corridor and link up with another pair clearing the corridor from the other end of the building.

The other two, followed by Karen, moved through a pair of blue fabric barrier doors on the right, the kind of doors you were supposed to be able to bump open and push through with a cart or a hand truck. On the other side of these doors was a product storage area with four long rows of empty ten-foot-high metal shelves. One man checked each row while the other covered the room. Karen, following orders, remained just inside the fabric doors, out of the way.

Was this the building where the Rainy Day Killer had held Theresa Olsen? The power had been shut down several years ago, but the incident commander had confirmed that the city had never turned off the water. Griffin believed the Rainy Day Killer didn't necessarily need electricity—the video camera could have been operated on battery power—but running water was a must for his clean-up procedures.

What the hell was the deal with the motorcycles? It bothered her that there was no sign of a van or SUV around the place, and the bikes didn't fit the picture. Could they have been left behind by the cannery staff? She shook her head. They had to belong to whoever had propped the doors open with the chunks of wood.

Maybe he used a van for his snatches and dumps, and a motorcycle for scouting and surveillance, giving him greater mobility.

One of the Tactical officers caught her eye and raised a thumb, indicating that the room was cleared. At that moment they heard the sound of distant gunfire.

"Thirty-one," a voice said in Karen's earpiece.

"Copy," the entry team leader acknowledged.

A third voice, which Karen recognized as belonging to the incident commander, said from his command post outside in the parking lot, "Go hot. Acknowledge."

"Copy that," the team leader replied, his voice calm. "We're hot. Rock and roll."

She heard the two team members in front of her acknowledge the change in tactics to a dynamic clearing method, in which force and speed were now key to accessing the objective. The closest man pointed at Karen.

"Stay put."

"Yeah, right," she muttered. She heard a sound coming from one of the rows. She crouched and aimed. A rat passed through the beam of her light, scuttling on a bottom shelf. She turned back to find herself alone in the room.

She moved cautiously into the next room. She looked at motionless, filthy conveyor belts, packing tables littered with garbage, a rusted push cart.

More shots were fired, in another part of the building.

"What the hell's going on?" she demanded. "Where is he?"

"Please stay off the channel, Detective," the team leader said. "Remain where you are until the situation has been resolved."

What the hell am I wearing body armor for? she thought, shaking her head. "I'm exiting the packaging area and entering the canning area."

"Negative, Detective. Remain where you are."

Crouching, she moved through the door into the next room, a large, cluttered area where the crab meat and baby shrimps had been packed into cans. Conveyor belts were everywhere, bending and twisting, rising and falling. Weak amber daylight from the rising sun filtered through a row of filthy windows on the far side.

She moved beside a hooded mass of machinery that must have been used to put the lids on the cans and vacuum-seal them shut. Now she could smell the foul odor of stale, rancid seafood. It wasn't one of her favorite smells.

She heard movement through the maze of conveyors at her two o'clock and a shot rang out. A bullet punched through the hood above her head and clanged around the machinery within.

"Taking fire in the canning room," she said calmly, crouching. "Not a good time for fratricide, folks."

Voices chattered in her earpiece as the team leader confirmed the location of each tactical pair. He assured Karen she was not taking friendly fire, and directed a pair to close in on the canning area. Suddenly, more gunfire rang out elsewhere in the building, and the tone of communications changed as another conflict erupted.

Edging along the side of the canning machine in a crouch, gun ready, Karen caught a glimpse of movement at her one o'clock. Someone scuttled past the end of her row and on to the next.

She held her fire.

It didn't make sense. The target she'd just seen was overweight, with long hair, a denim jacket, jeans, and cowboy boots. She hadn't read anything in any of the case files connecting the Rainy Day Killer to firearms, and this guy was firing a semi-automatic pistol at her.

Was he working with a partner? A fat slob who rode a motorcycle and was a really bad shot?

On a sudden hunch, she doubled back the way she'd come, scuttling through the doorway into the packaging area.

After a moment, the guy edged through—gun first, belly second, nose third.

As soon as he cleared the doorway she stepped behind him and stuck the muzzle of her SIG into the back of his neck, hard enough to leave a mark.

"Freeze, fuckhead."

Startled, the guy yelped and dropped his gun on the floor.

She took double-cuff disposable plastic locking straps from a pouch on her vest, swiftly secured his wrists, and then used her handcuffs to lock him to the end of a conveyor belt.

"One suspect apprehended and secured in the packaging area," she said.

"Copy," replied the team leader. "Situation has been resolved, Detective. Thought you were told to stay put."

"Don't be a crab."

He barked a short laugh that was mostly adrenaline. "On our way."

She holstered her gun and eyed her prisoner. "Thought you could bug out, did you?"

"I'm just a ride-along," the guy rasped, sweating profusely. "I don't count for nothing. It's not me you want. It's Lewis who's checking the place out. He's the one."

"Oh, and I guess Lewis was shooting at me from the other end of the fucking building, was he?"

"I didn't mean to. I was scared."

"You didn't *mean* to shoot at my fucking head? Exactly how stupid are you, you fucking moron?"

The room suddenly filled with bodies as the tactical team moved through on their way out of the building the way they'd come. They were leading another suspect, a taller, thinner version of the one she'd caught. This one, however, wore a leather jacket displaying gang colors, which explained the two motorcycles and ruled out the Rainy Day Killer as a possible squatter.

"Rest of the building's clear," the team leader told her. "We'll send Crime Scene in, but we didn't see any sign whatsoever that your guy was here. These two jokers were holding down the place for a meth lab. Just a happy coincidence we bumped into them."

Karen freed her prisoner and pocketed her handcuffs. "And a good time was had by all."

He winked at her. "Copy that." He grabbed her prisoner and hustled him out of the room.

Alone, Karen remained behind for a moment, looking around.

A damned false alarm, that's what it was. Nothing but a god-damned false alarm.

Theresa Olsen hadn't been here. But she'd been somewhere else like this. Filthy, poorly lit, foul-smelling, infested with rats, hope-lessly far away from help.

Karen's heart caught for a moment as she thought of Theresa ending her life in such a pitiless, desolate place at the hands of the Rainy Day Killer.

Two in the brainpan would be too good for an inhuman son of a bitch like that.

She looked forward to the moment when she had him in her sights, cold.

16

Hank was reading a report submitted by Detective Kaplan on the interrogation of his suspect in the drive-by shooting when the telephone on his desk began to ring. He looked at the call display:

10:48 AM   5-1

0-000-000-0000
UNKNOWN NAME

He hit the button on the call recording box attached to the phone and picked up the receiver: "GPD Homicide, Lieutenant Donaghue."

"Good morning, Lieutenant. I trust you're well today. It's a pleasure to finally make personal contact."

Hank looked at his computer screen. The call recording box was a USB device connected to his computer. In addition to recording the call and storing it on the departmental network server, it also activated software that logged the call and opened an instant message to Criminologist II Mickey Marcotte, Byrne's IT specialist, down in the lab. Hank grabbed his mouse and clicked on the "OK" button, which sent the instant message to Marcotte and activated a call-tracing routine.

"I recognize the voice," Hank said, "but I don't know your name."

"I told you, Lieutenant, it's Bill."

"In Louisville it was Paul. In Pittsburgh it was Charlie. What's your real name?"

"Actually, it *is* Bill." The voice sounded tired. "William. I won't give you my last name, though. Don't want to make it too easy." He laughed humorlessly. "Anyway, I assume you're recording this call and trying to trace it, so I won't spend all day on trivialities. I just wanted to say hello, make direct contact with you, so to speak, and let you know I saw the thing on the news about the raid on the factory. I laughed. It made my day."

"Glad to hear it," Hank said. "Where are you now?"

"Well, not there, that's for sure. Although I did actually scout the place, so it was a nice try on your part. I couldn't stand the stink. Eau de rotting crab. Not exactly conducive to romance. But your CSIs won't find any trace of me there. I'm careful. Very careful."

Hank glanced at his monitor and saw that Marcotte had responded to his instant message with one of his own, indicating that the trace was underway. "Where are you originally from, Bill? I'm listening to your accent. Is it St. Louis? Is that where you're from?"

"I saw that detective of yours on the news report," the man said, ignoring Hank's question. "The short blonde one. I think her name's Stainer, isn't it? When she gave the reporter a 'no comment' it was like she was biting through a steel rod. She looks tough. I saw her on the footage under the bridge, too. By the way, that spokeswoman of yours, Montgomery. She's quite a looker. Why don't you let her do the updates on me any more?"

"Never mind them, Bill. It's just you and me. This is between us now, isn't it? You and me."

"I expect that's Father Ed's doing. I think I remember reading about it in one of his books. Something about controlling the media and maintaining the UNSUB's focus on a single person. Oh, well. That's the way it goes. You'll have to do." The despondent tone was gone from his voice. "It was fun, though, being hunted by that woman cop in Louisville. Exciting. You may have noticed, both Stainer and Montgomery are my type. It could give me ideas, Lieutenant. You never know."

Watching his monitor, Hank saw another instant message pop up on the screen. "Tracing. Bouncing all over the place. Staying with it."

"That wouldn't be a good idea, Bill," Hank said, "unless you'd like to come in and talk to Detective Stainer one-on-one about it. You could go to any district police station and explain the situation to them, or you could come downtown here. I can give you the address."

"Oh, I've got the address, Lieutenant, but I don't think I'll be doing that. Detective Stainer looks like she'd enjoy nothing more than double-tapping me right in the middle of the forehead. I'll pass, thank you. Listen, I have to go. I know you're probably getting updates on the trace, which is bouncing through Europe and South America and all over the place right now. I just wanted to let you know that I'm trying to make up my mind who's going to be my next love friend. It's hard, because now I've got two more cute little blondes to consider. But there's no rush. Just keep your eye on the weather. Who knows? The next time it rains, someone else could be taking the ride of her life. Well, the last ride of her life, anyway."

The line went dead.

Hank rapped the disconnect button, got a dial tone, and called Marcotte. "Tell me you got him."

"Sorry, Lieutenant," Marcotte replied. "This guy must have some skills, or really good software. I'll analyze what happened but the bottom line is, we didn't get a location."

Hank hung up but kept his hand on the receiver. First, the package addressed to him with its grisly contents. Now, direct telephone contact. Griffin had been right: the Rainy Day Killer enjoyed making a personal connection between himself and the lead investigator, for whatever reason. The more often he contacted them, the more opportunities it created for him to make a mistake that would lead to his capture.

Hank didn't like the man's comments about Karen and Eleanor Montgomery. It was a disturbing new direction that he couldn't remember from any of the other case files. The killer had commented before about Lieutenant Kowpacki in Louisville and how he'd enjoyed being pursued by a female law enforcement officer, but Hank couldn't recall a prior instance in which he'd talked about stalking a female cop as his next victim.

He lifted the receiver and punched in Ed Griffin's number.

17

Hank's first clue that something was happening came immediately after lunch. He was on the phone with Ed Griffin, who'd responded to Hank's earlier voice message. They were discussing his telephone conversation with the Rainy Day Killer when Hank began to hear sounds of a disturbance through the interior wall that separated his office from the empty captain's office next door. When the noise showed no signs of letting up, he put Ed on hold and went out to take a look.

Workers were removing all the furniture from Martinez's old office. He asked one of the men what was going on.

"New stuff coming up from the fourth floor," the man said. "This is all going to the warehouse."

Hank went back to finish his call with Griffin. They'd sent the analyst a copy of the recording, and Griffin had been running through his impressions of the killer's words, tone, and overall emotional state.

"Bottom line?" Griffin said. "It's his early move in the chess game with you, not unlike the pattern he's followed with the others, but like I said, there are a couple of interesting things we need to think about. First, I believe him when he says his first name really is Bill, and I agree with you he's either a native of St. Louis or somewhere nearby in Missouri. That's been my working assumption all along, and I think you played it well. In other cases when the detectives have said something that's proven to be incorrect, he's tended to jump on it and work it for all it's worth like it's actually true, just for the sake of throwing them off track. You gave him a chance to do that again and he ignored you, which leads me to believe you might have hit the nail on the head. You're okay if I work that angle from this end? I'll ask our St. Louis field office if they can take a look at it. They owe me a few favors."

"Sure," Hank said, "no problem." Something crashed against the other side of the wall near his right elbow, causing him to jump.

"This other thing," Griffin went on, "talking about Stainer and Montgomery specifically by name and suggesting he's interested in them. I wouldn't put too much stock in it at this point, if I were you. He loves to work the emotional angle. Chances are pretty good he's pulling your chain just to raise the tension level and get you all hot and bothered. Still, I agree with your decision to tell them about it and, yes, I suppose they're going to be looking over their shoulders for a while but, hey, they're professionals. It goes with the turf."

"You think he's bluffing? We've seen him elevating his own personal risk level from one case to the next. Do you think this might be the next level up for him? Stalking a cop?"

"It's possible," Griffin admitted. "With these guys, anything's possible within the range of possibilities that go along with their type. As an organized offender who's shown a somewhat higher than average intelligence, he's definitely capable of upping the ante after he's had continued success at a lower level of risk, but having said that, even if this is a new fantasy of his, I'm not sure he's got the moxie to actually go through with it. Yet."

The line was silent for a moment as Hank thought about it.

"Increased vigilance is never a bad idea," Griffin said, "but I wouldn't invest too much emotional energy in it. He's pulling your chain."

"Okay."

Griffin ended the call by promising to send a written report for the Olsen case file by the end of the day.

Hank hung up the phone and went for another look into Martinez's office. It was now completely devoid of furnishings. The movers were gone. He walked to the elevators, rode down in a crowded car to the ground floor, and went for a walk to get a cup of coffee at the chip stand he usually frequented.

He leaned against a telephone pole and watched the traffic, sipping.

Time passed.

He found himself scanning the pedestrians for a white male

in a business suit, mid-thirties, well-groomed dark hair, short, slight build, not all that physically fit or strong but with good coordination.

He glanced up at the sky, which was beginning to fill with a flat sheet of cirrostratus clouds. A sign of approaching bad weather. Usually he paid very little attention to it, but now signs of rain on the horizon disturbed him. On the heels of that anxiety was annoyance that this guy had him watching the sky and scrutinizing passersby.

When his coffee was half-finished, he saw Detective Maureen Truly round the corner and walk down the sidewalk on the other side of the street. She wore a navy jacket-and-skirt combination Hank hadn't seen before. Her shapeless, straight brown hair was cut a little shorter than usual. When she reached a point directly across from the chip stand, she stepped between two parked cars and briskly jaywalked across the street. She bought a cup of coffee, stirred cream and sugar into it, and snapped on a plastic lid. Sipping, she strolled over to Hank's telephone pole and looked up and down the street.

"How's it going, Maureen?" he asked.

"Well, Lieutenant. You?"

"Peachy." He glanced up, hearing thunder. No, it was a jet taking off from the airport in Bering Heights. "How do you like it on the fifth floor?"

"Fine. Not much team work, but that's the nature of the beast, I guess." After having assisted Hank on the Jarrett case last year while on loan from the Cold Case Unit, Maureen had received a transfer to Intelligence, where she'd been assigned the organized crime desk. It was work that better suited her information-gathering skills than did active homicide investigation, in Hank's opinion.

"Something new this morning," Truly said. "Peter Mah's back in the country. He's in New York right now. He actually flew in on Monday. It takes a few days for me to get these reports, so I'm sorry I couldn't tell you sooner."

"That's all right, Maureen." He knew that all intelligence related to the Triad was being funneled through Lieutenant Jarvis and his Chinatown task force before reaching her desk, thanks to the current direction in which the political winds were blowing. Truly was very low on the totem pole, and was in the difficult position of having to establish her own information network without much help from her peers.

"Anyway," she went on, "I ran some checks this morning and it seems he's still there. He's staying at the Westin in Times Square."

Hank thought about it as he drained his coffee cup. When he'd saved the man's life two years ago, Peter Mah was the 426, the *Hung Kwan* or Red Pole of the local Triad brotherhood, responsible for enforcement and, when necessary, execution. He'd fled the country when William Chow was elected Dragon Head, knowing that Chow would conduct a bloody purge of all his rivals, including Peter, to consolidate his power as head of the local lodge. If Mah had chosen to return to the United States now, it must be for a very good reason. This particular lodge held its elections every three years. Was Mah coming back to begin a campaign to replace Chow next year?

"Thanks, Maureen. I appreciate the heads-up."

"Always, Lieutenant." She hesitated. "I hear you're getting a new captain."

"Apparently."

"It should be you. It's a mistake. I know her; she's a problem."

"We'll see." He shifted his shoulder against the telephone pole. "It's never a good idea to pre-judge a person."

"Karen won't like her. Not at all."

They watched the traffic for a moment. Truly stepped forward and glanced at him. "Take care."

Hank nodded and watched her cross the street. She retraced her steps up the sidewalk and around the corner. He finished his coffee, threw the empty cup into the trash can, and bought two more cups. He put them in a cardboard carrying tray, slipped a few packets of sugar, two creamers, and a stir stick into his pocket, and took them back to the ninth floor.

As expected, Helen Cassion was supervising the movement of her furniture into the vacant captain's office. As he entered the busy Homicide bullpen, he watched her, arms folded, frowning at the movers who were jockeying a large cherry wood desk through the narrow door. He'd never met her before, but Martinez had shown him her personnel jacket on Monday when Cassion's secondment had been announced. It wasn't exactly standard operating procedure for a subordinate to see the file of his new supervisor, but Martinez had repeated Bennett's desire that Hank assist Cassion as best he could while she was occupying the captain's chair.

"Do your thing, Hank," she'd said as he flipped through the pages of the file. "Work with her. It won't be easy, but then neither was Stainer, and look at the wonders you've accomplished with her."

Cassion unfolded her arms, flicked a lock of hair out of her eyes, and stepped into the doorway, watching the movers like a hawk. She was tall and slender, and looked younger than thirty-one. She wore a black blazer, a white blouse, a black skirt, and black high-heeled shoes. The skirt was too short for business wear, reaching only to mid-thigh, but she obviously believed her legs were worth looking at and wanted to show them off. Her medium-length hair was naturally dark and treated with blonde streaks, and it was cut in a careless-looking flyaway style that betrayed her love of the DC night life she reportedly enjoyed every weekend.

When she turned to look at him over her shoulder, Hank could see her Egyptian mother's DNA reflected in her dark complexion, black arching eyebrows, dark eyes, oval face, and long, straight nose. Unpleasant lines ran from the corners of her nose to the corners of her mouth, giving her an expression of impatience and disapproval.

"You must be Donaghue," she said, running her eyes up and down him before settling on the tray of coffee. "One of those better be for me. I need it right now."

He held out the tray, and she grabbed one of the cups. "Cream or sugar?" he asked politely.

She shook her head, opened the drinking hole on the plastic lid, and sucked at it greedily. When she came up for air, she nodded. "Bring me one of these every morning and we'll get along." She stepped into the office. "Hey! Not on that side, over there! Didn't you listen? Desk here, credenza there! Got it?"

Hank watched the movers wrestle the big desk back across the floor. He recognized it as having once belonged to Gerald White, the former chief for whom Hank had worked as a special assistant when he was younger than Cassion was now. It would have gone into storage when the new chief took over, but obviously had been plucked out again by someone in a senior position looking to furnish their office with the best available pieces without having to spend money that didn't exist in their budget. It was a part of the bureaucratic game that some people played, scouring for furniture above what was normally allocated to their rank and rating, in order to suggest power and influence greater than the next person's. That a former chief's desk had ended up in the office of a lieutenant supervising the Missing Persons Unit suggested that Cassion indeed had some political juice within the department, or at least was working hard on it.

"We need to talk," she said, walking up close to Hank. "Let's go into your office." She brushed by him, her breast making contact with his arm. "Now," she said over her shoulder.

He followed her into his office and watched her sit down in his chair behind his desk. He dropped into one of his visitor's chairs and leaned back comfortably, crossing his legs so that his left ankle rested on his right knee. He balanced his coffee cup on his calf and watched her look around the office.

"I love what you've done with the place," she said. "No photos, no nothing. Typical guy. You're not married?"

"No," Hank said, "but attached."

She shrugged, her eyes settling on him at last. "Older guys never know what to call it. They're so embarrassed and awkward. Whatever. Let's get a few ground rules settled right away before anything else. As supervising lieutenant, it's your job to do all the paperwork for this unit and have it ready for my signature on time, and make sure it's correct the first time. I'm not doing it for you, and I'm not signing anything that needs correction. Are we clear on that?"

"Crystal," Hank said, sipping.

"I've heard the talk about you and the commander," she went on, "and I won't put up with you going over my head to her on everything because you two are cozy or whatever. If you have something she needs to know, you tell me and I'll brief her on it as appropriate. Got it?"

Hank said nothing, but she plowed ahead without waiting for a reply. "I told her I disagree with you being the media contact on this serial killer case, because it should be the captain's prerogative to talk to the press on something that important, but the chief's signed off on it and there's nothing I can do, so I expect a full briefing on everything you and the PIO come up with for public statements. Nothing goes out without my prior approval. Got it?"

"Sure," Hank said.

"And another fiasco like what went down at the factory yesterday isn't going to happen on my watch. You're going to brief me ahead of time on every step you take from now on, and if I tell you to stand down, you stand down."

Hank smiled, in a friendly sort of way.

She opened his top drawer and rummaged around in it. "Got any Aspirin? My head's killing me."

"Second drawer," he said.

She continued to paw around in the top drawer until she'd seen everything there was to see in it, then she slammed it shut and opened the second drawer. She rifled it expertly, taking a quick inventory, and finally came out with his bottle of Aspirin. She popped the lid, swallowed four tablets with her coffee, and tossed the bottle back into the drawer. As she closed it, she looked at him sideways.

"You don't say a lot, do you?"

"I don't get paid by the word," Hank replied.

She laughed lightly. "I asked around about you. You're a nice guy with a black cloud over your head that capped your career. You've reached your ceiling but it hasn't made you bitter like it does a lot of the older guys who see women like me passing them by on the way up. I like that part." She sat back. "You're popular with the ladies, I'm told. You've got that big, worn-out teddy bear thing going. I like charm, it makes it easier to put up with the other crap, but at the end of the day, charm doesn't get the job done, so keep a cork in it and concentrate on making me look good, and I'll make sure you get all the credit you've got coming to you."

He realized he felt sorry for her. She was in over her head and she knew it, and in her fear and insecurity she was drawing on the bullshit posturing and sharp-edged fencing that probably made her a hot commodity in the DC night clubs and high-end parties she was known to frequent. Her father was a senior official in the State Department, and she was a pampered youngest child. In Martinez's opinion, her upbringing had thrown her into social circles that were, ultimately, a little more than she could handle. She was fluent in Arabic and had worked for two years with the FBI in Washington as an analyst before following Bennett and Barkley into the GPD, but at their insistence she'd taken the ground-floor route, becoming a sworn officer through the academy and putting in the minimum field duty before earning steady promotions into headquarters. She'd chosen law enforcement as a career, according to Martinez, because of discrimination she'd encountered as a teenager after 9/11 and a desire to prove her detractors wrong by waving a badge in their faces, but the chip on her shoulder was a little too obvious and merely served to highlight her shortcomings. Hank wasn't sure what he was going to do with her, but he'd promised Martinez he'd help her out, so that's what he intended to do.

"There's rain coming in the next day or two," he said.

She made a face. "So? Did I ask for a weather report?"

Hank got up, unlocked his filing cabinet, and removed a binder from the top drawer. "I've made you a copy of the Olsen murder book." He handed it to her. "They're not sure of his periodicity, because it's believed he commits other rapes and murders between his signature Rainy Day Killer offenses, but when he called me this morning he made it clear he was getting ready for another one. When it rains—and it's going to, soon—we'll have the districts increase their vigilance in terms of pedestrian traffic. Officers will get a copy of the composite sketch and the profile at the beginning of their shift. He wears a suit and carries an umbrella when he snatches them, so when it rains," he leaned on the words, to make sure she understood his point, "we're going to be extra busy because they'll likely be stopping and questioning possibles all over the place. It's a big city with a lot of businessmen who carry umbrellas. Stainer and Horvath will interview them and I'll observe, whenever possible. It'll cause a commotion, it'll likely generate complaints, and at the very least I'll be making an impromptu statement to the press before and after, explaining what we're doing, and why. It'll happen fast, but I'll keep you up to speed as best I can. How's that sound?"

She shrugged. She had put the binder down on his desk without looking at it. "Like I said, Donaghue, the media strategy's been explained to me, and while I don't like it, I have to live with it. Just show me your statements before you make them."

"I'd like your cell phone number," he said.

She gave him a look.

"If we arrest someone," he explained patiently, "you'll need to know we've got a suspect in custody. I need to be able to reach you whenever. You'll want to come in to consult with the assistant state's attorney on next steps."

She rolled her eyes, grabbed a pen on his desk, opened the binder, and wrote her number on the top page of the murder book. "Don't call asking me out for a drink. I don't do the after-hours thing with subordinates." She closed the binder with a flip of her hand, stood up, and tossed the pen down on his desk. "Let's make sure there are no more screw-ups."

She walked around his desk to where he stood, next to the filing cabinet. "This could go really well, Donaghue. If we catch this guy, it'll be a real feather in my cap. Yours, too. So let's be smart and do things the right way. Okay?"

"Sounds good to me," Hank said.

She patted him on the arm and walked out.

He quietly closed his door, sat down in the visitor's chair, picked up his coffee, and closed his eyes.

I promised, he told himself.

18

Karen had finally bitten the bullet. She'd called Faye's Flowers and made an appointment to drive over and pick something out of their damned books to keep Sandy's mother from blowing a gasket. She was greeted by Faye herself, a plump, middle-aged woman with a white Margaret Thatcher hairstyle and a British accent. Karen allowed herself to be led into a viewing room where several oversized books were waiting for her on a long table covered with a clean, white cloth. The room was filled with flowers. Reluctantly, Karen sat down as Faye ran through her introductory patter.

"Do you have anything particular in mind, Ms. Stainer?" she finally asked.

"Nope. I don't go to a lot of weddings."

"Do you have a favorite flower, for instance? We can feature it in the various arrangements and, of course, in your bouquet."

"I don't really do flowers," Karen said. "Sandy sometimes buys me roses."

"I see." Faye turned a few pages in the book. When Karen glanced at her watch, Faye smiled politely. "I believe Mrs. Alexander said you're a police officer. Is that right?"

"Yeah. Homicide detective."

Faye leaned back, away from the book. "Really? I think that's amazing. You must live a fascinating life."

"Yeah, it's fascinating, all right."

"I have the utmost respect for anyone who puts their life on the line for the sake of society," Faye said, "but especially for a woman who does so. Such a difficult and challenging career to have chosen." She reached out and touched her on the arm. "Mrs. Alexander has given us carte blanche, so how about if I help you spend a little of her money this morning? Then you can get on to much more important things."

Karen looked the woman in the eye, saw genuine humor and sincerity, and nodded. "Sounds good to me."

Faye reached for another book and opened it on top of the first one. "Do you have a favorite color?"

"Not really. Red flowers are nice, I guess."

"Ah." Faye grabbed about an inch's-worth of pages and turned to a section near the back. "I have an idea. What do you think of this?"

Karen looked at a photograph of a slender model in a white wedding dress holding a bouquet of red and white flowers.

"Your posy could feature roses, Asiatic lilies, alstroemeria, and dahlias, just like this. Isn't it lovely?"

Karen admitted that it was.

"The posy's a popular choice for a bouquet because it has a very contemporary look. Plus, it's much more convenient to hold."

"Sounds good," Karen said. "It'll make it easier for me to draw my gun without dropping the flowers."

Faye tittered, turning the page. "These would make nice bouquets for your bridesmaids and matron of honor."

"Okay."

"This is a lovely accessory," Faye said, pointing. "Two red garden roses attached with hairpins make an attractive fascinator."

"No thanks," Karen replied. "I'd look like I had flowers growing out of my head. My brothers would never let me live it down."

"All right." Faye turned the page.

By the time Karen had completed Lane Alexander's shopping list and chosen corsages, boutonnieres, flowers for the church, flowers with the guest book, outdoor urn arrangements, chair-back arrangements, table centerpieces and garlands, she felt as though she'd just blown six months' salary and had a great time doing it. Faye shook her hand firmly at the front door, they exchanged business cards, and Karen left feeling a little better about the whole wedding thing.

She hustled through the rain to her Firebird, started up the engine, and switched on the windshield wipers. Her hand reached out and flicked on the police radio as she pulled into traffic. The rain had lessened somewhat from earlier in the morning, and was now a steady drizzle. She drove slowly, thinking about the flowers. Her brother Brad had already begun the renovation of the barn on the Alexander property. Faye had recommended arrangements of red peonies and white hydrangea to complement the unusual height and depth of the venue, and Karen thought they'd look nice. Brad was a genius when it came to interior design, and—

"—Dispatch, we are ten-nineteen with possible felony suspect. Wearing a suit and carrying an umbrella as reported."

"Three twenty-six, HQ now requests you transport to their twenty."

"Ten-four, Dispatch."

Karen grabbed the mike and keyed the button. "Dispatch, this is thirty-four seventy-two, off-duty. Where was the felony suspect picked up?"

"Thirty-four seventy-two, we received a report of a suspicious pedestrian matching description of possible felony suspect on the five-hundred block of Cooper Street, west side, near Clovis."

"Got it," Karen said. "Three twenty-six, what's your ETA at HQ?"

"ETA ten," came the reply.

"Ten-four," Karen said. "Attaboy."

When Karen arrived at the ninth floor, the suspect had already been put into an interview room. Horvath sat at his desk, on the phone, head resting in his hand, intent on something in front of him. Officer Wilcox was parked nearby, in Karen's visitor's chair, shaking raindrops from his hat. Seeing that Hank's office door was open, she looked in and saw him at his desk. A woman sat in one of his chairs, her back to the door. She was doing all the talking.

Karen walked back to Wilcox. "What's the story?"

"The witness is Nicole Sample, thirty-four. She works as a receptionist in a dog grooming place on Clovis. She went out to mail some stuff and was on her way back when the suspect accosted her."

"Accosted her how?"

"According to her, the suspect approached her on the sidewalk and asked her if she was busy this afternoon. He held his umbrella over her when she stopped, and handed her a post card. He told her he was working for a cosmetics company that had a booth at a trade show for women, the one this weekend at the Roosevelt Trade Center in Bering

Heights. When she tried to walk around him, he made physical contact with her by pressing the card against her forearm, trying to get her to take it."

As she listened, Karen leaned back for another peek into Hank's office. From what she could see, Nicole Sample looked as though she was about five feet, seven inches tall and weighed about one hundred and sixty pounds. Her hair was brown.

"Then what?"

Wilcox shrugged. "She ran across the street to get away from him and called nine-one-one. Said she'd just been attacked by the Rainy Day Killer. My partner's in the washroom right now, if you want to talk to him when he comes out, but that's basically it."

"Thanks." Karen strolled over to Hank's office and leaned on the door frame.

"He said if I took the card to their booth," Sample was sobbing, "I'd get 10 percent off any purchase. I thought I'd never see my husband again!"

Hank stood up, excused himself, and motioned Karen to step out into the bullpen. "He's carrying a Maryland driver's license in the name of Thomas Peter Kirk, Baltimore address, DOB eleven twenty-two eighty-eight."

"Twenty-five years old," Karen said.

"A little on the young side," Hank agreed. "DiOrio was already in the building," he said, referring to the assistant state's attorney, "so she's waiting in the observation room. He was Mirandized and waived the right to call an attorney."

"Cocky bastard."

Hank shrugged. "Horvath's running down the ID. Why don't you see what you can get from this guy?"

Karen turned on her heel and strode down the hallway to the interview room. Hank followed, letting himself into the observation room. Horvath brought Nicole Sample out of Hank's office and sat her down in his visitor's chair while he continued his work.

The suspect sat at the table with his head in his hands. He wore a navy double-breasted suit, a white shirt, a red tie, and black leather shoes. He had a scrape on the left side of his forehead, and the front of his suit was soaked and covered with dirt and grit, no doubt the result of having been taken down on the wet sidewalk by Wilcox and his partner. His hair was longer than she'd expected.

"My name's Detective Stainer," she said, sitting down across the table from him. "You've already heard your Miranda rights, but I'm going to explain them to you again." She recited them briskly. "Do you waive your right to an attorney at this time?"

"I told the others, I don't know any lawyers and I don't need one. I didn't do anything wrong."

"We can send for a public defender."

"I told you, I don't need a lawyer. I didn't do anything!"

"Yeah, sure. How'd you come up with this bullshit about cosmetics?"

"At a job fair."

Karen paused a beat. "What's that again?"

"I got the job at a job fair last month. I've been out of work for a year. My girlfriend left me because I had to sell my car and move back with my parents. Do you know how humiliating that is? So I went to this job fair and these guys were hiring practically everybody who stopped at their booth with a CV. The only catch is you have to dress up and travel to the places where they're doing the trade shows and stuff. I don't get paid unless at least twenty people turn in the post cards at their booth. Can I have the rest of my cards back? I really need the money."

"You've got to be kidding me."

"I'm not! I'm practically broke."

"She's a little off your usual type, isn't she? What were you doing, slumming?"

"I don't know what you mean."

"Just a warm-up rape? Couldn't find a blonde on short notice?"

"Oh my God, you think I was attacking her?"

"You must think we're complete fucking idiots, Bill. Or whatever your real name is. Where'd you hold Theresa Olsen, you bastard? Where'd you do her?"

"Oh my God, this isn't happening. My name's not Bill, it's Tom. Tom Kirk. I live in Baltimore. I'm here with a group for the convention."

"You're here with a group." Karen paused a beat. "Okay, door-knob, I'll bite. Who's this group? Who hired you? What's your boss's name?"

"The company's called Tremont Products. My supervisor's name is James. I don't remember his last name, but his card's in my wallet. They took it. My wallet. Can you call him and tell him what's going on? I'm scared they're going to fire me."

"You're scared they're going to fire you. That's rich."

"They will! They fire you for practically anything."

Karen put her hands flat on the table, staring at him. She popped air through her lips, pressed her tongue against a back molar, then suddenly stood up.

"Sit tight." She left the room and went out into the hallway, narrowly avoiding a collision with Hank and DiOrio, who were coming out of the observation room.

"Let's see how Horvath's doing," Hank said.

"Okay, here it is," Horvath said quietly, glancing at the witness as they gathered around his desk. "The photo on the driver's license matches what's in the DMV database. I spoke to this James Repple, who answered the number on the business card, and a patrol car's bringing him and another person supposedly from the company down from the convention center. He confirms they have a guy with this name and general description working for them, handing out post cards down-town. We'll have to wait and see if he makes a positive ID. I think he's going to. This seems off, to me."

When James Repple arrived, he took one look through the one-way glass in the observation room and shook his head. "His ass is completely fired. What'd he do?"

Karen confronted him. "You confirm that this is Thomas Peter Kirk of Baltimore? An employee of yours?"

"Lorraine hired him, I didn't. But yeah, that's him. Complete doofus. What'd he do, trespass or something?"

Karen turned to the woman who'd accompanied Repple from the convention center. "What about you?"

"I hired him, yeah. Big mistake, obviously."

"How long have you known him?"

"About a month," Lorraine replied. "I gave him his training, along with six other guys. We brought three of them down here with us last night to work the show. They put their initials on the back of their cards; that's how we know who's driving the traffic up to us. We only saw one of his cards, so far. He's not working out." She glanced at Repple.

"Complete dope," he agreed.

"Can you confirm his whereabouts on Wednesday, April 24?"

Repple thought about it. "A week ago last Wednesday?" He pinched his chin. "That would be Bowie, I think. Right, Lorraine? Yeah, a Thursday-Friday-Saturday show at the Rec Center. Wednesday was our travel day. He rode down with me and John Ferris."

"Thanks for your time," DiOrio said.

Karen's shoulders dropped as the observation room began to empty.

"Cut him loose," DiOrio ordered. "A swing and a miss."

"God damn it," Karen muttered.

"I know. We all want this one real bad, but it's not him."

"I know it isn't. But for a short, sweet minute, I thought we'd nailed the fucker."

At that moment Helen Cassion walked into the room.

"I've called the press," she announced. "They should be here any minute." She looked at the one-way glass. "Is that him? Is our statement ready?"

Karen looked at DiOrio and, despite herself, began to laugh.

19

The following Friday morning, six days later, Eleanor Montgomery parked her Chevrolet Suburban in the lot of the Food Basket, a rather expensive grocery store in the Springhill neighborhood where she lived. It was a bright, fresh, sunny morning, and it was her day off.

As she walked through the sliding glass doors, she caught a glimpse of her reflection. She was wearing her Ralph Lauren fringed suede jacket over an indigo-striped t-shirt, faded blue jeans, and suede oxford wingtip lace-ups. Slung over her shoulder was a leather tote bag that matched the shoes. Her blonde hair was tied in a neat ponytail draped over her shoulder. It was a look that pleased her, all the more so because it was very different than what people saw of her on television. She preferred not to be recognized when off duty.

She grabbed a shopping cart, removed the tote from her shoulder, and put it in the cart's fold-out flap. She stayed close to her bag at all times while shopping, not only because it contained her cell phone and wallet but also because she had her off-duty service weapon in it, a Glock Px4 Storm nine millimeter. She began to fill her cart with a selection of greens, bags of baby carrots, fresh cilantro and curly parsley, fresh lemons, a sack of basmati rice, a bag of freshly-made tortilla shells, and a half-dozen bagels.

She was thinking about her boyfriend, Jerry Garrett, as she shopped. A reporter for the Glendale *Mirror* who worked the entertainment beat, he'd just written a blog post covering a recent tattoo arts convention held in Baltimore. Always fascinated by the fringes of modern society, Jerry had done a very good job exploring the culture, and had worked in several intriguing character sketches of the people who inhabited that world. She'd liked the post very much, but he'd come back from the convention with a large tattoo of a spider on his forearm that she didn't like at all. On top of that, he was pestering her to get a tattoo of her own; something small, he said, where the cameras wouldn't see it.

It wasn't going to happen.

She wasn't the kind of person who was into body art. She preferred to augment her appearance in more conventional ways, with clothing, accessories, makeup, and hair style. She knew they referred to her at work as The Ice Princess, a nickname she'd picked up as a patrol officer in Granger Park for her firm refusal to notice the advances of her male colleagues. While it bothered her to be thought of as aloof and disinterested in others, she preferred it to the alternative. She kept her personal and professional relationships separate. If Jerry had worked the city beat, she probably wouldn't have agreed to go out with him. As it was, their jobs occupied separate orbits that never intersected, which was just fine with her.

She was in the middle of an aisle when she realized she'd passed the tea without remembering she needed more. She grabbed her tote bag and walked back to the end of the aisle, where she chose a box of her preferred green tea. She paused, running her eye along the shelf to see if there was anything else she wanted. The store was not very busy for a Friday morning. An old James Taylor song, "Fire and Rain," played lightly on the store audio system. The lyrics began to track through her head as she slowly returned to her cart.

A man passed by the far end of the aisle. She saw a brief glimpse of a dark windbreaker, jeans, and a camera with a large lens on a shoulder strap.

Someone moved behind her and passed her in the aisle, jostling her: a large-hipped African-American woman in a flower print dress, arms filled with loaves of bread, heading for the check-out.

Montgomery tossed the box of green tea into her cart, put the tote bag back in the fold-out flap, and continued to shop.

She thought about Lieutenant Donaghue. Although he was twenty years older, he was still an attractive man. She liked tall men, and she definitely liked men with curly hair. Of course, she preferred men her own age. What she appreciated about Donaghue, though, was his attitude. He kept his eyes where they were supposed to be, he spoke to her with respect and genuine interest in what she had to say, and he had a certain style about him that mixed professionalism and humor in a way she liked. He'd kept her in the loop on the serial killer case, he appreciated her daily reports on the information she was culling from the TIPS line calls, and he used the statements she drafted for him with very few changes.

She decided she would ask him for a letter of reference when she applied for the upcoming detective competition this summer. Word was, the chief was finally going to do something about the acute shortage of detectives on staff. She was already studying for it.

She was lost in thought as she reached the check-out and began unloading her cart. Fresh fish, boneless chicken breast, the sack of rice, Tetra boxes of chicken stock, bundles of fresh green lettuce.

She paid for her purchases, piled the bags into her cart, and left the store.

She pushed the cart across the parking lot toward her Suburban, parked down the row on her left. Her eyes were drawn to movement in a parked white van on her right. She saw a man sitting behind the wheel of the van. He was lowering a camera out of sight, onto his lap, and his head was turning away from Montgomery to look straight ahead through the dusty windshield of the van. As she drew even, he flipped down the sun visor, which prevented her from seeing his face. She glanced behind her and ran her eyes in a one hundred and eighty degree arc across what would correspond to the man's field of vision. She saw nothing whatsoever that would be worth photographing.

She reached her Suburban, thinking hard. Yes. It was the man she'd seen briefly in the store, passing the end of the aisle with the camera slung over his shoulder. She opened the hatch and began unloading her cart.

An engine chuffed to life behind her.

She began to hurry, lifting several bags at once.

A Honda rolled behind her, heading for the parking lot exit at the front of the store.

Gears shifted behind her. She looked over her shoulder and saw the van ease out of its parking space.

The man turned the steering wheel with his left hand, watching the Honda, ignoring Montgomery. He rubbed the side of his face with his right hand, blocking Montgomery's view of his features.

She could tell that he was white, neither large nor small, and perhaps in his early thirties. His hair was short and dark. His hairline was slightly high and a little rounded, with a part on the left side. Exactly the way it looked in Esther Banks's composite sketch, which she'd distributed to hundreds of people already.

It was him. It had to be.

The Rainy Day Killer.

All she could see now was the rear end of the van as it followed the Honda. The license plate was coated with dust, but she was able to decipher the shapes of the numbers and letters. She committed them to memory.

She threw the rest of her groceries into the Suburban, slammed the hatch, and shoved the cart away. It bounced against the bumper of the pickup truck parked next to her and rolled away, down the lot.

"Hey!" yelled a man across the lot who was loading cases of beer into the trunk of his car.

"Sorry!" she called out, hurrying up to the door of the Suburban. As she fumbled in her tote bag for her keys, she looked around and saw the van turn right, at the front of the store, still following the Honda out of the parking lot. Her eyesight was good enough to see the man's face move briefly in her direction, but it was too far away to get a good look at his features.

Keys in hand, she got behind the wheel and gunned the engine to life. She backed out of her space, cutting off another vehicle trying to leave the parking lot. A horn sounded. She spun the wheel, waved apologetically in the rear view mirror, and hit the gas. She whipped around the corner, passed the front of the store in a blur, exited the parking lot and turned right, onto the side street. Ahead of her, at the intersection, the van was making a right-hand turn from a stop sign into the heavy traffic on MacArthur Avenue. She hurried up to the intersection.

She looked left at a steady, unbroken stream of traffic with no openings. A block away the traffic light was green. She'd have to wait for it to turn red, apparently, before she'd get an opening.

She grabbed her cell phone from her tote bag, plugged it into the hands-free system, and speed-dialed a number.

"Donaghue."

"Lieutenant, it's Eleanor Montgomery."

The light down the street turned red. She eased forward as two cars approached, anticipating the hole in traffic behind them.

"Hi, what can I do for you?"

She turned the wheel and stepped on the accelerator, racing out into traffic. "Lieutenant, I think I've got a visual on our suspect in the Olsen case."

"Are you sure?"

"Pretty sure." She jammed on the brakes. Traffic was stopped ahead of her, waiting for another red light. The van was second from the right, in the inside lane. "I've just left the Food Basket on MacArthur Avenue in Springhill. We're stopped at a light at the corner of, ah, Wilson Boulevard. It's a white delivery van, I think a Dodge Grand Caravan, no markings, dirty, three to five years old, Maryland tag eight bravo lima, alpha zero five. We're heading east on MacArthur. The light just turned green. He's moving straight ahead."

"I'm putting you on hold." The line went quiet as Montgomery shifted her foot from the brake to the accelerator and began to move forward to the intersection. The van was out of sight ahead of her. She checked her mirrors and over her shoulder, saw a gap on her left, and moved into it. She floored the gas pedal, trying to make up the distance between her Suburban and the vanished van.

She tensed as Hank's voice came back over the radio speakers. "Eleanor, I've called it in. The district is initiating pursuit, so stand down. You should hear the sirens in a moment. Stand down, you're not authorized to pursue."

"But he's right here," Montgomery said, craning toward the windshield, trying to spot the van. "He's right ahead of me. I'll stay on him until they get here."

"Do you still have a visual?"

"Not at the moment. The traffic's heavy and I'm trying to get closer." She grunted, shifting lanes, accelerating around a delivery truck and shifting back into the left lane. She'd gained three car-lengths. She saw a flash of white as a vehicle changed lanes about six car-lengths ahead of her. "Wait, I think I see him."

"Eleanor, stand down. Right now."

A white vehicle turned right, onto Blair Street. She reached the corner, turned, and saw the vehicle moving away from her. It was a white passenger car. It turned into a driveway halfway down the block. She put her foot on the brake, slowed down, pulled over to the curb, and shifted into Park.

Behind her, on MacArthur, she heard a sudden commotion of sirens, a blatting klaxon, and roaring car engines. Red and blue lights flashed in her rear view mirror.

"I've pulled over," she said. "I'm on Blair, just off MacArthur. I lost him somewhere back there on MacArthur."

"Come in, Eleanor, and we'll do a debrief. In the commander's board room."

Montgomery closed her eyes for a moment, gripping the steering wheel tightly with both hands. Her heart was racing and her breath was short. She opened her mouth and drew in air, held it for a moment, then released it slowly. She closed her mouth and inhaled deeply through her nostrils, held it, released it slowly.

"Eleanor? Are you all right?"

She opened her eyes and looked out the window.

A woman walked past along the sidewalk, holding a little girl by the hand. The little girl stared at Montgomery through the window, mouth open, eyes wide.

"Yes, Lieutenant," she said. "I'm fine."

20

Commander Ann Martinez got up from her desk and strolled out of her eighth-floor corner office, eating a spoonful of yogurt from the disposable plastic cup in her hand. Her secretary and administrative assistant didn't bother looking up from their cluttered desks. The secretary was on the telephone with the deputy chief's secretary, comparing schedules to book a meeting later that afternoon. The administrative assistant was making corrections to correspondence that Martinez would take to the meeting for Barkley's signature. They didn't look up, but they were aware of her movement through the outer office and knew where she was going.

She paused in the corridor. The workstations in this corner of the floor were taken up by civilian administrative staff assigned to Detective Services Bureau, and most of the people had already disappeared for lunch. She liked this time of day because it was a little quieter. There was a lull in the bureaucratic chaos, a pause for breath that gave her a few precious minutes for the police work she still loved. She dabbed her lips with the napkin trapped between her little finger and ring finger and walked into the commander's board room, where Cassion and Hank waited in uncomfortable silence.

Using her foot to move out the chair at the head of the board room table, Martinez sat down and dipped her spoon into the yogurt, looking at Cassion. "I understand there's been some progress."

"That's correct." Cassion sat up straighter. "There's been a sighting of the UNSUB. He was observed earlier this morning at a location in Springhill, and I've learned that the vehicle he was driving, a 2011 Dodge Grand Caravan, is a rental vehicle registered to a leasing company located at 879 Cooper Street. I've directed a forensics team to that location, with orders to obtain the original rental documents, video surveillance recordings, fingerprints, and any other physical evidence I can get from there. Stainer's questioning staff as we speak, in case they remember him."

"Cooper Street," Martinez said, dropping her napkin on the table. "That's only a few blocks from here."

Cassion hesitated. "I guess it is."

Martinez glanced at Hank. "Cheeky bastard."

Hank said nothing, his expression neutral.

"This will be the first involvement in the case by the FBI evidence recovery team," Martinez said.

Cassion looked confused.

"You said you directed a forensics team to that location, Captain," Martinez prompted.

"Yeah, I called Byrne and ordered him out. Are we supposed to call the FBI, too?"

"Criminalistics will," Martinez said, "as you should remember. They'll expect to receive the Bureau's lab reports within twenty-four hours. I want to know if there are any hitches from Homicide's perspective."

Cassion shrugged. "Whatever. Sounds like a pain in the ass to me."

"Hopefully it'll prevent a few pains in the ass," Martinez said. "Continue with your update."

"The UNSUB was sighted by Patrol Officer Montgomery. She was off duty at the time and unfortunately let him get away. God knows why she didn't call nine-one-one instead of Donaghue. I guess it's his charming smile. I've ordered her to sit with a sketch artist to do a composite likeness. We'll see how it compares to the sketch from the witness last week. Hopefully her memory's a little better than her understanding of procedure."

Vertical lines appeared between Martinez's dark eyebrows. "We don't use a sketch artist in the GPD, Helen. She'll have to sit with a technician trained in the software."

"That's what I meant," Cassion said. "The district's conducting a sweep for the van, and as soon as it's located, I'll personally supervise a tactical intervention on site. I don't want a repeat of the fiasco at the cannery, which went down before I came on board, or the screw-up downtown last weekend where people reacted without thinking, arresting the wrong guy. We're finally making some real progress, and I intend to nail this sonofabitch with by-the-book, solid police work this time."

Martinez thoughtfully ate another spoonful of yogurt, keeping her eyes on Cassion. "I signed off on the tactical intervention at the cannery, Helen," she said finally, "as you're well aware. We have to act on every possible lead to find where this guy holds his victims, and if we're wrong nine times in a row I don't care, as long as we're right the tenth time. Understand what I'm saying? That's how investigations proceed, one step at a time, one lead at a time. And as for Mr. Kirk, the district responded to a complaint from a citizen who thought she was in danger. That's what police officers do, Helen. It's my understanding Mr. Kirk has no interest in filing a complaint, and even if he did, it wouldn't amount to anything. I'm not worried about it, so you shouldn't be."

"If you say so. I've also spoken to ASA DiOrio, and we've gotten a warrant for the video recordings at the grocery store. Horvath's interviewing staff there now, and we're hoping to get some live footage of this bastard, since Montgomery reported seeing him inside the store while she was shopping. Personally, I think the lieutenant and his Bureau headshrinker give this guy far too much credit. It was stupid to show himself to a cop like that. I think he wants to be caught, and it's just a matter of being ready to jump on his next screw-up and nail him."

"I see." Martinez glanced at her watch. "I'm not sure that I share your assessment, though. You'll send copies of everything we get to Ed Griffin?"

"I hadn't planned to."

"It's important to keep SSA Griffin in the loop. We need his analysis of the offender's behavior each step of the way."

Cassion shrugged. "I've been in the Bureau, Commander. I've seen it from the inside, and this behavioral analysis stuff is just a lot of smoke and mirrors. They're not real psychologists, you know. They're just agents who read about this stuff and make elaborate guesses with all kinds of jargon thrown in for effect. It doesn't fool me, or a lot of other people I've talked to about it."

"Your opinion's noted and appreciated. I still want Griffin kept in the loop." Martinez stood up, scraping the inside of the plastic cup for the last bit of yogurt, then she tossed the cup and plastic spoon into a blue recycling bin against the wall next to the open board room door. "Is there anything else you want to tell me?"

"Not at this time," Cassion said, getting to her feet.

Martinez watched her cross her arms, fists clenched into her armpits in a classic defensive posture. She saw the tight lips and the narrowed eyes that flicked to Hank and back to her, and she didn't need to be telepathic to know what Cassion was thinking. Six days ago, Martinez had chastised her for contacting the media directly when Thomas Kirk was arrested, rather than leaving that to Hank, as per the chief's explicit wishes. Today she'd screwed up twice in a relatively short meeting, forgetting the FBI was now handling crime scene processing on the case and not knowing that the GPD used software to generate composite sketches rather than a forensic artist. Then she'd butted heads with her on keeping Griffin in the loop and taken a swipe at her for authorizing the tactical intervention at the cannery which, while non-resultant, had been a no-brainer. On a roll, she'd also sniped at Hank while criticizing Montgomery's failure to call 911 when she first spotted the Rainy Day Killer.

The chip on Cassion's shoulder was large and obvious, and it had as much to do with her inexperience and lack of attention to detail as it did with her jealousy that Hank and Martinez worked well together. She was making mistakes, and they were not being swept under the carpet.

Martinez looked at Hank, knowing he'd been told to keep his mouth shut and let Cassion handle the briefing. He looked back at her, eyes patient. He was honoring her request to work with Cassion. She appreciated it.

"Keep me informed," she said, heading out the door.

21

Hank and Horvath stepped off the elevator onto the third floor, heading for the video lab in the back corner where Mickey Marcotte was waiting for them with footage from the Food Basket and the car rental outlet on Cooper Street. Unfortunately, their route took them past Turcotte's office, and Hank wasn't altogether surprised when the captain fell into step behind them.

"Donaghue, a word."

"I'll be right there," Hank said to Horvath. He slowed to let Turcotte catch up.

"Are you on board with this protocol with the FBI?" Turcotte asked. "They've taken complete charge of the van. Allenson's reduced to a spectator. We found it; now they act like it's theirs."

Hank's cell phone began to vibrate. He took it out and looked at the call display. It was Karen. He and Turcotte were standing in front of an empty workstation near Turcotte's office. It was unassigned—a clean desk, a clunky, outdated computer monitor, an empty waste paper basket. Hank stepped into the workstation, held up his hand for Turcotte to wait, and answered the call.

"The Bureau's taking over the van out here," Karen said. "Byrne's so wound up he's ready to give birth to fucking kittens."

Hank turned away from Marcotte, "Byrne has functional authority and can dictate what they do, but the Bureau people will handle all the processing, and they'll do it their way."

"Yeah, well, Butternut's in the middle of it, trying to keep the peace."

"Is it the van Montgomery saw at the grocery store?"

"Oh, yeah. It's the one we want, all right."

"Okay, well, make sure they don't miss anything at the scene, and stay out of the crossfire."

"They're hauling the van away now. Oops, Butternut's stepping between Byrne and the Bureau guy. I'm watching this. Christ, Byrne looks like he's going to knock the guy's fucking head off. I should give Butternut a hand before somebody hits her by mistake."

"Karen, let them straighten it out themselves."

He was talking to a dead phone. Putting it away, he said to Turcotte, "They're removing the van from the scene now, Mike."

Turcotte rubbed his face, sitting down on the corner of the desk. "Do you have any idea what our budget looks like?"

Hank did, having seen it while helping Martinez with the divisional round-up in March, but he kept his mouth shut. He knew that Criminalistics had vacancies they were not being allowed to fill, but Homicide and every other area of the department were in exactly the same position. A shrinking population and lower median income in Glendale meant an eroding tax base which, when combined with less state aid, created a widening gap between revenues and expenditures, a shortfall that directly threatened the police budget along with every other essential service in the city.

"I can't believe what's happening in this country," Turcotte went on. "Cities are declaring bankruptcy, and they have no idea how they're going to pay for their police departments. New Jersey's homicide rates are through the roof, but cities there are shutting down municipal forces and outsourcing to the county, which has to turn around and create a new police department from scratch. In Colorado, they've got cities going through idiotic prioritization exercises and deciding to spend their police dollars on mall and university units instead of bomb squads, crime analysis, and SWAT. Look at this workstation." He waved his hand around. "Empty square footage and no body to fill it. I've got two units in this section, Donaghue, and Byrne's my only Criminalist Three supervisor. He's stretched so thin I'm afraid he's going to snap. I'm short three Criminalist Twos in the crime scene response unit, so I have to ask Allenson, Marcotte, and Beverley to double up from their regular duties in the forensic services unit whenever there's a call, because we can't send the Ones out on their own, unsupervised. We have to skimp on training and conferences, we have to use up all our obsolete supplies before ordering new stuff, and my second mobile unit needs a transmission overhaul and I have no idea how to pay for it."

He shook his head. "We've got no choice but to cooperate with the Bureau. I mean, take DNA processing as an example. We got a tiny piece of the federal pie a couple years ago when they were handing out funding through the backlog reduction program, but it was so small I had to make a choice—upgrade our obsolete equipment or hire new bodies. I had to go with the equipment because you guys need reliable results. And it's not just DNA, it's trace, toxicology, documents, the whole deal. We have less time per sample for analysis than I'd like, certainly a lot less than Byrne would like, but we have to keep attacking the backlog. Throw it under the microscope, give it the once-over, and move on to the next one."

Hank nodded, understanding the dilemma.

"It's a question of accreditation," he went on. "We're about to come up for renewal, and I'm going to have to ask for an extension because we won't be able to pass all the assessment criteria, the shape we're in right now. Do you have any idea the impact that could have when our cases go to court? A nightmare. My people are brilliant, Donaghue, but even if they work twenty-four-hour days they still can't break even. Look at turnaround time. Our average for DNA analysis is one hundred and ten days. We can do it in five days if we jump the queue on an urgent basis, but if we keep jumping the queue our turn-around time will get even worse."

He rubbed his face vigorously. "I'm sorry, I'm ranting. Eventually, I know damned well somebody in the chief's office is going to get the bright idea that we don't need in-house Criminalistics at all, that we could out-source to the state or the Feds tomorrow and save a ton of cash. I'm sure it's already being discussed. But it's a bad idea, Donaghue. We need to stay in-house. If we give this up, we lose control of our evidence, and if that happens, we lose control of our cases." He laughed humorlessly. "Hey, it's no skin off my ass. If they fold us up, they could move me into the vacant captain's seat in Major Crimes tomorrow, send that idiot Cassion back where she came from, and my life would be a hell of a lot easier. I could end up being your new boss, Donaghue. Think about that one for a minute."

Hank smiled faintly. "You wouldn't want that, Mike. Trust me. You think your headaches are bad right now?"

Turcotte shrugged and walked away.

In the video room, Horvath was watching a black-and-white loop of a man standing at the counter of the car rental place. The man was bent over, signing the paperwork. He was right-handed. He wore a baseball cap and dark glasses. He wasn't all that much taller than the woman who stood on the other side of the counter, pointing to the fields on the form that he was required to sign or initial.

"He kept his head down," Marcotte said, "so all we're getting is the lower half of his face. I'll run it through some facial-recognition software. It'll probably match your composite sketch, so at least you'll know it's the guy."

"We know it's the guy," Horvath complained, "what we want to know is who he is." He turned around to Hank. "The video from the grocery store was worse. He acted like he knew where the cameras were, and gave them nothing. To rent the car, he used the name William Cassidy. Showed a Maryland driver's license with an address in Frederick, and used a credit card in the same name. The address is a pizza joint. They don't know anyone named Cassidy. They're all Lebanese."

"So he has a connection to get fake ID," Hank said.

"Or he's a forger as well as a serial rapist and killer."

"He'll need another vehicle," Hank said.

"I called Montgomery. She's going out to all the rental companies with a still from this video, plus the composite. But here's what I don't get. Why rent a vehicle and expose himself like this instead of stealing one? Wouldn't that be a hell of a lot easier?"

"Maybe he doesn't have the skill set," Marcotte said.

"What do mean, skill set?" Horvath frowned. "What's so hard about stealing a damn van? Do you know how many are stolen every day?"

Marcotte shrugged. "I couldn't do it. I wouldn't know how."

"You're kidding me."

"Well, no. You see guys on TV take apart the steering column and twist two wires together, but how the heck do you do that? And which wires? Maybe he hasn't a clue how to hotwire a car, but he's got IT skills and the equipment to dupe plastic."

"It take five minutes on the Internet to find out how to steal a car, Mickey."

"I guess so. But I wouldn't bother. I hate cars. I won't even raise the hood on mine. I pay guys to do that. Maybe he hates cars, too."

Hank's cell phone vibrated. He answered without looking at the call display, thinking it was either Karen or Roubidoux.

"Hello, Lieutenant Donaghue," said the voice. "That was fun this morning, wasn't it?"

Hank snapped his fingers, catching Marcotte's attention. He rotated the phone away from his ears, raised his eyebrows, and motioned with his head.

Marcotte slid his chair down to another computer workstation and began to pound the keyboard.

"How'd you get this number?" Hank asked.

"Come on, Lieutenant. I'm not supposed to talk to anyone else except you, according to the edict from Father Ed. Right? Anyway, never mind the trivia. I just want you to pass on my compliments to Officer Montgomery for making me at the store. She's got a good eye. Great body, terrific wardrobe. Sweet stuff. I'm definitely considering her."

"So, is William Cassidy your real name? Is that what I should call you?"

"Please, Lieutenant. Give me a break."

"We were just talking about you here."

"I'll bet you were."

"We were wondering why you rented a van instead of stealing one. We thought maybe you don't know how to hotwire a vehicle. Is that the case?"

"Oh!" The voice sounded genuinely surprised. "Hey, that's really good, Lieutenant."

"So? Is that the case? Are we right?"

"Finally! Finally, a real challenge. I was beginning to think all cops are stupid donut-eaters, and then you come along. Terrific. Two things. One, don't fool yourself into thinking Montgomery's the only one I'm surveilling. Two, tell Father Ed he's right that I'm raising the risk level, but not because I want to be caught."

The line went dead.

Hank looked at Marcotte, who shook his head.

22

The Starlight Lounge in the downtown Hilton featured live piano music performed by a middle-aged guy in an evening jacket and bow tie. In different company, Karen might have called him a lounge lizard and made fun of the music, but since she was the guest of honor at a table including a city councilor, a magazine editor, a professional stand-up comic, and Commander Ann Martinez, she tried to mind her manners and enjoy her martini.

The martini was a gesture of good will on her part. When she'd arrived, fifteen minutes late, she'd asked for a beer, as usual, and was immediately subjected to a round of good-natured kidding about needing to try something a little more upscale, just for the occasion. Since she never drank mixed drinks, she suggested a bourbon on the rocks, but her new friends insisted on the martini. She decided to play along, smiling as Karla Strong, the comic, ordered it for her in a droll imitation of Sean Connery's Scottish burr.

Earlier in the day, Karen had cast around for a suitable excuse to escape after a drink or two, and had asked Sandy if he'd be willing to call her pretending to be Hank, ordering her to a crime scene.

"No way," Sandy shook his head. "This is your shower, Karen. Face the music."

"No, it's not. I don't do showers. I don't do this girlie stuff."

"Fine, call it something else. Call it whatever you want. Go have a little fun. Relax. Meet some new people. Enjoy yourself, for crying out loud."

Karen didn't socialize very well as a general rule, and Martinez didn't really understand how distasteful these things were for her, but her heart had been in the right place when she'd set it up after hearing that Karen was skipping most of the rituals brides-to-be usually experienced, including the traditional shower or bachelorette party or whatever it was called nowadays. After speaking to her friends, Martinez had instructed Karen to show up here this evening.

"Relax, Stainer. There won't be any male strippers or cheesy gifts or booze-drinking games. Just a nice evening with a few of my friends and a really great meal. You'll enjoy it. Trust me."

Karen drained the martini, and this time they let her order a beer.

"When I got married," said Donata Parker, the magazine editor, who looked like Dionne Warwick, "my husband and I were grad students at UNC. We couldn't afford a real wedding, so we made an appointment with a justice of the peace and took our landlady along as a witness. We had our reception at a steak joint in Chapel Hill and rented a motel room for the weekend. That was our honeymoon. Then we had to eat chicken hotdogs and Kraft dinner for two months until our student grants were renewed."

"That's so romantic," said Karla.

"I suppose it sounds that way," Donata replied, "but at the time, I was scared to death. What business do two students have getting married with no money and no job prospects? I thought there was no way we'd survive."

"But you did," Martinez said.

"Yes, we did. Twenty-two years and counting."

"Donata's husband retired last year," Martinez explained to Karen. "He was a professor of history at the University of North Carolina, and now he's a book editor."

"That's right." Donata smiled. "He edits books on the Civil War for UNC Press and MSU Press, so they let him use an office on campus at State. That way, he's not underfoot." She winked at Karen. "I do a lot of my work from home."

"I wish I could work from home," Karla said, wistfully. "Mostly I do strip joints and lounges that make this place look like the Taj Mahal."

"You could work from home," Donata said. "Just set up one of those webcam things and do podcasts."

Karla snorted. "Oh, no. Webcams are out. I'd end up doing porn. Do you know how much money you can make in front of a bedroom sex cam? All you have to do is sit in front of the mirror with nothing on, combing your hair. Even I could do that."

"Careful," advised Brooke Wilson, the city councilor. "Don't forget you're having dinner with two police officers."

Karla laughed.

Martinez leaned over to Karen. "She has her own late-night television program. She makes more in a week than you and I make in a year."

"I've never been to Virginia," Brooke said. "What made you decide to get married there, Karen?"

"That's where Sandy's from. He grew up a few miles outside of Covington."

"I don't know where that is."

"It's a little hole in the wall in the Alleghany Highlands, near the West Virginia border. His family has a couple-hundred-acre property. It's been in the family since the Civil War, or some damned thing." She grabbed her glass of beer. "His father made a bunch of money in real estate and now he's a gentleman farmer. Lane, Sandy's mother, struts around like she's some kind of faded southern belle."

As she drank her beer, there was silence at the table. Karen realized they weren't embarrassed by what she'd said but were simply waiting for her to continue.

"I know, I know, I'm being unfair. A little. People are who they are. I'm a cop's kid from northeast Texas and they're Virginian gentry. I shouldn't judge. They came here for a visit after Sandy told them we were getting married, and they made a huge effort to be really nice to me. I appreciated it. They'll make another huge effort next month when we show up for this dog-and-pony show Lane's got planned. Hopefully I won't shoot anybody and we'll all live happily ever after."

Everyone laughed politely.

"Your fiancé's with the FBI?" asked Brooke.

Karen nodded, draining her glass.

"Let me get you another one," Karla said. "I need another one. Another round?"

"Yes," said Donata.

Karla left the table to order at the bar.

"How'd you two meet?" Brooke asked. "On a case?"

Karen laughed. "God, no. In a Walmart parking lot. The little prick cut me off while I was turning into a parking spot. Nearly put a scratch on my Firebird. So I got out and sounded off at him. He got out and sounded off right back. Then he said something about stupid blondes who couldn't find their ass with both hands, and I threatened to pop him on the nose."

They began to laugh.

"What happened?" Donata exclaimed.

"He says, 'Oh my God, I'm in love.' He pulls out his FBI ID, laughing his fool head off, and asks me to have dinner with him. Turns out he already knew who I was, from some big fundraiser marathon we both ran in the year before, and had asked around about me. I had no clue. That morning he cut me off on purpose, just to get in my face. And ask me out, I guess."

"How romantic," Brooke said.

Karen shrugged. "If you say so. I just thought it was stupid, and told him to fuck off." She glanced at Martinez. "Sorry, I shouldn't use language like that in here, I guess."

"But you did end up going out with him," Donata said.

"Yeah, he wouldn't give it up. He's a persistent little shrimp."

"And now you're having a country wedding in the mountains."

"Yeah."

"The reception will be on your in-laws' farm?" Martinez asked. "Didn't I hear that your brother's renovating a barn for them?"

"Yeah."

"Really?" Karla said, slipping back into her seat. "A barn?"

"Yeah. Not the real barn, with cow shit and animals and stuff, but some other big barn they've got. Lane's trying real hard to be nice, and she decided that if we have a Texas-style ranch wedding reception, I'll feel more comfortable about the whole thing. It's supposed to look like a Texan barn dance. There'll be a gazebo and log benches, a big barbecue pit for the brisket and ribs, horseshoe pits, horseback riding, a softball diamond—you name it. She's going all out. My brother Brad's a contractor and his partner's a designer, so they did up a plan for her, and she just loves it."

"Sounds like a hoot," Karla said, leaning back as their drinks were served to them.

Karen rolled her eyes. "I was just going to blow her off, but Darryl—he's my oldest brother—told me to back off and let her have her moment. The country hoedown stuff's enough to embarrass any real Texan, but he kept saying to me, 'she means well, Karen.' We'll just make sure she hires this friend of Brad's as the caterer, so at least she gets the barbecue right. That's the most important part, anyway. That and the booze. Brad's got that duty on behalf of us Stainers, so he'd better not screw it up."

Donata reached over and handed her a business card. "Give this to your photographer. Tell him or her I'd love to see some shots of it. I might be able to run one in the magazine."

When their table was ready, Donata and Karla detoured to the washroom while Karen followed Martinez and Brooke Wilson into the dining room. When they were settled, the city councilor unfolded her napkin and looked at Karen.

"Forgive me for talking shop," she said, "but I understand you're working the Olsen case."

"Yeah," Karen replied, looking up as a server arrived to set out menus and glasses of ice water.

"We'll order when the others are back," Martinez said.

The server nodded and disappeared.

"This is a chance for me to tell you," Brooke went on, "as a politician, that I appreciate the work you and Ann do on these cases. I've been an active supporter of the S*T*O*P Violence Against Women Grant Program at the state level and the federal Violence Against Women Reauthorization Act, which, as you know, was signed by the president this year. You might say I work the front end and you work the back end." She looked at Karen. "Ann had the chance to provide input into the updated national protocol for sexual assault medical forensic examinations. As I'm sure you know, it's supposed to standardize the quality of care given to sexual assault victims across the country."

"Yeah," Karen said, looking at Martinez. "I've read it."

"They did a lot of consultation," Martinez said, "including law enforcement. I was happy to participate."

Karen raised an eyebrow. "I didn't know that. Good stuff."

"The updated protocol includes some important improvements," Brooke said, "in the areas of confidentiality, how to treat victims with disabilities, and reimbursement for forensic exams. But I feel like it's not enough. It's never enough."

Karen said nothing, watching her. She was the quiet one in this group of friends, even quieter than Martinez. When the others laughed, she merely smiled. She wore no jewelry at all, very little makeup, and her clothing, while expensive, was plain and not especially flattering. Waiting for her to continue, Karen realized that while she, herself, had relaxed into this small group and had begun to enjoy the evening, Brooke Wilson was the kind of person who never relaxed, who took everything very seriously, and who socialized the way someone else took prescription medication, because it was necessary to do so.

"This is very personal for me," Brooke finally went on, "and I know that's not a good idea. But like so many other women, I've also experienced sexual assault. Do you realize that one out of every five women in Maryland has been raped in their lifetime? For me, it changed my life. I was twelve." She picked up her wine glass and drained it. "I never married. My life went in another direction. I'm not anti-male, don't get me wrong. And I'm very happy for you that you've found someone who's obviously such a perfect match for you. But I just decided my life would be better spent working for change at the political level."

"I admire you," Karen said. "It takes moxie to make that kind of stand."

"Thank you. Ann and I have talked about this many times. For a while, the rumor went around that I'm lesbian, which I'm not. I'm a civil politician with her eye on the state legislature. That's all. But the reason I mention the Olsen case—"

"I can't discuss an active investigation," Karen said.

"Of course you can't. I quite understand. My point is, Ann knows she has my help, for what it's worth, if she ever needs it, because our work never ends. Does it? With her blessing, I'm making the same offer to you. If you ever reach a point in one of your cases where I can be of assistance, you only have to ask."

"Just keep the rest of us in the loop," Martinez said.

"Absolutely," Brooke agreed. "I'm not suggesting you jump the chain of command. I understand law enforcement's a very hierarchical environment. I'm just saying, if you reach out to me and I can help, I will."

"I appreciate that," Karen said.

"Oh oh," Karla said, dropping into her seat across from Martinez, "Brooke's getting all serious about stuff again. Time to lighten the mood, girls. Did you hear the one about the horse that walked into a bar and ordered a drink?"

"Please," Donata said, sitting down. "Not again."

Karla grinned at Karen. "The bartender serves him and says, 'So, why the long face?'"

23

"It's embarrassing," Hank said, shifting on the park bench.

"No, no," Ed Griffin shook his head, leafing through the eight-by-ten prints in the file folder on his lap. "Don't worry about it. She sounds like a real piece of work, but I don't take that sort of thing personally. I wouldn't last very long in this job if I did."

They were sitting in a small, unnamed park on Cooper Street, a few blocks from departmental headquarters. Across the street and down at the corner, they could see the car rental outlet where their unknown subject had been video-recorded while renting the unmarked white van, stills from which were included in the file Griffin was now reading. Hank watched the traffic, giving Griffin a chance to digest the contents of the folder.

After their briefing of Martinez on Friday, Cassion told Hank she would update Ed Griffin herself, since she had "more experience decoding BAU bullshit" than Hank. This morning, when he'd asked her what Griffin's reaction had been, she'd waved him off. She hadn't bothered calling the FBI analyst; it was a low priority that could wait.

Hank asked for permission to brief Ed himself. She refused. He pressed. She ranted about losing focus on a case rapidly growing cold. He replied that they'd collected information Griffin should share with other jurisdictions who'd also investigated the Rainy Day Killer, to which she retorted that Hank could feel free to share that information himself with them if he wanted to waste his time. When he pointed out that Griffin already had a dissemination protocol in place, she looked at her watch and said, "Whatever, Donaghue. Just make something happen and stop bothering me with trivia."

"You're correct," Griffin said, tapping a photograph of the man signing the rental form, "he's right-handed. Pathology reports have all consistently indicated that the removal of the breasts was done by someone who's right-handed, and there it is." He flipped back to a photo from the Food Basket. "He's got the camera slung over his right shoulder." He held the two pictures side by side. "Your technical guy's sure it's the same person?"

Hank nodded. Mickey Marcotte had run both video clips through analysis software and concluded there was a 95 percent chance, give or take 5 percent, that the man videotaped in the Food Basket was the same man videotaped while renting the white van.

"Unbelievably, none of the others came up with a picture of this guy," Griffin said. "Not even Pittsburgh." He flicked the photograph in his hand. "I mean, if he walked by me on the street I couldn't hold this up and say, 'Hey, it's him!' But just the same, it's progress, and that's a good thing."

Hank described the conversation between Marcotte and Horvath about whether or not the killer knew how to steal a car, and the reaction he'd gotten when he'd mentioned it during the telephone call.

"It was a good thought." Griffin folded his hands on the file, watching a young woman stroll by with a small boy. The boy was walking a Pomeranian dog on a leash. "In Pittsburgh, he leased a vehicle using an online service and had it delivered to a blind address in the suburbs. He used it for the two confirmed murders with the Rainy Day Killer signature, and God knows how many other rapes in between. Then he torched it in a quarry on his way out of town. I know you saw that in the file, Hank. I'm just thinking out loud. Indulge me for a minute."

"Go ahead," Hank said.

"I've skipped the West Virginia case because no one knows what vehicle he used, since he followed the Witten woman home and then took off. In the Towson case in Louisville, the white van he used was stolen from a construction company's yard on a Friday evening. The keys were left in it, behind the sun visor. It had been sitting there for a week, along with other vehicles, all with the keys in them, none of them used on a regular basis. We know he invests a fair amount of time in surveillance, so he probably earmarked the yard as an easy place to grab a low-risk vehicle without much effort."

"In Evansville," Hank said, "they never did figure out what he used, did they?"

Griffin shook his head. "No rental or leasing companies reported any missing vehicles during either time period. If he stole something, either it was never recovered or it was recovered and returned without ever being connected to the murders. In the first one, in St. Louis, all they know from witnesses who were out on the street when the Mortenson girl was picked up is that it was a dark-colored, mid-sized passenger car."

"I've included a copy of the FBI report on our van."

"I saw it. I take it they didn't recover any meaningful physical evidence, otherwise we wouldn't be here enjoying a peaceful afternoon in your beautiful city."

"No, it was clean. No fingerprints, no hair, fibers, soil, footwear impressions, biological fluid stains, tissue fragments, or any other physical evidence that the Bureau could find. Since it was found in the parking lot of a do-it-yourself car detailing place, it stands to reason he cleaned it up before walking away from it."

"It's not his first time around the block," Griffin said.

Hank hesitated a moment. "I've been wondering what his regular vehicle is, Ed. What does he drive in between? How does he move around from city to city? Could he travel from place to place by bus, for example, then pick up a vehicle when he gets to a new location?"

"I don't think so," Griffin replied. "He rented the van here only three days before he grabbed Theresa Olsen. When you consider the amount of surveillance he did, not only of Olsen herself but several potential captivity sites and various dump sites, I'd be willing to bet he put in at least two weeks, maybe more, in preparation. He comes across as a highly-mobile, restless kind of suspect. I've started wondering whether that dark-colored, mid-sized passenger car in St. Louis is his own vehicle. Maybe he figured he'd taken an unnecessary risk with it that first time and decided to use different, disposable vehicles after that."

"Do you think he has the skill set required to steal a car?"

"Who knows? It's a good thought. With these newer cars, the remote keyless entry devices are easily hacked, so maybe he steals them using high tech skills. We don't have enough data to make an educated guess at this point. The fact remains that here, in Glendale, he rented a white van and let himself be recorded doing it. That tells us something new."

"He's raising the risk level, as he said, but not because he wants to be caught."

Griffin sighed, closing the file folder. "Letting himself be videotaped, showing himself to Officer Montgomery, calling you on your cell phone when he's not supposed to know the number. Yes, he's being much more overt this time, a lot more daring."

"Why, if he doesn't want to be caught?"

Griffin shrugged. "Bored? Becoming desensitized and wants to increase the thrill factor? Arrogance, egotism? Feeding a narcissistic urge to appear smarter and better than the people hunting him? It could be any or all of these things."

Hank watched a motorcycle roll past with the characteristic growl of a Harley Davidson engine. The rider wore a shiny black helmet, a navy business suit, and cowboy boots. It was too far away for Hank to read the tag number.

"We're still trying to get a lead on where he's staying," he said. "The districts are canvassing hotels and motels with the composite and profile, but nothing solid's turned up. We've checked with property rental agencies and followed up on classified listings, in case he rented a house or an apartment, and we've gone through trailer parks and campgrounds in the area. A lot of legwork with nothing to show for it. Maybe he sleeps in his damned car."

"These aren't like your typical cases," Griffin said. "The domestic arguments or gang-related drug shootings where you can have a suspect in custody within three or four days if everything comes together. These cases take a long time to work, a very long time. I have cases in my filing cabinet, Hank, that have been open for fifteen years. Don't get me wrong; I'm not trying to discourage you. I'm just saying, cases like this can take a lot of time, a lot of patience, and a long memory."

Hank nodded. It would be three weeks tomorrow since Theresa Olsen had died, and he wasn't any closer to finding her killer than he'd been on the first day. Cases that stayed open for a long period of time inevitably became institutionalized, like wallpaper you looked at every day until you no longer saw it, or coffee in the bullpen coffee pot that you smelled but no longer bothered to pour because you knew you wouldn't drink it. Like Karen and most other detectives he knew, he preferred to immerse himself in a case, live it and breathe it twenty-four hours a day, seven days a week, until a suspect was in custody. A case like this, strung out over several weeks, with long periods of inactivity, was like a slow form of torture. He understood this type of offender was difficult to catch. He knew that sometimes they were never caught. He appreciated Griffin's point of view, that he needed to bring unusual patience and doggedness to bear this time around, and he knew his unit, like every other department, had open-unsolved cases which had grown stone-cold. It happened.

That didn't mean he had to like it.

Both men looked up as an empty tractor trailer rumbled through the intersection a block away. For a moment, it had sounded like distant thunder. Involuntarily, Hank glanced at the sky.

Bad weather was coming.

"We don't know his periodicity," he said. "We don't know when he'll be due again."

"No. There are months between his signature homicides, but he's said several times he commits other sexual offences in between. As far as I can tell, there's no real reason that he waits so long on the Rainy Day victims other than availability and timing."

"If he found another victim quickly, worked through his planning and preparations, and then a storm hit—"

"He could strike again at any time," Griffin completed the thought for him.

24

Three days later it was raining as Karen drove downtown to turn herself in at Richard's Bridal Salon for her dress fitting. Overnight, several isolated thunderstorms had moved inland over the city from Chesapeake Bay, but now it was raining steadily, although the downpour was supposed to ease into scattered showers later in the afternoon. Fortunately, she found a parking spot for her Firebird two doors down from the shop. She fed the meter like a good citizen and ran inside, handbag over her head.

Because he didn't know her, or know anyone who knew her, Richard had been otherwise occupied when Karen had made her appointment last week. The woman she'd dealt with, though, whose name was Mrs. George, had been very nice. They'd exchanged e-mail addresses. Karen reluctantly sent her several photographs of herself, along with her measurements (taken by Sandy, with much groping and fooling around), and a general description of what she'd like in a wedding gown. They went back and forth several times, and Karen tried to be patient in her replies. Finally, Mrs. George declared herself "ready with several lovely prospects, one of which is sure to win your heart."

Dreading the phony gushiness that would soon be inflicted on her, Karen hesitated inside the door, looking around the shop. The entire place was done in white. White walls, white ceiling, white fake Greek columns, white seating arrangements for bored fiancés to sit in, white lighting fixtures suspended from the ceiling, white carpet underfoot, and, of course, rack after rack of white wedding gowns.

She made her way toward a white reception desk behind which a twenty-something who looked as if she'd just stepped out of *Vogue* magazine pouted skeptically.

"Yes?"

Karen forced a smile. "The name's Stainer. I have a ten o'clock with Mrs. George."

Mrs. George was summoned, and Karen was led into a show-room where three mannequins were set up to display different models that would compete for Karen's heart. She sat down on a settee and accepted a cup of coffee while Mrs. George went to work, describing the three models and suggesting how each might be a match to Karen's particular body style and taste.

"As I mentioned, given your petite size, I believe the trumpet- or mermaid-style gowns will give you the best silhouette," Mrs. George said. "You'll want a waistline above your natural waist so that the lower portion of the dress looks somewhat longer, so as not to over-empha-size your shortness. We must also make sure the detailing stays small, so no enormous bows!"

"I'm not a real big fan of bows," Karen said.

"Then we're definitely on the same page, aren't we? We've stayed away from strapless gowns, as you requested. Does any one of these three particularly catch your fancy?"

Karen set down her cup of coffee. She didn't wear a dress very often, and her level of enthusiasm for the task ahead was not exactly where it should be. She was doing this more for other people than for herself, because she'd never been one to fantasize about being a glow-ing bride in a long, white gown. She'd been serious when she'd said to Sandy that she would prefer to be married in her Class A uniform, but she knew that option was definitely out. She had to go the traditional route with all this stuff. Everyone was expecting her to play along and be the nice little bride.

Sighing, she ran her eyes over the mannequins. The one clos-est to her seemed harmless enough. She stood up and walked over for a closer look. The first thing she did was find the tiny price tag, dangling on a thread, and turn it over.

Twelve hundred dollars. *Jesus H. Christ.*

Mrs. George beamed. "This is lovely. It's by Melissa Sweet, in-spired by the movie remake of *The Great Gatsby.* It's a fit-and-flare gown. The layering of the skirt in tulle and chiffon gives an airiness and shape that will ensure a lovely silhouette. I just love these cap sleeves. The corded lace has been hand-applied, and here, this illusion net at the neckline is very wispy and romantic. It's one of our more affordable models as well, so hopefully it'll fit your budget nicely. Would you like to try it on?"

Karen nodded. If twelve hundred was affordable, she was afraid to look at the prices of the others. While she was wondering how long it would take to remove the dress from the damned mannequin, Mrs. George led her over to a long table outside the dressing stalls where several gowns had been laid out for her.

"Based on your measurements, this should do." Mrs. George picked it up and held it draped over a forearm. "We'll make whatever alterations are necessary, of course."

"It's nice," Karen allowed.

"Yes, it is." Mrs. George raised her eyebrows. "You remembered to bring your shoes?"

"Yeah." Karen grabbed her handbag and pulled out the white shoes she'd bought for the ceremony.

"Perfect." Mrs. George led her into a stall, hung up the gown for her, and waved a hand. "Take your time. I'll be out here."

Left alone, Karen eyed the dress. Twelve hundred bucks, and she was paying for it. Was she insane? Twelve hundred for a dress? Did they know how many pairs of jeans she could buy in the Walmart for that kind of money?

She fingered the cap sleeve on the dress. It *was* beautiful.

What the hell.

She removed her jacket and hung it on a hook. She peeled off her top and hung it on another hook beside her jacket. She sat down on the bench and began unlacing her shoes. She took them off and set them aside, then stood up and removed her jeans, hanging them by the belt loop next to her top. She sat down again and unfastened the brand-new DeSantis elasticized rig around her ankle in which was holstered her new sub-compact 9mm pistol, a SIG Sauer P-290. She set the weapon on the bench beside her. She liked the style of the ankle rig, which was essentially an elasticized leg band secured by a Velcro thumb strap. Now that it was off, she was able to remove her white crew socks. She took out a pair of pantyhose from her handbag and struggled into them, then wrapped the ankle holster back on, adjusting its position so that the gun was situated on the inside of her lower calf, above the ankle bone, where she could easily reach it.

She stood up and glanced at herself in the mirror: bra, panties, pantyhose, and concealed-carry weapon.

She reached back into her handbag, took out an ankle-length slip she'd been instructed to bring, and stepped into it. Finally, reluctantly, she reached for the dress.

When she stepped out of the stall, Mrs. George appeared from thin air and gave her a once-over. "How does it feel?"

"Okay."

"Do you like the way it looks?"

Karen walked over to a three-sided dressing room mirror and looked at herself. "Yeah. It's nice." She turned around, looked at her reflection over her shoulder, and turned back. "Very nice."

The neckline came down in a v-shape that was a little lower than she'd anticipated, but her bust was able to handle it just fine. She really liked the way the cap sleeves covered the top halves of her deltoid muscles, leaving the lower half of her shoulders bare, and the way the neckline came up over her collarbone and around the base of her neck in back, almost like a very short collar. She rolled her head around. It felt good, not buggy at all. The corded lace made it look very feminine.

Holy shit. I look pretty in this thing.

Mrs. George asked her to turn around, then put her hands at each side of Karen's waist. "It could stand to come in just a touch here. You have a lovely figure, so you might as well show it off."

She ran her hands down the layers of the skirt, assessing how well they draped as they fell from Karen's thighs toward her shoes. Her hand brushed the holster as it passed across her ankle. She removed her hands and straightened up.

Karen hiked up the skirts and her slip to show her the gun. "I'm a cop. Where I go, it goes."

"I see." Mrs. George stared at her for a moment, then laughed. "That's a first for me. It definitely is. You'll be wearing it at the ceremony, will you?"

"I'll be carrying it, yeah. You don't wear a gun, you carry it, but yeah, I'll have it there. For sure."

"Then you're right to wear it—sorry, have it on—right now." She stepped back a few paces. "Twirl around for me. Pretend you're dancing the first dance with your husband."

Karen turned in a circle self-consciously. Her shoes, ivory peep-toe pumps, had two-and-a-half-inch heels, and she wasn't used to them. She was pleased, at least, to discover that she was athletic enough to be able to move in them without looking like Dumbo the elephant.

"Pretend you're dancing. No one can see you but me, Karen, and I'm busy watching the gown, so pretend you're all alone."

Karen obligingly moved around a little, rocking back and forth at the waist, then threw caution to the wind and pirouetted, dipped, whirled, and stepped back and forth. Sure enough, Mrs. George's eyes were following the movement of the gown with complete absorption. Karen took a few more steps and then stopped.

"Does it look okay?"

"Oh, yes. It looks fabulous on you. There's no interference from the gun at all that I could see, thanks to the slip. Would you like to try on one of the others?"

"No. I want this one."

Mrs. George raised an eyebrow. "Are you sure? There's plenty of time. It's always good to compare."

"No. First time lucky." She glanced at herself in the mirror. "It won't get any better than this."

"Confidentially, Karen, I don't think it will either, but that's because I believe this gown looks absolutely stunning on you. You're going to be a beautiful bride."

"Thanks."

Back in the stall, she looked at herself for a moment, hands on her hips. She shook her head. It was unbelievable. She looked great. Who would've thought?

She removed the shoes, the dress, the slip, the gun, and the pantyhose. She strapped the gun back on, having decided to skip the socks, and was pulling up her jeans when there was a tap on the stall door.

Zipping up her fly, Karen opened the door. "Yeah?"

Mrs. George stood there, an apologetic expression on her face. She held out a small white envelope. "Please excuse me, but the gentleman said it was urgent."

Frowning, Karen took the envelope. It was small, about five

inches by three-and-a-half inches, and had some kind of card in it. *Detective Stainer* had been written on the front with a fountain pen in an elegant hand. She turned it over. The flap had been folded inside the envelope, rather than sealed.

Puzzled, she removed the card from the envelope. *For the Bride* was printed on the front in gold cursive. She opened it and read:

> *Such a beautiful bride-to-be. I regret I cannot introduce myself in person at this time, but most selfishly I've made ar-rangements to spend the weekend with someone else. Perhaps next time.*
>
> *Your admirer,*
>
> *RDK*

It took her a precious moment to decode the initials: *Rainy Day Killer.*

She looked up at Mrs. George. "Where is he? Is he still out there?"

"No. He left."

"What'd he look like?"

"A pleasant-looking gentleman."

"Suit? Umbrella?"

"Yes."

Karen drew the gun from her ankle rig and pushed past Mrs. George, running out into the front of the shop.

The twenty-something behind the reception desk stared at her.

"Where is he? Which way did he go?"

"Who?"

"Jesus Christ," Karen snarled, running to the front door, "the guy with the suit and umbrella. Did he go left or right?"

"I don't know. Right?"

Karen burst out onto the sidewalk, threw a quick look to her left, then turned right. She ran down the block, gun held at high ready, her bare feet slapping the wet pavement. Her eyes darted from one pedestrian to the next, searching for a suit and an umbrella. There were several umbrellas, but no men in business suits. She reached the corner and stopped, looking in all directions at once.

People waiting for the light to change turned and stared at her.

"Anyone see a guy in a business suit with an umbrella?" she called out.

No one spoke.

"Guy with an umbrella!" Karen shouted. "Which way?"

People backed away from her, alarmed.

"Jesus!" She ran across the intersection, dodging traffic, gun in the air. "Police!" she shouted, starting down the next block. "Looking for a guy in a suit! Umbrella!"

People backed away from her.

A siren blipped behind her. She stopped and turned around as a patrol car pulled up, lights flashing, and two uniformed officers tumbled out, guns drawn.

"Drop your weapon!" the nearest cop shouted, aiming at her. "Right now! Put it down on the sidewalk and put your hands on top of your head!"

"Police! Homicide! In pursuit of a suspect!" Karen shouted back as she knelt and set the gun down on the sidewalk.

"Turn around! On your knees! Hands on top of your head!"

"Badge and ID in my right front pocket!" Karen called out, complying, as the other cop, a young woman, raced around to cover her from the front. "Can I remove it?"

"Don't move!" the female cop screamed.

The cop behind her grabbed her right wrist, cuffed it, pulled it back behind her back, grabbed her left wrist, pulled it down and back, and completed the handcuffing job. Applying upward pressure, he instructed her to stand.

She stood up. The female officer, whose name plate said *Barnes*, holstered her sidearm and stepped forward. "Right front pocket?"

"Goddamn it," Karen growled, adrenaline pumping, "he's getting away!"

Barnes reached out, felt the outside of her pocket, then reached in and took out the wallet containing Karen's badge and identification. She opened it, looked at Karen to compare her to the photograph on the ID card, then held it up to her partner. "She's GPD."

The officer behind her removed the cuffs.

"Detective," Barnes asked, "can you explain why you're running around in the street wearing only a bra?"

Karen looked down at herself. It was true. She'd run out of the dress shop in her bare feet without having put on her top. Her upper body was completely wet, her skin slick with rain, her bra soaked. Rain dripped from the tips of her hair down onto her bare shoulders. The adrenaline disappeared from her system as though it had been flushed down the drain.

"Jesus Christ," she said. "The rest of my clothes are back at the dress shop. I'm picking up my gun now, okay?"

"Feel free."

Karen rescued her new P-290 from the sidewalk. "Give me a tissue. You need to call in a possible sighting of the felony suspect the Rainy Day Killer. Get backup, get this area cordoned off, and have them contact Lieutenant Donaghue in Homicide. This guy may still be in the area. We need to move fast."

The male cop, whose name plate said *Krevinski*, handed her a tissue while Barnes stepped away, speaking into her portable radio. "What dress shop did you say this happened at?" he asked.

"Richard's Bridal Salon. Back a block. The guy walked in, left me a note." She scrubbed her gun with the tissue. "Look, he may be still in the area; we need to move fast."

Barnes came back. "Back-up's on the way. Is the suspect on foot or in a vehicle?"

"I have no idea," Karen replied, exasperated. "I couldn't get anyone to speak up outside the shop. That's what I was doing, trying to find someone who'd seen him."

Barnes rolled her eyes and keyed her portable radio again.

"Get in," Krevinski said, pointing to the cruiser. "We'll take you back to the dress shop."

"He could still be in the area," Karen insisted.

"And he could be long gone," Barnes said, shaking her head at Karen. "We can't exactly lock down the entire downtown."

"We have to set up a perimeter! He was here!"

"Let's start by getting you back to the dress shop," Krevinski said.

"Yeah," Barnes chipped in, "you could even finish getting dressed, if you want."

25

The daytime civilian staff who worked outside her office had already gone home for the evening by the time Ann Martinez stepped off the elevator on the eighth floor. The voices coming from her board room could be heard clearly as she made her way through the rows of workstations to her corner of the floor.

"So what?" Helen Cassion said. "It's the eastern seaboard, Lieutenant. It rains all the time."

"That's not the point," Ed Griffin said. "This note to Detective Stainer clearly indicates his intention to take another victim this weekend."

"That's bullshit and you know it," Cassion said. "He's obviously jerking our chain."

Martinez caught her own reflection in the locked glass doors leading into her office. She wore a red knee-length cocktail dress with a plunging neckline and high heels, and she carried a matching evening bag that was large enough to include her badge, identification, off-duty weapon, and credit cards. She and her husband, Oscar Sanchez, had been on the way to Baltimore for a dinner with a group of Oscar's important clients when Hank had called her with the news of Karen's near-encounter with the Rainy Day Killer. They'd been forced to stop at Annapolis, where Martinez arranged for a ride back to Glendale while Oscar, very much annoyed by the change in plans, continued on to Baltimore.

Her career had always been a sore point between them, and had caused him to break off their relationship before they were married. It had happened when she was still a detective and Hank was her supervisory lieutenant. A series of successful high-profile investigations had led to very favorable media attention, and she'd been a rising star in the division until Hank's enemies in Internal Affairs decided that her stellar performance appraisals had been given to her by Hank in return for sexual favors. Although false, the allegation had provided the media with enough toxic sludge that her reputation had taken a hit. The unexpected publicity had shocked Oscar, and he'd broken off their engagement.

She shifted her purse to her other hand and walked away from her reflection. Their affair, brief and intense, had come nearly two years later, when she was a sergeant assigned to Midtown district and Hank was working a desk in Public Relations. A year later, she and Oscar resumed their relationship.

"I don't think we can take that chance," Hank was saying as she reached the open door. "We need to move proactively."

"We need to keep our heads and not panic," Cassion retorted.

"Nobody's panicking," Griffin said. "Hank's right, you need to make the next move right now, right away."

Hank sat with his back to the door. Cassion stood at the head of the table, hands on her hips. Across from Hank, Griffin stared at Cassion, chair tipped back against the wall, legs crossed, arms folded. Karen Stainer paced back and forth at the far end of the table, hands shoved into the pockets of her jeans. Tension was thick in the room.

Martinez walked behind Hank, tapping him lightly on the shoulder, and sat down in the chair on his left, allowing Cassion to keep the symbolic head of the table. "Sorry I'm late, Helen. It was a bit of a drive back. Where are we?"

"The FBI lab has Stainer's card," Cassion replied, "but I'm not hopeful it'll give us prints or DNA. The store employees confirmed it was our suspect after looking at the composite and the video stills. We think he took a taxi after leaving the store, and we're canvassing the cab companies for confirmation."

"Or," Griffin said, "he has another vehicle already, and he drove it to wherever he's staying between captures."

"Whatever." Cassion folded her arms. "As far as I'm concerned, this is a lot of noise and hot air over nothing. He's playing games with Stainer just like he played with Montgomery last week. We're wasting time running around like chickens with our heads cut off while this guy sits back and laughs at us."

Griffin's face clouded and he opened his mouth, but Hank interceded. "I disagree, Helen," he said. "It's been nearly a month since he abducted Theresa Olsen. He's probably going to use the same captivity site again, since we haven't found it, so he's had four weeks to select and study another victim. We can't afford to assume he isn't ready to make his next move this weekend. Conditions are perfect."

"That's what he said," Karen said, stopping her pacing to confront Cassion. "In the note? 'I'll be spending the weekend with someone else?' Duh?"

"Sit down, Detective," Cassion said, pointing at a chair. "You're getting on my nerves. As I already said, he's playing games with you."

"Jesus." Karen pulled out the chair next to Griffin and dropped into it.

"Our investigation has been conducted so far on a proactive basis," Martinez said, deciding it was time to weigh in. "Community outreach, increased patrols in target areas, surveillance cameras along the river. We need to stay in that mindset." She looked across the table at Griffin. "Comments?"

"Absolutely," Griffin said. "It's the best approach you've got."

"If we assume he'll take someone again this weekend," Martinez said to Cassion, "what can we do to get ahead of the curve on this guy?"

Cassion shrugged. "I suppose we could try another media release. Get Donaghue to hand out the posters, that routine. 'Stay vigilant, be cautious with strangers,' blah blah blah."

Martinez waited.

"We can get the districts to brief their patrols again on what to look for," Cassion went on. "But they're not going to like it when it turns out we got them all cranked up crying wolf yet again."

"For the luvva—" Karen started.

"Detective," Martinez interrupted, without taking her eyes from Cassion, "please." She raised an eyebrow. "What else?"

Cassion sat down. "We can keep a channel open to Missing Persons, so they'll inform us right away if they get a report on someone matching the victim profile."

"Who's your replacement down there? Winston?"

"Yeah. I'll instruct her to call me when they get a hit."

"Call Captain Williams instead. Tonight. Tell her I want Winston to call Hank immediately. He'll brief her on the situation and explain what he needs. We want direct lines of communication in place if a report comes in matching the victim profile. Hank will be the boots on the ground this weekend. Right?"

Cassion looked at her. "Yeah. Right." She looked at Hank. "Wait for Winston's call. Tonight."

Hank nodded.

Martinez looked at Karen. "Did you get anything at all that could help us? Are we any further ahead?"

"Other than knowing he's gonna grab another one, probably tomorrow?"

"Other than that."

Karen's face clouded. "No. He's a careful bastard. Even with his face plastered all over town he still parades around like he's King Shit, waving his suit and damned umbrella under our noses. What we need to do is trap the sonofabitch. He's so arrogant, I'll bet we can walk him into something he won't walk out of."

"Such as what? Using you or Montgomery as bait? That's not going to happen."

Karen looked away.

Martinez understood that Karen wanted to make it personal, wanted to bait the subject into coming after her instead of some un-suspecting victim, but it wasn't going to fly. As much as she admired Karen's courage, Martinez would never sanction that kind of tactic.

"It's bad enough," Cassion said, "charging around in the street half-naked. You need to act a little more like a professional, Stainer, and not like some TV bimbo."

Hank's cell phone buzzed. He looked at the call display and got up from his chair to answer it, walking down to the far end of the board room.

"Stainer's actions are not in question, Helen," Martinez said, before Karen could open her mouth. "She acted in haste, yes, but I think given the circumstances I would've probably done the same thing. We all feel the urgency to catch this bastard." She turned to Griffin. "Why do you think he'll strike again this soon?"

"He feels at the height of his power right now," Griffin said, "like he can do no wrong. Karen's right, he's arrogant and self-confident. I think he's ready, he wants us to know he's ready, and I think he's so sure of himself, so addicted to the adrenaline from the greater risks he's taking, that he can't pass up the opportunity to make another move right now, right under our noses."

"You're over-reacting," Cassion said. "You're too subjective."

Griffin looked at her. "Subjective? Because I know this guy's profile inside and out?"

"If we're going to catch this guy, we need to concentrate on the evidence and not a bunch of headshrink guesswork."

"*Guesswork?*"

"Come on, Griffin. It's all guesswork. You're guessing at what's going on inside his head and you're guessing he's going to make another move, when it's obvious to anyone who's objective about it that he's pulling on your dick and having a big laugh."

"Can you take that chance?" Griffin asked. "Gamble with someone else's life that I'm full of shit," he waved his hand at Karen, "that *we're* full of shit and you're the one with the correct read on the situation?"

"We have to be proactive," Martinez interrupted, looking at Cassion. "Hank will brief the media, I'll contact the district commanders, and Helen, you make that call to Williams tonight so Missing Persons is briefed and ready to go."

Hank returned to his chair, putting away his cell phone. "That was Byrne. The FBI lab just sent over a set of reports on the Olsen evidence. They found something."

"Oh?" Martinez sat up straight. "What?"

"A hair. Imbedded in the manila rope from the package with Theresa Olsen's effects. Byrne's upset they missed it."

"I have to wonder about their competence down there," Cassion said. "Sounds like a pretty fundamental oversight."

"I don't think that's fair," Hank said. "The lab's under enormous time pressure and working with a serious backlog. Anyway, that's why we're using the FBI lab in this case, so we have a safety net. Byrne shipped everything from the Olsen case over to them two weeks ago, on the chief's orders, and they've been going through it since then."

"And?" Martinez prompted.

"The hair's a small one," Hank said. "According to their micro-scopical analysis, it's an eyelash hair. The theory is, it was dislodged at some point when he was using the rope, maybe when he rubbed an eye without thinking, and it worked its way into the fibers while he was ty-ing the rope around the package."

"Finally," Griffin exulted, "he makes a mistake!"

"Hard to believe," Cassion said. "He's been very careful so far."

"He's good, but he's not a genius by any means."

"Fucking right he's not," Karen said.

"They know it's an eyelash hair?" Martinez asked.

"Byrne, being Byrne, gave me the mini-tutorial," Hank replied. "Under the microscope, they can usually tell by appearance what part of the body a hair comes from. This one's short, stubby, saber-shaped, and with no significant difference in the shaft diameter from one end to the other. Eyelash hair."

"It could be from anyone," Cassion said. "A worker in the fac-tory, a clerk in the store where it was bought."

"But it's not," Hank disagreed, "because there's more."

"I was hoping there would be," Martinez said.

"The follicle was intact," Hank went on, "so they were able to extract nuclear DNA. But Sandy, on a hunch, got them to take a sample of mitochondrial DNA as well."

"I've never understood the difference," Cassion complained. "Is this telling us anything useful?"

"Nuclear DNA," Griffin said, "is found in the nucleus of the living cells in your body. It contains the recombined genes you inher-ited from both your parents. You know, the famous double helix? It's unique to you as an individual—unless you have an identical twin, of course. Mitochondrial DNA, on the other hand, is in the mitochondria inside your body's cells. It contains the same gene structure as your mother and your siblings, if you have any. So not unique, but definitely identifiable."

"Yeah? So?"

Hank leaned forward. "They ran the nuclear DNA sequence through CODIS," he said, referring to the Combined DNA Index System, a database of DNA profiles at local, state, and national levels.

"They came up empty. Whoever he is, he's never donated DNA to the system."

"So it's a dead end."

"Not at all." Hank glanced at Karen. "On a hunch, Sandy went through the other Rainy Day Killer files and discovered that in the Harrisville case they collected a lot of hair evidence."

Cassion frowned. "Which one is that, again?"

"Harrisville, West Virginia," Griffin said. "His previous stop before coming here. The victim, Annabelle Witten, was followed home from work and confined in her barn for three days before he killed her. It's the only case so far in which we know his captivity site." He looked at Hank. "Sheriff Anglehart was out of his depth and he knew it, but he was a smart cookie, just the same. He called in the state police and they spent a couple days in that barn. They came away with a real good collection of animal hairs, at least."

"Human, as well," Hank said. "They got a match on mitochondrial DNA between our eyelash hair and one of the hairs they analyzed from that barn."

Griffin slapped the table with his palm. "Outstanding!"

"Okay," Cassion said, "so that gives us a connection between the parcel you got and a previous case, but we still don't know who the hell this guy is."

"Come on, Cassion," Karen growled, "get with the program. Now we've got physical evidence we can take into court and ram down this bastard's goddamned throat."

"Thanks to Sandy," Martinez said. "It's a start, anyway."

"Our first break on the evidence," Hank agreed.

Martinez looked at Cassion. "Are you still going to be in DC this weekend?"

"I have to be," she said. "It's a long-standing commitment."

"That's fine. Leave your cell phone on so you can be reached at all times, but I want Hank fully empowered to make whatever decisions are necessary if something goes down. Understood?"

Cassion shrugged. "Sure. His responsibility."

Martinez looked at Hank. "Comfortable with that?"

"Of course."

She could see in his eyes that he hadn't known Cassion was

leaving the city tonight. Cassion had already told Martinez about her plans to attend a weekend film festival in the capital in the company of several celebrities, none of whom were familiar to Martinez. She'd given her blessing to it, as much to clear the decks for Hank this weekend as for any other reason.

She could see, as well, that Hank suddenly understood Cassion's unwillingness to take the killer's threat seriously as a reluctance to put her weekend plans in jeopardy. She saw him reacting to the lack of professionalism it revealed, and she raised an eyebrow.

Let it ride, Hank, she thought. *Now you have the green light to handle things your way without interference.*

He nodded, getting the message.

Martinez stood up. "Keep me informed." She walked out and headed straight for the elevator without looking at her reflection this time. She was all dressed up and had nowhere to go. Oscar was in Baltimore and she was here, wearing a red cocktail dress, about to call a taxi to take her home. She punched the elevator button and stepped back, watching the arrows, waiting for the one pointing down to light up.

26

The headache woke Hank at 4:26 A.M. He spent ten minutes trying to get back to sleep, then gave up and eased out of bed. In the bathroom he found a bottle of analgesics and took a couple with tap water, then went back to bed. He tossed and turned, then eventually got up again, accepting the fact that he wasn't going to be able to get back to sleep.

In the living room, he pressed the button that drew back the vertical blinds. It was still dark outside. Down in the quiet street far below, the black pavement glistened with wetness. Droplets clung to the outside surface of the window. The bad weather of the past several days was evidently going to continue for another day.

He fixed a pot of coffee in the kitchen, and while it was percolating he went into the bathroom. While he was there, he turned on the wall-mounted flat-screen television and found the weather channel. Showers today, and for the next three days. The current temperature was 64 degrees Fahrenheit. After showering he turned off the television and returned to the bedroom. He walked into the closet and chose a pair of dark-brown cotton trousers, a violet linen shirt, and a two-button, medium-brown cotton sport jacket. Warm from the shower and the clean, fresh clothing, he felt a little better.

He poured a cup of coffee and took it into the living room. Contemplating his music collection, he chose an album featuring fifteenth- and sixteenth-century plainsong, slipped the disc into the player, and settled down in an armchair in front of the window, closing his eyes against the pain in his head as the male chorus performed a *Sanctus* attributed to Henry V.

He sipped the coffee.

The music was quiet, simple, soothing. It complemented the

darkness outside, the tranquility of an early Sunday morning, the search for release from pain.

The telephone rang.

Setting aside his cup, he got up and walked over to answer it.

"Donaghue."

"Another one," Karen said. "I'm downstairs. How long will you take?"

"I'm ready," Hank said. He glanced at his wrist, which was bare, and made a mental note to put on a watch before he left. "I'll be down in a minute."

"It's not far."

"Oh?"

"City hall."

Hank said nothing, frowning.

"It's him," Karen said. "You'll see. Hang up and get a move on."

27

This time, there was no overpass to huddle beneath while the scene was being worked by the medical examiner and the FBI crime scene technicians. Hank held an umbrella over his head, given to him by Butternut Allenson, and stood between Dr. Jim Easton, the ME, and Ed Griffin as they watched the corpse being placed into a body bag for transportation back to Easton's morgue. The victim was another young, blonde female, and the nude, mutilated, chalk-white body was slick with rain.

Easton was uncharacteristically somber, rain dripping from his Tilley hat onto his raincoat, as Chalmers supervised the lifting of the body bag onto the gurney. He'd traveled to the scene himself, despite the earliness of the hour, because they were all aware of the impact that a second homicide by this serial killer would have on the city, and he felt that Chalmers should have his supervision and guidance. Once he'd arrived and inspected the body for himself, however, he'd stepped aside and motioned for Chalmers to proceed, his jaw clenched.

They stood in the open plaza facing the southern façade of city hall on Market Street, in the oldest part of the city. The center of the plaza was dominated by a large, ornamental fountain. The fountain consisted of an upper basin that was twenty-four feet in diameter, a middle basin that was sixty feet in diameter, and a lower basin that was one hundred and three feet in diameter. When turned on, as it had been for the past week in anticipation of the summer tourist season, water shot about fifty feet into the air from the jets in the upper basin and cascaded down to fill the middle and lower basins. The retaining wall around the lower basin was two feet high, made of concrete, and decorated at the key points of the compass with foot-long bronze sea creatures, including a sea horse, a dolphin, a crab, and a leaping fish.

The killer had seated the body on the edge of the retaining wall next to the crab, had lowered it backward until the upper body was submerged, had positioned the legs so that they were widely splayed open, feet on the paving stones, and had positioned the hands on the inner thighs. Again, the positioning of the corpse was intended to be obscene.

"What's his thing with the rain?" Easton suddenly asked. "Is bad weather a trigger to his perverted sexual behavior?"

Griffin shook his head. "I don't think so. He'd like us to think it's part of his signature, part of some murky compulsion that begins with sex and ends with murder, but it comes across more and more like an MO he's deliberately following. Studies have looked for a connection between rainy weather and rape, and rainy weather and homicide, but there's no significant link."

Easton shook his head and left to follow Chalmers and the body bag to the waiting ambulance.

Hank turned around at the sound of his name. Karen and Martinez crossed the plaza, umbrellas over their heads. Martinez walked up to Griffin.

"He's early this time, isn't he?"

Griffin nodded. "The victim must have died on him ahead of schedule. From the looks of her, she wasn't in the best of health to begin with."

"Based on body temp and the absence of rigor," Hank said, "Chalmers believes time of death was between four and five this morning."

"Karen tells me there are other differences," Martinez said, turning to watch the gurney disappear into the back of the ambulance.

"Yes," Hank said, following her gaze. He saw Chalmers hand Easton a tablet, which the medical examiner studied intently. "The mutilation this time included not only the breasts but the lower genitalia, and there were multiple stab wounds, about twenty of them, all postmortem."

"Rage," Martinez said.

Griffin shifted his weight. "I agree. He expected another full day with her, and she let him down. He lost his temper. Uncharacteristically."

Martinez looked around the plaza. "So maybe he made mistakes this time? Left evidence behind that will help us find him?"

"Byrne's not hopeful," Hank said. "The rain, again." He turned and pointed behind them at Market Street. "There's a ramp on the curb, by the corner. City vehicles use it to drive up onto the plaza. He came up that way, drove up to the fountain, left the body, and drove across the plaza to another ramp at the far corner." His finger followed a path that was delineated with yellow evidence markers. "They're working the tire tracks, but they're mostly gone, washed out."

Martinez shook her head.

"Plus, the municipality worker who was at the scene—"

"That was at six oh eight?"

"Correct. One minute before the responding officers arrived. First thing he did was drain the fountain, on orders from his supervisor. Byrne's very upset."

"I talked to Urban Eye," Karen said. "They're waiting for us."

Martinez's eyebrows went up. "They have something?"

"Oh, yeah." Karen pointed at the city hall building. "The camera's over there. On the clock tower."

They all turned to look. Urban Eye was a relatively new municipal surveillance program that was still in the pilot phase. Modeled after similar projects such as Baltimore's CitiWatch program, Urban Eye currently consisted of forty cameras and five civilian employees watching real-time video feeds on eight-hour shifts. Because it was run by the mayor's office with funding in part from Homeland Security, it was currently headquartered off-site in office space rented by the city.

"The supervisor's a retired cop, Bill Judge," Karen said. "They caught the dump on video."

"Well, that's something," Martinez said.

"Here's something else." Joining the circle, Easton handed Hank the tablet Chalmers had given him. "We caught a bit of a break, given the way the hands were posed, with the fingertips down on the thighs and clear of the water. There wasn't any *Waschhaut*, or washerwoman's hands, to speak of, so Chalmers was able to scan the prints and run them right away. We got a hit."

"Elizabeth Mary Baskett," Hank read from the screen. "a.k.a. Liz Baskett. DOB five-eight-eighty-nine—"

"Twenty-three years old," Martinez said, upset.

"Place of birth, Denver, Colorado," Hank went on, eyes scanning the record on the screen. "Her sheet includes loitering, shoplifting, misdemeanor possession of marijuana. That's it. Occupation listed as musician. Address is an apartment in Springhill, not all that far from the university campus."

"A kid," Martinez said.

"Panhandler, from the looks of it," said Easton.

"Busker," Karen said. "Maybe she had a license. They specify the location they're allowed to work."

"Might give us the capture site," Griffin said, hopefully.

At that moment, Eleanor Montgomery edged between the umbrellas. "I've got a media statement ready for you, Lieutenant—"

"We've got an ID," Martinez interrupted. She turned to Hank. "Do you want to release the name right away?"

Hank handed Montgomery the tablet and looked at Griffin. "Ed?"

"Go for it," Griffin said.

"Damned right," Karen agreed. "Let's get wheels up on this one right away."

Hank looked at Martinez, who nodded. "Add it to the statement, and make it clear we believe it's linked to the Theresa Olsen case."

"Using the Rainy Day Killer nickname?" Montgomery said, looking from Hank to Griffin.

"No," Griffin said. "I wouldn't. The media will add it anyway, but it's important that it doesn't come from you."

Montgomery looked at Hank, who nodded. She gave him the tablet. He passed it back to Easton. As the medical examiner turned away, Martinez shifted her feet.

"Jim, this is at least a day early. Is it possible she died from something other than strangulation, like cardiac arrest?"

Easton smiled thinly. "I got the memo, Ann. Sarah and I will look closely at her heart along with everything else. Don't worry, we won't miss anything."

As they watched the medical examiner walk away, Martinez's smart phone buzzed. She took it out, looked at the call display, and turned away to answer it.

"Where's Horvath?" Hank asked Karen.

She motioned toward the crime scene tape along Market Street. "Talking to witnesses."

"Let the others finish that. Grab Horvath and go see what Urban Eye's got."

"Will do."

"Follow up on the busking and see if she had a license. If so, find out where it was for."

"Will do."

"I'll call Springhill and run down there to take a look at where she lived." He looked at Griffin. "Want to come?"

"Sure," Griffin said.

Martinez turned back, putting away her phone. "That was Cassion. She just got your voice message. She's coming back from DC this morning."

Karen snorted.

"She's very upset," Martinez said, still looking at Hank, "and very contrite."

"She wants to be," Karen said.

"This is your captain we're discussing," Martinez snapped. "Show a little basic respect."

Karen reached out with a forefinger and jabbed Hank on the forearm. "*This* is my captain. I don't care what anybody else says."

"Not at the moment, he's not."

"Fucking politics—"

"Karen," Hank interrupted, "take a breath. Get Horvath and go watch some tape."

"This is—"

"Beat it! Now!"

Karen turned on her heel and stalked away in the direction of Market Street, umbrella bouncing up and down as she crossed the plaza in a huff.

"What time will Cassion get here?" Hank asked.

"About noon," Martinez said.

"I'll do the media statement, then go down to Springhill."

"You think she was taken from her home, like Olsen?"

"I don't know."

"Maybe there," put in Griffin, "or maybe where she did her busking. If we're lucky, we can find out right away."

"I thought you didn't do field work," Martinez said, eyeing him.

"This time," Griffin said grimly, "maybe I'll make an exception."

28

The Urban Eye Project was located in a strip mall on Osgoode Road in Bering Heights, in a unit out of which the city had previously operated a family-planning clinic until cutbacks two years ago had closed it down. Since Urban Eye's funding went mostly into hardware and human resources, the rent for the unit was low enough that it fit into the project's budget. Unfortunately, it was situated in a rough neighborhood with a lot of muggings, burglaries, and car theft. The joke was that the first of the forty cameras had been installed on the roof of the strip mall when the project moved in, and the crime rate within a four-block radius had already decreased by 60 percent.

The other good news for the civilian staff of Urban Eye was that the mall also featured a twenty-four-hour pizza joint and a Thai restaurant that served the best chicken Pad Thai in the city. As Horvath got out of the car, he looked longingly at the front window of the restaurant, which was closed.

"Ah, man, I love Thai. I wonder if they're open for lunch on Sundays."

Karen locked the Taurus and led the way down to the unit with the City of Glendale logo painted on the glass door. She wasn't in a very talkative mood. Three days before, she'd been close to the son of a bitch. Although she was never one to beat herself up over what might have been, she dearly wished it had played out differently. Maybe if she'd turned left instead of right when she'd left the dress shop, the kid she'd looked at this morning would still be alive.

A sign hanging on the door was turned around so that the CLOSED side was facing out, but Karen opened the unlocked door and walked into a reception area with a counter, a clock on the wall, a flag on a gold-colored plastic pole in the corner, tube chairs along the wall, and a potted rubber tree that had died some time during the past year.

A man with gray hair and a red cardigan sweater stepped through the doorway behind the counter and looked at them.

"Stainer, Homicide," Karen said, showing her badge. "This is Horvath."

"Bill Judge, glad to meet you." Judge shook her hand, shook Horvath's hand, then motioned them down to the end of the counter, where he lifted the flap and opened the cattle door for them. He led them down a short corridor. Karen looked at four doors, two on each side, that were labeled with strips of masking tape on which had been printed in black felt pen: SERVER RM. 1; SERVER RM. 2; UTIL; WASHRM (COED). At the end of the corridor they entered a large room filled with workstations cluttered with desktop computers, laptops, and other assorted hardware. Marks on the floor suggested where temporary room dividers had been removed to create a single, open work space. Along the far wall was an impressive bank of widescreen monitors showing various shots of city streets, the airport's arrivals and departures entrances, a dockyard, and other locations.

Judge introduced them to a pudgy young man wearing a black t-shirt, jeans, and scuffed white sneakers.

"This is Scott Bump. He was the monitor on duty this morning. He'll show you the feed from City Plaza."

Horvath looked around. "How many people work here?"

"We have two monitors on each shift, plus a supervisor. Our total staff is nine monitors and four supervisors, plus two part-time IT guys. All the supervisors are ex-cops, like me. The monitors are trained civilians who work eight-hour shifts on a seven-on and three-off rotational schedule. The night shift ended at seven this morning, but I asked Scott to stay on to walk you through it."

"Tomorrow's my day off," Bump said, "so it's okay."

"Glad to hear it." Karen looked at Judge. "What about the supervisor?"

"That would be me," Judge said. "The day shift supervisor called in sick, so I'm pulling a double. We also serve as analysts, since we're former sworn officers. The monitors are trained in stuff like narcotics, crime reporting, and that, but they tend to be techies who already have experience in CCTV operation. We need the help with bug fixes and technical problem-solving, since we've still got a year to go on the pilot and just keeping the feeds running is a big challenge."

Behind them, the washroom door opened and a skinny young man in a gray hoodie and jeans took a seat in front of the bank of monitors. "That's Danny. Day shift."

Eyes on the monitors, Danny raised a hand and rotated it back and forth.

"Where's the other day-shift monitor?" Horvath asked.

"In the server room. Daily maintenance."

Horvath frowned at the back of Danny's head. "Nobody was watching the monitors just now?"

"The thing you have to understand," Judge said apologetically, "is that they can't all be watched, all the time. In Baltimore they've got more than five hundred cameras, and there's no way you can have eyeballs on every screen every minute of every day, so they use a monitoring plan that we've copied for our pilot. That's where analysts like me come in. We sit down with crime stats from GPD Intelligence, target high-risk times and days for each camera, and deploy monitoring resources accordingly."

"Show us what you got," Karen said.

Bump led them over to a desk with a large monitor and keyboard. "This is our review workstation," he said, sitting down and pulling over the keyboard. "It's a dumb terminal, don't worry."

"What?"

"He means it's only for viewing footage," Judge explained. "There's no computer attached to it with a hard drive or a port for a USB drive or other means to save the data. We wouldn't be able to maintain chain-of-custody control of our evidence if someone could save it on a thumb drive and walk out the door with it. Server Room Two is specifically set up for the purpose of burning footage for evidence, and it's kept locked at all times, with restricted access only."

"Here's what you want to see," Bump said, pointing to the monitor.

Karen leaned forward. She was looking at a wide-angle shot of the plaza behind city hall that provided a good look at traffic moving along Market Street in the distance. "It's in color," she said.

"Well, yeah," Bump said. "The cameras are color, all-weather jobs with low-light and PTZ capability. They record twenty-four-seven at thirty FPS, although, as you can see, the monitors we watch display live at fifteen FPS. Some of the cameras are wireless, but this one's fiber, since city hall's on the dedicated fiber optic municipal backbone."

"In English," Karen said, her bad mood leaking out.

"PTZ means pan, tilt, and zoom," Bump said. "The cameras can do all three. FPS is frame rate, how many frames per second you see. Films are normally shot at twenty-four FPS, for example." He pointed at the bank of monitors. "Fifteen's a little jerky, like a Charlie Chaplin movie."

"Great," Karen said. "Shut up and let me watch."

Numerals at the bottom-right corner of the screen indicated a time of 05:54:08 hours. Traffic was very sparse. A passenger car moved from left to right across the top of the screen in the near lane of Market Street. At 05:54:39 a delivery truck moved from right to left in the far lane.

At 05:54:51, headlights slowed at the top left corner. They watched a dark-colored passenger van mount the curb and slowly cross the plaza to the fountain. Red brake lights flared as the van pulled up next to the fountain, then went out again as the driver shifted into Park.

"Zoom in," Karen said.

"I can't," Bump said.

"I thought you said you could."

"Yeah, in real time, but we're watching a recording."

"We can stop the playback if you want, Detective," Judge said, "and Scott can crop and enlarge the image on the screen, but you might want to watch it through without stopping the first time, then we can isolate certain frames when you go through it again."

"Yeah, okay. Whatever."

A man walked around the end of the van from the passenger side. He wore coveralls and a baseball cap. He opened the back doors of the van and reached in. After a moment, he pulled out a board and set one end down on the paving stones, then pulled out a second board and set it down parallel to the first.

"A ramp," Horvath said.

The man disappeared into the back of the van.

Karen glanced at the time display: 05:57:04. Three minutes before six o'clock in the morning. Nine minutes before Urban Eye called it in. Time enough for a patrol car to get there if it had been called in at this moment in time, instead of nine minutes later.

"It's getting light," Horvath said.

"Sunrise was at five fifty-four this morning," Judge replied.

A hand truck rolled slowly down the make-shift ramp out of the back of the van, pushed by the man in overalls. A large, black body bag was strapped to it. At the bottom, he turned for the first time to face the camera as he rolled his burden up to the fountain.

"Fuck," Karen said.

"Keeping his head down," Horvath agreed, "so the bill of the cap hides his face. Must've known the camera was there. Smart bastard."

They watched him remove the bungee cords holding the body bag in place. He lowered the bag to the ground behind the retaining wall, out of sight. After a moment, he moved around and bent down again. He moved up and down several times.

"What's he doing?" Horvath asked.

"Taking the body out of the bag," Karen said.

At 05:58:12, the nude body became visible as the man maneuvered it into a seated position on the edge of the retaining wall of the fountain.

Lights passed from right to left across the top of the screen. The man paused, looking over his shoulder.

"A car," Horvath said.

"They couldn't see him," Karen said, pointing. "The van blocked their view."

"Unless they looked back at the last minute, here," Horvath said, pointing at the top left corner of the image.

The man was now lowering the body backward into the water in the outer basin of the fountain. He shifted position several times, adjusting his balance, and slowly eased the head and shoulders down below the surface. He was careful to keep his face down, so that the camera would not record it.

"No rigor," Horvath observed.

Karen grunted.

The man stood for a moment, admiring his work, then at 06:00:19 stooped to gather up the body bag. He wheeled the hand truck back into the van, pulled up the board ramps, and closed the back doors from inside the van. At 06:01:06 the back lights flickered as the man shifted gears into Drive. The van rolled slowly away from the fountain on a diagonal course across the plaza. As it disappeared out of the frame at the top right corner, the image jerked, zoomed, and panned right, as though pursuing the van. But it was too late—the van was gone. The view panned back and zoomed in on the body in the fountain.

The time was 06:01:58. Four minutes before Urban Eye called it in.

"Stop it there," Karen said.

Bump reached for the keyboard and froze the playback.

Karen turned on Judge. "So walk me through this," she said, her voice tight. "This guy drives up off the street onto the plaza at five minutes before six, drives up to the fountain, unloads a body and positions it, and nobody here notices what's going on until six minutes after it starts. Have I got that right? Scotty Bumpkin here was picking his nose or taking a whizz or whatever the fuck and didn't clue into what was happening for *six* minutes? *Six minutes*? Then the best he can do," she pointed at the screen, "is ogle the fucking body?"

"Jesus," Bump said, putting his hands on top of his head.

"Now hold on, Detective Stainer," Judge said, "that's out of line. I already told you, it's not possible to have eyeballs on everything, every second. We're lucky to have what we have."

"We're not *lucky*," Karen retorted, "because he obviously picked this dump site so he could get on camera. He knew it was there." She turned on Bump. "What the fuck were you doing?"

"I'm sorry," Bump said, "I really am. I told Mr. Judge I'll quit if he wants me to. I'm so sorry I didn't see it until it was too late."

"What the fuck were you doing?"

"Pouring a cup of coffee. I'm really sorry."

"A cup of *coffee*?"

"He was almost through his shift," Judge said defensively. "It's exhausting work, watching these things for eight hours straight. You have to understand, city hall isn't a high-risk zone after four A.M. Even if he'd been planted in front of the monitors, his attention would've been focused elsewhere. At least we've recorded the incident and, like I said, we can crop and enhance to give you every bit of detail we possibly can."

"Another thing," Karen went on, "it takes you guys another four minutes to call it in? What's up with that? It took the district only four minutes to reach the scene, but it took you the same amount of time to realize you had something you needed to call in?"

"I didn't see it real time," Judge said. "I'm the one who authorizes call-ins, and it took a few minutes to retrieve the footage and for me to take a look at it. Ideally, we see it as it's happening and call it in right away. That's happened before, and you can look it up. Our record's good. It just didn't happen that way for us this time, unfortunately."

"We appreciate what you can give us," Horvath said. "C'mon, Stains. Calm down. Let's watch it again."

Karen took a breath, counted silently to five, then stabbed a finger at Bump. "Sit," she commanded. "Play it again."

"Yes, ma'am," Bump nodded, reaching for the keyboard.

29

"Look," Griffin said, glancing over at Hank, "I don't want you to feel like I'm crowding you, here."

"I don't," Hank said from the passenger seat of the FBI-issue, black, unmarked Chevrolet Suburban.

"Because despite what I said to your commander in the heat of the moment, I'm not jumping into field work."

"I understand."

"How'd I end up doing the driving, by the way? Isn't this your gig? Aren't I supposed to be the passenger, literally as well as figuratively?"

Hank smiled. "I don't own a car, Ed, and they won't let me sign one out of the motor pool. For my own protection."

"Oh, wait. I remember that about you now. You *can* drive, you just don't. Why is that, anyway?"

"Just an eccentricity, I guess."

"No, seriously. It interests me."

Hank shrugged. "Almost everyone drives, Ed, so it's not too hard to get a ride wherever I need to go. Which leaves me free to concentrate on other things without worrying about rear-ending the guy in front of us."

Griffin's eyes flew back to the street ahead of them and his foot moved to the brake pedal, but he was several car-lengths behind the car in front of them. He exhaled, shaking his head.

District had dispatched a car to Liz Baskett's address, and the apartment was sealed. By mutual agreement between the FBI and Captain Turcotte, Butternut Allenson had been assigned to process it. When Hank called, Butternut assured him she was nearly finished, since it was a just a small studio apartment. Everything was photographed, and the fingerprinting was almost done. He would be free to poke around, pick things up, or turn them on.

Hank ran a hand through his frizzy hair, glancing at Griffin. "Tell me something, has there been any indication so far that he visits his victims' residences, either before or after?"

"If he does, he's not leaving any physical evidence behind. Hegman in Pittsburgh was particularly interested in that question as well. He thought maybe the UNSUB was entering their homes as part of his targeting and surveillance work. Came up empty. No jimmied locks, no forced window frames, no missing keys, no witnesses reporting strangers at the victim's door."

"Anyone have any idea if anything had been taken?"

"Again, zilch. You're thinking trophies."

Hank shrugged. "He bundles up their clothing and jewelry, purse, keys, wallet, whatever they had with them, and he sends it to us. I know it's impossible to tell if he's holding anything back as a souvenir or trophy, but wouldn't it be much simpler for him just to throw their stuff away instead of taking the risk involved in sending a parcel through a local courier? My point being, it seems important to him that we receive everything he strips from them, possessions and body parts. To demonstrate his complete control over them."

"I'd say that's a pretty fair assessment." Griffin braked for a red light. "They take souvenirs for a variety of reasons. Sometimes it's displacement, like when they take a victim's ring or necklace and give it to their wife or girlfriend without telling them where it came from. It gives them an unspoken sense of control over them, and they fantasize about being able to kill them, instead. On the other hand, it may have some kind of symbolic meaning for them, like when they take a trophy from one victim and leave it with the next one. And sometimes it's a memento that lets them relive the experience over and over again afterward."

"Do you see anything like that with this guy?"

"If he's keeping any kind of souvenir, I'd have to say it's the video. It stands to reason he's recording more than just his statement to police, don't you think? If he wants to relive the experience afterward, I can't see him bothering with rings or lockets or other stuff like that when he could just play video recordings. As for transfer, I'm still not convinced the victims are a substitute for some other intended victim, like his mother or a baby sitter or some other female in his childhood. He made that claim to Hegman in the first Pittsburgh murder, but then in the West Virginia video he retracted it, along with all that Native American bullshit he'd been spinning in Evansville."

"Yeah, he'd talked about the blonde baby sitter who'd abused him when he was a boy."

"Then came out and admitted to Hegman it was crap. Stuff people were expecting to hear. A logical explanation for his serial tendencies. Sensing that people need a rational motivation for something like this, when there is no reason that makes sense to a normal person."

"I've studied the motivational models for serial killers," Hank said, staring out the rain-streaked window. "I've read about dysfunctional social environments in their childhood, unstable parents, formative events like direct or indirect trauma, abuse or neglect, disturbing early sexual experiences, negative personality traits like chronic lying, fetishism, or aggression, negative cognitive patterns that lead to antisocial behavior. I've read about the so-called criminal gene, the extra Y-chromosome, or other possible genetic causes, brain structure abnormalities, and on and on and on. It seems like for every killer there's another theory and another psychiatrist or scientist trying to make a career out of this stuff. In your books you discuss a basic motivational model, Ed, but I've never understood where you actually stand on it."

"That's because you've been avoiding my lectures," Griffin joked. "Bottom line? I'm not a psychiatrist, I'm not a geneticist, I'm not a neurologist. I'm law enforcement, period. Cassion's right about that, as far as it goes. I study their behavior so I can describe it to others and, hopefully, predict future behavior based on past behavior, but that's the *what*, not the *why*. I'm not the guy—we're not the guys, you and I—who'll figure out the why, and frankly, I don't care. My focus is on catching them and making sure they don't do it again. Ultimately, I don't give a shit if their brain has a piece missing or they have an extra chromosome or they collected pornography as a kid. If it tells me who they are—name, date of birth, last known address, current location—then hey, great. Otherwise, I'll let other people nurse that headache. They can call me a pragmatist all they want. In my lexicon, that's not a dirty word."

The building in which Liz Baskett had lived on Davis Road was six blocks away from the university campus in a residential area dominated by students, the elderly, and low-income families. It was a three-story, Federal-style brick house that at one time had been the home of a prominent merchant. It was now divided into as many separate living spaces as possible.

Unit 1-C was a studio apartment on the ground floor, to the left of the main central staircase. The door opened into a six-foot hallway. When Hank walked in, he found his way blocked by the bathroom door, which opened out into the hallway. He rapped on it with a gloved knuckle.

"I'm just finishing up," Butternut Allenson said from inside.

"It's just me," Hank said. "Coming through."

"It's okay, I'm in the shower."

Hank moved the door out of his way and walked into the main room. The apartment was a thirty-by-thirteen rectangle with old-fashioned plaster walls and high ceilings. On the left was a bedroom area dominated by a double bed and a wooden wardrobe. The bed was unmade. There was barely enough space to pass between the foot of the bed and the wall to get to the wardrobe, which might have explained in part the clothing that was haphazardly strewn about the place. Paperbacks were stacked against the wall. An old suitcase, standing on end, served as a bedside stand.

To the right was the living room/dining room/kitchen portion of the room. Against the wall was an old couch that looked like it might have been picked from the garbage and should be carried back out there to be hauled to the dump. A large wooden spool from a construction site doubled as a coffee table and dining table. Hank looked at the remains of a breakfast—an open box of Froot Loops cereal, a bowl with a bit of milk in the bottom and a few stray loops, a glass with about an inch of orange juice left in it. Next to the juice glass was the classified section from last Thursday's edition of the Glendale *Mirror*, folded to the Articles for Sale section.

Hanging on the wall over the couch was a framed poster advertising a Neil Young concert at the Shakespeare Theatre in Stratford, Connecticut, on January 22, 1971. Pinned on the wall above the bed was another poster for the Big Sur Folk Festival in 1968 featuring Joan Baez and Judy Collins. Hank looked around in vain for photographs of Liz Baskett or anyone else.

"Hard to call this a kitchen," Griffin said, behind him.

Hank looked at a counter, a few overhead cupboards, a sink, and a refrigerator. A small hotplate was plugged into an outlet above the counter.

The far wall was dominated by a cheap, white particle-board desk and shelving unit. The surface of the desk was completely covered with stuff. Front and center was a Mac laptop. The lid was open, but the computer was not turned on. There was a film of fingerprint dust on it. Connected to the laptop was an expensive-looking USB microphone on an adjustable stand. Attached to the stand was a round pop screen, which vocalists use to filter out the popping sounds that can occur when singing words beginning with a "p" or "b." Also attached to the laptop was a battered set of speakers and a pair of headphones. The mouse was wireless. Elsewhere on the desk, Hank saw a handheld digital recorder, a container of blank DVDs, and other assorted paraphernalia. Liz Baskett was obviously recording herself, perhaps preparing a demo disc of her music.

"Looks like she was serious enough about it," Griffin said, pointing at the corner of the room, between the end of the couch and the end of the desk, where an acoustic guitar in excellent condition stood on a metal stand.

"That's a Martin twelve-string," Hank said. "Even used, they're not cheap. And a mandolin, behind it. The cases may be under the bed." He hesitated. "You'd expect to see a six-string, as well."

"Maybe she had it with her, if she was busking."

Horvath had learned that she'd applied for, and received, a license to busk at a nearby mall. It would be their next stop.

They turned at a sound behind them. Butternut Allenson had emerged from the bathroom with her case in her left hand. She smiled at Hank and held out her hand to Griffin, looking at the FBI identification card hanging on a lanyard around his neck.

"Hi, I'm Butternut. You must be the BAU guy."

"Ed Griffin." He shook her hand, raising his eyebrows. "Butternut?"

She smiled at him. "My husband's a carpenter. On our first date, he took one look at my hair and said, 'butternut.' His favorite color of wood. So, Butternut it is."

"Glad to meet you."

"Anything interesting turn up?" Hank asked.

"The usual," she replied, shifting her case to her right hand. "At this point I'm collecting, not analyzing, so I'll run stuff when I get back. Lots of prints, of course, but probably mostly hers. Hairs in the drains, hairs on the furniture, miscellaneous fibers. I'm going to grab the bed-clothes now, and I left the desk for you to look at. I'll take the laptop, of course, but tell me what else you want me to bring."

"The musical instruments," Hank said. "The microphone set-up, headphones, the digital recorder. I see you printed the laptop. Did you turn it on?"

"Not yet," Butternut said. "Be my guest."

Griffin had drifted away, and was opening cupboard doors in the kitchen area. Butternut began removing the sheets from the bed. Hank powered up the laptop. While it was booting, he took a closer look at the shelves above the desk. There were trade-sized paperbacks, including *The Idiot's Guide to Getting Rich*, a biography of Al Pacino, and *The Hotplate Cookbook*. A plastic magazine holder was crammed with sheet music. Hank pulled out a one-inch black binder and flipped through pages of handwritten music notation and lyrics. He put the binder back and looked at bottles of vitamin C, salmon oil, and Aspirin, a cheap inkjet printer not attached to the laptop, and a tomato can filled with pencils, Sharpies, and ballpoint pens.

He looked at the laptop, which had finished booting up. It wasn't password-protected. The desktop was crowded with icons. Several kinds of recording and mixing software were installed on it. He looked at several icons for sound files and noticed one called "End of the Day." He double-clicked on it.

Griffin opened the refrigerator. "She must have eaten some-where else. There's almost nothing in here."

A six-string acoustic guitar played the introductory notes of a quiet song. A female voice began to sing:

> What did you think
> When you started this game,

You could just run away,
When the loneliness came?

"She had a nice voice," Griffin said.

Hank spotted a small photo album behind a large bottle of vitamin C. He pulled it out and looked at photos of a small girl, presumably Liz. There was a family group, likely with her mother and older sister, and what must have been a recent photo of Liz taken on a beach somewhere. She was sitting on a rock, holding a guitar. He looked closely and counted the number of tuning pegs on the head. Six. She apparently did own a six-string guitar which wasn't here now. He slipped the photo out of the album and put it in his pocket.

And what can you do
At the end of the day,
When the darkness arrives,
And the crowd slips away?

She had a pleasant, strong singing voice, her pitch was perfect, and her playing was skilled and confident. Hank knew it wasn't easy to break into the business as an independent with no connections or contacts, and he imagined she'd chafed at playing for spare change at the mall. Hank closed the audio player and shut down the laptop. He looked at Butternut, who was bagging the bedclothes.

"Bring everything," he said, waving at the desk.

The superintendent of the building, Magda Olkowech, lived on the third floor. In her early sixties, she looked as though she might have been a matron in an eastern European prison for women before the fall of the Iron Curtain. She frowned at the mention of Liz Baskett's name.

"Noisy," she said in a thick accent. "Trouble, like I say to officer. Tell her all time, people try sleep, no make music at night. Never listen."

When Hank asked her if she saw or heard anything on Thursday or Friday suggesting that Liz had had a visitor, Olkowech shook her head. "Only know very quiet now. Much better."

"It's quiet because she's dead," Griffin said, annoyed. "Doesn't that bother you at all?"

The woman shrugged. "Nobody to me. Always late with rent." She put her hands on her hips. "Make sure stuff's out by middle next week. Want to show room right away."

On the way back downstairs, Griffin said, "I should keep my mouth shut."

"Don't worry about it," Hank told him.

At the front door, a uniformed officer gave them a list of other tenants in the building. "I spoke to one guy upstairs, a Mr. Malek. Retired, on a pension. Never goes out. Didn't know the vic at all. The tenant in the back apartment on this floor waits on tables in a coffee shop just off campus. Knew the vic to see her, complained a few times about noise to the old bat upstairs, but didn't see or hear anything since Thursday morning. Nobody else is home right now."

"Thanks," Hank said, putting the list in his pocket. "We'll track down the others later."

He followed Griffin outside. "Let's go to the mall," he said.

Griffin unlocked the Suburban with his remote fob.

"Her six-string guitar's not there," Hank said, thinking out loud. "She was pushing to make some extra money. There was something she wanted to buy."

They got into the Suburban. Griffin started the engine. "The newspaper."

"Yeah, she was checking the classifieds while she was having breakfast. Looking to pick up something second-hand. So she needed to raise the cash for it."

Two blocks farther down on Davis Street they reached the Southpoint Mall, a single-level enclosed shopping center that, at its peak, had featured more than one hundred stores. It was anchored by J.C. Penney at one end and a Shoppers grocery store at the other end. The economic downturn had drastically increased the number of vacant units, but the mall still featured several shoe stores, a drug store, jewelers, and numerous clothing stores. At an information kiosk inside, Hank showed his badge and asked the woman to call the mall manager.

The manager was a tall, pear-shaped, prematurely bald man who introduced himself as Cam McLeod. "I'm the operations manager," he said, shaking Hank's hand. "I work for Kefoll and Williams. We're the property management firm that runs this place."

"This is FBI Supervisory Special Agent Griffin," Hank said.

"Wow, FBI," McLeod said, raising his eyebrows as he shook hands with Griffin. "I always wondered what it would be like to work for the FBI. Probably not like it is on TV, all action and car chases and stuff like that. Probably a lot of paperwork, right? God knows I have enough of that right now. What can I help you guys with this afternoon?"

"We're investigating the homicide of a young woman named Liz Baskett. She had a busker's license for this location." Hank took the photo out of his pocket and showed it to him.

McLeod shook his head. "Name doesn't mean anything to me. Wait, is that what I heard on the news this morning? She was found downtown, at city hall? Terrible. My sister called me about it when I was getting ready for work. She was really upset."

"You didn't know Liz Baskett personally?" Hank asked.

McLeod shook his head again. "We have a number of people with permission to perform on mall property. We screen them ourselves, did you know that? Even if they already got their license from the city, they have to do an audition with our general manager, Mrs. Charlene Tennant-Pecaskie. If she doesn't think they're appropriate for our clientele, she won't give them permission. It *is* private property after all, license or no license." He held up his hands. "But don't get the wrong idea. Mrs. Tennant-Pecaskie's really, really nice to them. Nicer than other property managers I know. We have a seating area up in the north court, close to the entrance to Shoppers, where most of the units are vacant right now. She set up an area for them with a little stage, and they come into the office and reserve time slots on the board. They're also allowed to perform outside the east entrance, but we have our security staff check on them to make sure they're not bothering anybody."

"Was Liz Baskett scheduled to use the stage on Thursday?"

"I'd have to look."

"Could we do that now?" Hank asked, politely.

"Oh! Yeah! Sure! Sorry! This way." He pirouetted on his heel and led them down the main concourse. "This Payless shoe store is one of the original tenants," he said, pointing. "This one here, Crazy Pops, is newer. They sell all kinds of flavored popcorn." He leaned close to Griffin. "How about blueberry-flavored popcorn? Sound good to you?"

"Not really," Griffin said.

"I tried it once. Nearly barfed. But the kids apparently love it. It's their best-seller. Life will always be a mystery to me."

"I hear that," Griffin said.

"Just down here." McLeod swung around the corner into a side passage. "This is where our offices are. Washrooms there," he waved his hand at doorways on the left, "and we just go in here." His identification card was attached to his belt by a retractable lanyard. He stopped at a door on the right, pulled out the card, swiped it through a card reader, and opened the door. He pointed to a buzzer mounted on the door frame. "They ring to come in when they want to schedule themselves." He turned and pointed at the ceiling. "We have a little dome camera there, see? So staff know who it is before they buzz them in."

He led them into the office and around a reception counter to a whiteboard mounted on the wall. Drawn with black marker on the board was a seven-day calendar divided into one-hour slots from 9:00 A.M. to 5:00 P.M. "We're open until nine o'clock on weekdays, but Mrs. Tennant-Pecaskie prefers to have the evening hours quiet for shoppers."

Names were handwritten on magnetic strips of different colors. "Yellow for musicians, blue for magic acts and jugglers, red for mimes."

"What about fire-eaters and sword-swallowers?" Griffin asked.

McLeod laughed nervously. "Oh, Mrs. Tennant-Pecaskie doesn't allow them. Liability issues."

Hank saw that the schedule for Thursday didn't include Liz Baskett. In fact, someone named Johnson had reserved four different time slots on that day. When he pointed this out, McLeod nodded.

"That's Angus Johnson. He's a retired aircraft mechanic who plays the accordion and sings all those corny songs old folks love. You know, 'The Beer Barrel Polka,' that kind of stuff. He's popular around here. Margie, she's the one looks after the board during the day, she doesn't work Sundays but she sits right here"—he pointed at a desk—"she's kind of sweet on the guy and lets him get more than his fair share. When the others complain to me, I just tell them it's out of my hands. Maybe they should learn the accordion, too."

"I hate the accordion," Griffin said.

McLeod nodded. "Me too."

Since they seemed to be getting into a groove, Griffin touched him on the elbow and turned him away from the board. "You guys obviously have security cameras all over the place here. How about getting us a copy of your feeds from last Thursday? It could be very important to the investigation."

"Oh, I couldn't do that without a warrant," McLeod replied. "Company policy. I'd get fired in a heartbeat."

"A warrant won't be any problem," Hank said, unperturbed. "We wouldn't want to cause you any trouble. If Liz Baskett wanted to busk here last Thursday but couldn't get on the schedule, you said she'd be allowed to play outside the east entrance? That right?"

"Yeah, exactly. There's a bit of overhanging roof when you walk outside, and they're allowed to do their thing under there. We let them stay a couple of hours, then one of our security guys asks them to leave. If they stay too long, we get loitering complaints from customers, irregardless of their licenses. We move them out and give somebody else a chance."

Hank looked at the schedule for today. There were several blank spots. Someone named Keyton was performing in the north court at the moment. Taking out his notebook and pen, he jotted down a few notes.

"We're worried that the young lady's killer might've snatched her right here from the mall," Griffin said. "If it comes out later, it could cause a big public relations problem for your company. It'd help the lieutenant if he could get out ahead of the curve."

Hank closed his notebook and reached into his pocket for the composite drawing of the Rainy Day Killer. He showed it to McLeod. "We're looking for this guy. We'd like to confirm on the video that Ms. Baskett was here at the mall last Thursday, but we also want to find out whether this guy was here."

McLeod stared at the drawing. "I don't know. I worked on Thursday, but I wouldn't remember. Hundreds of people come in and out all day."

"That's why we need to see the video."

McLeod hesitated, wrinkling his brow again. The office door opened behind them. They turned around as a young man in a security guard's uniform walked through the office without looking at them, heading for a room at the back. McLeod looked at Griffin and shrugged. "I can't burn a copy right now, but I can ask Warren to play it back. You're welcome to watch over his shoulder, in case you see anything you might need to subpoena from us later. For evidence. Whatever you guys do."

Griffin looked at Hank. "I don't mind, if you want to call for the warrant and look around."

Hank nodded. "Karen will come down and relieve you as soon as she can."

"Whatever." Griffin turned to McLeod. "So introduce me to this Warren guy."

Hank left them and walked back out into the mall. He was closest to the east entrance, so he headed in that direction first, removing his cell phone and calling Karen as he walked.

"I'm at the morgue," she said. "They're putting her through x-ray right now, but I thought I'd stick around in case they find anything more this time. Horvath's downtown with Montgomery, checking out the hotline tips. They're getting a ton of calls, and he wanted to look through the slips."

"Sounds good. I'll give him a call and have him do the warrant. You stay with the body."

"Roger wilco. You looked good on TV at noon. Very captain-like."

"Don't start on that."

"I'll call you when I know more." She ended the call.

Hank speed-dialed Horvath. It rang a number of times, and when Horvath finally answered it, his voice sounded harried.

"Yeah, Hank. Can you hold a minute?"

"Sure," Hank said, but Horvath had already lowered the phone and was continuing the argument he'd been in the middle of when Hank called.

"It doesn't matter," he said, "it's already done. If she says no one called it in, then there's nothing she could do. You know that."

Hank could hear Cassion's voice replying to Horvath, but he couldn't make out the words.

"With all due respect, Captain," Horvath said, "we need to focus on what's in front of us now and not start flaming Missing Persons for something they couldn't—"

Cassion's voice rose angrily. "—incompetence!"

"Jim," Hank said, trying to get his attention.

"She's not incompetent," Horvath argued, "they just didn't get a report on the vic. End of story."

"Jim," Hank repeated, stepping into the doorway of a vacant unit and cupping the phone with his free hand. "Jim!"

"No, it's not like that at all," Horvath was saying.

"*Jim!*"

"Sorry, Hank," Horvath said, coming back on the line, "the captain and I are—"

"Put her on."

"Sure, just a moment. Captain, it's Lieutenant Donaghue."

Cassion took the phone. "Donaghue, give me a sit-rep."

"I'm following a lead. What's going on?"

"I'm heading into a briefing with the chief, and I'd like to be able to say we're on this guy's ass already."

"Helen, we checked with Missing Persons multiple times Friday and Saturday. There were no reports anywhere close to the victim profile, let alone for this specific individual."

"I find that hard to believe, Donaghue. We've been broadcasting this guy's MO all over the city for nearly a month. I can't believe someone didn't report her missing. Winston fucked it up—"

"The victim was a loner," Hank interrupted. "I interviewed her building super. Nobody there knew her well enough to care if she went missing. Her family's in Colorado. I'm at the mall where she busked right now to see if anyone here knew her at all, but the bottom line is, she was a high-risk victim with no known personal attachments and, apparently, poor awareness of personal safety. Low-hanging fruit, to cross us up after all the high-risk crap he's been pulling. Do you need Horvath right now?"

"Horvath? What for?"

"For the briefing."

"Why would I need him for that? What I need is to hear you've got a solid lead on this UNSUB."

"Detective Stainer's pulling footage from the Urban Eye camera covering the plaza," Hank said. "I'm at the mall in Springhill right now"—he caught himself before mentioning Griffin's name—"and I need Horvath to get a warrant for their video surveillance system. The victim was a busker licensed to perform here, and we think there's a possibility this is where the suspect grabbed her. We might get lucky."

"Okay," Cassion said, sounding mollified, "okay, that's good. Maybe people working in the stores saw something. You could question them. Maybe they remember seeing the UNSUB with her. Show them the composite."

"Good idea," Hank replied, patiently. "I'll follow up on that. You saw the media statement?"

"Yeah, you went out with the victim's ID and connected it right away to the Olsen case. Are you sure that's wise? Won't it piss him off?"

"It shouldn't. He's been through this before, and remember, he wants to elevate the fear level in the community. It's one of his sources of gratification."

"Right, I know that."

"Assure the chief that we've got a day, maybe two or three, before we receive his package with Liz Baskett's effects and body parts. He probably won't call before that, so there's a bit of time for us to do our job and get ahead of the curve. Tell the chief we're on top of it."

"Okay. I hope Bennett's not too worked up over this. I heard the mayor already called to give him shit."

"The chief can handle it, Helen. It's what he does for a living."

"Yeah, but you know how they like to pass the stress down the line."

"You'll be fine. Assure the chief the unit's working twenty-four-seven following up on all leads. He's more interested in how you're doing than anything else, Helen. He knows we're working it hard. Project your usual self-confidence, and it'll go well."

"You don't have to coach me, Donaghue. I know what I'm doing."

"Good to hear. Put Jim back on."

When Horvath came back on the line, Hank told him to secure a warrant for all video surveillance records at the Southpoint Mall for the past seven days. He gave Horvath the name of the property management company, the name of the general manager and operations manager, and told him to bring the warrant down as soon as he had it in his hands.

"I'll bring Mickey. Look, Hank," he lowered his voice, "I'm friends with Sharon Winston, and she doesn't deserve to be flamed by senior management over this. You checked with her, I checked with her, Stains checked with her. We drove her nuts, and there was nothing. I was just coming out of Montgomery's office and Cassion was here in the hallway blowing her frigging horn to What's-his-name, the chief's EA—"

"Glennon."

"Yeah, him, about how she should've never turned her back on Missing Persons, Winston's a fuck-up, and—"

"Jim," Hank interrupted, "it'll be fine. Cassion just over-reacted a little. She's fine, now. Winston's ass is covered. Look, I need you to get that warrant ASAP and get down here to this mall to secure the video. Griffin's viewing it unofficially right now, but I need you here to establish chain of custody, okay?"

"Absolutely," Horvath said. "I'm on it."

Hank ended the call and resumed his walk toward the east entrance. The mall was very quiet, with few shoppers that he could see, and he imagined that the various stores were struggling to make their rent each month, given the current state of retail in the country. He reached a broad intersection. To his left, a corridor ran down to the east mall entrance. Straight ahead, he saw the check-out lanes of the Shoppers grocery store. A woman pushed a cart filled with plastic sacks between the metal stiles and headed down toward the exit. Idly, as though putting in time while his wife shopped, Hank stuck his hands in his pockets and followed her, glancing up at another dome camera about halfway down.

He walked through the double set of automatic glass doors and found himself outside under the truncated overhanging roof McLeod had mentioned. There was no video surveillance camera out here.

A young man huddled in the corner, smoking a cigarette, a guitar hanging by a brightly-colored strap around his neck. His guitar case was open, the bottom spattered with coins and a few folded one-dollar bills. A city license, plasticized, was propped up at the wide end of the case. With his wool sweater, headband, and scruffy beard, he looked like a refugee from a *Scooby-Doo* cartoon.

"Rough weather," Hank said, feeling in his pocket for his bill clip.

"You're telling me." The kid pitched away his cigarette and pulled the guitar around.

"Are you here often?"

The kid shrugged, sliding his left hand up and down the neck of the guitar, as though double-clutching before fingering a chord. "Time to time."

"Were you here last Thursday?"

"Who's asking?"

Hank took the photo of Liz Baskett from his jacket pocket and held it out. "Know her?"

The kid nodded. "She's damn good. Who's asking?"

Hank held up the wallet containing his badge and identification. "She was murdered this weekend. Do you know if she was here last Thursday?"

"Ah, fuck." The kid shook his head. "Ah, fuck. She was sweet. What a fucking shame. No, I wasn't here, so I don't know if she was. Tommy would, though."

"Tommy?" Hank put his wallet away and slipped the photo into his pocket.

"Tommy Keyton. He's playing center stage right now. You could ask him. He was, you know, interested in her."

Hank remembered the surname from the schedule board in the office, and he assumed that center stage referred to the area in the north court that the general manager had set up for the use of the buskers.

He took out the composite of the Rainy Day Killer. "Ever seen this guy around?"

The kid stared at the picture, and shook his head. "Looks like a mean fucker. That him? The guy who did it?"

"He's someone we're interested in talking to."

"I haven't seen him, but that don't mean much. I don't make a lot of eye contact when I'm here, know what I mean? I just play and let the coins fall where they may."

Hank smiled. "You any good?"

The kid pulled out a pick that was wedged between the strings at the head of the guitar and launched into the opening chords of "A Horse With No Name."

Were all the kids into retro folk rock these days? Hank's fingers found his bill clip and removed the top bill. He dropped it into the guitar case without looking at it.

"Twenty," the kid said. "Righteous."

Hank went back inside the mall and headed for the north court. Tommy Keyton was another twenty-something musician trying to make ends meet. He wore a black sports jacket, a white shirt, blue jeans, and Nike sneakers. A good-looking young man, he was tall and slender, and his wispy blonde hair, high forehead, and mutton-chop sideburns reminded Hank of a young Stephen Stills. He was playing a six-string Yamaha guitar and singing a song Hank didn't recognize.

Because the mall was quiet, he had no audience and his open guitar case had very little cash in it. Hank took out his bill clip, found another twenty, and dropped it into the case. Keyton's eyes checked out the denomination, flashed up to Hank's, and then he nodded without skipping a beat in the song he was singing.

When it was finished, Hank took a step closer. "Are you Tommy Keyton?"

"That's right. Tell me you're from a record company."

"Sorry." Hank showed him his badge and identification. "Lieutenant Donaghue, GPD. Were you here at the mall last Thursday?"

"Yeah, but not to play. Why? Some kind of trouble?" Tommy stepped down from the little stage.

Hank took out Liz Baskett's photo. "Know her?"

Keyton took the photo from him. "Yeah, that's Liz." He looked at the photo for a long moment, then frowned. "Why're you asking?"

"She was murdered over the weekend," Hank said, taking back the photo. "We're trying to trace her movements on Thursday, which is the last time she was seen."

Keyton swung the guitar strap over his head, put the instrument into a small folding metal stand, and sat down on the edge of the stage. He covered his face with his hands. His shoulders moved up and down.

Hank gave him a few moments, then sat down beside him. "Was she here on Thursday, Tommy? It's important to us to verify that."

Keyton nodded, then dragged his fingers down over his face to remove the tears and shook his head. "Sorry, man. I really liked her. I thought maybe we would. . ."

"Were you seeing her? Going out with her?"

"No, nothing like that. I was taking it slow, looking toward the future. She wasn't into relationships at all, just her music. But we were friends. What happened to her?"

Hank hesitated. It was obvious he didn't follow the news and hadn't heard the morning report of Liz's death. There was something about this kid that he liked, a vulnerability and sensitivity that radiated from him in waves and filled the music that Hank guessed he'd written himself. He knew there was no way to avoid hurting him.

"We think someone may have taken her from here last Thursday. Her body was found downtown this morning, at city hall plaza."

"Why? Why would someone do that? I don't understand. She was gentle and shy, she didn't mean anyone any harm."

"Did you see her here last Thursday? Anything you can tell us may help us find the person who did this." He took out his notebook and pen.

"Yeah." He jammed a thumb into the corner of his eye to wipe away another tear. "I knew she'd be here, outside. She wanted to up-grade her recording software, but it was going to cost two hundred bucks, and she needed to raise the cash. The old walrus, Johnson, was hogging center stage all day, so she decided to play outside. I came around because I wanted to see her."

"Why was that? Something specific?"

Keyton stared at his boots. "No, I just wanted to talk to her. She composed her own stuff too, and I wanted to run a few ideas past her. I have a music degree, but she's self-taught. It's her lyrics that really shine, and I thought maybe we could do a few songs together. Plus, I knew she was putting together a demo, and I was going to tell her I'd play rhythm for her and do some background vocals, if she wanted."

He fell silent, eyes closed.

"Tell me about Thursday," Hank prompted.

"I got here a bit late, about eleven. She was already here, but she wasn't making anything. The rain was a bitch. She was soaked because it was blowing in under the roof. Nobody wants to be out there in bad weather, but she was desperate for the money. I hung around with her, but we didn't really talk very much. A few people came in, but nobody was paying for play. Weather like that, everybody's head's down and they're walking too fast to see you. After a while she said screw it, let's go get a coffee. So I came inside with her and we hung out at the food court for a while. I bought her coffee and something to eat. Then I had to go. I had an ophthalmologist's appointment. I need glasses."

"About what time was this?"

Keyton shook his head. "Not sure, some time around noon, I guess."

"What did Liz do?"

"She went back outside. She was determined to raise some cash."

Hank took a moment to catch up on his notes. "Was there anyone else here who might have talked to her after you left? Any other buskers?"

"No, just old man Johnson, and he doesn't talk to us. He calls us snotty-nosed punks, the bag of pus. Sorry."

"No one else was hanging around?"

"No. People tend to stay away in bad weather. No money to be made. Maybe someone came after I left."

Hank brought out the composite drawing. "What about this guy? Ever see him around the mall?"

Keyton studied the drawing. "I don't know. Could be. Lot of guys like that around. I don't pay attention to what people look like. I guess I should. That's what you do, isn't it? Facial recognition? Cops are supposed to be good at that."

"Most are," Hank agreed.

"I'm aurally-oriented. I have perfect pitch, and I can identify any sound I've heard before. Visually, I'm not very good. Guess that's why I need glasses."

Hank put away the composite and closed his notebook. He slipped it into his jacket pocket with his pen and touched Keyton's knee lightly with the heel of his fist. "Thanks, Tommy. I appreciate your help.

I'm sorry for your loss."

Keyton raised his head and looked at him. "Thanks, man."

The young man's damp cheeks told Hank that Liz Baskett would at least be missed by someone in this town.

30

They gathered in Martinez's board room to discuss the new shipment from the Rainy Day Killer, which an FBI team had processed after its arrival this morning. It included another cardboard carton tied with manila rope, and a guitar case containing a Ramirez six-string guitar in good condition. Everything had been fingerprinted and examined for hair samples, fibers, soil, and any other trace evidence. After the break with the eyelash hair, they were a little more optimistic this time around.

The carton had contained a knapsack belonging to Liz Baskett, into which the Rainy Day Killer had stuffed the victim's clothing and sneakers, a cheap turquoise ring, a silver chain, a Casio digital sports watch, her wallet, and a re-sealable plastic container holding her breasts and genital tissue. Under the knapsack, at the bottom of the carton, was another DVD.

The evidence recovery team had duplicated the disc after processing it, and as Mickey Marcotte loaded the copy into the board room DVD player, he avoided eye contact with the others in the room. "I only watched the first few seconds. It's really awful."

Martinez gestured to Karen. "Close the door, would you?"

As Karen got up, Cassion frowned at Griffin. "Don't you have somewhere else to be?"

"Charmed, I'm sure," the analyst replied.

Karen closed the board room door and sat down next to Horvath.

Hank pressed the green button on the remote.

Unexpectedly, the video began with a shot of Liz Baskett's naked body on a large metal table. Her arms were pulled up, tied at the wrists to the corners of the table, and her splayed legs were similarly bound. She was dead. A naked male appeared in the frame, visible from the waist up, his back to the camera. As they watched, he plunged a large KA-BAR knife into the abdomen of the body several times. He then approached her right breast, fondled it, and with practiced movements sliced it off from the bottom up.

"My God," Martinez said, her eyes moving involuntarily away from the television screen.

Karen bared her teeth. Cassion paled, mouth open. Horvath raised a hand to his forehead and watched from beneath the protective canopy of his fingers. Marcotte kept his head down, staring sightlessly at his hands, folded in his lap.

Martinez forced her eyes back to the screen as the killer removed the second breast and tossed it callously on the table next to the body. He stabbed the body, viciously, several more times, then circled it, like a predatory animal, before moving in on the exposed genital area.

"I can't watch this," Martinez said.

She did, nevertheless.

They all did, except for Marcotte, because it was their job to watch it.

At no time did the killer expose his face to the lens, nor did they see his body below the waist. No distinguishing features, such as scars or tattoos, were visible. After several more minutes with the knife, he walked out of the frame and the screen went blank.

Two seconds later, a new image replaced it, one almost identical to what they'd seen in the previous video. Faint light from the top right-hand corner of the frame fell across the killer, who sat once again in a chair, facing the camera. The table on which the mutilated body lay was once more a dark shape at the left of the frame.

"Hello, Hank," the killer said. "I'm sorry for the outburst. I wanted you to see what happens when I'm disappointed. She deeply disappointed me by giving up far too early. At the same time, I'm disappointed in myself for having chosen her to begin with. I thought she was in better physical condition than that. Turns out she was slim because she was underfed and undernourished. I should have seen it a mile away. I wonder, though, if there was something wrong with her heart. Would you do me a favor? Find out from your medical examiner if she had some kind of heart defect, and let me know.

"I'd love to talk to you about a lot of things. I admire you, and I hope you'll understand me better than the others because we're very much alike, you and I. Unfortunately, though, I have to cut this short. It ran very late—oh shit, I forgot to turn on the date and time stamp. I leave it off for my own filming and switch it on for you." He paused for a moment. "Oops, shouldn't have told you that, but you and Father Ed have probably already put two and two together. Whatever. Anyway, my point is, it's late and I need to move her quickly before she stiffens up, so there isn't a lot of time for conversation right now. We'll have to wait for the next one.

"And yes, as advertised, the next one's going to be a cop. I've been teasing you about it, but I've decided it's time to pull the trigger, figuratively speaking. Your challenge, should you choose to accept it, is to guess which cop I'm talking about. Is it the lovely Karen Stainer? The gorgeous Eleanor Montgomery? I'd definitely consider that new captain of yours, Helen Cassion, or the commander, who's the hottest Latina in a uniform I've ever seen outside a porn film, but they're not the Rainy Day Killer's type, are they? Sorry, ladies. Maybe next time. No, our lovely blonde cops are the ladies in competition to become the Rainy Day Killer's next luscious love.

"So, gotta go. I'll call you later. Bye for now."

The screen went blank again.

There was silence in the room as they waited. When it was obvious there would be nothing more, Hank used the remote to shut it off.

"He's mine," Karen said. "Just so we're clear. The first shot takes his gonads, the next two kneecap him, and then he gets to beg for the kill shot."

"Stand in line, Stainer," Cassion said, staring at the blank television screen. Tears ran down her cheeks, and her jaw was tightly clenched.

"That's enough," Martinez said. She looked at Hank. "I want around-the-clock protection on both Stainer and Montgomery, starting immediately. Understood?"

"Forget it," Karen said. "If anybody needs protection, it's that fucking mutt when I catch sight of him."

"You're not leaving the building tonight without a protection detail," Martinez said. "Understood?"

"I'll take care of it," Hank said.

"I want that captivity site found," Martinez went on. "I'm going to talk to the chief and get an overtime budget for the districts to step up searches of these abandoned factories and warehouses until we find this place and cut him off. I will not allow him to do this to another woman."

She suddenly pounded the table three times with her fist, furiously.

"NO! MORE! VICTIMS! Am I understood?"

"Absolutely," Hank said.

She stood up abruptly and locked eyes with him.

"Put an end to this. That's an order."

31

The following afternoon, a sharp-eyed patrol officer noticed a new-looking padlock on the side door of an abandoned warehouse belonging to Helpern Logistics, a licensed and bonded freight shipping and trucking company. Helpern had been out of business for almost a decade, but their assets were still tied up in bankruptcy proceedings and had been sitting unused for a long time. The warehouse was a ramshackle brick building on Howson Street in South Shore West. Its windows were boarded up, the walls were decorated with graffiti, and the cracks in the pavement of the parking lot were sprouting thistles and quack grass.

Howson Street ran north and south through the district, passing through block after block of neglected rowhouses, until it reached O'Connell Street, where a rail line running from the dockyards crossed it diagonally. On the other side of the tracks was an industrial area including a scrap metal yard, a chemical processing plant, a packaging factory, and the empty remains of Helpern Logistics. Directly across the street from the warehouse was an empty lot where another building had once stood.

The police officer, whose name was Matt Valpone, sat on the passenger side of the cruiser while Jim Choi, his partner, drove. They were halfway through their shift, patrolling the residential portion of their beat north of O'Connell, when they decided to cross the tracks on this particular pass. The duty sergeant was badgering everyone to watch for any suspicious activity or signs of entry that might connect to the hunt for the Rainy Day Killer, and Valpone and Choi wanted to be able to say they had at least taken a look.

It was a clear, windswept afternoon, a break from the rainy weather, but the temperature was unseasonably cool, and they both wore their jackets over their uniform shirts. The tires of the patrol car splashed through puddles left behind by the recent storm as Choi drove across the tracks. He rolled through the O'Connell Street intersection and continued down the next block.

The Helpern warehouse crowded the sidewalk on the right side of the street. As they cruised alongside it, they listened to the usual chatter on the radio between Dispatch and other patrol cars in other neighborhoods. They were a little bored and a little distracted by the radio, but as they passed the employee entrance halfway up the side of the warehouse, Valpone's eyes jumped.

"Hey, stop for a minute."

Choi glanced in the rear view mirror, saw nothing behind them, and slowed to a stop.

"The side door. Back up."

Choi backed up and stopped even with the door. It was a typical metal door, painted light green. The weather had darkened it with mildew. Rainwater leaking down from the lintel had left wide rust streaks on it. There were several dents in the door where someone had hammered on it with a baseball bat or tire iron, chipping the paint in the process and creating more rust marks. Even the gang tag spray-painted on the door with white paint was faded and streaked.

A padlock had been attached to the door about a foot above the doorknob, probably when Helpern had gone into bankruptcy and the warehouse had become a seized asset. The hasp was rusted and scratched, but the padlock itself looked new and expensive, as though the original lock had been removed and replaced with this one. It was the sort of thing that would go unnoticed ninety-nine times out of a hundred, but as they'd rolled past the door, light from the setting sun had caught the shank of the padlock and flashed at Valpone like a signal.

Looking at it again, he saw that his initial impression had been on the money—the padlock's newness was out of synch with the general appearance of the rest of the door.

Choi drove down to the entrance of the parking lot at the far end of the warehouse. The lot was big enough to accommodate two tractor trailers at the same time. Choi stopped a few yards short of the entrance, flipped on the cruiser's light bar, and shifted into Park.

The parking lot was empty of vehicles. There were two dumpsters on the far side against the chain link fence running along the back of the warehouse. Litter was packed against the fence like the remnants of last winter's snow. The doors and windows of the main entrance of the building were boarded up and undisturbed.

"Tracks," Valpone said, pointing into the lot.

Choi nodded, looking at parallel ribbons of grit and wetness that ran from the sidewalk to the closer of the two loading docks, where they could see another padlock securing the roll-up door. The tracks and the two padlocks made it obvious that the warehouse had seen some sort of recent activity.

They called it in.

When Tactical breached the building, they discovered that cheap alarms had been set up on the roll-up doors and all other street-level doors and windows. Fortunately, however, there were no explosive devices or other booby-traps. Inside, they found two different areas set up by the killer. One, just inside the loading dock, contained a metal butcher's table, a plastic folding table holding jugs of industrial cleanser, a rubber hose attached to a water tap, three 1200-watt halogen portable lights on tripods, a portable generator and a gas can still one-third full of gas, extension cords, a wheelchair, and a hand truck. In what had once been the employee lunch room they found a double-size bed, manila rope, two more halogen lights on tripods, another portable generator, extension cords, another plastic folding table containing an assortment of syringes and ampoules, a stun gun, a mini-fridge, and a microwave oven.

The district set up a perimeter at each end of the block and established a command post in the empty lot across the street as a staging area for the crime scene. Standing just out of earshot at the edge of the command post, Hank watched Turcotte and Byrne argue with FBI Special Agent Jack Carson, who was in charge of the evidence response team.

Although the protocol had been in place for several weeks now and had been followed several times, Byrne and Turcotte both seemed to suffer from a pathological inability to get along with others, and their shared compulsion to make things difficult was now being exercised on Carson, who listened patiently to their criticisms and tried to say the right things. For someone like Butternut, who got along well with others, the situation was complicated but workable. For Byrne and Turcotte, however, it was a screw-up in the making.

Hank was staying out of it. As lead investigator, he had the clout to intervene if he thought it necessary in order to straighten things out, but Butternut was working nicely with her Bureau counterpart in the parking lot across the road, which would shortly be cleared so that Karen and Horvath could go over for a closer look. The discussion in front of him, on the other hand, was like watching bighorn sheep butt heads on the Nature Channel while mindlessly obeying their territorial imperative. That kind of headache he didn't need.

"Uh oh," Karen said. "Incoming."

Down at the intersection of O'Connell and Howson, an unmarked black Taurus passed through the barrier.

"Martinez?" Griffin asked.

Hank nodded. With Cassion in tow. He watched a uniformed officer direct Martinez to a parking area set up at the far edge of the empty lot in which they were standing.

He felt a twinge of guilt as he saw Cassion get out of the car, slinging her handbag over her shoulder. He watched her adjust her sunglasses and say something to Martinez as the commander took out her cell phone and looked at it. The rank of captain was the highest in the department that was staffed by a competitive process, everything higher being staffed through appointment by the chief. At noon today, the deadline had passed for the process that would be used to fill several captains' vacancies. Cassion had been bubbling for a week about it, having submitted her application the same day the process opened, and she was already talking about changes she intended to make when Homicide became hers on a permanent basis. More than once, Hank had been forced to take Belknap and Karen aside for a quiet word to calm them down. Surely to God, he kept telling them, she'll end up somewhere else. Surely to God they'll slot an experienced hand into Homicide.

This morning at 11:51 A.M., Hank had gone up to the tenth floor and submitted his own application package to Human Resources. As they'd stamped and logged the envelope, he'd felt a small current of satisfaction that had surprised him.

He wanted the job, after all.

As he watched Cassion and Martinez pick their way across the cracked concrete toward the command post, his cell phone began to vibrate. He took it out of his pocket and looked at the call display:

4:34 PM   5-23

0-000-000-0000

UNKNOWN NAME

"Call Mickey," he told Karen urgently, showing her the phone. "Get him on it."

She nodded, turning away to take out her own phone.

"Donaghue," he said, answering the call.

"You guys are good," said the Rainy Day Killer. "I'll give you that."

"Where are you, Bill? Can I send someone to pick you up?"

The killer laughed. "I haven't had this much fun in a long time. I'm still riding the adrenaline."

"How close were we to nailing your ass?"

"Very close, I don't mind telling you. I was there to pick up some things, but I didn't stay more than a few minutes. A gut feeling, Hank. A sense of alarm I've trained myself not to ignore. It's almost like a sixth sense, really. When I get the jitters, I take off, good and fast. I won't be back, so you can have the rest of my stuff."

"Oh, we'll take it, trust me." Hank paused. "Does that mean you're leaving Glendale?"

"I don't know, Hank. You tell me. It's going to be either Montgomery or Stainer next. Is either of them going to be out of town in the next month or so?"

"I don't believe you. You don't have the balls." From the corner of his eye, Hank saw Griffin frown.

"Father Ed doesn't like you challenging me like that, Hank, but don't worry. I won't take offense. We're past that. We're almost like brothers now, you and I."

"No, we're not." Hank spun around in a slow three-sixty, searching the horizon. There were numerous tall buildings in all directions. He could be on the roof of any one of them, watching with

193

binoculars. Hank caught Karen's attention and raised his eyebrows. "Can you see me right now, Bill? Are you watching us right now from somewhere close by?"

Karen nodded and turned away again, lifting the cell phone back to her ear.

"Of course I am, Hank, so I won't stay on the line very long, since it looks like the lovely Miss Karen's calling in the choppers as we speak. And, by the way, I know she has plans coming up that will take her out of state. If you were me, would you choose her, or the lovely stay-at-home Officer Montgomery?"

"Why don't you just show yourself, Bill, and one of the helicopters can pick you up. We'll talk about it then."

"Oh, thanks for the offer, but I think I'll pass. Decisions like this are so hard to make. I do have another place set aside as a back-up love nest, but on the other hand, a road trip to the Alleghany Highlands does have its appeal. I'll let you figure it out, Hank. Maybe Father Ed has some insight for you. Gotta go. Later."

The phone went dead.

"What's going on?" Cassion said, walking up to him. "Are you talking to him?" She held out her hand. "Let me talk to him."

Ignoring her, Hank looked at Karen, who shook her head.

The sound of a helicopter rose in the distance.

Hank put the phone in his pocket and looked at Martinez. "He's nearby. He had a visual on us." The helicopter passed overhead and moved in a slow arc over the surrounding buildings.

"What did he say to you this time?" Cassion demanded.

The duty sergeant in charge of the scene joined their circle and held out a cell phone to Martinez. "Commander, I have Commander Morency on the line for you."

Martinez nodded, took the phone, and walked away.

"He's still playing the game," Hank said to Griffin. "Still threatening to try for a cop."

"Stainer and Montgomery?"

Hank nodded. "Made it sound as though he'd settled on Karen. Said he knew she was about to leave town for Virginia."

Karen stepped out from behind him, putting her phone away. "Hunh. Bring it on."

Hank shook his head. "He also said he had another captivity site ready, so he's probably bluffing. Mickey didn't get anything?"

"No," Karen replied, "same old bullshit. Hank, we *want* this guy to come after me. All I need is one opening, and I'll put two right in the middle of his fucking nosebrow."

"We want him alive to stand trial," Cassion said.

"You're taking a week's leave," Hank said to Karen. "You're getting married, for God's sake."

"Maybe we'll get lucky," Griffin said, watching the helicopter circle around for another pass. "Maybe they'll catch him today."

"Not likely," Cassion said. "Not with just one bird in the air."

Martinez rejoined them, with Turcotte beside her. She handed the cell phone back to the duty sergeant, who'd been wordlessly listening to the ongoing discussion, then held up her own phone. "I just spoke to the chief. He just met with Exler," she said, referring to State's Attorney Warren Exler, "and they convinced a judge to issue a John Doe arrest warrant based on the DNA profile from that eyelash hair. The chief turned around and used the warrant to call in the capital-area task force."

Cassion frowned. "Task force?"

"A joint task force with the state, the county, the FBI, and the U.S. Marshals Service," Hank explained. "We're a participating member, but I don't remember us calling them in before."

"I don't get it," Karen said. "What the hell does that mean to us?"

"It means," Martinez said, "that we no longer have the lead, internally. This case is now being run by Special Ops."

"Oh, fuck me," Karen spat.

"But it's a homicide investigation," Cassion protested. "It belongs to me."

Martinez shook her head. "It's now a fugitive apprehension operation, as far as the chief's concerned. Everything gets turned over to Miller right away," she said, referring to Lieutenant Ted Miller, who was in charge of the unit within Special Operations that handled liaison with outside agencies. She hiked a thumb at the crime scene across the street and looked at Turcotte. "The one and sole objective of all that work over there now is to get this guy's ID for Miller. Understand?

Either you and Byrne play nice with Special Agent Carson, or the FBI'll be talking directly to the task force and leaving the GPD completely out of it."

"This is bullshit," Cassion said.

"It's a done deal," Martinez said. She glared at Turcotte. "Go. Get on it." She turned back to Hank. "You all right?"

Hank shrugged. What was there to say? His position as lead investigator in two homicide cases had just disappeared. At best he would be a post office, forwarding information from the FBI lab to Special Ops while the task force honchos carried out the hunt for the bastard who'd just spoken to him on the phone a few minutes ago. What was he supposed to say? That he was relieved he no longer had the responsibility? That he was looking forward to a nice little break?

"I agree with Cassion," he said. "It's bullshit."

"You know it isn't. It's a question of resources, like every other damned thing. We've been running after this guy blindfolded with both hands tied behind our backs. Now there's an army after him. This is how he'll get caught, Hank, and you know it."

A second helicopter swooped overhead. It bore the markings of the U.S. Marshals Service. Hank was surprised at how quickly they'd gotten airborne and on the scene. He knew Martinez was right. He knew that Chief Bennett had made the correct decision.

But he was damned if he was going to admit it.

32

One week later, Karen stared out the window in the passenger seat of Sandy's black Suburban as they tooled along the I-495 toward the Woodrow Wilson Memorial Bridge, which spanned the Potomac River south of Washington. They'd been on the road for forty-five minutes, it was a bright, cloudless morning, the Beltway was busy but moving, and they were just beginning a week's leave. Sandy was humming something under his breath as they approached the bridge, but Karen felt uneasy, as though she were sitting on a bag of broken glass.

It had nothing to do with the fact that she wasn't behind the steering wheel, since sharing the driving with her beloved spouse-to-be was something she'd already conceded would be a part of her new life as a married woman. It was other stuff, and she'd been stewing about whether she should come out with it now or wait for a better time. She'd been waiting so long now, she thought she'd waited a little too long.

"What are you thinking about?" Sandy asked, his eyes on the traffic in front of them.

"Nothing."

"Come on, it's not nothing. I heard you on the phone with Hank this morning. Don't tell me you're still upset about that case."

She snorted. "What a load of crap. All they've done is flush him out of wherever he was holed up. Now he's in the wind, and who knows where the hell he'll turn up next."

"It wasn't a bad move," Sandy said, "using the DNA profile as the basis for a John Doe arrest warrant. More and more jurisdictions are doing it now."

"Yeah, but in rape cases where the statute of limitations is about to kick in. We're talking homicides, Sandy. And not even two months old."

"I know, but the fact of the matter is, a judge signed off on it and your chief called in the Marshals. The case is out of your hands now. That's all there is to it."

Karen bit her lip as they passed beneath big orange signs that warned of the drawbridge ahead. Traffic was slowing down as they moved across the bridge. The Woodrow Wilson was the most heavily-traveled crossing on the Potomac, and a major traffic trap when the drawbridge was up. Thankfully the warning lights weren't flashing, meaning that the drawbridge was down, but volume was heavy, and brake lights were flaring in all six lanes ahead of them. They were facing a four-hour drive to Sandy's parents' place in Virginia as it was, and this wasn't helping her mood.

Looking at the Washington Monument in the distance, she thought of Ed Griffin's crack a month ago about federal agents marrying local cops. She knew at the time that it was a joke, and she didn't have a thin skin when it came to stuff like that, but she did worry about how Sandy felt. Would he find it hard to relate to local priorities when he was busy chasing The Big Picture?

Don't be a knob, she told herself. She was transferring anxiety to other stuff, and she knew it. The fact of the matter was that she wasn't pissed this morning because the Rainy Day Killer case had been re-assigned, and she wasn't feeling angsty about Sandy's professional perspective versus her own. What a load of crap.

The truth was that she was worried about what lay ahead. By getting into the passenger seat of the Suburban, shutting the door, and fastening her seat belt, she'd committed to a series of events that would change her life forever. At the end of this long-assed drive, she'd unbuckle the seat belt, get out of the Suburban, and walk into something that was way outside her comfort zone. While everyone watched, she'd have to look Sandy in the eye and make the commitment, while hoping she'd read him right over the last two years. Was he as wonderful as he seemed? Would he suddenly have gigantic regrets and change his mind?

A wedding wasn't supposed to be such a horrific ordeal, was it?

Maybe somewhere on the Alexander ranch she could get in a little target practice. Shred a few silhouettes, put the new baby SIG through its paces, work off some stress. After a few dozen rounds she'd start to feel more like herself again. Nothing like a little firearms recoil to jolt you back to your senses and remind you of who you really are.

The tires of the Suburban clacked over the metal seams at the edge of the drawbridge segment. Ahead, the drawbridge operator's control tower jutted up in the middle of the bridge like the prow of a tugboat. She knew they'd just reached an important and very interesting spot on the map. The Woodrow Wilson was the only bridge in the United States that passed through three different jurisdictions—Maryland behind them, Virginia ahead of them, and for the next three hundred feet, the southernmost tip of the District of Columbia. It was like a convergence of the most important influences in her life at the moment, right there at that spot, high above the Potomac River.

"I don't think I should have a kid," she blurted. "I don't think it'd be the right thing to do."

Sandy took a moment to respond. "Because of the schizophrenia and your mother? You don't want to pass it on?"

"Correct. I don't. And I'm not out of the woods myself. I could still crash, up to the age of forty, or whatever the hell it is." She looked at him. "That'd be awful enough for you, but add a kid to the mix? Another kid with a mother checking out of her life and into the bughouse? And passing the genes on to her? I can't take that gamble with someone else's life, Sandy, I just can't. It's not fair, no matter how much I want a kid. It's not fair to be that selfish."

"I understand."

She stared at his profile, watching his eyes flick from the rear view mirror to the side mirror to the traffic ahead. His expression was completely neutral. How could he be so goddamned calm?

"I know you want kids, Sandy."

"I want kids if you want kids," he said, glancing at her. "If you want to adopt, we can adopt. But if you want it to be just you and me, then it's just you and me."

"You'd be happy with just that?"

He smiled then, glancing at her again. "I'd be happy with that, and no 'just' about it. Karen, you're more than a handful for me. You're everything. Absolutely. Trust me on that one. Do you want to look into adoption?"

"No. I want it to be you and me."

He nodded. "Then it's you and me. End of story."

They passed beneath a big white sign with a cardinal on it that said, "Virginia Welcomes You." On the right, Karen could see the waterfront of Alexandria, the colorful rowhouses of Old Town, and the jutting spire of the Masonic Temple. Just ahead, as they approached the end of the bridge, was Jones Point Park.

"Well," she said, "I guess we better finish this drive and make it all official-like."

"Roger that," Sandy laughed.

33

A day later, Hank was listening to Martha Scanlan's album *The West Was Burning* in the CD player of his rented Cadillac as he drove south on the I-95 on his way to Quantico to pick up Ed Griffin. It was another bright and sunny day, traffic was typical of a Friday morning, and Hank was grateful to have some time off.

Before leaving, he'd briefed Helen Cassion on the active cases that would require attention while he and Karen were away. Horvath had decided at the last minute he wanted to attend the wedding, but Cassion had denied his leave request, so he would be there to continue working active cases with Belknap and Kaplan. With the Rainy Day Killer case in the hands of Special Ops, the workload would hopefully be manageable.

Cassion, for her part, was ebullient. She'd gone through her interview in the competitive process for the position of captain on Monday, and was feeling particularly good about herself. She half-listened as Hank walked through the next steps the detectives would be taking on their most important cases, then impatiently waved a hand.

"Yeah, yeah, Donaghue, I got it. I sign off on their reports, remember? I know all about this stuff."

As he listened to Scanlan's cover of the Dylan song "I Went to See the Gypsy," his thoughts tracked back to Wednesday, which he'd spent in the hands of Human Resources. In the morning he'd written an in-basket test as part of the competitive process. He was given an information package containing an elaborate scenario in a fictitious police department, including an organization chart and a set of letters, memos, and reports, and his task was to respond to each document in what he judged to be the appropriate manner, whether by writing memos, delegating tasks, planning meetings, or whatever else might occur to him over the course of the three-and-a-half hours he was given to complete the test. Because he understood how in-basket exercises were designed, he hadn't experienced any difficulty with them before. In the past, he'd racked up a perfect score. This time around, he expected the outcome to be the same.

After a quick lunch at a chip wagon down the street, he'd ridden the elevator back up to the tenth floor for his interview with the three-person selection committee, consisting of the director of Human Resources, Mrs. Mona Bloodworth, Commander Jason Stone of Midtown District, and Commander Henry Dalzell of Intelligence. Both Stone and Dalzell were wearing their Class A uniforms, while Bloodworth, a civilian, wore business attire. Hank, although a sworn officer like Stone and Dalzell, was not required by departmental policy to wear his uniform, being assigned to plain clothes duty, so he wore a navy Armani suit he particularly liked, a crisp white shirt, a cobalt tie, and black oxfords polished to a high shine.

Hank was the last candidate to be interviewed, they explained as he sat down, and the chief expected an eligibility list from them by next Monday.

The first portion of the interview consisted of a situational judgment test, in which scenarios were described and Hank was required to explain how he'd respond to each of them if he were the captain responsible for the area involved. In a way, it was a duplication of the in-basket exercise in that it assessed his ability to analyze a situation and exercise good judgment, but instead of a paper exercise he was faced with departmental superiors watching his body language like hawks, ready to jump on his every word.

Again, though, because he understood that situational judgment tests would assess his leadership skills, his personal aggressiveness, and his initiative in solving problems, he was able to anticipate the key words and phrases that would be printed on the answer sheets they were using to grade his performance. Solid preparation, an excellent memory, and a high IQ once again brought him through this test without a scratch.

A sign warned him that he'd reached the off-ramp for Exit 150A to Quantico. As he crossed the overpass, he glanced down and saw that traffic in the east-bound lanes of Joplin Road was moving briskly. He braked and took the ramp at a slow pace, spiraling down clockwise onto Joplin and under the overpass he'd just crossed.

A white tractor trailer passed over his head as he moved beneath the overpass, and for an instant he flashed on the enclosed space beneath the Howard K. Chase Bridge where, more than a month ago, he'd huddled in his trench coat, hiding from the rain as they'd worked on Theresa Olsen's body.

Still an open case, with a suspect's DNA profile but no identity to go with it.

For Hank, the lack of progress made him feel as claustrophobic as the tons of concrete looming above his head. Two dead young women. A string of others before them. And the threat of more lives that would end in unspeakable horror.

Up ahead, he saw traffic lights that marked the intersection of Joplin Road and the Jefferson Davis Highway.

Wednesday's interview had become more difficult when they moved from the situational judgment test to the portion intended to assess his personal suitability for the position. These questions were intended to gauge his loyalty and dedication to the department, his ethical judgment, and how his professional experience qualified him for the position. Bloodworth began with a series of soft questions about his education and his accomplishments as a child prodigy, his decision to forgo a career in the office of the state's attorney for a cop's life, and a few of his recent and more prominent cases in homicide. He'd answered similar questions when he'd been promoted to lieutenant and knew what to say. A few minutes later, however, Dalzell changed the pace by pressing him about his connections to the local Triad brotherhood.

"Have you met with Lam Chun Sang, a.k.a. Uncle Sang, a known Triad figure, on at least one occasion in the recent past?"

Hank acknowledged that he had.

"Do you really expect us to believe that your conversation was limited to questions relating to the Jarrett case?"

Hank explained that, as the commander well knew, in any opportunity to obtain information from a CI, one asked all sorts of questions.

"What information did you pass on to Lam to repay him for

being a 'confidential informant,' as you put it?"

Hank responded calmly that in such a situation, as the commander also knew, the idea was to ask the questions and not answer them.

Dalzell then demanded that he explain his connections to the Mah family, including Jerome Mah, the wealthy shipping magnate who was believed to be an associate of Lam, and his son Peter Mah, the former Red Pole enforcer whose life Hank had saved while investigating the Martin Liu case.

"Peter Mah believes he owes me a debt of honor," Hank replied, "because Detective Stainer and I prevented a Triad hit squad from assassinating him."

"Again, does part of that debt of honor involve the exchange of money or confidential departmental information?"

"Absolutely not."

"Speaking of the Martin Liu case," Dalzell went on, "how do you explain the fact that you're currently in an intimate sexual relationship with Meredith Collier Liu, the mother of the victim in that case, who is herself a known associate of Peter Mah?"

Hank paused, knowing he was supposed to rise to the bait. He suspected that everything else Dalzell had asked had been intended to lead up to this question, which was supposed to cause him to lose his composure and betray a lack of professional self-control.

"How do I explain it? Love, I guess."

Bloodworth bit the inside of her cheek to hide a smile.

"That's it?" Dalzell huffed. "That's how you explain a relationship that could severely compromise your ability to maintain confidentiality and protect the interests of this department?"

"Yes, sir. That's how I explain it."

Commander Stone, whose district included Chinatown, shifted uncomfortably. "Are you trying to be flippant, Lieutenant?"

"Not at all, sir. At all times I respect the confidentiality of information that comes into my possession through my duties as a sworn officer of this department, and I will always, every day, do everything in my power to protect the interests of the GPD. My relationship with Ms. Collier is personal, and her relationship with Peter Mah is, to say the least, cool."

"Moving on—" Bloodworth began.

"One more question on the subject," Stone interrupted. "Lieutenant, if the chief were to assign a captain to the current Chinatown task force attempting to address the violence that continues to plague that neighborhood, and you were that captain, what steps would you take to carry out your new duties?"

Surprised, Hank hesitated before responding. He could tell from the look on Bloodworth's face that Stone had just deviated from the script they'd been following up to that point. He glanced at Dalzell, who stared at him intently, obviously having expected Stone to ask this question at the last moment.

Hank knew there was constant friction between Lieutenant Jarvis, the current head of the task force, and Dalzell's analysts in Intelligence, whose reports and advice Jarvis preferred to ignore. He also knew the relationship between Jarvis and the district was even worse. Stone's people felt, with good cause, that their toes were constantly being stepped on. He suddenly understood that he'd already passed the test as far as both uniformed members of the committee were concerned. They were asking this final question now in order to have his response on the record. Perhaps they hoped it would give them some sort of leverage down the road against the task force and the way it conducted business. Perhaps the chief did, in fact, intend to have a captain take charge of the task force, and they wanted it to be him.

Hank disliked playing political head games, but he had very strong opinions about the way Jarvis had been running the show in Chinatown, and if Stone and Dalzell wanted something on the record, he was more than happy to oblige them.

"The first thing that would happen," Hank said, "is that the elders would invite me for tea. As I understand it, there's a nice little garden behind a grocery store down on Lexington where they like to get together." He glanced at Dalzell, who nodded slightly. "I'd accept that invitation and have a cup of tea. I might try one of those pastries they're all addicted to. I'd ask about their health, pat the dog on the head, and admire the flowers."

Bloodworth frowned, not following him at all.

"Go on," Stone prompted.

"The elders only want peace and quiet to pursue their business," Hank said, looking at Bloodworth. "They hate these home invasions and drive-by shootings and all the rest of the violence."

"I thought they thrived on it," she said.

"Just the opposite. They hate it when one of their own goes rogue and starts making waves. It draws the spotlight to them and brings unwanted police attention that plays serious hell with business. Believe it or not, they want good relations with us. They understand it's our job to shut them down, but they have this ideal vision in which it's an honorable game played by honorable men according to a well-defined set of rules."

He saw Bloodworth's frown and leaned forward. "These men are criminals, make no mistake. Their businesses include drug trafficking, human smuggling, prostitution, and pornography. As a sworn officer, it's my duty to shut them down and send them to prison. But if we understand how they think, we can use it to our advantage. To them, relationships are extremely important. It's what they refer to as *guanxi*, a network of family and business connections. Within this network they operate according to a principle called *renqing*, which implies not only emotional commitment but also an exchange of favors or other considerations."

He sat back again. "The commander asked earlier about my relationship with Peter Mah. Unfortunately, because I protected him from a Triad hit team in 2011, Mah feels I'm now part of his *guanxi* network and that he has a *renqing*-type obligation to me. While he's been out of the country, one of his employees has been hovering around, feeding me information and watching my coattails. Commander Dalzell's quite right to question whether or not I'm reciprocating in some fashion but, believe me, I've gone out of my way to make it clear to the Mahs that I don't buy into it and I won't play along. Just the same, if they want to continue treating me as though this relationship actually exists, I'd be a fool not to take advantage of it.

"So, yes, I'd have a cup of tea with the elders and listen to what they felt obligated to say to me. I'd respond with respect, and I'd suggest that if we were to consider some kind of reciprocal agreement, it would have to involve the cessation of all this violence right up front. If they were to remove the troublemakers themselves, send them back to Hong Kong or Fukian province or wherever they come from, and they took care of this in such a way that I had no personal knowledge of it that I'd be obligated to report to Homeland Security, then I could probably live with it. The mayor could probably live with it. In exchange, perhaps I wouldn't go blundering around down there like Dogberry on speed, the way Jarvis is right now. In fact, if they took care of it themselves and got rid of all the troublemakers, we wouldn't need the task force at all, would we? Which would make them very happy."

He looked at Dalzell. "Then you could go back to working your intel on their businesses, and you," he looked at Stone, "could go back to policing them the way they're supposed to be policed."

"It sounds to me as though you're saying that if you were appointed to head up the task force, you'd actually try to get rid of it," Bloodworth said.

"In a nutshell, I guess that's correct."

"Thank you for your answer," Commander Stone said.

"You're welcome," Hank replied. "Just make sure they don't put me on the damned thing, because there's no way in hell I want *that*."

Bloodworth smiled, but Stone and Dalzell merely nodded.

Hank stepped on the brakes. He'd passed through the intersection at the Jefferson Davis Highway and was now on Fuller Road, slowing to a stop at the sentry post that marked the entrance to the land controlled by the United States Marine Corps, land that included the town of Quantico, where Ed Griffin was waiting for him, the FBI Academy, and the Marine Corps base.

As he edged forward in the lineup of cars waiting to be greeted by the Marine sentry, he pulled out the wallet containing his badge and departmental identification. Although he'd passed through this checkpoint several times in the past, he knew his status as a law enforcement officer meant very little to the sentry who exercised the jurisdiction granted to the USMC by Congress and the state over the town of Quantico, Virginia.

He was about to become just another ten-second event in the life of a bored Marine.

34

The town of Quantico consists of only seven streets and just under five hundred people, but because it's bordered on three sides by one of the largest U.S. Marine Corps bases in the world, the town has seven barber shops, seven laundry and tailoring businesses, and four stores specializing in military apparel and gear, not to mention twelve restaurants and coffee shops. Hank decided that civilians running a business in Quantico apparently had no trouble understanding what their patrons were looking for in terms of goods and services.

He was not surprised to find that Griffin was waiting for him in the driveway of his tiny, two-bedroom bungalow. He got out and opened the trunk of the Cadillac, and Griffin tossed in his travel bag.

"You travel light," Hank said, closing the trunk.

"Always. It's part of the life."

They climbed in and Hank started back through town.

"I would've invited you in," Griffin said, "but I don't have a housekeeper and I don't do housework. You can do the math."

"That's all right," Hank replied.

"I really need another coffee. Just don't stop at any of these places in town, I beg of you. You have to remember, their clients are almost exclusively military personnel and law enforcement officers, none of whom could care less what coffee tastes like as long as it's hot and in constant supply. There's no point in inflicting it on our livers. I know a place about an hour from here where we can stop. I'll show you."

Hank turned onto Fuller Road. As they drove past the base bachelor housing quarters, Griffin cleared his throat.

"You sure you're okay with this?"

"With what?"

"With driving. We can switch, if you like. I don't mind doing it, if it'll make you feel more comfortable."

Hank grinned at him. "Nervous?"

"No, no! Not at all. I just thought you didn't drive, is all."

"I drive when I'm on leave. I love highway driving. It's very relaxing. I'm fully-trained in defensive driving, advanced precision driving, pursuit driving, and every other course it's possible to take, so you're perfectly fine, Ed. Just make sure your seat belt's fastened, and you'll be okay."

"I feel so safe now."

Hank made his way back to the southbound I-95. His plan was to jump onto Route 3 at Fredericksburg and work his way southwest to Charlottesville, then take the I-64 the rest of the way to Alleghany County. They had a long drive ahead of them, and when Griffin's coffee joint came up they both bought jumbo sizes.

"Our next stop will be a roadside rest area," Griffin said as they pulled back out onto the highway. "You don't buy coffee, you just rent it."

Hank laughed.

"It was nice of the happy couple to invite me like this at the last minute," Griffin remarked between sips.

"It's a Bureau wedding. Half the Glendale field office is probably invited."

Griffin groaned. "Say it ain't so. Too many navy suits gives me blurred vision. That reminds me, did I pack my eye drops?"

They drove in silence for a mile, then Hank pointed at the Cadillac's music system. "You can turn that on, if you like. There are CDs in the console."

"I'm fine, thanks." Griffin rubbed his chin. "Tell me something. Do you think our friend Bill's still in Glendale?"

"No. I don't."

"Montgomery's still under protective surveillance, isn't she?"

Hank nodded. "For a while longer."

"But you don't think she's in any danger."

Hank hesitated, then shook his head. "No, I don't."

"I happen to agree with you. I think the bastard's on his way here, just like we are." He turned sideways in his seat to look at Hank. "You know, I'm starting to wonder if he wants to get caught now, if he's been elevating the risk level to bring about some kind of end game. I think it's fair to say at the very least that the post-offense excitement he's feeling is reaching the point where it's equal to, if not exceeding, the excitement of the offense itself. Maybe he's actually getting bored with the sexual component and is ready to give up his anonymity in exchange for fame and personal recognition."

"You think he's getting a bigger thrill out of the risk than the rape and murder?"

"We've seen instances before where behavior escalates as they go through a kind of desensitization to the act of rape, and even to the murders. I hate using the drug analogy, because I don't like equating sexual homicide with addiction, but it *is* almost like the way the body develops a tolerance for drugs and other chemical sources of pleasure, requiring larger and larger doses to maintain a certain level of satisfaction. It could be that he's reached a stage where the act itself no longer supplies him with the kick he needs."

"That's difficult to appreciate, Ed."

"I know. It's a horrible, twisted world these guys inhabit. But I think this may be what's going on. He called you more than he called the other lead investigators."

"Lucky me."

"They like the thrill of power that comes with injecting themselves into the investigation and contacting the police, but he was even more anxious than usual to develop a relationship with you, even obtain your approval."

Hank said nothing, staring at the highway ahead of them.

"He's on his way here," Griffin said finally. "He has some way of surveilling Karen's activities. Maybe computer spyware, listening devices, I don't know. He's aware of this trip, and I think it's his intention to grab her right out of the middle of it and turn her into his crowning achievement. He's probably fantasizing about the book and the movie deals he'll get for his story after he pulls it off."

"He won't stand a chance."

"You may be right. But as I've said before, he's not stupid. He's shown an amazing ability to evade pursuit up to now. He'll be extremely confident he can pull it off. And if he doesn't, he no doubt figures he'll be famous anyway."

A mile later, as Hank mulled over Griffin's words, a thought occurred to him. The Cadillac was equipped with a hands-free communication system to which he'd paired his cell phone, and now he touched the button to activate the service.

"Mickey Marcotte," he said, and the phone dialed the number for him.

Thankfully, Marcotte was at his desk and took the call on the third ring.

"Mick, it's Donaghue. Can you do something for me?"

"Sure, Lieutenant. What's up?"

"Can you get someone to sweep my office for bugs?"

"Bugs? You mean listening devices?"

"That's what I mean. Can you get someone in there right now, today?"

"Um, I think so. I could take a shot myself, but I know a guy who'll do it right. I should be able to get him in."

"Do it. Tell Byrne to charge it to our unit and I'll take care of it. He can call me if he wants, but I need it done today. It's extremely important."

"Will do, Lieutenant."

Hank ended the call and glanced at Griffin, who was looking at him with eyebrows raised

"A hunch," Hank said.

"Oh?"

"I've got a bad feeling I've already met the Rainy Day Killer. In person."

35

"The day before the ceremony," Lane Alexander said, pushing aside the remnants of her chicken caesar salad, "is supposed to have a lighter schedule than the Big Day, so I've taken care of several tasks for you already." She reached down and brought out a wicker handbag. "Let's go through a few things now, so we can just strike them right off that old checklist."

Karen nodded grimly. They were sitting on the patio behind the Alexander ranch house, at a glass-top dining table Lane had explained was part of a set she'd personally chosen because she liked the references to eighteenth-century furniture design, including the metal lattice work with decorative acanthus leaves, the serpentine detailing on the arms of the chairs, and the simple ivory color of the cushions, none of which Karen understood or gave a damn about.

Karen had already devoured her BLT and downed the two glasses of wine Lane was permitting them to have before the rehearsal, scheduled for later in the afternoon, and she'd been picking restlessly at a bowl of cashews as her mother-in-law-to-be filled her in on the latest gossip as it related to the guests she'd personally invited to the wedding. Effortlessly, in accordance with her professional training, Karen had committed each detail to memory, but her mind was elsewhere.

Escape is futile, Stainer. We have you completely surrounded. Come out with your hands on top of your head. This is your last warning.

Lane touched her hair unconsciously. It was thick, black hair, coiffed and sprayed rigid in a style that reminded Karen of Ann Landers, the gossip columnist from her youth. Tidy and perfect in a powder blue jacket and skirt, her makeup and lipstick flawless, Lane was a compact, alert Virginian with a soft accent and a sharp glint in her eye.

"I've taken the liberty of printing out your schedule for tomorrow," she said, holding up a folded piece of paper. "I'll put it right in here."

She opened the wicker bag and took out Karen's clutch, which Karen had thought was still in her room but had obviously found its way into Lane's hot little hands. Lane slipped the piece of paper into the clutch and gave Karen a toothy smile.

"I've assembled your wedding day kit for you," she said, removing things one at a time with a little flourish. "Mini-deodorant, breath mints, tissues, a package of safety pins, thread and needle, and a few other emergency items to make sure you get through the day without a scratch."

"Is there still room for my gun?"

Lane's smile brightened crisply. "I do love your sense of humor, dear. It absolutely brightens up everything."

She put the clutch back into the wicker handbag and took out two small boxes. "I have the rings, so don't fret about them." The boxes went back in the bag in exchange for another small box. "I've purchased your gifts for the wedding party. Swarovski brooches for the ladies, Rolex wrist watches for the gentlemen. Would you like to see them?"

Karen shook her head. "I'm trusting you here, Lane. I know you'll make me look good."

"You'll look better than good, sweet. You'll look fantastic." The wicker handbag disappeared again beneath the table.

"Sandy packed your getaway bag this morning," Lane went on, "so that's done. The manicurist will be here at two, so don't forget. Your friend, Miss Archer, arrived in town an hour ago and got settled into her room at the hotel. Mr. Donaghue is expected to arrive here at three, and your brother Darryl telephoned to let me know he'll meet us at the church at four. Brenda, of course, is in town. That's everyone in the wedding party, so hopefully we'll be able to start the rehearsal right on schedule. We've reserved the back room at Lee's in town for the rehearsal dinner, so everything should fall into place nicely."

"Thank God," Karen said.

"One other thing." Lane held out her hand. "I'll take your cell phone now."

"Excuse me?"

"Your phone, dear. We don't want you bothered by a lot of nuisance calls or texts or whatever people pester you with. I'll keep it right with me, so it'll be safe. Don't worry about that."

Karen blinked. "Sorry, Lane. No can do."

"Of course you can."

"No, I can't. I don't stop being a cop just because I'm on vacation. The cell stays with me."

"It's not a vacation, for heaven's sake. It's your *wedding*. The Most Special Day Of Your Life."

Karen stared at Lane's outstretched hand and shook her head. "Sorry. I tell you what, though. Compromise. I'll turn it over to you tomorrow before I walk into the church, as long as you promise to hand it back to me at the reception. Deal?"

"After you throw your bouquet," Lane offered.

"After the photographs are taken."

"After the first dance."

"After dinner."

Lane sighed, withdrawing her hand. "After dinner." She picked up her glass of wine and drained it, shaking her head. "I wonder if all Texan girls are like you."

"I severely doubt it."

"So do I." Lane set down her empty glass. "Just one more thing."

"Uh oh."

"Try to relax, dear."

"Okay, Lane, I'll try. I know you've got my six on this. I appreciate it."

"I've got your what?"

Karen laughed, despite herself. "Never mind."

36

"Welcome to the Alleghany Highlands," Bill Alexander said, shaking their hands in the foyer of the craftsman colonial that served as the main house on the Alexander ranch. "This is my nephew, Stephen Walton. He's helping us out this weekend. Don't know what we'd do without him."

Hank shook hands with the shy-looking blond teenager who'd answered the door when they rang the bell. "Nice to meet you, Stephen. Beautiful place you have here, Mr. Alexander."

"Please, please, call me Bill. It's Hank, right? And Ed? We don't stand on ceremony, here. Except for the Big One tomorrow, of course." He laughed. "Your luggage is still in the car? Good. Hank, you'll be staying in the guest house, and Ed, we've reserved a room for you at the hotel in town. We've practically taken over the place. All at our expense, of course. Y'all are our guests this weekend. Stephen will run you in when you're ready to go, but I was hoping you might have a few minutes for a drink first."

"Of course," Ed said. "I'd love to. I imagine Hank would love a bourbon after that drive, but I'll stick to something non-alcoholic, if you don't mind."

"Sure enough! We've got everything here, don't worry about that." He led them down the hall and into the great room. "Twenty-two-foot ceiling," he said, waving a hand, "floor-to-ceiling stone fireplace, wrought-iron chandelier hand-forged up in Warm Springs a hundred and fifty years ago, dark oak floors. Built by my great-great-grandfather before the Civil War, during which it miraculously survived an attempt by the Yankees to burn it to the ground." He grinned at them. "My apologies. I was in real estate a lifetime ago, before I retired and became the humble gentleman farmer you see before you."

When they'd been fixed up with drinks and had chosen seats in the great room around the spectacular fireplace, Alexander leaned back in his chair, crossing his legs. "Either of you smoke? I forgot to ask. I'm an occasional smoker, myself, but I'm not allowed to smoke in the house. We can sit outside on the patio, if you like."

"Just the odd cigar," Hank said. "Maybe later."

"Sounds like a plan. Ed?"

"Caffeine's my only vice," Griffin said, holding up his glass of Coke. "I'm all set."

"That's fine. How do you fellows like this little part of heaven?"

"It's beautiful," Griffin replied. "How high up are we?"

"This little hollow's thirteen hundred and sixty feet above sea level. Pleasant Mountain, which I expect you saw to the northwest of us, is two thousand feet. Our ranch is a forty-acre parcel that's been in the Alexander family for five generations now. When he inherits it, Sandy will be the sixth."

"It's still an operating ranch?"

"We keep a few horses, and the rest of the acreage is in clover, timothy, and a few other grasses. Our main cash crop is honey. We have a big apiary on the property. I hired a good man to look after it for me, and we supply honey as far east as Staunton and all the way down to Roanoke. As Lane likes to say, we're very sweet around here."

"Fascinating," Griffin said, sipping his Coke.

"If you gentlemen are interested in local history, there's plenty to see. That cemetery you passed when you turned off Jackson River Road? That's the Pleasant Mountain United Methodist Cemetery. I'm the administrator, mostly because no one else has the time or interest to take on the responsibility, but all my family's buried there, including Robert Alexander, who built this house, and his wife Marietta. Most of the tombstones are lost, but Robert's, thankfully, is still there. Has a very touching inscription: 'Beyond the sunset's radiant glow, there is a brighter world, I know. Beyond the sunset we shall spend, delightful days that never end.' I memorized it when I was a young man. It was my job to cut the grass back in those days. Now I hire a man from Covington to do it. A townie."

Hank's cell phone, which he'd unplugged from the car before

coming in, vibrated in his pocket. He slipped it out and looked at the call display.

"If that's something you need to take, Hank," Alexander said, "go right ahead. Business is business."

"Sorry," Hank said, standing up.

"Don't apologize. Ed and I are just getting warmed up."

Hank walked out into the empty hallway and stood at the bottom of the staircase. "Donaghue."

"Lieutenant, it's Mickey. I hate to tell you this, but we found a listening device in your office. In the overhead lights. It's a wireless Infinity that operates on a SIM card. The way it works, the guy calls the device from a cell phone, the SIM card answers, and then he can hear everything in the office."

"And?"

"It traced back to a throwaway, Lieutenant. Dead end. Sorry."

"Okay, Mick. Thanks."

Hank disconnected and speed-dialed Jim Horvath.

"Hey, Hank. Are you there yet?"

"Yeah, Griffin and I are at the Alexander ranch. How's it going?"

"Right now I'm having a cup of coffee in a great little place called Ellen's Diner, on Market Street. What's up?"

"I want you to think back for a minute. Do you remember the day we got the Theresa Olsen package?"

"Yeah, I guess so."

"You came in with some reports from Byrne and we went out into the bullpen to talk because some guy was changing the overhead lights in my office. Do you remember?"

"Yeah, sort of. The fluorescent tubes. Right. We were talking when the mail clerk came along with the package. Then all hell broke loose."

"That's right. Do you remember the guy who was changing the light bulbs?"

"Not really. Why?"

"He had a visitor's badge. He kept calling me chief. The Public Works guy came along and asked him where the other guy was."

"I remember. He said the other guy was upstairs, didn't he?"

"Yeah. Do you remember what the guy looked like? Not the DPW guy, the guy in my office changing the light bulbs?"

"Not really, Hank. Caucasian. Small to medium build, clean-shaven. Ball cap, I think. Overalls or something. That's about it."

"Think you'd recognize him again if you saw him?"

"Nope. Why? What's this all about?"

"I'm having trouble remembering him, myself," Hank said, "and it's really important. Mickey just found a bug in the overhead lights in my office. I think that guy may have put it there."

"No shit. What the hell for?"

"For one thing, to insert himself into the investigation. For another, I think he wanted to be there when the package arrived. To witness all the commotion."

"The package? I'm not tracking you, Hank."

"The Rainy Day Killer, Jim. I think it was him."

37

When Hank returned to the great room, Bill Alexander was describing to Griffin the importance of the railroad in the history of the Alleghany Highlands. He broke off when he saw the look on Hank's face.

"Is there a problem?"

"Ed and I should have a word together."

Alexander stood up quickly, holding up his glass. "I need another drink." He walked over to Hank's chair and picked up his glass. "Refresh yours?"

"Thanks."

"Bear in mind, Hank, that although Sandy doesn't come home very often, when he *is* here, he's always taking calls on his cell phone. I've developed selective deafness when it comes to you law enforcement types. I'll just be over here." He headed for the bar in the corner of the room.

Griffin stood up. They moved to the opposite corner of the room. "What's up?"

"You were right when you said that the Rainy Day Killer must have some kind of surveillance on us. We just found an Infinity wireless listening device in the overhead lights in my office, the kind you access with a throwaway cell phone. He may have been listening when Karen was talking to me about her wedding plans here."

"If he's followed us," Griffin said, "we need to distribute copies of the composite right away. We should contact the sheriff and get him on board. The task force has jurisdiction down here, as far as Roanoke, anyway. Maybe they'll extend their parameters."

Hank glanced across the room. "We need to bring Mr. Alexander in on this. We'll need his help to make sure everyone's aware and watching, just in case."

"I suppose you're right."

Hank caught Alexander's eye and beckoned him over. "SSA Griffin and I are concerned that some unfinished business may have followed us from Maryland. A possible threat to Karen. We need your help to spread the word quietly and arrange some kind of security procedures."

"Who's the sheriff?" Griffin asked. "We'll need to make contact and bring him up to speed."

"His name's Crull. Dan Crull."

Griffin raised an eyebrow at his tone. "You don't seem too enamored of him."

"He and I are on opposite sides of the political fence," Alexander said uncomfortably. "I've been pretty noisy about supporting his opponents in the last two elections. I don't expect he'd be willing to suddenly leap into action on our account."

"Okay, well, we still have to make him aware of our concerns and brief him on the case. I take it he's in town?"

Alexander nodded.

"Fine." Griffin looked at Hank. "We should go there now, right away. I've got the composite and some other stuff with me. Maybe they'll take care of the printing and distribution for us this afternoon."

"Uh," Alexander said, "Hank, don't forget you have to be at the church in a few minutes for the rehearsal. You've got just enough time to drop your bag off at the guest house before Stephen runs you down to Clearwater Falls."

"You go ahead," Griffin told Hank. "Fulfill your ceremonial obligations." He looked at Alexander. "Could your nephew take me on into town after dropping him off at the church?"

"Of course. What's this all about, anyway?"

"A case we've been working on in Glendale," Hank answered. "Someone murdered two young women bearing a general physical resemblance to Karen. We believe the same individual's responsible for other murders in several other states. There's a task force pursuing him right now in Maryland, but SSA Griffin and I are concerned that this individual may have followed Karen here. We need to make sure we're ready for any contingency."

"You think a mass murderer is here? Right here? Is that what you're saying?"

"Please stay calm, Mr. Alexander." Griffin said. "If he's followed her here, he's made a major mistake, wouldn't you say? Just count the number of FBI agents and police officers in the wedding party and on the guest list. We just need everyone alert and aware, and we need the sheriff's office involved on an official basis, in case they need to coordinate with the task force and make an arrest if he shows up."

"Does Sandy know about this?"

"Sandy's been involved in the case, yes," Griffin replied, "and he's aware of the possibility, but we haven't talked to him yet about our present concerns. We just got here."

"If you stir up everyone and turn this into some kind of police circus, Lane will blow a gasket. Can't you do this discreetly? So she doesn't hear about it? She's trying very hard to like Karen, but, well, frankly, the girl's quite a bit outside Lane's normal comfort zone, if you know what I mean."

"We'll do everything we can to minimize the disruption to the wedding," Hank said. "We may be wrong and nothing will happen. We hope that will be the case. But we can't take a chance. You understand, don't you?"

"Yes, I understand," Alexander said. "We *are* a law enforcement family after all, in a manner of speaking, with a son in the FBI. It's just that, up to now, it's all been at arm's length, something to brag about, and Sandy's always assured us he spends most of his time doing paperwork and attending courses. I know he downplays it for his mother's sake, since he is a field agent and all, but..."

"I know your son quite well," Griffin said. "He's been a participant in several courses I've taught, and we talk on the phone. He's the local coordinator who deals with us analyst types at Quantico. He's always got a thousand questions, and not one of them dumb. I've spoken to his boss about him, Special Agent in Charge Roubidoux. I don't know if you've ever met her? Sharp woman. Speaks very highly of Sandy, but I've told her, and I'm telling you now, I feel very strongly his future's at Quantico, in the Behavioral Analysis Unit, at some point down the road. He's got the smarts, he's got the drive, and he's getting the necessary field experience right now, at this point in his career, that will make him a complete analyst. Why am I telling you all this? Because, when Sandy understands the situation and our present concerns, we'll be relying on him to be our inside man, so to speak. To make sure your wife and the rest of your family and the wedding party aren't unduly upset. Can you let him take care of that, while you keep the rest of us on schedule?"

"Sure, yeah. I guess so. Of course."

Griffin patted him on the arm. "Fine. That's the spirit. Now where's that nephew of yours? We need to get our tails in gear."

38

The sheriff's office was a typical brick building on a typical street in a typical Virginia town. Thankfully, it was within walking distance of the hotel, so Griffin was able to check in and dump his bag in his room before showing up at the front desk, portfolio under his arm. An administrative assistant wearing a black polo shirt with the crest of the sheriff's office embroidered on it took his name and politely asked him to take a seat along the wall until someone was available to speak to him.

The only other person with him in the waiting area was a young, uncomfortable-looking woman wearing a flowered blouse, dark-colored jeans and toeless shoes. She was overweight, her fingernails and toenails were painted blood red, and the white purse she held on her lap was scuffed and worn. She kept her eyes down, avoiding eye contact.

The administrative assistant chatted behind the counter with another woman in an identical black polo shirt. After a moment, the second woman lifted the flap on the counter, pushed through the little swinging cattle door, and walked out into the waiting area. She was short, in her mid-forties, with short, brown hair and a sober expression on her face.

Griffin looked at her expectantly, but she walked past him and held out a hand to the young woman in the other chair. "Are you Natalie? I'm Susan Raymond, nine-one-one coordinator. Sorry to keep you waiting."

Natalie shot to her feet and shook the offered hand. "That's okay. I was here early. I mean, I don't mind waiting."

"We'll do the interview in my office. Right this way."

Griffin watched them disappear into the back.

A uniformed sheriff's deputy mooched up to the counter, shot Griffin a look, and drifted away. The dispatcher's voice murmured in the background. Replies popped on the speakers attached to her equipment. When there was a lull in the action, he listened to the humming of the overhead fluorescent lights.

The man who finally came out to speak to him wore a crisp brown uniform with the gold epaulettes and insignia of a senior officer. He was about twenty years younger than Griffin, six inches taller, and fifty pounds heavier.

"You wanted to speak to someone?" he asked politely.

Griffin stood up, showing his identification. "Supervisory Special Agent Ed Griffin. I'm attached to the Behavioral Analysis Unit of the FBI in Quantico."

The man took the identification and gave it a long look before handing it back. "I'm Lieutenant Colonel Mike Ames, chief deputy, sheriff's office, Alleghany County." He shook Griffin's hand with a firm, aggressive grip. "What can we do for you today, sir?"

"Is there somewhere we can talk?"

"My office." Ames led him through the cattle door and back to an office where he pointed at a visitor's chair, inviting Griffin to sit.

"I was hoping to speak to the sheriff," Griffin said. "Is he here?"

"Not at the moment. And I've only got a few minutes before I have to leave, too." Ames sat down and leaned back, folding his hands behind his head.

"I see." Griffin unzipped his portfolio, removed a copy of the poster with the composite drawing, and passed it over. "We have reason to believe this individual may be in your county at the moment. We're concerned he may have targeted a female police officer from Maryland who's here to get married this weekend."

Ames took the poster and looked it over. "The Rainy Day Killer. Glendale, Maryland. And you think this person may have traveled from there all the way over here to chase someone. That it?"

"Yeah, that's it."

Ames dropped the poster on his desk. "Here's something I don't understand. You say you're from Quantico. Why am I hearing about this from you instead of the Roanoke office?"

"Several reasons. One, as an analyst in the BAU, I've been working this case for, oh, about three years now, when he showed up in Kentucky to rape and kill a young woman after kidnapping her right off her own doorstep. I've followed him to Pennsylvania, West Virginia, Maryland, and now here. Two, the potential victim I mentioned is one of the investigating detectives from Maryland, and I happen to be an invited guest at her wedding. Three, this guy's the target of a fugitive pursuit task force in Maryland, which still believes he's back there, and I think it might be a good idea if an update on his current whereabouts came from your office instead of from me. Your sheriff will probably want to call the Roanoke Bureau office to get the ball rolling. I could call them, but I don't have investigative responsibility. Plus, I'm trying to extend you a professional courtesy, since this is your jurisdiction."

Ames thought about it for a moment. He picked up the poster, read it again, and put it back down. "So, what's your 'reason to believe' he might have followed this detective here instead of running anywhere else in the known universe, seeing as he's got this task force climbing all over his back?"

"He threatened to make her his next victim. Part of his post-crime behavior is to establish contact with the lead investigator. In this case, Lieutenant Hank Donaghue of the GPD."

"Mentioned right here," Ames said, tapping the poster with his index finger.

"That's correct. In his last communication with Donaghue, he stated that Detective Karen Stainer or one other police officer would be his next victim. He made it clear to Donaghue he knew Stainer was coming here to get married and was looking forward to a road trip. We believe he's going to try to make good on his boast."

"So you're saying this Detective Karen Stainer's the next victim, and she's getting married. Who's she marrying?"

"Sandy Alexander. His family lives—"

"Up on Pleasant Mountain Road, yeah. I know them. Sandy was a year ahead of me in high school. I heard he was a Feeb. How come I'm not talking to him about this?"

"Because he's getting married, for crying out loud. Donaghue and I haven't had a chance to bring him up to date. We felt it was a higher priority to get you boys on the job."

"That was your 'expert analysis' of the situation, was it?"

"Yes, dammit, it was. Look, can we put aside the games for a minute and focus? You may be enjoying yourself putting down the stuffed-shirt federal agent, but women are dying very horrible deaths because of this guy, and the odds are extremely high he's just come into your jurisdiction for his next kill. You need to circulate that poster, or get out one of your own with that guy's face on it, this afternoon. Without delay. The wedding's scheduled for tomorrow and Stainer will be leaving tomorrow night, so if this guy's planning to kidnap, rape, and murder her here, which we strongly believe he is, it's going to happen within the next twenty-four to thirty hours. That doesn't give you a lot of time. Every deputy needs this face burned into his brain right away because I guarantee you he's here, right now, possibly in town, having a cup of coffee in one of your restaurants or scouting out abandoned buildings in the area or buying new stuff for his kit. His time's short, so he's going to keep it simple, which means if you get busy you might catch him in a mistake and nail his sorry ass before Stainer or someone else gets hurt. Does that maybe sound like a plan to you?"

During this speech Ames had listened attentively, without expression. As Griffin angrily closed the zipper on his portfolio, the chief deputy shrugged. "I'll talk to the sheriff about it."

"Wonderful. When might that happy event take place?"

Ames glanced at his watch. "In about ten minutes. He's over at the high school right now, giving a talk to the kids on the baseball team. I'm heading there now to spell him off. I'll let him know about it. Where can you be reached?"

Griffin reached into his pocket and tossed a business card on the desk. "My cell number's there. I'm checked in at the Day's Rest, just down the street. He needs to call me right away so we can get this thing in motion."

Ames stood up, grabbed his hat from a hook, and clapped it on his head. "We'll be in touch."

As Griffin stood up, Ames strode out of the office, leaving him behind. The deputy who'd earlier eyeballed him over the counter stepped into the doorway and gestured.

"This way, sir."

Griffin shook his head. "Delighted, I'm sure."

39

That evening, the screen porch just off the ranch house dining room was taken over by the Stainer family. Darryl, who seemed to feel the cold more than the others, had built a fire in the fireplace, the temperature having dropped down to 60 degrees Fahrenheit after the sun disappeared behind Pleasant Mountain. Karen sat in another of Lane's expensive wrought-iron patio chairs, her feet up on a matching foot rest, while Bradley, as the youngest Stainer present, was elected to serve drinks to everyone. Delbert was stretched out on a three-cushion lounger, his eyes closed, but when Brad held out to him a Jack Daniels and cola, his hand found and gripped the glass firmly.

"Del could be in a coma," Brad remarked to Karen, "and still hook onto that JD and C."

"He'd get it intravenously," joked Rebecca, Darryl's wife, who was sitting at the round patio table.

Beatrice Roberts, Del's girlfriend, laughed. It was a low, throaty sound that operated on a frequency felt by men in the marrow of their bones. A double for Diana Ross in her prime, she was a night club singer in Houston often compared by the local media to Etta James in terms of vocal style. She and Del had lived together for twelve years now. Karen liked her.

Del swung around on the lounger and sat up, making room for Darryl, who dropped down beside him. "You make me sound like a lush." He sampled his drink, then held it up. "A toast. To our little baby sister, who's all grown up. Here's to you, Little Kay."

They all drank solemnly.

"You guys are the best," Karen said.

"We know." Brad sat down at the table across from Rebecca and Beatrice. "Did you get a tour of the barn?"

"I peeked in through the door. It looks amazing. But it's so damned big!"

"Seating for a hundred and twenty. That's not so bad, is it?"

"Two hundred and forty fucking eyeballs staring straight at me. Jesus Christ."

"You'll be fine, darlin'," Brad soothed. "Just pretend we're all naked."

"Please," Del complained, rubbing his forehead. "I've got a migraine already. Don't make it worse by forcing me to picture you naked."

"What're you talking about? You saw me naked all the time when we were kids."

"Yeah, before puberty, pal. Before you crossed the *ne plus ultra*. Don't take me down that road, man."

Brad laughed.

"I can't wait to see your wedding dress," Beatrice said to Karen.

"It's nice. It really is. I paid for it myself, Bea. Twelve hundred bucks, and I don't regret a single dime."

"Who would've thought?" Brad said. "My big sister, a blushing bride."

"Leave her alone," Beatrice said, pretending to be stern. "I think it's wonderful. They're a perfect couple."

"Wait a minute," Brad said. "How can you afford a twelve-hundred-dollar dress on a cop's salary? Are you on the take?"

"Fuck off, Brad," Karen laughed. "You just wish you could try it on. You want me to leave it in your room after, so you can see what you look like in it?"

Everyone laughed.

"For your information, I do *not* wear women's clothing. Ever. Just so you know."

Karen winked at him, her face softening. Two years younger, Brad was the brother she'd always looked after in school, a kid who'd always been picked on for his passive manner, a brother for whom she'd often fought other boys, breaking one kid's nose when he caught Brad in the schoolyard and started to whale away on him. The kid was fifteen and Karen only twelve, but she'd dropped him with a single punch.

Blond like Karen and smaller than Darryl or Del, Brad had always been the different one, the one not interested in cars or guns or law enforcement or living up to their father's expectations. He was his own man and lived his life on his own terms, and Karen loved him for it.

"You didn't tell me how the rehearsal went," Beatrice said, leaning over to pat Del on the knee.

As Del ran a hand through his long, wavy black hair, Karen noticed that it was starting to show some gray. Uncombed and parted in the middle, hanging in his eyes and touching his shoulders, it gave him the look of an aging rock musician or college professor, but the long-fingered hands with their small cuts, rapped knuckles, and chronic dryness betrayed his actual profession.

"It was a happening, baby," Del said. "I thought I'd joined the army. First we all had to line up, and in the right order, no foolin'. Darryl thought we should be tallest to shortest, but that'd put Karen closest to the door and we don't want her running off on us."

"Darryl!" Rebecca laughed at her husband. "You didn't."

Quiet as always, Darryl gave her a shy smile.

"After that," Del went on, "we had to practice the *re*-cessional and the *pro*-cessional, up and down, back and forth, by the numbers. I thought I'd joined the Foreign Legion by mistake."

"Delbert, you do exaggerate,' Rebecca said.

"So we're doing the processional, and I'm up at the front with Hank, Sandy, and the minister. They start the music, and the two bridesmaids start coming down the aisle, that blonde chick—"

"Louise, the minister's daughter," Karen supplied.

"Right, and your friend—"

"Molly."

"Molly. She comes down next, and right after her Brenda, Sandy's sister."

"She's the matron of honor, isn't she?" Beatrice asked.

"You got it. So then Darryl and Karen start down, and out of nowhere Molly breaks into these Michael Jackson dance moves and you"—he pointed at Karen—"start laughing, and I'm breaking up, and the minister's giving me a dirty look, but all I can see is the look on poor Mrs. Alexander's face, like, 'who *are* these people and what planet did they beam down from?' Poor woman."

"She's having a hard time with Molly's piercings and tattoos as it is," Karen said. "I told her Molly's a really outstanding parole officer, one of the best, but it's not really getting through. All she can see is the lifestyle stuff."

"I thought she was going to have a stroke," Darryl said.

"I thought *I* was going to have a hernia." Del drained the last of his drink and waggled his glass at Brad, who got up and took it from him. "Anyway, baby, it was all downhill from there."

"You have to be nice to these people," Beatrice said. "They're not used to people like us."

"What, gay people?" Brad said, coming back with Del's drink and taking Karen's glass for a refill.

"Gay people," Beatrice said, "lesbian people, black people, hard-ass cop people. We're different from them. It's not easy."

"You're right, baby," Del said. "We're like the circus coming to town. They've got these plastic smiles on their faces, like they're trying real hard to like us and it ain't working."

"They're okay," Karen said. "Anyway, Lane really likes you, Brad. She went on and on about the great job you did on the barn. I heard James made it up here, by the way. I absolutely love his barbecue."

"Yeah, he drove up with me. I had to help him load all his damned coolers of meat into the van."

"You know it's going to be worth it."

"Damned right. Lane wants Texas barbecue, she's getting Texas barbecue."

They fell quiet for a moment, lost in their own thoughts. Karen listened to the sound of crickets and frogs in the darkness beyond the window screens, feeling better about things now that she was spending a little time with her brothers. Having them with her made the Alexanders, and all the other strangers who'd be watching her tomorrow like a bug in a jar, that much easier to face.

She looked at Darryl and caught him exchanging a shy smile with his wife. Hard to believe he was now forty-four years old and a father of three teenaged kids. She hadn't gone back to Texas over the Christmas holidays because she'd been working, and when she thought about it, she realized it had been at least a year and a half since she'd seen any of them. She saw the gray in Darryl's dark, slicked-back hair, the lines on his handsome face, the few extra pounds beneath his black polo shirt as he lifted his glass to his mouth, and her heart went out to him.

"Darryl, I swear you look more like Daddy every day," she blurted.

Darryl swallowed and looked down, nodding.

"He does, doesn't he?" Del said. "Me, I look like somebody's pet possum, but isn't he just the spitting image of Trooper Bobby Stainer?"

"One more of these," Brad said, holding up his beer, "and I'll be asking him to read me my bedtime story."

"Sometimes," Darryl said, smiling at Karen, "when I get up in the morning, I'm scared to look into the mirror in case I see him instead of me."

"You've done him proud, Darryl," Del said fervently. "Don't you ever think otherwise. You made lieutenant and took over the motorcycle troop, and you got that award for bravery. You know he's looking down on you and glowing with pride, man. You've gone twice as far already as he ever did, and that's a fact."

"You're going to make his head swell," Rebecca said.

Rain began to patter softly on the other side of the dark window screens.

"So how's she doing?" Karen finally asked, having put off the question for long enough.

"She's all right," Darryl said. As the oldest, he'd accepted the responsibility of holding their mother's power of attorney, and he visited her twice a month at the institution where she was kept in Dallas. "She's doing okay."

"You told her about it? About the wedding?"

Darryl nodded. "She was pleased, I think. There was a moment there. She looked at me and focused on what I was saying. It didn't last long, but it was there."

"Good," Karen said. "That's nice."

"Next time you're down," Rebecca said, "you should come visit her with us. She'd like that. She's very quiet, Karen. Her health's good and her behavior's just fine. We talked to her psychiatrist—when was that, hon?"

"January," Darryl said.

"January. He said her episodes are getting a lot less bad than they used to be. They like the meds they've got her on now. They seem to keep her, you know, okay without knocking her right out. He said they've come a long way with the drugs from how it used to be."

"How it used to be was pretty damned ugly," Del said.

Karen nodded.

"We had a real good talk with him," Rebecca went on. "Darryl's been a little worried about the kids, now they're into puberty and all, but he told us the chances are real good nothing bad'll happen. He gave us a copy of this article that said there's only a 5 percent chance that a grandchild of a person with schizophrenia will get it themselves. That's if only one grandparent had it and neither parent does."

"I thought it was a lot higher than that," Karen said.

"No, that's what the doctor said. Darryl was pretty relieved. Weren't you, hon?"

"Yes," Darryl said. "It was good news."

"That's good," Karen said, not convinced.

Rebecca glanced at Darryl and shut her mouth.

Del, however, was smiling as he stared at what was left of his drink. "Remember that little trip we all took down to Galveston? When was that, eighty-four?"

"Nineteen eighty-five," Darryl said.

Del nodded. "I think I was fourteen. Poor Daddy, he never had any fun in life, but that summer he was bound and determined we'd go on a little vacation."

"I remember," Karen said. She'd been ten years old at the time.

"He packed up the car," Del went on, shifting on the lounger to tell the story to Beatrice, "and drove us all the way down there. Got a cheap motel room for the night, rented a boat, and took us out fishing. Nobody caught a damn thing. Brad and Karen spent the whole time fighting about whether we should keep the fish or throw them back."

"I don't remember," Brad said.

"You would've only been eight," Del said, draining his glass. He winked at Beatrice. "He wanted to keep them, and Little Kay wanted to throw them back. Anyway, it was a moot point since we didn't catch anything. After a while, Daddy just reeled in his line and brought us back to the marina. Darryl took off to go girl-watching on the beach, and Daddy and I threw a football around in the motel parking lot."

Karen nodded. She'd spent the time on the beach as well, looking for seashells. She held up her glass and Brad, taking the hint, got up to refill it for her.

"I can still remember the smell of the Gulf," she said. "Sometimes when I'm down on the boardwalk and I smell the Chesapeake, I think of that day."

"Yeah." Del leaned back, massaging his temples.

"It sounds nice," Beatrice said.

"Mama spent the whole night crying," Del said. "We were all sacked out on the floor, me, Darryl, Brad, and Jimmy Bob, and Karen was in the armchair, but I don't think any of us slept. We just lay there staring at the ceiling all night, listening to Daddy's voice trying to make her feel better, and her crying. Not loud, not carrying on, just quiet crying. She never stopped, the whole night. The next morning he packed the car up and we went back home to Fort Worth. So much for his weekend holiday."

As Brad handed her glass to her, Karen hastily brushed away a tear, hoping he hadn't noticed.

"Thing was," Del went on, "we were all helping Daddy put the stuff in the car, and nobody was keeping track of her. When we were ready to go, we looked around and she was nowhere in sight."

"You found her," Darryl said.

"I did." He looked up at Brad, who was holding out his hand. "Surely, son, you are a mind reader." He gave him his empty glass.

"What happened?" Beatrice asked. "Where was she?"

"We looked all over the place. Daddy checked the other motel rooms, to see if she'd gone into one that was unlocked. Darryl walked up the road in case she'd started hitch-hiking, which she sometimes did. I went down to the beach, and that's where she was. I found her swimming a few yards offshore, in all her clothes, just breast-stroking along without a care in the world."

"My goodness." Beatrice patted his knee.

"I'll never forget the look on her face, Bea. I kept calling out to her, 'Mama, you gotta come in now. Mama, Daddy wants to leave.' She just kept swimming along. So I waded out to get her. By the time I reached her, I realized the water was only just up to my waist. I thought it was deeper. I reached out and caught hold of her, and she stopped swimming. She stood up in the water and looked at me with this incredibly peaceful look on her face and said, 'Delbert, it's just so lovely. It's all so very lovely.' I'd never seen her look so serene. Before or since."

They listened to the rain, which was now falling much harder.

It was Darryl, though, Karen remembered, who'd gone with their father that day when she was finally institutionalized for good. Bobby had packed a small suitcase for her with a few things, some clothing, photographs, and a few keepsakes, and Darryl carried it as they came downstairs that morning, the three of them. There'd been a lot of fighting the night before, as Mary Beth had been terribly upset about what lay ahead of her—a sudden, last-minute shift from her normal apathy—but in the morning calmness had thankfully returned. Karen watched from the front hallway as they came downstairs, her father in the lead, Mary Beth following docilely, and Darryl bringing up the rear, carrying the suitcase.

Her father walked past her, opened the front door, and led the way out to the car, which was waiting in the driveway with the engine running. His face was expressionless, a cop's face, impassive, but she'd seen the pain in his eyes as he avoided her stare.

Her mother, wearing her best blouse and ankle-length skirt, also passed Karen without looking at her, then hesitated at the door. She turned back.

"You look pretty today," she said.

Then she was gone.

At the bottom of the stairs, Darryl shifted the suitcase from one hand to the other. "What are we going to do, Kay?"

Karen remembered how angry the question had made her. "What we've always done, Darryl. Do it all ourselves. That's what we're gonna do."

It was painful to remember how Mary Beth had been abused, mentally and physically, in that first hospital before Bobby had been able to move her to the place where she lived now. If Bobby felt guilty for having signed the papers and taken her there on that morning, closing a door behind them that could never be reopened, Karen felt equally guilty for having been so angry at her mother, for having, in that moment, not given a damn what happened to Mary Beth as long as all the turmoil and heartache ended, right then and there.

She knew now, in retrospect, that it never ended.

After a long silence, Rebecca stood up and walked over to the bar to get herself another beer from the mini-fridge. "It's a good job you guys decided not to have the ceremony outside in the gazebo. It's raining pretty hard out there right now."

"Yeah," Karen said. "I'd look like a drowned rat."

"I went over to see Jimmy Bob," Darryl said.

"Oh, God," Brad said, sitting down again with a fresh bottle of beer.

Del frowned, rubbing the back of his head.

Karen said nothing, wiping her eyes with a tissue.

"He's all right," Darryl soldiered on. "As good as you could expect."

Jimmy Bob, the youngest of the Stainer children, was serving a life sentence in a maximum-security prison in Abilene for armed robbery. Eleven years ago, when he was twenty-four, he and two buddies robbed a savings and loan in Lubbock, during which act of incredible stupidity one of the others shot a guard. The man survived, but remained paralyzed from the waist down.

"He's taking a welding course."

"Good for him," Del said. "As long as he doesn't try to cut his way out of there, he can do whatever the fuck he wants."

"I say a prayer for him every night," Darryl said. "I know how lame that sounds, but Daddy asked me to, just before he died. I promised him I would, so I do."

"Darryl," Brad said, "if God listens to anyone on this damned planet, he listens to you. But he isn't going to listen to a single word about Jimmy Bob. Not a single goddamned word."

"That makes two of us," Karen said. "Can we change the fucking subject?"

"Good idea," Del said. "How's your Firebird driving, Little Kay?"

"Just lovely," Karen said. "I'm taking real good care of it, trust me."

"Oh, I do. You didn't go snooping around behind the guest house, did you?"

"No, of course not. I haven't been down there."

"Good. I've got your wedding present stashed back there, so stay away."

"Oh, Del. Another car?"

"What else would it be?" Beatrice laughed. "This man's got a one-track mind."

"Now you know, baby, that ain't true." Del winked at her, then pointed at Karen with his glass. "Sandy already saw it, so it's too late to ask for something else. Anyway, when you see it, it's going to abso-fuckinlutely knock you out. You'll see."

"What is it?"

Del shook his head. "Tomorrow. Darryl's driving you to the church in it. Right, big boy?"

"You bet," Darryl said. "If it starts."

"If it starts?" Del sputtered. "If it *starts*? Do you know how many hours I slaved over that engine? Just the starter motor itself, which had to be replaced, mind you, was a total bitch. Made me late on two other restoration jobs. Man, I had to take off the engine mounts, jack up the engine, take off the carb and the tranny linkages *and* both exhaust manifolds. Not an easy job, kids. But what a sweet engine. It's the optional 430 V-8, the bigger one, cranks out 350 HPs at 4400 RPMs, and goes from zero to sixty in nine-point-nine seconds. Nine-point-nine seconds!"

"Nobody knows what all that means, hon," Beatrice said.

Del nodded at Karen. "She does. Don't you, Little Kay?"

"Are we talking about a T-bird, Del? What year? A '59?"

"I'm not saying," Del said. "It's a surprise."

"Not any more," Brad said. "Blabbermouth."

"What color? Black? Red?"

"You just never mind."

"Convertible?"

"Never mind."

Brad stood up. "Come on, Karen, let's go find a flashlight and check it out."

"Don't you dare!" Del held out his hand, palm down. "It's a surprise. She'll see it tomorrow."

"Okay, Del," Karen said, letting him off the hook. "I'll wait."

"You're gonna love it," he grinned at her. "You're gonna be *so* happy."

40

The next morning, Karen broke another of Lane's little rules by meeting with her husband-to-be on their wedding day. Earlier, the two women had trooped into town for their hair and nail appointments, and as they pulled into the long driveway at the Alexander ranch at fifteen minutes before noon, freshly coiffed and manicured, Karen was bravely trying to keep up her end of the conversation, which had gravitated to Lane's ongoing interest in fashion. She had a mental list of suggestions she wanted to make to Karen for improving her wardrobe and look, and she was only halfway through it when they reached the ranch. With a sense of relief, Karen saw that Sandy was waiting for them at the front door of the house. One look at the expression on his face, however, told her something was wrong.

"Sandy, what are you doing?" Lane demanded as she got out of the car. "Don't you know it's bad luck for the groom to see the bride before the ceremony?"

"I thought that was just the wedding dress," Sandy replied lightly, gesturing with his head that Karen should step aside so he could speak with her.

"Nonsense, dear. The groom shouldn't see the bride at all until she and her escort walk down the aisle."

"Karen and I need to talk, Mom. Business."

Lane stopped in the doorway and turned around to look at him. "Business? What kind of business could you possibly have today, of all days?"

"Police business, Mom. It'll only take a minute."

"I see." Lane looked at Karen. "Please remember that Mary Lou will be here at noon to do our makeup. She can start with me, but you mustn't be late."

"Okey doke." She watched Lane sail off into the house and turned to Sandy. "What's up?"

"Not here. We're in the barn."

"We?"

The caterer's staff had begun setting up the tables inside the barn for lunch for the groom and his party, but at a word from Hank, they quietly slipped outside to give them privacy. Karen looked around at Ed Griffin, Darryl, and Marie-Louise Roubidoux.

"What the hell's going on?" Karen asked.

"I got a call on my cell an hour ago," Hank said. "From him."

In her defense, Karen had been struggling for several days to make the mental transition from law enforcement officer to bride-to-be. It was the morning of her wedding, and she'd just about convinced herself that today, for one day, she could be someone normal, someone who did something normal such as marry the man she loved, like any other normal, ordinary woman. The fact that it took her a moment, then, to realize what Hank was talking about was understandable.

"He's here," Hank went on, when he saw in her eyes that the penny had dropped. "He said he was watching you, in town. Saw you go into May's Salon with Lane and took photos of you through the front window." Hank held out his phone. "He sent me one."

Karen took the phone and looked at a shot of herself, taken through the big picture window of the beauty salon, smiling at someone. As though she had a right to smile and laugh and be happy.

"The fucking goddamned son of a bitch. I'll kill him."

"I notified the SAC in Richmond," Roubidoux said, "and spoke to Special Agent Hudson Barnett in the Roanoke office. He's on his way, and he'll coordinate with Sheriff Crull. We'll get people at the church, in town, and here at the ranch. Everyone's on high alert. He won't bother you, Karen. If he tries, we'll get him."

"Let him through," Karen said, handing back Hank's phone.

"I don't think—" Hank began.

"No, I'm serious. Let him through. Let him try. I swear to God, I'll take that smug, vicious, lowlife piece of shit—"

"Karen," Sandy said quietly, "let them handle it. Take a step back."

"I'm not going to take a step back, Sandy. I'm going to give that fucking bastard a taste of his own fucking medicine."

"Take a step *back*, Karen," Sandy repeated. "Marie-Louise just said the Roanoke office is sending an agent. He and the sheriff's office will take care of it. That's what they're paid to do. You and I are going to be busy, remember? With something we've planned for a long time. Let these other people do their thing so we can do ours. Okay?"

"All I'm saying is, if I get the shot, I'm taking it."

"Please, Karen?"

"If I get the shot, I'm *taking* it."

Sandy stared at her for a long moment, then looked at Darryl and shook his head. "Was she always this intense?"

"Oh yeah," Darryl said.

"The sheriff got a poster out with the composite," Griffin said, "although it took some convincing. It seems," he looked at Sandy, "he doesn't like your father very much."

"I'm aware," Sandy said.

"It's circulating around town as we speak," Griffin went on, "and his deputies have a copy with them on their patrols. If he makes any mistakes at all, they'll grab him and this will all blow over like a puff of smoke from a bad cigar. You two need to concentrate on your families and friends. Do you think you can do that?"

Karen fixed him with a laser-beam stare. "Sure enough. And if I get the shot, I'm taking it."

"We just thought you should be aware, Karen," Hank said. "That's all."

"I understand."

"Don't let it spoil the day."

She bared her teeth at him, but said nothing. She picked up a linen napkin from the table next to her and wadded it into a tight ball.

"Do you think this guy's serious enough to try something?" Darryl asked Griffin.

The analyst shrugged. "We can't be 100 percent certain, but why take a chance on being wrong? You saw the weather. Overcast sky, those scudding, low-hanging clouds making it all smoky and misty, the intermittent drizzle. It's perfect for him."

"Maybe it's a bluff," Roubidoux said. "Just trying to get under everyone's skin. Maybe tomorrow he'll be in Kentucky or Tennessee."

"We have to be sure."

"Of course. I agree. I just don't think he'll be able to get close. I think it's all talk. Playing games. Then he'll move on."

"I hope you're right," Griffin said.

"I don't," Karen said. "I hope he shows."

"Go," Sandy said, "back to the house. Lane will never shut up if you keep the makeup girl waiting."

"Like hell. I want a piece of this." She fired the wadded napkin across the barn.

"Not a chance. Go get your makeup done with Lane. Come on, Karen. Please?"

"While you get to stay out here? How's that fair? It's me he wants. I should be the one taking point."

"Shut up and beat it."

As they watched her storm out of the barn, Roubidoux folded her arms and rocked back on a heel. "Feisty girl."

Sandy sighed. "She is that."

"I'll tell you one thing," Roubidoux said, "from where I'm standing, I kind of hope she gets the shot. The son of a bitch would never know what hit him. But don't quote me on that. I'll deny the words ever came out of my mouth."

Sandy's eyes creased at the corners, but he merely shrugged.

41

While Sandy had lunch in the barn with his father, Hank, Horvath, and Darryl, Karen was stuck in the main dining room of the ranch house with Lane and the other women, forced to smile politely and grind her teeth while listening to prattle about flowers, booze, and chocolate.

What made it worse, the photographer had shown up, much to Lane's delight, and was snapping pictures of them forking salad into their mouths and nipping at the single glass of white wine Lane had begrudgingly allowed them to have with the meal. He was a sharp-eyed, rat-faced twerp with an effete, phony-looking Vandyke beard and an annoying habit of giving them directions on how to pose by pointing without speaking. Karen watched grumpily as he gestured to Molly, seated on Lane's left, to lean over so that he could shoot the two of them together. Lane smiled grimly and Molly, thank God, gave the creep a decent smile to get it over with.

He snapped a couple of shots of Karen, then lowered his camera, put a hand on his hip, and raised an eyebrow at her.

"Who the hell *is* this guy?" Karen demanded of Lane.

"He comes highly recommended," Lane replied. "He has a studio in Roanoke."

"Do you know him? Have you met him before?"

"No, but his reputation's wonderful."

Karen eyed him. "Did anybody check your ID coming in here, pal?"

In response, the photographer put his little finger in the corner of his mouth, pulled it up to simulate a smile, and raised the camera, squeezing off several more shots.

"What is this guy," Karen groused, "a fucking mute?"

Molly choked, spraying a mouthful of wine across her salad.

"Karen!" Lane stared, horrified. "I'm sorry," she said, turning to Louise Tench, the minister's daughter. "She's under so much pressure."

Rebecca and Beatrice, whom Lane had also invited to the lunch, knew better. They looked at each other and hid smiles beneath their napkins.

At that moment, one of those chance interactions took place that might pass unnoticed by someone not sensitive to such things but that acted as a trigger for Karen. Turning away from her, the photographer lowered his camera, looked at her, and fluttered his eyelids in contempt.

In an instant, Karen was out of her seat and behind him. She grabbed his right wrist and shook it violently, sending the camera bouncing across the table onto Molly's plate. She twisted his right hand behind his back and forced him over the table, then grabbed his left wrist and doubled it back over the right one.

"Don't move, asshole," she hissed in his ear, removing a plastic locking strap from the pocket of her blazer and securing his wrists tightly behind his back.

Lane was on her feet, shrieking. Louise Tench, the minister's daughter, had dropped from her chair and rolled under the table. Rebecca covered her mouth with her hand, staring. Beatrice watched, eyes wide, mouth open, while Molly calmly picked the camera out of her salad and held it aloft with her thumb and index finger, pinkie extended, while salad dressing dripped from the lens.

"Are you insane?" the photographer shouted, suddenly finding his voice. "What do you think you're doing? You're hurting me!"

"Let's see what you got, pal." Karen ran her left hand over his body while pressing her right hand into the small of his back to hold him down. "Let's see now, keys," she threw them on the table, "gum, change," on the table, "ah-ha, wallet." She fished it out of his pocket and straightened, pressing her knee against his buttock to hold him in place while she opened the wallet.

"Thought you could waltz right in, huh?" Karen pulled out a credit card. "Nelson P. Wister. How the hell'd you come up with that one?"

"It's my name! I was born with it, you idiot!"

"Sure you were." She pulled out a Virginia driver's license with his photo on it. It was in the name of Nelson P. Wister, with a Roanoke address. She looked at a Roanoke public library card with his name on it, a Wister Photography business card, an AAA card with his name on it, a Roanoke Quik Lube courtesy card with his name and three holes punched out of it, and a Virginia Wedding Photojournalist Association membership card with his name on it. When she found the condom in a side pocket, she reluctantly accepted the fact that she'd made a mistake.

She picked up the knife from beside Louise Tench's plate and slit the locking strap, freeing Nelson P. Wister's wrists. She pulled him up by the shirt collar and brushed at pieces of lettuce clinging to the front of his shirt.

"Sorry, pal. Honest mistake."

"Mistake? Are you insane? I'll sue your ass! You idiot!"

"Calm down. I'm a police detective. We're looking for a homicide suspect. You came off the wrong way, pal."

"Detective? Homicide? I'll sue your department's ass, too. My camera!" He pushed away from Karen and hurried around the table to grab his camera from Molly. "It's ruined. How am I supposed to work now?"

"Come on, buddy," Molly said. "You've got at least two others in your bag over there. Use one of them."

"Lane," Karen said, "reason with him."

Lane, who had thankfully stopped shouting, was staring at Karen with her hands pressed to her cheeks. "What just happened? What did you just do?"

"Look, I'm real sorry, Lane. I really am. Stuff's going on, and I kind of blew my top. I didn't mean to. Can we just say sorry and move along?"

"I'm out of here," Wister said, grabbing his bag from the corner of the room and shoving the ruined camera into it. "I'm gone."

"Please," Lane said. "Please don't leave."

"Oh, I'm leaving, all right."

"Nelson," Karen said, stepping toward him. "Look, I'm real sorry. I apologize. I'll make it up to you."

"You certainly will. In court."

"No no, you meathead. I can make it up to you. Wait a sec." She grabbed her handbag from under the table, making eye contact with Louise Tench while she was down there and motioning for her to come back out, and pulled out a business card from her wallet.

"This is the card of a real important magazine editor," Karen said, extending the card. "Donata Parker? *Mid-Atlantic Monthly*? She told me to give it to you. She said she's interested in seeing your work from the wedding and maybe would use a couple shots if they're any good. Are you any good?"

"You've got to be kidding me." Wister looked at Lane. "Is she kidding me?"

"Please listen to her," Lane begged. "She's an important police detective from Maryland. If she says this woman's a friend, then she's a friend. Please. Please stay."

Wister hesitated, then glared at Karen and pointed at the table. "Don't come any closer. Put it down."

Karen put the business card down on the table and moved back a step.

Wister picked it up and looked it over.

"The magazine sells all over the damned place," Karen said. "Baltimore, D.C., Philadelphia, Raleigh-Durham. Great exposure for you, huh?"

"This is bullshit," Wister said, dubiously. "You're bullshitting me."

"No, I'm not. I had drinks with her a couple weeks ago, her and Brooke Wilson, a city councilor. Donata gave me the card and told me to make sure to give it to you. She's interested."

"Please say you'll stay," Lane said. "I'll replace your camera and make sure to add a bonus to your payment."

"I'll replace the camera, Lane," Karen said.

"If I call her," Wister said, holding up the card between his index and middle fingers, "and I give her your name, she's going to know what the hell I'm talking about?"

"Of course. Call her. Mention my name."

"Oh, I'll mention your name, all right. And she'd better know what I'm talking about."

"Then you'll stay?" Lane asked, hopefully.

Wister slung his bag over his shoulder. "If this is legit," he waggled the card between his fingers, "I'll stick around. In any case, I've got enough shots of lunch, don't you think?"

They watched him stalk out of the dining room on silent, sneakered feet.

Molly grinned at Karen and put a hand to her throat in a choking gesture.

"I need a drink," Karen said. "And not this pissy grape juice shit. Vodka. Straight."

Lane stared at her for a moment, then nodded.

"I'll have one with you," she said, "along with an explanation."

42

The photographer made his call and stuck around. At 1:45 P.M. he pushed his way into Sandy's room and shot him buttoning up his black tuxedo jacket and running a comb through his hair, then followed him downstairs, where he took photographs of him at the front entry with Hank and Del, now also wearing their tuxes. Having heard of Wister's altercation with Karen, they were very careful to be tolerant of his wordless stage directions and overall intrusiveness, while exchanging knowing smirks behind his back.

Bill Alexander came in and announced to everyone that the best man had arrived. Hank followed Sandy and Del outside. The sky was overcast, and low-hanging clouds trailed large, dark streamers through the tops of the trees, but for the moment the drizzle had stopped. Hank was introduced to a tall, skinny redhead in yet another black tuxedo.

"This is John Bolingbroke," Sandy said. "He's not bad, for a journalist."

Hank shook his hand. "You publish the local paper, Sandy said."

"Publish, edit, write the odd feature, take classified ads over the phone, and handle some of the artwork, including photos." Bolingbroke eyed Wister with distaste as he circled around them, squeezing off shots.

"This is Del Stainer, from Houston," Sandy said. "Karen's brother."

"Guilty as charged." Del shook hands. "You guys covering this bash for the paper?"

"Oh yeah." Bolingbroke ran his eyes around the circle. "You're all cops, right? If my reporter asks you questions, please don't give her the 'no comment' thing, okay, just out of habit? Try to feed her some juicy stuff on this guy. There'll be something in it for you later if you do."

"Hey, wait a sec, I'm no cop," Del protested. "Do I look like a cop to you?"

"No, come to think of it," Bolingbroke said, "although you could be undercover."

"When I go undercover, man, it ain't those kind of covers."

"Del does vintage auto restoration," Sandy explained. "If you're nice to him, he might be able to hook you up with that '67 Shelby you always dreamed about."

"I know one," Del said promptly, "but it needs a hell of a lot of work."

"We should talk about it," Bolingbroke said. "Later."

"John and I go way back," Sandy said. "Best buddies in high school. Camera club and the yearbook club, all that stuff. Went to UVA together. He took over the university paper and I was the late-night DJ on the radio. Great times."

"How'd you end up turning into a Feeb, Sandy? I still haven't figured that one out."

"Guess I zigged right when I should have zagged left."

Bolingbroke laughed, but his mind was obviously elsewhere. He turned to the photographer, who was still taking pictures. "Nelson? Nelson? Hello?"

Wister lowered the camera, frowning.

"Can you give us a few minutes? Maybe take someone else's picture inside?"

"He already tried that," Del said. "It didn't go so well."

Wister made a bit of a production out of putting his lens cap on and slinging the camera over his shoulder. Shaking his head, he wandered off across the courtyard toward the barn.

"I got copies of a bulletin on a serial killer from Maryland," Bolingbroke said. "Do you gentlemen know anything about it? Can you tell me what's going on?"

Hank gave him a basic description of the Rainy Day Killer and his activities, and explained in general terms their reasons to believe he'd followed them here from Glendale.

"Are we in some kind of danger?" Bolingbroke asked,

alarmed.

"The way I understand it," Del interjected, "this guy doesn't rape and murder male redheaded news guys, so I think you're relatively safe."

"He's shown absolutely no use of firearms in any of his previous offenses," Sandy said quickly. "The threat is specific to Karen, and it would involve finding her alone and abducting her, using a stun gun and some kind of sedative like midazolam. No one else is in any danger, John. The idea is to carry on with the day as planned and make sure Karen's never alone."

"Can I quote you on this?"

"We'd prefer that you keep things general right now," Hank said, "and concentrate on public awareness of this guy's face and behavior. The details can wait until later."

Bill Alexander stepped outside and joined them. "Hank, according to Lane's timetable, you and Delbert need to leave for the church now. Is everything all right?"

"Everything's fine." Hank looked at Sandy. "Break a leg."

"Thanks."

Hank and Del walked across the courtyard, avoiding the puddles. Hank unlocked the Cadillac with the fob and got in behind the wheel. Del slid into the front passenger seat. As Hank was fastening his seat belt, Del rolled toward Hank and moved the edge of his tuxedo jacket, revealing a handgun in a clip-on holster fastened to his belt on his right hip.

"Just so you know," Del said.

"Jesus, Del. Why didn't you tell me you were carrying?"

"I just did." Del straightened and fastened his seat belt. "Don't worry, I've got the non-resident permit with me, and I stopped into the sheriff's office in town when I got in yesterday to let them know about it. It's all copasetic."

"We need to let them take care of this," Hank said, starting the engine. "We can't go flying off the handle."

"Hey, man, I never fly off the handle. And I carry it whenever I travel. Some of the places I go car hunting, you can't be too careful. Don't worry about it, okay? I may not be a cop, but I'm a Stainer. Daddy taught me how to shoot just like Darryl, Karen, and Brad. Besides, you don't expect me to believe you're not packing too, do you?"

Hank shook his head. Stainers. Sighing, he slowly lifted his right trouser cuff. Strapped to his lower leg, on top of his over-the-calf black silk hose, was the SIG Sauer P-225 he'd purchased on his last visit to Virginia.

"What'd I tell you?" Del said. "Little Kay's going to be covered six ways to Sunday."

At the end of the driveway they passed a parked cruiser. The sheriff's deputy eyeballed them silently. Del gave him a friendly wave without receiving a response.

Hank retraced his route from yesterday, driving back down Pleasant Mountain Road to the t-intersection at the Jackson River Road, then turned south. It was a beautiful drive despite the poor weather, along a two-lane highway with virtually no shoulders on either side. They were hemmed in on the right by overhanging trees and a rising bank that continued all the way up to the top of a sixteen-hundred-foot mountain peak they couldn't see because of the low clouds. On the left, the land sloped down to the river.

"Where'd you go to school, Del?"

"A&M. I'm an Aggie."

Hank nodded, watching the highway. "What'd you take?"

"Mechanical engineering. Paid my way through by working part-time at an auto body shop in Bryan. The real fun, though, was philosophy. Most of my electives were philosophy and logic courses."

"Really!" Hank glanced over at him.

"Yep."

"So where do you stand? Philosophically speaking?"

"I'm a pragmatist, Hank. Only way to fly."

Hank laughed. "I hear that."

Del shifted, watching the trees suddenly close in on either side as the road began to bend. "I'm glad Karen and Sandy are going ahead with it. Married life will be good for her."

"I think so, too." Hank drove around another bend, and they emerged from the trees and crossed a bridge. On the other side, they passed a gas bar and a sign that told them they'd reached Clearwater Falls. Hank started watching for Wallace Street, his right-hand turn that would take them to the Paradise United Methodist Church.

"Is she doing okay?" Del asked, glancing over at him. "Is she happy there, Hank?"

"I think so," Hank said. "She's a hell of a detective."

"She'd have to be. She's a Stainer."

Hank slowed and turned onto Wallace, which was so obscured by trees he'd thought at first it was someone's driveway. "She has a relentlessness and tenacity about her that's unparalleled. I don't know anybody, and I mean anybody, I'd rather walk onto a crime scene with than your sister. When it gets tough, I know she's got my back. Sometimes she takes too many risks, and I worry about that, but I know she can handle herself better than anyone else wearing a badge."

"She told me you're her guardian angel. That true?"

Hank glanced at him. "She said that?"

"Uh huh."

"I suppose it's true."

"The family appreciates it that you're looking out for her."

"Glad to." Hank braked as they reached the parking lot beside the church. "Looks like we're here."

Getting out of the car, Hank glanced at his watch. It was ten minutes past two o'clock. There were a few other vehicles in the parking lot, but no marked cruisers. The guests would soon be arriving, and Hank had expected to see more of a police presence already. They walked across a patch of lawn and found Griffin waiting for them at the top of the stairs leading into the church.

Hank introduced Del. As the two men shook hands, he looked up and down the street. "Where's the sheriff?"

Griffin shook his head. "Otherwise occupied. Was there a car at the ranch house?"

"Yes."

"I'm afraid that's the extent of their contribution. They'll follow her in and park out here. It's the best we could do."

"What about the staties?"

Griffin shook his head. "Marie-Louise is inside, talking to Special Agent Barnett, so at least the Bureau has supplied a body, but that's it, Hank. Crull just isn't taking it seriously. I talked to him this morning, and he said the state police laughed at him. They contacted the task force, and the prevailing wisdom is that the UNSUB's still in

Glendale. They're following up on some quote unquote very hot leads. Looks like we're it."

"You told them about the phone call and the photo?"

"I did. They don't buy it. They think we're wrong and he's still in Maryland."

"Damn it," Hank said.

"We can handle it ourselves," Del said.

Griffin looked at him for a long moment. "I hope so." He glanced back into the church. "I should remind everyone that, according to Virginia Code 18.2-283, it's a Class 4 misdemeanor in this state to carry a gun into a place of worship during a religious ceremony without having good and sufficient reason for doing so."

"I'd say we have a damned good and sufficient reason, wouldn't you?"

"I'm just saying," Griffin said.

Del nodded and walked into the church.

A green car turned into the parking lot. As they watched, an elderly couple got out. As they were smoothing their clothing and shutting their doors, a Grand Cherokee turned into the lot and parked next to them. A white van followed. Hank and Griffin watched a family pile out of the van. A young woman in a long flowered dress began to organize three small children while her husband, obviously uncomfortable in a safari jacket and black jeans, looked on.

"I'm going inside to grab a pew," Griffin said. He patted Hank on the arm. "Looks like it's show time for you, big guy."

Alone in the church doorway, Hank watched the mother fuss with her children, tucking in shirts and finger-combing hair.

A light rain began to fall.

A man got out of the Grand Cherokee and began removing equipment from the back. It was the videographer, Hank realized, a small, nondescript individual in his mid-thirties. He wore a neat blue suit and his head was shaved bald. As he lugged his equipment bag and tripod across the parking lot, he turned around, walking backward, and looked up at the sky. He pulled a gray tweed driving cap from his bag and clapped it over his head, then turned back and chose a spot on the lawn to dump his stuff.

Watching him set up his tripod, obviously intending to film the impending arrival of the bride, Hank hoped that Karen wouldn't attack him, too.

As the family approached the church, walking briskly to get out of the drizzle, the smallest child, a little girl in a bright yellow dress, broke away from her mother, ran up the stairs, and landed in front of Hank with a joyful little hop.

"Hi! I'm Amanda!"

Hank smiled uncomfortably. "Hi, Amanda. Friends of the bride or the groom?"

"I dunno. What's your name?"

"My name's Hank. That's a nice dress you're wearing, Amanda."

"It was Lisa's but it's mine, now. I'm three years old. How old are you?"

One hundred, Hank thought, noting with dismay that the videographer was filming the encounter, holding an umbrella above his head with his free hand to protect his equipment.

Thankfully, Amanda's mother was coming up the stairs with another girl in tow. Lisa, no doubt.

Hank smiled at her, trying to put more conviction into it. "Friends of the bride or the groom?"

43

Meanwhile, at the ranch house, Nelson P. Wister worked his camera from a safe distance as Karen walked out the front door and embraced Darryl, looking very handsome in his black tuxedo.

"You look lovely, Little Kay," he whispered in her ear.

"Speak for yourself. You look like a million bucks."

"Check out the ride." He stepped aside and held out his hand.

Parked in the courtyard, engine idling, ready to convey her to the Paradise United Methodist Church, was a Baltic blue 1959 Ford Thunderbird convertible, as spotless and perfect as the day it rolled off the assembly line, with a flawless blue-and-white interior, power seats, power windows, and automatic transmission. In deference to the inclement weather, the top was up.

"A Square Bird," she said, staring. "He actually did it. He got me a Square Bird."

"He did," Darryl agreed. "Let's go get you married, darlin'."

In the middle of a convoy that included Lane and Bill Alexander, a collection of Sandy's aunts and uncles, Molly Archer, Nelson P. Wister in his white van, and the sheriff's office cruiser bringing up the rear, Darryl and Karen made the drive down Jackson River Road, windshield wipers beating rhythmically.

"I'm very proud of you," Darryl said.

"Thanks."

As they crossed the bridge over the river, Karen cleared her throat. "I'm not going to have kids, Darryl."

He stared out the windshield, guiding the Square Bird around the bend past the Petticoat Junction gas bar. "I understand."

"I'm sorry. You probably wanted nieces and nephews to play with and buy presents for and all that stuff."

Darryl shook his head. "Rebecca's got nieces and nephews. They're more than enough. Little monsters."

"I know her psychiatrist said your kids should be safe, and I'm so glad to hear that, Darryl. You have no idea. But I'm still scared. Maybe the odds are worse for daughters of schizophrenics or something, I don't know. I just can't do it. I'm sorry."

He frowned over at her. "You don't owe nobody nothing. Understand? You paid your dues after she went away, trying to be a mother to Bradley and Jimmy Bob. You did your best. For God's sake, Kay, live your own life. Be your own woman. Don't say you're sorry, ever again."

"Aye-firmative." She gave him a crooked smile, trying to mean it.

"That's better."

At the church, she fretted in the passenger seat as Darryl followed his instructions from Lane, waiting until everyone else had parked and entered the church before rolling over to the spot closest to the entrance that had been left vacant for him.

Over his shoulder he saw the sheriff's office cruiser pull up to the curb.

He shut off the engine. "You okay?"

"Let's do this thing." She watched him get out, walk around the front of the car, and open the passenger door for her.

She slid out and took a moment to collect herself. She had her bouquet of flowers. Her gown was on properly, and zipped all the way up in back. Her shoes fit. She'd turned her cell phone over to Lane just before leaving the ranch, as promised. She'd covered off the something old, new, borrowed, and blue thing with the old Thunderbird, a pearl necklace borrowed from Lane, a blue garter on her left thigh and, most importantly, the new SIG Sauer P-290 on her right ankle under her gown. She knew where she was supposed to stand and what she was supposed to say.

She pictured Sandy's face, smiling at her, and confirmed for the millionth time that she loved him completely and had made the right decision. She'd gotten past the incident with the photographer, who was now snapping shots of her from the lawn next to the videographer, who looked like another insufferable creep.

Darryl was right here, holding out his arm, a perfect, incredible stand-in for her father who was watching, hopefully, from somewhere peaceful as she went ahead and did this thing she thought she'd never, in a million years, do.

She slipped her hand through his arm and let him guide her across the lawn, up the stairs past the lenses, and through the doors into the Paradise United Methodist Church.

44

The ceremony, Hank thought, had gone very well. The church was nearly filled to capacity, a testament to the reach of the Alexanders, who seemed to have invited most of the town. He and Del had initially followed Lane's instructions to the letter, asking each arrival if they were friends of the bride or the groom. Before long, however, the groom's side of the church was packed and the bride's side was a yawning expanse of empty pews, so they abandoned her insistence on tradition and filled up the other side with the latecomers.

He and Del paid close attention to unaccompanied men, of which there were ultimately three. Only one, however, was of the approximate age and body type of the Rainy Day Killer. Hank kept an eye on him during the ceremony. The man sat quietly, head up, singing when everyone else sang and praying when everyone else prayed, maintaining an alert, interested expression throughout.

Hank was astonished at how beautiful Karen looked in her wedding gown, clutching her bouquet with a shell-shocked expression as Darryl escorted her down the aisle. The contrast between this woman and the hard-assed, foul-mouthed homicide detective he loved so much brought a fond smile to his face.

They'd written their own vows, which were simple and filled with meaning. The minister, the Reverend James Tench, was humorous and personable. The flower girl and ring boy, children of Lane's nephew, were sweet and stole everyone's attention. Bolingbroke, clowning around, pretended to drop Karen's ring before handing it to Sandy, drawing chuckles from everyone except Lane, who rolled her eyes and shook her head. When the minister finished his business and Sandy took Karen into his arms, their kiss was long and single-minded, and Hank doubted they heard the clapping and catcalls that accompanied it.

The videographer had set up his camera and tripod at the back to film the ceremony, and as the newlywed couple were introduced to the congregation by the minister, Hank noticed out of the corner of his eye that he'd removed his camera from the tripod and was holding it on his shoulder, apparently intending to precede them out of the church. Hank made a mental note to get a copy of the video later, although it appeared as though the Rainy Day Killer had wisely chosen to avoid the ceremony altogether.

It took forever for the church to empty, as everyone inched forward toward the receiving line squeezed into the nave to avoid the drizzle outside, but eventually cars began to work their way out of the parking lot. Reverend Tench slipped into his little cubbyhole to remove his vestments and sneak a quick cigarette. The videographer disappeared.

Lane and Wister began calling out directions to the wedding party regarding arrangements for the shooting of the official wedding portraits. Originally planned for the gazebo Brad had built next to the barbecue pit, the photos were now being taken in a spot inside the barn he'd set up this morning.

Hank and Del found Griffin outside in the parking lot, sharing an umbrella with a middle-aged woman who seemed to have a lot to say to him. As Hank approached, Griffin looked relieved to be rescued. He shook the woman's hand and hurried out from under her umbrella.

"Mrs. Tooley, the head librarian in town. It seems she recognized me from the jacket cover photo of my latest book."

"A fan," Hank said.

"Yeah. What can I say? I promised to stop by the library before I leave."

"You have fans?" Del asked, puzzled.

Griffin rolled his eyes. "Don't ask."

Hank unlocked the Cadillac with the remote fob. "Want to ride with us?"

"Yes, please."

Inside the car, as Hank started the engine, Griffin leaned forward from the back seat. "There was only one possible that I could see. The guy sitting two rows behind me on the left side, first seat in."

"We saw him," Del said.

"Turns out he's Sandy's friend," Hank said. "They held up the receiving line getting re-acquainted. Pissed off everyone behind him, but cleared him as someone I might have needed to shoot."

"So he didn't show."

Hank put the Cadillac in gear. "Not that I could see. Let's check with this guy before we go." He rolled forward and pulled up behind the sheriff's office cruiser. Leaving the engine running, Hank got out and rapped on the driver's side window, pressing his badge against the glass.

The deputy buzzed down the window and nodded politely. "What can I do for you, sir?"

"Any sign of our fugitive out here?"

The deputy shook his head. "Not a thing. Dead as dirt the whole time, sir."

"You going to stick with her back to the Alexander ranch?"

"That's the plan."

"And you're it?"

"I'm it," he said.

"This guy called me this morning on my cell," Hank said. "He's been doing that because I was the lead investigator on the two homicides he committed in my city. He said he'd followed Stainer here and intended to make her his next victim. He sent me a photo of her taken in town this morning, so I believe him. He's looking for the ultimate challenge, and as far as he's concerned, this is it. Are you up for it, Deputy?"

"I think so, sir."

"You don't look like you are, Deputy. You don't look like you take this whole thing very seriously. Your eyes look like you were dozing. Were you dozing, Deputy?"

"Not exactly."

"Chief Crull told you to humor us and go through the motions, did he?"

"Not exactly, sir."

"What's your name, Deputy?"

"Preston, sir. Sheriff's Deputy Steven Preston."

"Listen up, Deputy Preston. This guy captures women just like

Karen Stainer in broad daylight on days just like this one, when people are preoccupied with getting out of the rain and not paying much attention to their surroundings. He holds them for three or four days in a remote location, an abandoned building, and rapes them repeatedly. He strangles them to the point of unconsciousness, rapes them again, revives them, and then does it again. They're naked, drugged, injured, violated, humiliated, and terrified. When he's finished with them, he strangles them to death, cuts off their breasts and genitalia, then dumps them naked on a river bank or in a fountain. He feels nothing but contempt for people wearing uniforms like you and for homicide investigators like me. He believes he's smarter, faster, and infinitely more courageous than we are. Is he right, Deputy? Are we just a bunch of dull, slow-footed morons who haven't a clue and couldn't catch him if he stood in front of us with his hands held out, asking to be cuffed?"

Preston swallowed. "No sir."

Hank stared at him for a long moment. "Time to man up, Deputy Preston."

"Yes sir."

Hank put his badge back in his pocket and walked back to the Cadillac. He slammed the door, shifted into Drive, and accelerated around the cruiser and down the street.

"So?" Del said.

"He didn't see anything except the insides of his eyelids," Hank ground out, gripping the steering wheel tightly.

"Christ," Del said.

"I suppose it's too far outside their experience," Griffin said. "I didn't get the sense that they were stupid people, just unable to believe something like this could come up here into their county. They've handled murders before, but the conventional kind with a body and a dumb-ass husband or drinking buddy or whatever with the murder weapon stashed under the front seat of his car."

"If you say so," Del said.

Hank kept his mouth shut, trying to clear the anger from his mind as he drove. He knew that anger would sap his focus and concentration when he needed it the most. In a situation like this, when upset or deeply disturbed by something, he often forced himself into mental routines that had originally been ingrained in his mind as a patrol officer. He'd taught himself to focus intently on doors and windows, locks and bolts, garbage bags and cardboard cartons while on foot patrol, noting every detail, every sight and sound and smell, until the anger or depression or fear had been compartmentalized somewhere at the back of his brain where it wouldn't interfere with his ability to do his job. Another trick was to note and memorize license plates. It was something he usually did mechanically, out of habit, but sometimes he reached for it deliberately as a technique to push away emotion and focus his mind.

As he negotiated the narrow streets toward Jackson River Road, he locked onto every license plate he could see. It was possible the Rainy Day Killer was driving a vehicle with Maryland tags, so he watched for those in particular, but it was more likely he'd switched to Virginia plates at some point, so he looked at them all, committing the numbers to memory.

By the time he turned off the highway onto Pleasant Mountain Road, his anger had resolved into cold determination.

45

After returning to the ranch, Hank dutifully participated in the photo session orchestrated by Nelson P. Wister. By then, his mood had eased up enough that he was able to appreciate more fully the job Brad had done renovating the barn for the Alexanders.

It was a large structure that had originally been used to store dry feed and hay. It was in excellent condition, with large, solid timbers, sturdy walls, wooden flooring, and a hay loft. Brad had insulated the walls and covered them with more barn board. He converted the area under the loft on one side into a galley-style kitchen, and turned grain bins on the other side into booths for private seating. The loft, accessed by a metal winding staircase from a salvage yard in Roanoke, now featured a separate lounge area and bar. The main floor space was filled with round tables that would seat one hundred and twenty people. At the back of the barn, he'd built a false wall to mask the area the Alexanders had earmarked for the washrooms, and it was in front of this false wall that he'd set up a tableau for the photograph session. The centerpiece of the tableau was a beautiful antique cutter, the kind of sleigh pulled by a single horse in winter. Bill had purchased the cutter from Lane's brother-in-law, Stuart Porter, a local antiques dealer. Arranged around it were other items from Porter's shop, including a wagon wheel, a church pew, a buffalo robe, and an assortment of collectibles intended to recreate a nineteenth-century rural look and feel.

Behind the false wall and next to the entrance to the washrooms was a set of double doors that led outside. Beyond them, several vehicles belonging to Porter, the catering crew, and others were parked behind the barn.

When Hank walked in, Wister had already convinced Sandy and Karen to pose in the cutter. As he stood next to Bill Alexander, he was relieved to see that Karen's smile was genuine. She looked happy. He watched her squeeze Sandy's hand affectionately and laugh as he said something to her.

"This is Stuy Porter," Bill said, indicating a short, white-haired man standing next to him. He wore a navy suit, a white shirt open at the neck, and black cap-toe shoes polished to a high shine. "Stuy, meet Lieutenant Hank Donaghue."

Stuy shook Hank's hand. "Lieutenant, is it?" he said with a distinct British accent, giving the rank the English pronunciation 'leftenant.' "In the army, are we?"

"Hank's a homicide detective in Maryland," Bill said. "He's Karen's commanding officer."

"Homicide? You don't say. Brilliant."

"Stuy's married to Lane's sister, Petra. She's around here somewhere. You're originally from Stamford, England, aren't you, Stuy? Near London?"

The antiques dealer ruffled his thinning white hair, which looked as though it had already received quite a workout. "You Yanks. It's in Lincolnshire, lad, quite a bit north of London. Between Peterborough and Nottingham."

"Anyway, Stuy's stuff looks great, doesn't it?"

"It does," Hank agreed.

"You look like a man who knows a few things about fine furniture," Stuy said, handing Hank a business card. "We specialize in Georgian, but I can fix you up with whatever you like. Ship it back home to Maryland for you. Stop by the shop and look us over."

Hank slipped the card into his pocket and obeyed a summons from Lane to join the rest of the wedding party, who were gathering around the cutter.

It took an hour for Wister to be satisfied that he'd taken every possible photograph of everyone from every conceivable angle. He shot them lined up at the railing up in the loft while he stood on a table downstairs, he shot them on the winding staircase, he shot them standing before the big front doors, open to the drizzle outside, and he shot them in a corner with barn board on either side.

When he finally gave up and waved them away, it was 4:36 P.M. Hank went looking for Marie-Louise Roubidoux, and found her sitting at a table with Hudson Barnett. He pulled out a chair and sat down.

"Where are we?"

"Just finishing background checks on all the catering staff," Barnett said. "There's the guy from Texas, James Watson, the chef. He's apparently a friend of Detective Stainer's brother. He checks out. The local crew was hired from a catering company in Roanoke to do the prep and serving and stuff. They all check out so far."

"Good," Hank said.

"The photographer, Wister, checks out. The videographer, his name's, uh," he glanced at a notebook on the table, "Gerald Mansfield. We got his business card from Mrs. Alexander and we're running a check on him. He's not here right now, but I'll talk to him later. John Bolingbroke knows Wister but never heard of Mansfield before. We'll get him checked out, though."

He consulted his notebook again. "The musicians for the live entertainment tonight are scheduled to show up at six thirty. I actually know these guys, the Steve Eakin Band. Four Roanoke ex-hippie types who play country swing, bluegrass, you name it. Got one of their CDs. As far as the guests are concerned, Mrs. Alexander gave me a list and we're proceeding on them. I got all the tag numbers from the church and we're running them. That'll take a bit of time." He looked around the barn. "I'm getting DMV photos sent to my phone, and once they start showing up here I'll do visuals to match them up. We wanted to request ID at the door but Mrs. Alexander had a little hissy fit, so this is the best we can do."

"All right. What about the sheriff's deputy, Preston?"

"His orders from Sheriff Crull are to stay where he is right now, at the end of the driveway, off Alexander property. The sheriff *really* dislikes Mr. Alexander. Local politics."

"So I understand."

"Rather than try to go through their dispatcher if we need to communicate with him in a hurry, I gave Preston a spare cell phone and told him to keep it turned on." Barnett wrote on the back side of one of his business cards and gave it to Hank. "This is the number."

"Thanks. And the state police?"

"Are available in the event of an emergency," Marie-Louise replied. "Their position remains that the UNSUB's still in Maryland and the task force still calls the shots."

As Hank put the business card into his pocket, a group of people walked into the barn through the main entrance. Barnett checked his phone.

"No DMV pics yet."

"Let's see if Sandy can help out," Hank said, standing up.

46

Karen and Sandy were sneaking a beer behind the cutter tableau when Hank and Marie-Louise came looking for Sandy to give them a hand identifying the guests. People were now arriving for cocktails, which they'd started to serve ten minutes ago. As Karen watched them cross the floor, she saw Sandy flag down his father, likely to help identify people he and Lane had invited who were unfamiliar to Sandy. On impulse, she went up the winding staircase and got herself another beer at the bar. It was a free bar, entirely paid for by Bill and Lane, so there was already a bit of a crowd. She spotted Molly sitting at a table with Louise Tench. They both had glasses of beer in front of them.

"It's okay," Molly said, "I checked her ID. She's twenty-one."

"Dad said I could have one before dinner," Louise said, moving her glass self-consciously, "and one more later."

"Good for him," Karen said, standing beside their table. "Make sure that's all you have."

"We were just talking about you," Molly said.

"I'll bet." Karen slipped her right foot out of her shoe and flexed her toes, which were getting a little sore. Louise and Molly were not exactly a combination she expected to see together, the preacher's kid and a lesbian parole officer with piercings, tattoos, and spiky hennaed hair, but they seemed to have made friends. One of the reasons Karen liked Molly so much was her innate kindness and willingness to relate to people on their terms, rather than hers. It made her good at her job and good company, as well.

"Do you really investigate murders?" Louise asked, staring up at her.

"Yep."

"That must be *so* exciting."

"Not really, hon. Mostly it's mindless paperwork and endless phone calls and interviews with boring, stupid people. A lot of routine crap, just like any other job."

"Molly says you're the best shot in the police department and you've killed criminals in the line of duty."

"Molly runs her mouth altogether too much." Karen gave her friend a look. "Why don't you ladies talk about something nice, like puppy dogs or Justin Bieber?"

Molly snorted. "Get real. This little number wants to be a cop, just like the famous Detective Stainer."

"No, you don't," Karen said to Louise.

"Yes, I do."

"She thought it was too cool the way you took down Photo Boy in one-point-five seconds at lunch," Molly said. "She wants you to show her how."

"Can you?" Louise asked.

"No."

"Please?"

"No."

"Come on," Molly said. "Just show her how you did it. I would, but I don't have a clue. I didn't take that course."

"Maybe later," Karen relented. "After dinner. After I've got a few drinks in me."

Molly and Louise bumped fists together, grinning.

Rolling her eyes, Karen raised her glass of beer. "Later, girls. Stay out of trouble."

Downstairs, she ran into Lane, who took the glass from her hand.

"We're forming the receiving line in ten minutes. Let's get ourselves ready now, shall we?"

Karen groaned inwardly. More handshakes and brainless small talk. Would it never end? "Give me five, Lane. I have to pee."

"Please, as soon as you're done."

"I'll try to hurry," Karen lied.

Coming out of the stall, she checked her look in the mirror before going back out onto the floor, thinking about what Louise had said. *Molly says you're the best shot in the police department and you've killed criminals in the line of duty.*

She'd never wanted to be anyone other than who she was, but for five minutes she'd like to take a break from it and pretend she was a lovely, sweet bride from a magazine who lived in a swanky penthouse apartment and ate chocolate-covered strawberries all afternoon in bed while watching old movies and drinking champagne.

Maybe next lifetime, hon.

Pushing through the washroom door, she bumped into the videographer, who was standing behind the false wall, unloading his equipment from a small hand truck.

"There you are," he said, half-turned away from her as he fussed with his camera. "Listen, while I've got you, can I shoot a bit of footage of you by yourself, maybe in the sleigh or something?"

"They're looking for me at the receiving line," Karen said.

"I know, everybody's over there already, but I just got here and we won't have another chance once things get started. Just a minute or two, that's all."

"I don't know," Karen said, hesitating. She didn't want to piss Lane off any more than necessary, but the guy was a lot more polite than Wister had been, and she was feeling inclined to cooperate with him. "Just for a minute."

"Thanks." He set his camera down on the floor and stepped behind her. "Wait, you've got a piece of toilet paper snagged on the bottom of your gown. Can't have that, can we?"

"What?" Karen turned as he bent down behind her.

"Got it," he said, straightening up with a piece of toilet paper in his left hand.

"Man, that would have been embarrassing," Karen said, turning away.

"I know."

Out of the corner of her eye, she saw his right hand suddenly come up from his side. Instinctively, she turned her head back toward him and brought her elbow up in a reflexive, defensive movement.

She heard a snap below her right ear and felt intense pain as her elbow struck his forearm. Peripherally, she saw a stun gun fly from his right hand as her legs turned to jelly, her brain filled with noise, and she dropped to the floor like a shot steer.

47

A stun gun uses two nine-volt batteries to generate at least eighty-five thousand volts of electricity. The voltage travels like a thousand freight trains through the nervous system into the muscles, causing them to spasm. The movement is sufficiently violent to bring about an instantaneous spike in lactic acid levels, causing the muscles to feel as though they've suddenly turned to cement. At the same time, electrical signals to the brain are momentarily scrambled, triggering disorientation and confusion. A half-second of contact is enough to startle, frighten, and hurt someone enough to chase them away. Three seconds of sustained contact, on the other hand, will take down an adult male and leave him in a dazed mental state for up to fifteen minutes.

Because Karen had instinctively raised her elbow and knocked the stun gun out of the Rainy Day Killer's hand, she experienced only a full second of contact. It was enough, however, to cause intense pain, to generate enough lactic acid in her legs to cause them to fold underneath her, and to instigate rippling spasms across her body. The sheer unexpectedness of the attack, catching her in a moment when she'd been thinking about the receiving line, Lane's fussiness, and Sandy's patient smile, was as much responsible for her sudden confusion as the voltage itself.

She fell on her right side, her knees jerked up into a fetal position. Her left arm spasmed several times. Her head, fortunately, had bounced off the side of the killer's equipment bag before hitting the floor, which cushioned the blow and prevented a concussion.

She fought to understand what was happening.

She heard a voice whisper in her ear, "Just relax. You'll be my best girl ever."

What the hell, she thought. *I'm on the floor.*

The spasms passed quickly.

She tried to move her legs. Her left leg straightened slightly, but that was it.

"Hold still, darling," the voice whispered in her ear. "Don't move."

She tried to move her right arm, but it was trapped beneath her body. She moved her left arm. It flopped up and fell back again.

"Don't," the voice said. "This will only take a second."

She felt the hem of her gown slide up her left, uppermost calf.

Fuck, she thought. *It's him.*

She felt the hem being tugged as he tried to move it up to her knee. The tugging stopped. She felt her slip, which hadn't come up with her gown, begin to slide up her left calf. Under her right calf, however, it remained trapped between the floor and her ankle holster.

"Damn," the voice said. "Thigh is better, but calf will do."

She heard a rustling sound, the movement of his pants against the floor. She swung her left arm again, cutting it around in a weak arc, but it moved through empty air.

Missed him. Not there.

As her arm flopped down, the voice returned to her ear. "Hold still. This will just take a second."

She felt a sharp prick in her left calf, and immediately understood what was happening.

Stuns her and then pounds in a sedative right away.

Her own words, spoken to Chalmers, standing over Theresa Olsen's nude body.

Anger flooded her brain. Just as the brief shot of electricity had poured through her body moments before, robbing her limbs of energy, the surge of anger provided new fuel to her muscles and cut through the disorientation in her mind.

She swung her left arm again, but this time with more purpose and precision. For the second time, she succeeded in making contact, striking his hand as he was depressing the plunger on the syringe to inject the drug into her body. The syringe flew away, leaving a divot on her calf.

"Damn!" he yelped in frustration.

She heard him scramble around behind her head. Hands began to turn her over onto her back, fumbling for position under her armpits. He was going to try to drag her, perhaps to get her onto his hand truck and wheel her out the back door to his vehicle.

As she turned, she slowly drew up her right leg and groped with her hand, trying to find her gun.

Other voices, suddenly loud, burst through the washroom door. Women talking and laughing. The voices stopped in mid-sentence, mid-laugh.

The hands disappeared from her armpits and the back of her head thumped against the floor, but she was already rolling over, so she didn't feel it. Gown tangling around her thick and clumsy legs, she struggled to her hands and knees.

She looked up into the eyes of a woman she recognized as one of Sandy's cousins.

"Tell them," Karen croaked. "Sandy."

"Oh my God, are you all right?" The woman stared down at her, frozen in place.

"Tell them. Rainy Day Killer. Here."

48

The women hesitated, shocked expressions on their faces. They slowly edged around her, anxious to get away. They probably thought she'd had too much to drink. Falling-down drunk. What a scandal.

She made it to her feet and staggered, one shoe on and one shoe off. She shook her right foot and sent the remaining shoe skittering away. She bent down and managed to keep her balance as she freed the SIG Sauer P-290 from the holster on her ankle. As she straightened up again, swaying, she looked into the wide eyes of Stuy Porter.

"My goodness, love. What's happened to you?"

She opened her mouth, but before any words could come out, Hank appeared out of nowhere.

"Karen, we need to—"

She grabbed his forearm. "He's here. He ran. Out the back. Video guy."

Darryl materialized from behind Hank. "She may be in the wash—"

"Get the others," Hank ordered Darryl. "It's the videographer. He went outside." He pulled up the leg of his trousers, drew his weapon, and ran out the back door.

Darryl called out Del's name, then put a hand on her arm. "Did he attack you? Are you all right?"

Karen nodded, breathing deeply to clear her head, hoping he hadn't had time to get very much of the sedative into her tissue before she'd knocked the syringe away.

When Del appeared, Darryl said, "Go get the others, the FBI people. Tell them it's the video guy. He's the killer. Karen's all right. Tell them to cut him off at the front."

Del looked at Karen, nodded at Darryl, and hurried away.

Darryl ran out the back door after Hank.

Karen stood there, gun still in her hand, swaying slightly.

"Fuck this," she said, and ran out the door after Darryl.

"Hey," Stuy Porter said, suddenly coming to life, "wait for me!"

49

In the first few moments outside, behind the barn, Karen saw only parked vehicles, a confusion of vans and trucks, some marked with the insignia of local businesses, some blankly anonymous. She ran between a cube van and a pickup truck and saw Hank just ahead of her, cell phone pressed to his ear.

"Goddamn it, Preston," Hank was shouting, "just block the end of the driveway like I told you. He's trying to get past you right now. The Grand Cherokee!"

Karen saw Darryl sprinting across the wide expanse of lawn toward the driveway. Hank put the phone away and took off after him.

Karen worked her way clear of the parked vehicles and began to run across the grass. Ahead, she saw the cruiser slowly moving into the mouth of the driveway, blocking the way. The brake lights flared on the Grand Cherokee as it stopped, and the white rear lights came on as the driver shifted into reverse.

Her feet, soaked from the wet grass, began to slip and slide. She wobbled, threw her arms out, and went down, falling heavily on her left arm. She rolled and twisted, hearing the zipper seam at the back of her dress tear open. As she slid across the wet grass, Stuy Porter leaped over her like an improbable Olympic hurdler. As his black oxfords landed on the wet grass, they immediately flew out from under him and he went down hard.

Karen got to her feet, her left elbow and shoulder on fire, and ran over to him. "Are you insane?"

"I'm fine, love. Thanks for asking. Just a little winded. Help me up, will you?"

"Stay put, you dope. This is police business."

Pushing on his shoulder to emphasize her point, she ran on.

The Grand Cherokee now sat in the courtyard in front of the ranch house, the driver's-side door wide open. She angled across the lawn in that direction. Off to her right were Del and Brad, running furiously toward her. Behind them, just coming out of the front door of the barn, were Roubidoux, Barnett, and Sandy.

She kept going, but her footing was still uncertain, and by the time she reached the edge of the courtyard, Del and Brad had caught up to her.

"Where is he?" Del asked, a little breathless.

Darryl appeared in the open front door of the ranch house. "He went in here, but he may be cutting through to go out the back."

Roubidoux, Barnett, and Sandy arrived. Darryl pointed behind him. "Hank's inside."

Barnett looked at Roubidoux. "Cover the rear, I'll take the inside."

"We'll cover the rear," Karen said.

"I'll cover the rear," Sandy said. "You go back to the reception."

Karen glared at him.

"You three help Hank inside," Darryl said, "and we'll cover the rear. Hurry!"

"Come on," Barnett said, ducking through the door into the house. Roubidoux followed. Sandy looked at Karen.

She gestured sarcastically with her hand—*what are you waiting for?*

Sandy followed Roubidoux into the house.

"Come on," Karen said to her brothers, holding her gun at the high ready position. Leading the way along the side of the house, she edged up to a window, quick-peeked, saw nothing inside, and moved on. It occurred to her that her wedding gown was drenched, stained, and torn in back. Lane would be completely pissed off. She reached the corner of the house and raised a hand. Darryl, Del, and Brad stopped behind her.

She peeked around the corner of the house and saw the patio where she and Lane had enjoyed lunch yesterday. Beyond the patio was a long green lawn, meticulously groomed, and an in-ground swimming pool with white chairs, tables, yellow umbrellas, and an empty metal liquor cart.

She saw no movement. Nobody. No killer.

She spun around the corner, gun out in the Isosceles stance she favored, both arms fully extended, elbows locked. She moved forward slowly, heel and toe, heel and toe, the patio stones warm and wet through the soaked pantyhose covering her feet. The wedding gown, wet and heavy, made a swishing sound as she moved, but nothing could be done about it. Her hair and makeup were ruined. Lane would never speak to her again.

What the hell, folks. This is me. Karen Stainer. People can like it or fucking go fish.

Her eyes knifed around, searching, as the boys fanned out behind her, Brad toward the house on her right, Darryl and Del toward the swimming pool on her left.

The French doors burst open and the videographer, her assailant, the Rainy Day Killer, the son of a bitch, ran out onto the patio, arms pumping, mouth clenched, eyes darting back and forth. His hands were empty. True to form, he had no gun.

He passed Brad without seeing him, spotted Karen, and skidded to a stop as he realized her gun was aimed at his forehead. He knocked over a patio chair that clattered away from him and bowled over a potted plant. His feet went out from underneath him on the wet stone.

Down he went.

He rolled three times and stopped. When he looked up, he was staring into the muzzles of four semi-automatic pistols held by four grim-looking, barely-restrained, thoroughly pissed-off Stainers.

"Say your prayers," Karen gritted.

"Wait for Barnett," Darryl warned.

"I'm gonna grease him," Karen growled. "Turn away."

"Back off, Darryl," Del said. "I'll shoot off his balls, Kay, then you can double-tap him in the head."

"What's that leave me?" Brad complained.

"Shut up," Karen said. "All of you."

Hank burst through the French doors onto the patio. "Barnett! Preston! Out here!"

FBI Special Agent Hudson Barnett ran out, followed by Sheriff's

Deputy Steven Preston, who'd disobeyed orders to join in the pursuit. Suddenly all business, Preston leveled his gun at the prone fugitive.

"Gerald Mansfield, a.k.a. John Doe, you're under arrest for assaulting this woman. Detective Stainer, please lower your weapon. You others, I want you to do the same. I'm taking this man into custody." Karen stared down into the watery brown eyes of the Rainy Day Killer. He was a small, inconsequential little creep who didn't look very much like the damned composite drawing they'd papered half of the eastern seaboard with for the past month. Beside the fact he'd shaved his head, which was knobby and white, his nose was wider, his lips were thicker, and his ears were much larger than had been depicted on the poster.

He looked like a completely different guy.

So much for Esther Banks, their reliable eyewitness.

"Now I'm going to be famous," he murmured, a supercilious little smile at the corners of his mouth. "Thank you, Detective."

Karen growled, a low, throaty, animal-like sound.

She'd had the shot, and she hadn't taken it.

She lowered her gun and curled her lip.

"When they put the needle into your arm, you son of a bitch, I'm going to be there watching. For Theresa and Liz and all the others."

"They'll never get that far. The book will be a bestseller, Kevin Spacey will play me in the movie, and I'll still be around, haunting your dreams. You'll see."

She didn't bother to reply. Turning her head, she spat on the patio stones and walked away.

50

"So how does it feel?" Brad asked, putting his feet up on an empty chair.

Karen sat with her back against the wall, legs across Sandy's lap. "How does what feel?"

"To be a married woman. Plural, as opposed to singular."

"Feels great," Karen said.

"That's just the midazolam talking," Sandy said, rubbing her foot.

"It is not. I only got a tiny little bit of it."

"The vodka, then."

"Well, that." She ran a hand along the leg of her getaway jeans, into which Lane had allowed her to change before dinner, given that her wedding gown was a mess. "Anyway, I've been plural for a while. Sandy and me. Us. We."

"Now it's official," Darryl said, taking out a cigarette and rolling it between his thumb and index finger.

"Since when did you start smoking again?" Karen asked.

"Since about an hour ago." Darryl looked at Sandy. "It's your father's fault. He gave me a pack. Took pity on me."

"Where's Rebecca?" Karen asked.

"Dancing with your new captain." Darryl waved a hand at the dance floor, where a crowd was swinging around as the Steve Eakin Band belted out a lively version of "Bring It On Down To My House Honey." He stood up. "Anybody care to join me for some fresh air? The rain's stopped."

"Later," Brad said.

Darryl walked around and kissed Karen on the top of the head. "She's very proud of you, in her way."

"I know."

"Try to forgive her."

"I will."

Darryl patted Sandy on the shoulder and slipped off into the crowd.

Forgive her for being weak. Forgive her for being crazy, for having broken genes that she'd passed on to her only daughter, for going away, for leaving her without a mother, for forcing her to grow up before she was ready to, for forcing her to be stronger and tougher and meaner than anyone else. To be who and what she was today.

Karen closed her eyes, rubbing the lids. She was satisfied with who and what she was today, thanks. It was all good.

People could like who she was or fucking go fish.

When you looked at it that way, it was easy to forgive poor, crazy Mary Beth.

Poor Mary Beth.

Poor Mom.

She opened her eyes as Del and Beatrice spun off the dance floor and sat down at the table with them.

"Feeling okay?" Del asked.

"Yeah, I'm fine. Thanks." Karen shrugged it off. "A little whacked, but still ready to go."

Del reached over and handed Sandy a set of keys. "Darryl forgot to give you these. Can't make your getaway if you can't start the car, can you?"

"Thanks, Del," Sandy said. "We really appreciate it. It's a beautiful car."

"You're welcome." Del looked at Karen. "I hear Hank got a promotion. What's that all about?"

"It's not official yet. They'll post the list next week."

After Preston, Barnett, and Roubidoux had left the ranch with their prisoner, Hank had called Martinez to give her a situation report. When he was done, Martinez asked to speak to Karen. They were in Bill Alexander's study at the time, just Hank and Karen. The paramedics had been and gone. She'd checked out fine, Karen told Martinez, and didn't need to go to the hospital. There was a small burn on her neck from the stun gun and a small wound on her calf from the syringe. The paramedic had treated and dressed them, and that was it. Her head had cleared up and she was fine, thanks. A little weak, but getting better.

She accepted Martinez's well done and passed the phone back to Hank.

She tuned out at that point, brooding about Lane, wondering what she'd have to do to mend fences. The reception was going ahead as planned, if slightly delayed, and hopefully Lane would have a few wine spritzers and get over it.

When Hank put away his phone, he had an odd look on his face.

"What?" Karen said, sitting up. "What's wrong?"

"Nothing."

"It's not nothing. You look like you just fell down a well. What's wrong?"

"Ann told me they called her to let her know the results of the board."

"The captains' board? Don't tell me we're stuck with Cassion. *Fuck* me. Jesus *fucking* Christ. Hank, I can't stand that woman."

Hank shook his head. "Not Cassion. She's on the list, but at the bottom."

"So what's wrong, then?"

"The name at the top of the list."

"I give up, Hank. It's been a long day. Who's at the top of the list?"

"I am. The chief's going to offer me Major Crimes after they publish it next week."

She flew out of the chair and gave him the longest, hardest hug she'd ever given him.

"He'll be responsible for homicide, robbery, arson, and family-related," she told Del. "He deserves it. He's the smartest guy in the department, bar none."

"Will you still work for him?"

Karen nodded. "They'll bring in another lieutenant to replace him but yeah, he'll be my captain."

"What about the killer?" Beatrice asked. "What happens to him?"

"Ask the feds," Karen said, digging her heel into Sandy's

thigh.

"Ow." Sandy moved her legs away and lowered them to the floor. "It's a county bust at the moment, because they're charging him with assault on Our Little Package of Sugar, but that's just for starters, to hold him over until we can fast-track a DNA test and match him up with the John Doe warrant. Then the negotiations will start."

"I heard he may have killed the real video guy," Del said.

"Gerald Mansfield." Sandy nodded. "They're searching for him now. There were signs of foul play in his studio in Roanoke."

"So they think this guy killed him so he could come here posing as the videographer? Because no one here had ever met the real one?"

"Looks like. If that's the case, there'll be some arguing back and forth, but the Mansfield killing probably won't carry the death penalty, as the Olsen and Baskett homicides will in Maryland. Hopefully he'll end up back with us."

Beatrice picked up an empty glass on the table and looked at it meaningfully. Brad took the hint and went to the bar after taking orders from everyone else except Sandy, who would be driving later tonight when they made their getaway.

"Thank God I'm not the youngest," Karen said.

"You'd have the night off even if you were," Del said.

"So who is this guy, really?" Beatrice asked. "Do they know?"

"Ed Griffin thinks his real name's William Schenker," Sandy said. "Originally from St. Louis, where the first Rainy Day Killer murders took place. Apparently local police actually questioned him at one point, early in their investigation, but let him go."

"You're kidding."

"You have to understand," Sandy said, "they talk to a lot of people in these cases. Ed asked our St. Louis office a couple weeks ago to have St. Louis PD go back through all the files looking for someone named William something, and they came up with four. Only one was still in the city. They'd just started running down the others, but Ed thinks Schenker's the guy. He was an insurance claims rep, apparently, which is how they think he got close to his early victims before he started the Rainy Day Killer homicides."

The band suddenly launched into an up-tempo cover of one of Karen's favorite Hank Williams songs. She stood up and swatted Sandy on the shoulder. "Come on, good lookin', enough chit-chat. Let's go have our getaway dance."

He grinned at her and bounced to his feet.

Del stood up and kissed her. "Have fun, Kay. I love you very much."

"I know. I love you too."

She embraced Beatrice, grabbed Sandy by the hand, and pulled him out onto the dance floor.

Acknowledgments

I'm grateful to the authors of three reference sources: John E. Douglas, Ann W. Burgess, Allen G. Burgess and Robert K. Ressler, *Crime Classification Manual: A Standard System for Investigating and Classifying Violent Crimes* (San Francisco: Jossey-Bass Inc., 1992); Robert K. Ressler, Ann W. Burgess and John E. Douglas, *Sexual Homicide: Patterns and Motives* (New York: The Free Press, 1992); and Frederick A. Jaffe, *A Guide to Pathological Evidence* (Toronto: Carswell, 1976). Any misstatements, errors, or incorrect interpretations of their work are entirely my responsibility.

Once again, I'm deeply indebted to editorial reader Margaret Leroux for her superb work with the manuscript. Thanks as well to Gwenda Lemoine, my "Clive Cussler" reader. If there are any sections in this novel that you, the reader, skipped through because they were boring, it's not because Gwenda didn't point them out to me first.

Thanks go out to the real Stuy Porter and Charlene Tennant-Pecaskie for the loan of their names. Stuy, I hope you didn't mind that Karen called your counterpart a dope. Charlene, perhaps managing a mall would be an improvement on the SRS!

Finally, thanks go out to my wife, Lynn Clark, to whom this book is dedicated. Lynn has once again spent many hours as my editor, taking on not only developmental editing of the first draft but also the copy editing and proofreading of the revised manuscript and the final proofs. Thanks to her, as well, for the lyrics to the song "End of the Day," attributed in the novel to Liz Baskett. In addition to her work on this manuscript, she has also labored tirelessly as publicity and distribution manager for our imprint, The Plaid Raccoon Press—for which the raccoon is, believe me, eternally grateful (contact information available at www.theplaidraccoonpress.com).

For everything you've done, and for all your patience, love, and affection, this book is lovingly dedicated to you, Lynn.

About the Author

Michael J. McCann lives and writes in Oxford Station, Ontario, Canada. A graduate of Trent University in Peterborough, ON, and Queen's University in Kingston, ON, he worked for Carswell Legal Publications (Western) as Production Editor of *Criminal Reports (Third Series)* before spending fifteen years with the Canada Border Services Agency as a training specialist, project officer, and program manager at national headquarters in Ottawa. He's married and has one son.

He's the author of the Donaghue and Stainer Crime Novel series, including *Blood Passage*, *Marcie's Murder*, and *The Fregoli Delusion*, as well as *The Ghost Man*, a supernatural thriller.

If you enjoyed Michael J. McCann's

The Rainy Day Killer

you won't want to miss the other exciting novels in

THE DONAGHUE AND STAINER CRIME NOVEL SERIES

Blood Passage
by Michael J. McCann

ISBN: 978-0-9877087-0-0
eBook ISBN: 978-0-9877087-1-7

Would you believe a little boy who claims he was murdered in his previous life? The first Donaghue and Stainer Crime Novel.

Marcie's Murder
by Michael J. McCann
ISBN: 978-0-9877087-2-4
eBook ISBN: 978-0-9877087-3-1

Hank Donaghue is on vacation when he's jailed on suspicion of murder. Can Karen Stainer get him released and help him find the real killer before it's too late?

The Fregoli Delusion
by Michael J. McCann
ISBN: 978-0-9877087-4-8
eBook ISBN: 978-0-9877087-5-5

The only witness to the sensational murder of a Glendale billionaire suffers from a rare disorder that renders his testimony useless. Is Karen Stainer wrong to believe that he's telling the truth?

www.ingramcontent.com/pod-product-compliance
Lightning Source LLC
Chambersburg PA
CBHW021959010726
47494CB00003B/808